INTRODUCING A FRIEND

When I was asked to introduce Kurt Austin, Joe Zavala, and their friends who serve the National Underwater and Marine Agency, I accepted with great pleasure and enthusiasm. I've had the privilege of knowing Kurt and Joe for many years. We first met when they joined NUMA at Admiral Sandecker's invitation not long after Al Giordino and I came on board. Although we've never had the opportunity to work on the same project together, Kurt and Joe's escapades above and underwater have often fired my imagination and left me wishing I'd done that.

In some ways Kurt and I are similar. He's a few years younger, and we hardly look alike, but he lives in an old remodeled boathouse on the Potomac River and collects antique dueling pistols, a wise choice when you consider how much simpler they are to maintain and store than the old cars in my aircraft hangar. He's also into rowing and sailing, which sends me into exhaustion just thinking about it.

Kurt is resourceful and shrewd, and he has more guts than a white shark on steroids. He's also a genuine nice guy with two tons of integrity who believes in the flag, mothers, and apple pie. To my chagrin, the ladies find him very attractive, even more attractive than they find me. The only obscure conclusion I can reach—it pains me deeply to say so—is that between the two of us he's better looking.

I'm happy that Kurt and Joe's exploits are finally being chronicled from the NUMA Files. There is not the slightest doubt that you will find them entertaining as well as ~~~~~~~~~~~ ~~~~~ ~~~~~~~~ ay the time. I know that I hav~~~~~

Dirk Pitt® Adventures by Clive Cussler

By Clive Cussler and Craig Dirgo

CLIVE CUSSLER

with PAUL KEMPRECOS

SERPENT

POCKET BOOKS

LONDON · SYDNEY · NEW YORK · TOKYO · SINGAPORE · TORONTO

First published in the USA by Pocket Books, 1999
First published in Great Britain by Simon & Schuster UK Ltd, 1999
This edition published by Pocket Books, 2000
An imprint of Simon & Schuster UK Ltd
A Viacom Company

1 3 5 7 9 10 8 6 4 2

Simon & Schuster UK Ltd
Africa House
64–78 Kingsway
London WC2B 6AH

Simon & Schuster Australia
Sydney

A CIP catalogue record for this book is available
from the British Library

ISBN 0-671-02216-4

Printed and bound in Great Britain by
Caledonian International Book Manufacturing Ltd, Glasgow

ACKNOWLEDGMENTS

WITH APPRECIATION TO DON STEVENS
for taking us down to the *Andrea Doria* without getting our feet
wet, and for the work of two fine writers, Alvin Moscow and
William Hoffer, whose books *Collision Course* and *Saved* so vividly
describe the human side of that great sea tragedy. And for the
tenacity of that intrepid explorer John L. Stephens, who braved
mosquitoes and malaria as he trekked through the Yucatan discovering the wonders of the lost Mayan civilization.

PROLOGUE

SO QUICKLY DID THE PALE SHIP appear, she seemed to spring whole from the depths, gliding like a ghost across the silver pool of luminescence cast by the near full moon. Tiaras of porthole lights glittered along her bone-white sides as she raced eastward in the warm night, her sharply raked bow knifing through the flat seas as easily as a stiletto cutting through black satin.

High in the darkened bridge of the Swedish-American liner *Stockholm*, seven hours and 130 miles east of New York City, Second Mate Gunnar Nillson scanned the moonlit ocean. The big rectangular windows that wrapped around the wheelhouse gave him a panoramic view as far as he could see. The surface was calm except for a ragged swell here and there. The temperature was in the seventies, a pleasant change from the heavy humid air that weighed over the *Stockholm* that morning as the liner left its berth at the Fifty-seventh Street pier and headed down the Hudson River. Remains of the woolly overcast drifted in tattered shrouds across the porcelain moon. Visibility was a half dozen miles to starboard.

Nillson swept his eyes to port, where the thin, dark horizon line became lost behind a hazy murkiness that veiled the stars and welded the sky and sea.

For a moment he was lost in the drama of the scene, sobered by the thought of the vast and trackless emptiness yet to be crossed. It was a common feeling among mariners, and it would have lasted longer if not for the tingling in the soles of his feet. The power produced by the massive twin 14,600-horsepower diesels seemed to flow up from the engine room through the vibrating deck and into his body, which swayed almost imperceptibly to adjust for the slight roll. Dread and wonder ebbed, to be replaced by the omnipotent sensation that comes with being in command of a swift liner racing across the ocean at top speed.

At 525 feet stem-to-stern and 69 feet in the beam, the *Stockholm* was the smallest liner in the transatlantic trade. Yet she was a special ship, sleek as a yacht, with racy lines that swept back from her long forecastle to a stern as softly rounded as a wine glass. Her gleaming skin was all white except for a single yellow funnel. Nillson luxuriated in the power of command. With a snap of his fingers the three crewmen on watch would jump to his orders. With a flick of a lever on the ship's telegraphs he could set bells clanging and men scurrying to action.

He chuckled, recognizing his hubris for what it was. His four-hour watch was essentially a series of routine tasks aimed at keeping the ship on an imaginary line that would bring it to an imaginary point near the stubby red lightship that guarded Nantucket's treacherous shoals. There the *Stockholm* would make the northeasterly turn onto a course that would take its 534 passengers past Sable Island on a straight shot across the Atlantic to the north of Scotland and, finally, Copenhagen Harbor.

Even though he was only twenty-eight and had joined the *Stockholm* barely three months earlier, Nillson had been on boats since he could walk. As a teenager he'd worked the Baltic Sea herring boats and later served as an apprentice seaman with a huge shipping company. Then came the Swedish Nautical College and a stint in the Swedish navy. The *Stockholm* was one more step in achieving his dream, to be master of his own ship.

Nillson was an exception to the common tall blond Scandinavian stereotype. There was more of Venice than Viking in him. He had inherited his mother's Italian genes, along with her chestnut hair, olive skin, small-boned stature, and sunny temperament. Dark-haired Swedes were not unusual. At times Nillson wondered if the Mediterranean warmth lurking in his large brown eyes had anything to do with his captain's frostiness. More likely it was a combination of Scandinavian reserve and the rigid Swedish maritime tradition of strict discipline. Nevertheless, Nillson worked harder than he had to. He didn't want to give the captain a single reason to find fault. Even on this peaceful night, with no traffic, near flat seas, and perfect weather, Nillson paced from one wing of the bridge to the other as if the ship were in the teeth of a hurricane.

The *Stockholm's* bridge was divided into two spaces, the twenty-foot-wide wheelhouse in front and the separate chartroom behind it. The doors leading out to the wings were left open to the light southwest breeze. At each side of the bridge was an RCA radar set and a ship's telegraph. At the center of the wheelhouse the helmsman stood on a wooden platform a few inches off the polished deck, his back to the dividing wall, hands gripping the steering wheel, eyes on the face of a gyrocompass to his left. Directly in front of the helm, below the center window, was a course box. The three wooden blocks in the box were printed with numbers to keep the helmsman's mind focused on the heading.

The blocks were set at 090.

Nillson had come up a few minutes before his eight-thirty watch to look at the weather reports. Fog was forecast for the area near the Nantucket lightship. No surprise there. The warm waters of the Nantucket shoals were a virtual fog factory. The officer going off duty told him the *Stockholm* was just north of the course set by the captain. How far north he couldn't tell. The radio positioning beacons were too far away to get a fix.

Nillson smiled. No surprise here, either. The captain always took the same course, twenty miles north of the eastbound sealane recommended by international agreement. The route wasn't mandatory, and the captain preferred the more northerly track because it saved time and fuel.

Scandinavian captains did not do bridge watch, customarily leaving the ship in charge of a single officer. Nillson quickly settled into a series of tasks. Pace the bridge. Check the right-hand radar. Glance at the engine telegraphs on each wing of the bridge to make sure they were set Full Speed Ahead. Scan the sea from a wing. Make sure the two white masthead navigation lights were on. Stroll back into the wheelhouse. Study the gyrocompass. Keep the helmsman on his toes. Pace some more.

The captain came up around nine after having dinner in his cabin directly below the bridge. A taciturn man in his late fifties, he looked older, his craggy profile worn around the edges like a rocky promontory ground smooth by the unrelenting sea. His posture was still ramrod straight, his uniform razor-creased. Iceberg-blue eyes glinted alertly from the weathered ruins of his ruddy face. For ten minutes he paced behind the bridge, gazing at the ocean and sniffing the warm air like a bird dog catching the scent of pheasant. Then he went into the wheelhouse and studied the navigation chart as if in search of an omen.

After a moment he said, "Change course to eighty-seven degrees."

Nillson turned the oversized dice in the course box to read 087. The captain stayed long enough to watch the helmsman adjust the wheel, then returned to his cabin.

Back in the chartroom Nillson erased the ninety-degree line, penciled in the captain's new course, and figured the ship's position by dead reckoning. He extended the track line according to speed and time elapsed and drew in an X. The new line would take them about five miles from the lightship. Nillson figured strong northerly currents would push the ship as close as two miles.

Nillson went over to the radar set near the right door and switched the range from fifteen miles to fifty miles. The thin yellow sweep hand highlighted the slender arm of Cape Cod and the islands of Nantucket and Martha's Vineyard. Ships were too small for the radar to pick up at that range. He returned the range to its original setting and resumed his pacing.

Around ten the captain returned to the bridge. "I'll be in my cabin doing paperwork," he announced. "I'll make the course change north in two hours. Call me to the bridge if you see the lightship before then." He squinted out a window as if he sensed something he couldn't see. "Or if there is fog or other bad weather."

The *Stockholm* was now forty miles west of the lightship, close enough to pick up its radio beacon. The radio direction finder indicated that the *Stockholm* was more than two miles north of the captain's course. Currents must be pushing the *Stockholm* north, Nillson concluded.

Another RDF fix minutes later showed the ship nearly three miles north of the course. Still nothing to be alarmed about; he'd simply keep a close eye on it. Standing orders were to call the captain in case of drift off course. Nillson pictured the expression on the captain's seamed face, the hardly veiled contempt in those sea-bitten eyes. You called *me* up here from my cabin for *this?* Nillson scratched his chin in thought. Maybe the problem was with the direction finder. The radio beacons still might be too far away for an accurate fix.

Nillson knew he was a creature of the captain's will. Yet he was, after all, the officer in command of the bridge. He made his decision.

"Steer eighty-nine," he ordered the helmsman.

The wheel moved to the right, taking the ship slightly south, closer to the original course.

The bridge crew changed posts as it did every eighty minutes. Lars Hansen came in from standby and took over the helm.

Nillson grimaced, not altogether pleased with the change. He never felt comfortable sharing a shift with the man. The Swedish navy was all business. Officers talked to the crewmen only to give orders. Pleasantries simply were not exchanged. Nillson sometimes broke the rule, quietly sharing a joke or wry observation with a crewman. Never with Hansen.

This was Hansen's first voyage on the *Stockholm*. He came on board as a last-minute replacement when the man who signed on hadn't shown up. According to Hansen's papers he'd kicked around on a number of ships. Yet nobody could place him, which was hard to believe. Hansen was lantern-jawed, tall, broad-shouldered, and his blond hair was cropped close to the scalp. The same description could apply to a few million other Scandinavian men in their early twenties. It would be hard to forget Hansen's face. A fierce white scar ran from his prominent cheekbone nearly to the right-hand corner of his mouth, so his lips seemed turned up on one side in a grotesque smile. Hansen had served mostly on freighters, which might explain his anonymity. Nillson suspected it was more likely the man's behavior. He kept to himself, spoke only when he was spoken to, and then not very much. Nobody ever asked him about his scar.

He turned out to be a good crewman, Nillson had to admit, jumping smartly to orders and carrying them out without a question. Which was why Nillson was puzzled as he checked the compass. On past shifts Hansen had shown himself to be a competent helmsman. Tonight he was letting the ship drift as if his attention were wandering. Nillson understood that it took a while to get the feel of the helm. Except for the current, though, steering was undemanding. No howling wind. No giant seas breaking over the deck. Just move the wheel a little this way, a little that way.

Nillson checked the gyrocompass. No doubt about it. The ship was yawing slightly. He stood close to the helmsman's shoulder. "Keep a tight line, Hansen," he said with gentle humor. "This isn't a warship, you know."

Hansen's head swiveled on the muscular neck. The reflected glow from the compass imparted an animal glitter to his eyes and accentuated the deepness of the scar. Heat seemed to radiate from his glare. Sensing a quiet aggressiveness, Nillson almost stepped backward in reflex. He stubbornly held his ground, though, and gestured at the course box numerals.

The helmsman stared at him without expression for a few seconds, then nodded almost imperceptibly.

Nillson made sure the course was steady, mumbled his approval, then escaped into the chartroom.

Hansen gave him the creeps, he thought, shivering as he took another radio fix to see the effect of the drift. Something didn't make sense. Even with the two-degree correction to the south, the *Stockholm* was north of the course by three miles.

He went back into the wheelhouse, and without looking at Hansen he ordered, "Two degrees to the right."

Hansen eased the wheel to ninety-one degrees.

Nillson changed the course box numbers and stayed by the compass until he was satisfied Hansen had brought the ship onto the new tack. Then he bent over the radar, the yellow glow from the scope giving his dark skin a jaundiced tinge. The sweep hand illuminated a blip off to the left side of the screen, about twelve miles away. Nillson raised an eyebrow.

The *Stockholm* had company.

Unknown to Nillson, the *Stockholm*'s hull and superstructure were being washed by unseen electronic waves that rippled back to the revolving radar antenna high atop the bridge of a ship speeding toward it from the opposite direction. Minutes earlier, inside the spacious bridge of the Italian Line passenger ship *Andrea Doria,* the officer manning the radar scope called out to a stocky man wearing a navy beret and a uniform of evening blue.

"Captain, I see a ship, seventeen miles, four degrees to starboard."

The radar had been monitored constantly at twenty-mile range since three o'clock, when Superior Captain Piero Calamai walked onto the bridge wing and saw gray wisps hovering over the western sea like the souls of drowned men.

Immediately the captain had ordered the ship rigged for running in the fog. The 572-man crew had been on full alert. The foghorn was blowing automatically at hundred-second intervals.

The crow's nest lookout was reassigned to the bow where he'd have a clearer view. The engine-room crew was put on standby, primed to react instantly in an emergency. The doors between the ship's eleven watertight compartments were sealed.

The *Andrea Doria* was on the last leg of a 4,000-mile, nine-day voyage from its home port of Genoa carrying 1,134 passengers and 401 tons of freight. Despite the dense fog pressing down on its decks, the *Doria* cruised at close to its full speed, its massive 35,000-horsepower twin-turbine engines pushing the big ship through the sea at twenty-two knots.

The Italian Line did not gamble with its ships and passengers. Nor did it pay captains to arrive behind schedule. Time was money. No one knew this any better than Captain Calamai, who had commanded the ship on all its transatlantic crossings. He was determined that the ship would arrive in New York not one second beyond the hour it had lost in a storm two nights earlier.

When the *Doria* had rolled by the lightship at ten-twenty P.M., the bridge could pick the vessel up on radar and hear the lonely moan of its foghorn, but it was invisible at less than a mile away. With the lightship behind them, the *Doria*'s captain ordered a course due west to New York.

The radar pip was heading east, directly *at* the *Doria*. Calamai bent over the radar screen, his brow furrowed, watching the blip's progress. The radar couldn't tell the captain what *kind* of ship he was looking at or how big it was. He didn't know he was looking at a fast ocean liner. With a combined speed of forty knots, the two ships were closing on each other at the rate of two miles every three minutes.

The ship's position was puzzling. Eastbound ships were supposed to follow a route twenty miles to the *south*. Fishing boat, maybe.

Under the rules of the road, ships coming directly at each other on the open sea are supposed to pass port-to-port, left side to left side, like cars approaching from opposite directions. If ships maneuvering to comply with this rule are forced into a dangerous cross-over, they may instead pass starboard-to-starboard.

From the look of the radar, the other vessel would pass safely to the right of the *Doria* if the two vessels held their same course. Like autos on an English highway, where drivers stay to the left.

Calamai ordered his crew to keep a close eye on the other ship. It never hurt to be cautious.

The ships were about ten miles apart when Nillson switched on the light underneath the Bial maneuvering board next to the radar set and prepared to transfer the blip's changing position to paper.

He called out, "What's our heading, Hansen?"

"Ninety degrees," the helmsman replied evenly.

Nillson marked X's on the plotting board and drew lines between them, checked the blip again, then ordered the standby lookout to keep watch from the port bridge wing. His plot line had shown the other ship speeding in their direction on a parallel course, slightly to the left. He went out onto the wing and probed the night with binoculars. No sign of another vessel. He paced back and forth from wing to wing, stopping at the radar with each pass. He called for another heading report.

"Still ninety degrees, sir," Hansen said.

Nillson started over to check the gyrocompass. Even the slightest deviation could be critical, and he wanted to make certain the course was true. Hansen reached up and pulled the lanyard over his head. The ship's bell rang out six times. Eleven o'clock. Nillson loved hearing ship's time. On a late shift, when loneliness and boredom combined, the pealing of the ship's bell embodied the romantic attachment he had felt for the sea as a youngster. Later he would remember that clanging as the sound of doom.

Distracted from his intended chore, Nillson peered into the radar scope and made another mark on the plotting board.

Eleven o'clock. Seven miles separated the two ships.

Nillson calculated that the ships would pass each other port-to-port with more than enough distance in between. He went out on the wing again and peered through binoculars off to the left. Maddening. There was only darkness where radar showed a ship to be. Maybe the running lights were broken. Or it was a navy ship on maneuvers.

He looked off to the right. The moon was shining brightly on the water. Back to the left. Still nothing. Could the ship be in a fog bank? Unlikely. No ship would move that fast in dense fog. He considered decreasing the *Stockholm's* speed. No. The captain would hear the jangle of the ship's telegraph and come running. He'd call that frosty-assed bastard *after* the ships had safely passed.

At 11:03 radar on both vessels showed them four miles apart. *Still no lights.*

Nillson again considered calling the captain, and again dismissed the idea. Nor did he give the order to sound warning signals as required by international law. A waste of time. They were on open ocean, the moon was out, and visibility must be five miles.

The *Stockholm* continued to cut through the night at eighteen knots.

The man in the crow's nest called out, "Lights to port!"
Finally.

Later, analysts would shake their heads in puzzlement, wondering how two radar-equipped ships could be drawn together like magnets on the open ocean.

Nillson strode onto the left bridge wing and read the other ship's lights. Two white pinpoints, one high, one low, glowed in darkness. Good. The position of the lights indicated that the ship would pass off to the left. The red portside light came into view, confirming that the ship was heading away from the *Stockholm*. The ships would pass port-to-port. Radar put the distance at more than two miles. He glanced at the clock. It was 11:06 P.M.

* * *

From what the *Andrea Doria*'s captain could see on the radar screen, the ships should pass each other safely on the right. When the ships were less than three and a half miles apart, Calamai ordered a four-degree turn to the left to open up the gap between them. Soon a spectral glow appeared in the fog, and gradually white running lights became visible. Captain Calamai expected to see the green light on the other ship's starboard side. Any time now.

One mile apart.

Nillson remembered how an observer said the *Stockholm* could turn on a dime and give you eight cents change. It was time to put that nimbleness to use.

"Starboard two points," he ordered the helm. Like Calamai, he wanted more breathing room.

Hansen brought the wheel two complete turns to the right. The ship's bow went twenty degrees to starboard.

"Straighten out to midships and keep her steady."

The telephone rang on the wall. Nillson went over to answer it.

"Bridge," Nillson said. Confident of a safe passing, he faced the wall, his back to the windows.

The crow's nest lookout was calling. "Lights twenty degrees to port."

"Thank you," Nillson replied, and hung up. He went over and checked the radar, unaware of the *Doria*'s new trajectory. The blips were now so close to each other the reading didn't make any sense to him. He went to the port wing and, without any urgency, raised his binoculars to his eyes and focused on the lights.

Calmness deserted him.

"My God." He gasped, seeing the change in the masthead lights for the first time.

The high and low lights had reversed themselves. The ship no longer had its red portside light to him. The light was *green*. Starboard side. Since he'd last looked, the other ship seemed to have made a sharp turn to its left.

Now the blazing deck lights of a huge black ship loomed from the thick fog bank that had kept it hidden and presented its right side directly in the path of the speeding *Stockholm*.

He shouted a course change. "Hard a-starboard!"

Spinning around, he gripped the levers of the ship's telegraph with both hands, yanked them to Stop, then all the way down as if he could bring the ship to a halt by sheer determination. An insane jangle filled the air.

Full Speed Astern.

Nillson turned back to the helm. Hansen stood there like a stone guardian outside a pagan temple.

"Damn it, I said hard a-*starboard!*" Nillson shouted, his voice hoarse.

Hansen began to turn the wheel. Nillson couldn't believe his eyes. Hansen wasn't rotating the wheel to starboard, which would have given them a chance, even a slight one, to avoid a collision. He spun it slowly and deliberately to the *left*.

The *Stockholm*'s bow swung into a deadly turn.

Nillson heard a foghorn, knew it must belong to the other ship.

The engine room was in chaos. The crew was frantically turning the wheel that would stop the starboard engine. They scrambled to open the valves that would reverse power and stop the port engine. The ship shuddered as braking took hold. Too late. The *Stockholm* flew like an arrow at the unprotected ship.

In the port wing Nillson hung on grimly to the ship's telegraph.

Like Nillson, Captain Calamai had watched the masthead lights materialize, reverse themselves, saw the red portside light glowing like a ruby on back velvet. Realized the other ship had made a sharp right turn directly into the *Doria*'s path.

No warning. No foghorn or whistle.

Stopping was out of the question at this speed. The ship would need miles of room to skid to a halt.

Calamai had seconds to act. He could order a right turn,

directly *toward* the danger, hoping that the ships would brush each other. Maybe the speeding *Doria* could outrun the attacking ship.

Calamai made a desperate decision.

"All left," he barked.

A bridge officer called out. Did the captain want the engines shut down? Calamai shook his head. "Maintain full speed." He knew the *Doria* turned better at higher velocity.

In a blur of spokes the helmsman whipped the wheel around to port using both hands. The whistle shrieked twice to signal the left turn. The big ship struggled against its forward momentum for a half mile before it heeled into the start of the turn.

The captain knew he was taking a big risk in exposing the *Doria's* broad side. He prayed that the other vessel would bear off while there was still time. He still couldn't believe the ships were on a collision course. The whole thing seemed like a dream.

A shout from one of his officers snapped him back to reality. "She's coming right at us!"

The oncoming ship was pointed at the starboard wing where Calamai watched in horror. The sharp upturned bow seemed to be aimed directly at him.

The *Doria's* skipper had a reputation for being tough and in control. But at that moment he did what any sane man would have done in his position. He ran for his life.

The Swedish ship's reinforced bow pierced the metal skin of the speeding *Andrea Doria* as easily as a bayonet, penetrating almost a third of the liner's ninety-foot width before it came to rest.

With a weight of 29,100 tons, more than twice that of the *Stockholm,* the Italian liner dragged the vessel with it, pivoting around the point of impact below and aft of the starboard bridge wing. As the stricken *Doria* plunged ahead, the *Stockholm's* crumpled prow pulled free, ripping open seven of the liner's ten passenger decks like a raptor's beak tearing into the flesh of its victim. It scraped along the long black hull in a bright shower of sparks.

The gaping wedge-shaped hole that yawned in the *Doria*'s side was forty feet at the top and narrowed to seven feet below sea level at the bottom.

Thousands of gallons of seawater rushed into the massive wound and filled empty outboard fuel tanks torn open in the collision. The ship tilted to the right under the weight of five hundred tons of seawater that flooded into the generator room. An oily river poured through an access tunnel and manholes and began to rise through the floor gratings of the engine room. The struggling engine crew slid on the oil-slicked decks like circus clowns taking pratfalls.

More water gushed in, surged around the undamaged empty fuel tanks on the port side, and buoyed them up like soap bubbles.

Within minutes of being hit, the *Doria* had heeled over into a severe list.

Nillson expected to be flung to the floor by the impact. The jolt was surprisingly soft yet strong enough to jar him from his paralysis. He dashed from the wheelhouse into the chartroom and lunged for the alarm button that would close the *Stockholm*'s watertight doors.

The captain roared onto the bridge. "What in God's name happened?"

Nillson tried to mouth an answer. The words stuck in his throat. He was at a loss to describe the scene. Hansen ignoring his order to go to starboard. The blurred spin of the wheel to port. Hansen leaning forward into the wheel, hands tightly clutching the spokes as if frozen in time. No fear, no horror in his eyes. Only a glacial blue coldness. Nillson thought it was a trick of the light at first, the illumination from the gyrocompass housing catching the ugly scar. There was no mistake. As the ships hurtled toward certain disaster, the man was *smiling*.

There was no doubt in his mind. Hansen had *deliberately* rammed the other ship, aiming the *Stockholm* as if he were riding a torpedo. No doubt, too, that nobody, not the captain or anyone else on the ship, would ever believe such a thing could happen.

Nillson's anguished eyes shifted from the captain's angry face to the helm as if the answer lay there. The deserted wheel spun madly out of control.

In all the confusion Hansen had vanished.

Jake Carey was shocked from his slumber by a doomful metallic thunderclap. The hollow boom lasted only an instant before it was followed by the tortured shriek of steel against steel and a terrifying crumple and crunch as if the upper deck cabin were imploding. Carey's eyes blinked open, and he stared fearfully at what looked to be a moving grayish-white wall, only a few feet away.

Carey had drifted off to sleep minutes before. He had kissed his wife, Myra, good night and slipped beneath the cool sheets of a twin bed in their first-class cabin. Myra read a few pages of her novel until her eyelids drooped. She switched off the light, pulled the blanket close around her neck, and sighed, with pleasant memories of the sun-baked Tuscan vineyards still in her head.

Earlier, she and Jake had toasted the success of their Italian sojourn with champagne in the first-class dining room. Carey had suggested a nightcap in the Belvedere Lounge, but Myra replied that if she heard the band play "Arrivederci Roma" one more time, she'd swear off spaghetti forever. They retired shortly before ten-thirty P.M.

After strolling hand-in-hand past the shops in the foyer deck, they took the elevator one level up and walked forward to their large upper-deck cabin on the starboard side. They put their luggage out in the corridor, where the stewards would collect it in anticipation of the ship's arrival in New York the next day. There was a slight roll to the ship because the vessel had become more top-heavy as fuel in the big hull tanks was used up. The motion was like being rocked in a giant cradle, and before long Myra Carey, too, fell asleep.

Now her husband's bed lurched violently. He was catapulted into the air as if he'd been launched from a siege machine. He floated in free fall for several lifetimes before splashing into a deep pool of darkness.

Death stalked the decks of the *Andrea Doria*.

It roamed from the posh cabins on the higher levels to the tourist-class accommodations below the waterline. Fifty-two people lay dead or dying in the wake of the crash. Ten cabins were demolished in the first-class deck where the hole was at its widest. The hole was at its narrowest at the bottom, but the cabins below the waterline were smaller and more crowded, so the effect was even more devastating.

Passengers died or lived according to the whims of fate. A first-class passenger who'd been brushing his teeth ran back to the bedroom to find the wall gone, his wife vanished. On the deluxe foyer deck two people were killed instantly. Twenty-six Italian immigrants in the smaller, cheaper cabins of the lowermost deck were right in line with the collision and died in a mass of crushed steel. Among them were a woman and her four young children. There were miracles as well. A young girl scooped out of a first-class cabin woke up in the *Stockholm*'s crumpled bow. In another cabin the ceiling crashed down on a couple, but they managed to crawl out into the corridor.

Those from the two lowest decks had the toughest struggle, fighting their way up the slanting smoke-filled passageways against a stream of oil-slicked black water. Gradually people began to work their way to the muster stations and waited for instructions.

Captain Calamai was at the far side of the undamaged bridge when the ships hit. Recovering from his initial shock, he pulled the ship's telegraph lever to Stop. The ship eventually came to a halt in the deep fog.

The second officer strode to the inclinometer, the instrument that measured the ship's angle.

"Eighteen degrees," he said. A few minutes later he said, "Nineteen degrees."

Cold fingers brushed the captain's heart. The list should be no more than fifteen degrees, even with two compartments flooded. A tilt of more than twenty degrees would overwhelm the watertight compartments.

Logic was telling him the situation was impossible. The designers guaranteed that the ship would remain on an even keel with any group of two compartments flooded. He called for damage reports from each deck, especially on the status of the watertight doors, and ordered an SOS sent out with the ship's position.

Officers rushed back to the bridge with damage reports. The engine-room crew was pumping the starboard compartments, but water was coming in faster than they could get it out. The boiler room was flooded, and water was flowing into two more compartments.

The problem was at A Deck, supposed to serve as a steel lid over the transverse bulkheads that divided the ship into compartments. Water was flowing down those passenger stairways into the other compartments.

The officer called out the new reading. "Twenty-two degrees."

Captain Calamai didn't have to look at the inclinometer to know the list had passed the point where it could be corrected. The evidence was in the slant of the chart-littered floor right at his feet.

The ship was dying.

He was numb with grief. The *Andrea Doria* was not just *any* ship. The twenty-nine-million-dollar Queen of the Italian Line was the most magnificent and luxurious passenger vessel afloat. Barely four years old, it was launched to show the world that the Italian merchant marine was back in business after the war. With its graceful black hull and white superstructure, the rakish red, white, and green funnel, the liner looked more like the work of a sculptor than a marine architect.

Moreover, this was *his* ship. He had commanded the *Doria* on her trial runs and on a hundred Atlantic crossings. He knew her decks better than the rooms of his own home. He never tired of strolling from one end to the other, like a spectator in a museum, breathing in the work of thirty-one of Italy's finest artists and artisans, glorying in the Renaissance beauty of the mirrors, gilt, crystal, rare woods, fine tapestries, and mosaics. Surrounded by the massive mural that lionized Michelangelo and other Italian masters, he would pause in the first-class lounge before the massive bronze statue of Andrea Doria, second only to Columbus in greatness. The old Genoese admiral stood ready as always to draw his sword at the first sign of a Barbary pirate.

All this was about to be lost.

The passengers were the captain's first responsibility. He was about to give the order to abandon ship when an officer reported on the lifeboat situation. The lifeboats on the port side were unlaunchable. That left eight boats on the starboard side. They were hanging far out over the water. Even if they could be launched, there was room enough for only half the passengers. He didn't dare give the order to abandon ship. Panic-stricken passengers would rush to the port side, and there'd be chaos.

He prayed that passing ships had heard their SOS and could find them in the fog.

There was nothing he could do but wait.

Angelo Donatelli had just delivered a trayful of martinis to a raucous table of New Yorkers celebrating their last night aboard the *Doria* when he glanced toward one of the draped windows that took up three walls of the elegant Belvedere Lounge. Something, a flicker of movement, had caught his eye.

The lounge was on the front of the boat deck, with its open promenade, and in the daytime or on clear nights first-class passengers normally had a wide view of the sea. Most passengers had given up trying to see anything through the soft gray wall that enclosed the lounge. It was only dumb luck that Angelo looked up and saw the lights and rails of a big white ship moving through the fog.

"Dios mio," he murmured.

The words had barely left his lips when there was an explosion that sounded like a monster firecracker. The lounge was plunged into darkness.

The deck shifted violently. Angelo lost his balance, fought to regain it, and, with the circular tray clutched in one hand, did a tolerable imitation of the famous Greek statue of a discus thrower. The handsome Sicilian from Palermo was a natural athlete who'd kept his agility tuned to a fine edge weaving in and out of tables and balancing drinks.

The emergency lights kicked in as he scrambled to his feet. The three couples at his table had been thrown from their chairs onto the floor. He helped the women up first. No one seemed seriously hurt. He looked around.

The beautiful lounge, with its softly lit tapestries, paintings, and wood carvings and its glossy blond paneling, was in a turmoil. The shiny dance floor, where seconds before couples had been gliding to the strains of "Arrivederci Roma," was a jumble of squirming bodies. The music had stopped abruptly, to be replaced by cries of pain and dismay. Band members extricated themselves from the tangle of instruments. There were broken bottles and glasses everywhere, and the air reeked with the smell of alcohol. Vases of fresh flowers had spilled onto the floor.

"What in God's name was *that?*" one of the men said.

Angelo held his tongue, not sure even now of what he had seen. He looked at the window again and saw only the fog.

"Maybe we hit an iceberg," the man's wife ventured tentatively.

"An *iceberg?* For Chrissakes, Connie, you're talking the coast of Massachusetts. In *July.*"

The woman pouted. "Well, then, maybe it was a mine."

He looked over at the band and grinned. "Whatever it was, it got them to stop playing that goddamn song."

They all laughed at the joke. Dancers were brushing their

clothes off, the musicians inspecting their instruments for damage. Bartenders and waiters rushed about.

"We've got nothing to worry about," another man said. "One of the officers told me they built this ship to be unsinkable."

His wife stopped checking her makeup in the mirror of her compact. "That's what they said about the *Titanic,*" she said with alarm.

Tense silence. Then a quick exchange of fearful glances. As if they'd heard a silent signal, the three couples hastily made for the nearest exit like birds flying off a clothesline.

Angelo's first instinct was to clear the table of glasses and wipe it down. He laughed softly. "You've been a waiter too long," he said under his breath.

Most of the people in the room were back on their feet, and they were using them to move toward the exits. The lounge was quickly emptying out. If Angelo didn't leave, he'd be all alone. He shrugged, tossed his dish towel on the floor, then headed for the nearest doorway to find out what was going on.

Black waves threatened to drag Jake Carey under for good. He fought against the dark current tugging at his body, crawled onto the slippery edge of consciousness, and hung on grimly. He heard a moan and realized it was coming from his own lips. He moaned again, this time on purpose. Good. Dead men don't moan. His next thought was of his wife.

"Myra!" he called out.

He heard a faint stirring in the gray darkness. Hope surged in his breast. He called his wife's name again.

"Over here." Myra's voice was muffled as if coming from a distance.

"Thank God! Are you all right?"

A pause. "Yes. What happened? I was asleep—"

"I don't know. Can you move?"

"No."

"I'll come help you," Carey said. He lay on his left side, arm pinned under his body, a weight pressing on his right side. His legs were locked tight. Icy fear gripped him. Maybe his back was broken. He tried again. Harder. The jagged pain that shot up from his ankle to his thigh brought tears to his eyes, but it meant he wasn't paralyzed. He stopped struggling. He'd have to think this thing through. Carey was an engineer who'd made a fortune building bridges. This was no different from any other problem that could be solved by applications of logic and persistence. And lots of luck.

He pushed with his right elbow and felt soft fabric. He was under the mattress. He shoved harder, angling his body for leverage. The mattress gave, then would move no more. Christ, the whole bloody ceiling could be on top of him. Carey took a deep breath, and, using every ounce of strength in his muscular arm, he pushed again. The mattress slid off onto the floor.

With both arms free he reached down and felt something solid on top of his ankle. Exploring the surface with his fingers, he figured out it was the chest of drawers that had been between the twin beds. The mattress must have shielded him from pieces of the wall and ceiling. With two hands free, he lifted the dresser a few inches and slid his legs out one at a time. He rubbed circulation gently back into his ankles. They were bruised and painful but not broken. He slowly got up on his hands and knees.

"Jake." Myra's voice again. Weaker.

"I'm coming, sweetheart. Hold on."

Something was wrong. Myra's voice seemed to issue from the other side of the cabin wall. He flicked on a light switch. The cabin remained in darkness. Disoriented, he crawled through the wreckage. His groping fingers found a door. He cocked his head, listening to what sounded like surf against the shore and gulls screaming in the background. He staggered to his feet, cleared rubble from around the door, and opened it on a nightmare.

The corridor was crowded with pushing and shoving passengers who were cast in an amber hue by the emergency lighting. Men, women, and children, some fully dressed, some in their nightclothes under their coats, some bare-handed, others lugging bags, pushed, shoved, walked, or crawled as they fought their way toward the upper deck. The hallway was filled with dust and smoke and tilted like the floor of a fun house. A few passengers trying to get to their cabins struggled against the human river like salmon swimming against the current.

Carey glanced back at the door he had just come through and realized from the numbers that he'd crawled out of the cabin adjoining his. He must have been thrown from one cabin to the other. That night in the lounge he and Myra had talked to the cabin's occupants, an older Italian-American couple returning from a family reunion. He prayed that they hadn't followed their usual practice of retiring early.

Carey muscled his way through the throng to his cabin door. It was locked. He went back into the cabin he'd just come out of and pushed through the debris toward the wall. Several times he stopped to move furniture and push pieces of ceiling or wall aside. Sometimes he crawled over the wreckage, sometimes he wriggled under it, driven by a new urgency. The tilted deck meant the ship was taking on water. He got to the wall and called out his wife's name again. She replied from the other side. Frantic now, he groped for any opening in the barrier, found the bottom was loose, and pulled until he made a hole big enough for him to squeeze through on his belly.

His cabin was in semidarkness, shapes and objects awash in a faint light. He stood up and looked toward the source of the illumination. A cool salty breeze blew against his sweaty face. He couldn't believe his eyes. The outside cabin wall was gone! In its place was a gigantic hole through which he could see moonlight reflected on the ocean. He worked feverishly, and minutes later he was at his wife's side. He wiped the blood off her forehead and cheeks with a corner of his pajama top and tenderly kissed her.

"I can't move," she said almost apologetically.

Whatever it was that had sent him hurling into the next cabin had ripped the steel frame of Myra's bed from the floor and pushed it against the wall like the spring in a mousetrap. Myra was in a near upright position, luckily cushioned from the pressure of the tangle of bedsprings by the mattress but jammed against the wall by the frame. To her back was the steel shaft of a ship's elevator. Her one free arm dangled at her right side.

Carey wrapped his fingers around the edge of the frame. He was in his mid-fifties but still strong from his days as a laborer. He pulled with the considerable power of his big body. The frame yielded slightly only to spring back in place soon as he let go. He tried to pry the frame with a length of wood but stopped when Myra called out in pain. He tossed the wood aside in disgust.

"Darling," he said, trying to keep his voice calm, "I'm going to get help. I'll have to leave you. Just a little while. I'll be back. I promise."

"Jake, you have to save yourself. The ship—"

"You're not getting rid of me *that* easily, my love."

"Don't be stubborn, for Godsakes."

He kissed her face again. Her skin, normally so warm to the touch, felt clammy. "Think about sunshine in Tuscany while you're waiting. I'll be back soon. Promise." He squeezed her hand and, unlocking the door from the inside, went out into the corridor without the slightest idea what he was going to do. A strong-looking heavyset man came toward him. Jake grabbed the man's shoulder and started to ask for help.

"Outtamyway!" With a white-eyed stare the man shouldered Jake aside despite Carey's size.

He tried frantically to recruit a couple more men before giving up. No Samaritans here. It was like trying to snag a steer out of a thirst-crazed herd of cattle stampeding for a water hole. He couldn't blame them for running for their lives. He'd be dragging Myra for high ground if she were free. He decided his fellow passengers would be useless. He had to find someone from the crew. Struggling to keep his footing against the slant of the deck, he joined the throng heading for the higher decks.

Angelo had made a quick survey of the ship and didn't like what he saw, especially on the starboard side, which was dipping ever lower toward the sea.

Five lifeboats had been launched, and all were filled with crew. Dozens of frightened waiters and kitchen help were jumping into the dangerously overloaded boats and pulling toward a white ship. One look at the ship's crumpled bow and the gaping hole in the side of the *Doria* told Angelo what had happened. Angelo thanked God that many of the passengers were out of their cabins celebrating the last night aboard when the boats hit.

He headed for the port side. It was tough climbing up the slanted deck whose surface was slicked with oil and water from the shoes of passengers and crew. He pulled himself up inch by inch along a passageway by holding on to handrails and door jambs, and finally made it to the promenade deck. Most of the passengers had instinctively gravitated to the side farther from the water. There they awaited instructions. In the glare of emergency lighting they clung to deck chairs that were bolted to the floor or huddled apprehensively among the piles of baggage placed there earlier in preparation for docking. The crew did their best to tend to broken arms and legs. Bumps and bruises would have to wait.

Some people were dressed in evening wear, others in the clothes they wore to bed. They were amazingly calm except for those times when the ship shuddered. Then cries of anguish and anger filled the damp air. Angelo knew that composure would quickly change to hysteria if word spread that some crewmen were taking the only lifeboats and leaving the passengers behind on a sinking ship.

The promenade deck was designed so passengers could step through the sliding windows into the lifeboats that hung down from the boat deck. The ship's officers and what was left of the crew worked fruitlessly to unhook the lifeboats. The davits hadn't been made to work at a steep angle, and it was impossible to release the boats. Angelo's heart fell. That's why the passengers hadn't been instructed to abandon ship. The captain was afraid of a panic!

With one half of the lifeboats carrying off the ship's crew and the other half useless, there weren't enough for the passengers. Not even enough life jackets to go around from the look of it. There was no escape for the passengers if the boat sank. For a fleeting moment he considered sliding back to the starboard side and jumping ship with the other crewmen. He shook the thought away and instead grabbed a pile of life jackets from another crewman and started passing them out. Damned Sicilian code of honor. One of these days it was going to kill him.

"Angelo!"

A bloody apparition elbowed its way through the milling crowd, calling out his name.

"Angelo, it's *me*, Jake Carey."

The tall American with the pretty wife. Mrs. Carey was old enough to be his mother, but *mamma mia,* those big beautiful eyes and the way her middle-aged pounds had added a ripe voluptuousness to her once-youthful curves. Angelo had fallen in love with her instantly, a young man's innocent lust. The Careys had tipped him generously and, more important, treated him with respect. Others, even fellow Italians, looked down on his dark Sicilian skin.

That Jake Carey had been the picture of American prosperity, still fit in his mid-fifties, wide shoulders filling out his sports jacket, trim gray hair, tanned face. The well-dressed passenger he'd seen earlier that evening was gone. The wild-eyed man rushing toward him wore ripped pajamas caked with dust and dirt, the front smeared with a big red stain. He came over and grabbed Angelo, gripping his arm so hard that it hurt.

"Thank God, someone I know," he said wearily.

Angelo searched the crowd with his eyes. "Where is Signora Carey?"

"Trapped in our cabin. I need your help." Fire burned in his eyes.

"I come," Angelo replied without a moment's hesitation.

He caught the attention of a steward and shoved the life jackets at him, then followed Carey toward the nearest stairway. Carey put his head down and bulled his way through the tide of humanity streaming onto the deck. Angelo clutched the back of

Carey's soiled pajama top so he wouldn't lose him. They dashed down one staircase to the upper deck, where most of the first-class cabins were. By then only a few oil-covered stragglers were making their way along the hallways.

Angelo was shocked when he saw Mrs. Carey. She looked as if she were in a medieval torture rack. Her eyes were closed, and for an instant he thought she was dead. But at her husband's gentle touch her eyelids fluttered.

"Told you I'd be back, darling," Carey said. "Look, Angelo here has come to help."

Angelo took her hand and gallantly kissed it. She gave him a melting smile.

Both men grabbed the bed frame and pulled, grunting more with frustration than exertion, ignoring the pain from the sharp metal edge cutting into the flesh of their palms. The frame gave a few inches more than it had earlier. As soon as they let go, it sprang back into place. With each attempt, Mrs. Carey clamped her eyes and lips tight. Carey cursed. He'd gotten his way so often with simple strength, he'd become used to winning. But not this time.

"We need more men," he said, panting.

Angelo shrugged with embarrassment. "Most of the crew is already on the lifeboats."

"Jeezus," Carey whispered. It had been hard enough finding Angelo. Carey thought for a moment, looking at the problem from an engineer's point of view.

"We could do it, just the two of us," he said finally. "If we had a jack."

"What?" The waiter looked puzzled.

"A *jack*." Carey struggled for the right word, gave up, and made pumping motions with his hand. "For an automobile."

Angelo's dark eyes brightened with understanding. "Ah," he said. "A *lever*. For an auto."

"That's right," Carey said with growing excitement. "Look, we could put it here and pry the frame away from the wall so we'll have space to pull Myra out."

"*Si.* The garage. I come back."

"Yes, that's right, the garage." Carey glanced at his wife's stricken face. "But you must hurry."

Carey was never a man to take things for granted. Angelo might bolt for the nearest lifeboat as soon as he left the cabin. Carey wouldn't blame him. He gripped Angelo's elbow.

"I can't tell you how much I appreciate this, Angelo. When we get back to New York, I'll make sure you're rewarded."

"Hey, Signor. I don't do this for money." He grinned, blew a kiss at Mrs. Carey, and disappeared from the cabin, grabbing a life jacket on the way out.

He ran down the hallway, descended a staircase to the foyer deck, and got no farther. The *Stockholm*'s bow had penetrated almost to the chapel, leaving the foyer a mess of twisted metal and shattered glass. He moved away from the main damage area and followed a central corridor that took him toward the stern, then went down another set of stairs to A Deck. Again, many of the starboard cabins had simply vanished. Once more he made his way down to the next deck using a circuitous route.

Angelo stopped and crossed himself each time before he descended to another deck. The gesture gave him comfort even though he knew it was futile. Not even God would be crazy enough to follow him down to the bowels of a sinking ship.

He paused to get his bearings. He was on B Deck, where the garage and many of the smaller cabins were located. The fifty-car Grande Autorimessa was sandwiched between the forward tourist-class cabins. The air-conditioned garage stretched the width of the ship. Doors on both sides allowed cars to drive directly onto the pier. Angelo had only been below once before. One of the garage men, a fellow Sicilian, wanted to show him the wonder car Chrysler was shipping back from Italy. The streamlined Norseman had taken a year to design, and Ghia of Turin had spent another fifteen months hand-building the hundred-thousand-dollar machine. He could see the breathtakingly beautiful modern lines through openings in the crate that protected it. The two men were more interested in a Rolls-Royce that a rich American from Miami Beach was shipping home from his Paris honeymoon. Angelo and his friend took turns pretending they were the Rolls's chauffeur and passenger.

Angelo remembered being told that there were nine cars in the garage. Maybe one would have a jack he could get at. He wasn't hopeful after seeing the extent of the starboard damage. The other ship would have ripped right through the garage wall. He paused in the gloom to catch his breath and wipe the sweat from his eyes. Now what? Flight? *Mamma mia.* What if the lights go out? He'd never find his way. Fear tugged at his legs, tried to set them in motion.

Wait.

The day he visited the garage his friend showed him another vehicle, an oversized armored truck, in a far corner away from the impact side. No markings had been visible on the shiny black metal body. When Angelo asked about it, his friend simply rolled his eyes and shrugged. Gold maybe. He only knew that it was guarded day and night. Even as they talked, Angelo had seen a man in a dark gray uniform watching them until they left the cargo space.

The deck trembled under his feet. The ship listed another degree or so. Angelo went beyond fear and was now in the throes of genuine terror.

His heartbeat ratcheted up several notches. Slowed as the ship settled. He wondered how close it was to rolling over. He looked at the life jacket he'd been carrying and laughed. The vest would not do much good if the ship capsized and sank with him deep in its belly. Five minutes. That's all he'd give it. Then it was up to the top deck as quick as a rabbit. He and Carey would work something out. They *had* to. He found the entrance to the garage. He took a deep breath, opened the door, and stepped through.

The cavernous space was black except for yellow puddles from the emergency lights in the high ceilings. He glanced toward the starboard side and saw rippling reflections on the floor where the garage was taking on water. Water surged around his ankles. Seawater must be pouring in, and if the garage weren't filled yet, it would be so in minutes. Chances were that any cars in the way would have been crushed by the knifing bow. He wouldn't have much time. He started along a wall toward the far corner. He could see the boxy shape in the shadows and the glint of light off its dark windows. Logic was telling him it would be a dangerous waste of time to go any farther. Get out of the hold and to the top deck. *Pronto.* Before the garage became a fish tank.

The image came to him of Mrs. Carey, pinned against the wall like a butterfly. The truck was her last chance, yet no chance at all. Most likely the jack would be locked inside. He had convinced himself he would have to leave empty-handed and stopped to take one last longing look at the truck. That's when he discovered he wasn't alone.

A pencil-thin beam split the darkness near the truck. Then another. *Flashlights.* Then portable lamps flared and were placed on the floor so as to illuminate the truck. In their light he could see people moving around. There appeared to be several men. Some wore gray uniforms, others black business suits. They had the side and back door of the truck open. He couldn't see what they were doing, except that they seemed to be very intent on their work. He was about two-thirds of the way across the garage and opened his mouth to call out "Signores." The word never left his lips.

Something was moving in the shadows. Gray-clad figures appeared suddenly like actors on a darkened stage. Vanished into the darkness. Appeared again. Four of them, all wearing engine-room coveralls, moving across the breadth of the hold. Something about their furtiveness, like the stealth of a cat stalking a bird, told Angelo to remain quiet. A guard turned, saw the approaching figures, shouted a warning, and reached for the holstered gun at his hip.

The men in coveralls dropped to one knee with military precision and raised the objects they'd been carrying to their shoulders. That smooth and deliberate motion told Angelo he'd been mistaken about the tools. You didn't grow up in the home of the Mafia not knowing what a machine gun looked like and how it was aimed.

Four muzzle barrels opened fire simultaneously, concentrating on the immediate threat, the guard, who had his gun out and was aiming it. The fusillade ripped into him, and his gun went flying. His body virtually disintegrated in a scarlet cloud of blood, flesh, and clothing from the impact of hundreds of soft-nosed bullets. The guard gyrated, caught in a grotesque slow-motion death dance by the stroboscopic effect of the white-hot muzzle blasts.

The others tried to scramble for cover, only to be brought down by the merciless hail of lead before they could take a step. The metal walls echoed and reechoed with the ugly chatter and the mad whine of bullets ricocheting off the armored truck and the wall behind it. Even after it was quite clear that no one could have survived, the men with the guns continued to move forward, firing at the supine bodies.

Suddenly all was silent.

A purple pall of smoke hung in the air, which was thick with the smell of cordite and death.

The killers methodically turned over each body. Angelo thought he would go mad. He stood flat against the bulkhead frozen with fear, cursing his luck. He must have stumbled onto a robbery! He expected the killers to start removing sacks of money from the truck. Instead they did a peculiar thing. They lifted the bleeding bodies out of the rising water, dragged them one by one around to the back of the truck. Then they stuffed them inside, slammed the door, and bolted it shut.

Angelo felt a coldness at his feet that had nothing to do with fear. The water had risen to where he stood. He backed away from the truck, staying in the shadows. As he neared the door he'd come through, the water rose to his knees. Before long it was up to his armpits. He put on the life jacket he'd been clutching like a child's security blanket. Quietly breast-stroking, he made his way to the door. He turned around in the water for one last look. One of the killers stared briefly in Angelo's direction. Then he and the others cast their weapons aside, waded into the water, and began to swim. Angelo slipped out of the garage, praying they hadn't seen him. The corridor was inundated, and he kept swimming until he felt steps under his feet. His shoes and clothes were leaden with water. With a strength born of unbridled terror, he vaulted up the stairs as if the dark, thin-faced killer who seemed to sense Angelo's presence were right on his heels.

Moments later he burst into the Careys' cabin. "I couldn't get a lever," he sputtered breathlessly. "The garage—" He stopped short.

The bed frame had been pried away from the wall, and Carey was gently easing his wife out with the help of the ship's doctor and another crewman. Carey saw the waiter.

"Angelo, I was worried about you."

"She's gonna be all right?" Angelo said with concern. Mrs. Carey's eyes were shut. Her nightgown was wet with blood.

The doctor was taking the woman's pulse. "She passed out, but she's still alive. There may be internal injuries."

Carey noticed the dripping clothes and empty hands. "These guys found me. I got a jack sent over from one of the rescue ships. Guess you didn't find anything in the garage."

Angelo shook his head.

"My God, man, you're soaked. I'm sorry you went through all that."

Angelo shook his head. "It was nothing."

The doctor jabbed a hypodermic needle into the woman's arm. "Morphine for the pain," he explained. He tried to hide the worry in his eyes. "We've got to get her off the ship as soon as possible."

They wrapped the unconscious woman in a blanket and carried her up to the promenade deck on the lower side. The fog had miraculously disappeared, and a small flotilla surrounded the ship, blazing lights reflected in the sea. Coast Guard helicopters hovered above like dragonflies. A steady stream of lifeboats plodded back and forth between the stricken liner and rescue ships.

Most of the lifeboat traffic was between the *Doria* and a huge passenger ship with the words *Ile de France* on its bow. Searchlights from the *Ile* were trained on the *Doria*. Word to abandon ship had never come down. After waiting for two hours, passengers simply went over the side on their own. Women and children and older people were being taken off first. Progress was slow because the only way they could get off the boat was with ropes and nets.

Mrs. Carey was strapped onto a stretcher that was carefully lowered with lines down the side of the ship to a waiting lifeboat, where friendly hands reached up to receive her.

Carey leaned over the rail watching until his wife was safe, then turned to Angelo.

"Better get your butt off this ship, my friend. She's gonna go down."

Angelo looked sadly around him. "Pretty soon, Mr. Carey. I help a few more passengers first." Smiling, he said, "Remember what I say about my name." When Angelo first met the Careys he'd joked that his name meant "angel," someone who serves others.

"I remember." Carey enveloped the waiter's hand in his. "Thanks. I can never repay you. If you ever need anything, I want you to come to me. Understand?"

Angelo nodded. *"Grazie.* I understand. Please say good-bye to the *bella signora."*

Carey nodded, heaved himself over the side, and slid down a rope into the lifeboat. Angelo waved good-bye. He hadn't told Carey or anybody about the wild scene in the garage. This wasn't the time. There might *never* be a right time. Nobody would believe a fantastic story told by a lowly waiter. He remembered a Sicilian saying: *The bird who sings in the tree ends up in the cooking pot.*

The death watch was almost over.

The last survivors had been taken off the ship in the pinkish light of dawn. The captain and a standby crew stayed on the ship until the last minute to keep the liner from being claimed as salvage. Now they, too, slid down ropes into lifeboats.

As the warm morning sun climbed into a cloudless sky, the ship's list became ever sharper. By 9:50 A.M. she lay on her starboard side at a forty-five-degree angle. The bow was partially submerged.

The *Stockholm* hove to about three miles away, her prow a twisted mass of metal. Debris littered the oily water. Two destroyer escorts and four Coast Guard cutters stood by. Planes and helicopters circled overhead.

The end came around ten o'clock. Eleven hours after the collision, the *Doria* rolled completely onto her right side. The empty lifeboats that had defied all the crew's efforts to launch them floated away on their own, free of their davits at last. Foamy geysers exploded around the perimeter of the ship as air trapped in the hull blew out under pressure through the portholes.

Sunlight glinted on the huge rudder and the wet blades of the twin nineteen-foot propellers that had sent her steaming proudly across the ocean. Within minutes water engulfed the bow, the stern lifted at a steep angle, and the ship slid beneath the sea as if she'd been sucked under by the powerful tentacles of a gigantic sea monster.

As she sank, more seawater rushed into the hull and filled compartments and staterooms. The pressure tearing apart metal and rivets produced that spooky, almost human moaning that used to send chills up the spines of submariners who had just sunk a ship.

The ship plunged toward the bottom in almost the same angle and position at which she sank. Two hundred twenty-five feet below, she came to a jarring stop, then settled levelly onto her sandy bier on her starboard side. Bubbles seething from hundreds of openings transformed the normally dark water around the wreck to a light blue.

Rubbish whirled around a tremendous vortex for at least fifteen minutes. As the water returned to normal, a Coast Guard boat moved in and dropped a marker buoy where the ship had been.

Gone from the world's sight was the two-million-dollar cargo of wines, fine fabrics, furniture, and olive oil.

Gone, too, was the incredible artwork—the murals and tapestries, the bronze statue of the old admiral.

And locked deep in the ship's interior was the black armored truck with the bullet-riddled bodies and the deadly secret they had died for.

The tall blond man came down the gangplank of the *Ile de France* onto Pier 84 and made his way to the customs shed. Wearing a black wool sailor's cap and a long overcoat, he was indistinguishable from the hundreds of passengers who swarmed onto the deck.

Discharging its humanitarian duty had put the French liner thirty-six hours behind schedule. It arrived in New York on Thursday afternoon to a tumultuous welcome, stayed long enough to unload seven hundred thirty-three *Doria* survivors. After accomplishing its historic rescue, the ship did a quick turn-around, steamed back up the Hudson River and out to sea. Time was money, after all.

"Next," the customs officer said as he looked up from his table.

The officer wondered for a second if the man in front of him had been injured in the collision and decided the scar had healed long ago.

"State Department's waiving passports for survivors. Just sign this blank declaration card. All I need is your name and U.S. address," the customs inspector said.

"Yes, thank you. They told us on the ship." The blond man smiled. Or maybe it was just the scar. "I'm afraid my passport is at the bottom of the Atlantic Ocean." He said his name was Johnson and that he was going to Milwaukee.

The officer pointed. "Follow that line, Mr. Johnson. The Public Health Service has got to check you for communicable diseases. Shouldn't take long. Next, please."

The health inspection was brief, as promised. Moments later the blond man was through the gate. The crowd of survivors, relatives, and friends had surged from the steamship dock onto the street. There was a traffic jam of slow-moving, horn-honking traffic—cars, buses, and taxis. He stopped at the curb and scanned the faces around him until a pair of eyes met his. Then two more and another. He nodded to acknowledge that he had seen his comrades, before they headed off in different directions.

He moved away from the crowd toward Forty-fourth Street and flagged down a taxi. He was weary from the night's exertions and looked forward to the chance to rest.

Their work was done. For now.

1

NINA KIROV STOOD AT THE TOP OF
the ancient stairway, eyes sweeping the nearly stagnant green waters of the lagoon, thinking she had never seen a coast more barren than this isolated stretch of Moroccan shoreline. Nothing stirred in the oppressive, ovenlike heat. The only sign of human settlement was the cluster of putty-colored, barrel-roofed tombs that overlooked the lagoon like seaside condominiums for the departed. Centuries of sand drifting through the arched portals had mingled with the dust of the dead. Nina grinned with the delight of a child seeing presents under the Christmas tree. To a marine archaeologist, these bleak surroundings were more beautiful than the white sands and palm trees of a tropical paradise. The very awfulness of the mournful place would have protected it from her biggest fear: site contamination.

Nina vowed to thank Dr. Knox again for persuading her to join the expedition. She had refused the initial invitation, telling the caller from the University of Pennsylvania's respected anthropology department that it would be a waste of time. Every inch of Moroccan coastline must have been explored with a fine-tooth comb by now. Even if someone *did* discover an underwater site, it would have been buried under tons of concrete by the Romans, who invented waterfront renewal. As much as Nina admired their engineering skills, she considered the Romans Johnny-come-lately spoilers in the grand scheme of history.

She knew her refusal had more to do with sour grapes than archaeology. Nina was trying to dig herself out from under a mountain of paperwork generated by a shipwreck project off the coast of Cyprus in waters claimed by the Turks. Preliminary surveys suggested the wreck was of ancient Greek origin, triggering conflicting claims between these old enemies. With national honor at stake, the F-16s from Ankara and Athens were warming up their engines when Nina dove on the wreck and identified it as a Syrian merchantman. This brought the Syrians into the mess, but it defused the potential for a bloody encounter. As the owner, president, and sole employee of her marine archaeological consultancy firm, Mari-Time Research, all the paperwork ended up in Nina's lap.

A few minutes after she told the university she was too busy to accept the invitation, Stanton Knox called.

"My hearing must be going bad, Dr. Kirov," he said in the dry nasal tones she had heard a hundred times issuing from behind his lectern. "I actually thought I heard someone tell me you were *not* interested in our Moroccan expedition, and of course that can't be true."

Months had passed since she had talked to her old mentor. She smiled, picturing the snowy shock of hair, the near manic gleam behind the wire-rimmed spectacles, and the roué's mustache that curled up at the ends over a puckish mouth.

Nina tried to blunt the inevitable charm offensive she knew was coming.

"With all due respect, Professor Knox, I doubt if there's a stretch of the North African coast that hasn't been overbuilt by the Romans or discovered by somebody else."

"*Brava!* I'm glad to see that you recall the first three lessons of Archaeology 101, Dr. Kirov."

Nina chuckled at the ease with which Knox donned his professorial robe. She was in her thirties, owner of a successful consulting business, and held almost as many degrees as Knox did. Yet she still felt like a student within his aura. "How could I ever forget? Skepticism, skepticism, and *more* skepticism."

"Correct," he said with obvious joy. "The three snarling dogs of skepticism who will *rip* you to pieces unless you present them with a dinner of hard evidence. You'd be surprised at how often my preaching falls on deaf ears." He sighed theatrically, and his tone became more businesslike. "Well, I understand your concern, Dr. Kirov. Ordinarily I would agree with you about site contamination, but this location is on the Atlantic coast well beyond the Pillars of Melkarth, away from Roman influence."

Interesting. Knox used the *Phoenician* name for the western end of the Mediterranean where Gibraltar bends low to kiss Tangier. The Greeks and Romans called it the Pillars of Herakles. Nina knew from bitter classroom experience that when it came to names, Knox was as precise as a brain surgeon.

"Well, I'm terribly busy—"

"Dr. Kirov, I might as well admit it," Knox interjected. "I need your help. Badly. I'm up to my neck in land archaeologists who are so timid they wear galoshes in the bathtub. We *really* need to get somebody into the water. It's a small expedition, about a dozen people, and you'd be the only diver."

Knox's reputation as a skilled fly fisherman was not undeserved. He dangled the Phoenician connection under her nose, set the hook with his sympathetic appeal for help, then reeled her in with the suggestion that as the only diver she would get sole credit for any underwater finds.

Nina could practically see the professor's pink nose twitching with glee. She shuffled the folders on her desk. "I've got a ton of paperwork to finish . . ."

Knox cut her off at the pass. "I'm well aware of your Cyprus job," he said. "Congratulations, by the way, for averting a crisis between NATO partners. I've taken care of everything. I have two highly competent teaching fellows who would love to gain experience in dealing with the red tape that is such a substantial part of archaeology these days. This is a preliminary survey. We'll only be a week or ten days. And by then my trusted young Myrmidons will have dotted all the *I*'s and crossed all the *T*'s.

You don't have to decide this minute. I'll fax you some material. Take a peek at it and get back to me."

"How long do you need, Dr. Knox?"

"An hour would do. Cheerio."

Nina put the phone down and laughed out loud. An *hour*.

Almost immediately, paper began to spew from the fax machine like lava from an erupting volcano. It was the project proposal Knox submitted with his funding request. He wanted money to survey an area for Greco-Roman or possibly *other* ruins. The standard Knox sales pitch, a tantalizing mix of facts and possibilities, designed to make his project stand out in bold relief from all the others competing for funds.

Nina breezed through the proposal with a practiced eye and shifted her attention to the map. The survey locus was between the mouth of the Draa River and the western Sahara on the Moroccan coastal plain that stretched from Tangier to Essaouria. Tapping her teeth with the tip of her ballpoint pen, she studied an enlarged section of the area. The coastal indentation looked as if the cartographer had hiccupped while drawing the shoreline. Noting the site's proximity to the Canary Islands, she leaned back in her chair and thought how she needed to get out into the field before she went insane. She picked up the telephone and dialed.

Knox answered in mid-ring. "We leave next week."

Now, as Nina surveyed the lagoon, the lines and squiggles on a map translated themselves into physical features. The basin was roughly circular, embraced by two pincers of blasted brick-red rock. Beyond the entrance were shallows that at low tide revealed rippling mud flats. Thousands of years ago the lagoon opened directly onto the ocean. Its naturally sheltered waters would have attracted ancient mariners who commonly anchored on either side of a headland to wait for good weather or daylight. Nearby was a dry riverbed, what the locals called a *wadi*. Another good sign. Settlements often grew near a river.

From the lagoon a narrow, sandy path led through the dunes and eventually terminated at the ruins of a small Greek temple.

The harbor would have been too tight for Roman ships and their massive jetties. She guessed the Greeks used the inlet as a temporary anchorage. The steep shoreline would have discouraged hauling goods inland. She had checked the old maps, and this site was miles from any known ancient settlement. Even today, the nearest village, a sleepy Berber encampment, was ten miles away over a rutted sand road.

Nina shielded her eyes from the sun and stared over the water at a ship anchored offshore. The vessel's hull was painted from waterline to superstructure in turquoise green. She squinted, just making out the letters *NUMA,* the acronym for the National Underwater and Marine Agency, emblazoned on the hull amidships. She idly wondered what a vessel belonging to a U.S. government agency was doing off a remote shoreline in Morocco. Then she picked up a large mesh bag and descended a dozen worn stone steps to where the water gently lapped the bottom stair.

As she removed her UPenn baseball cap, sunlight glinted off braids the color of ripe wheat woven together behind her head. She slipped out of an oversized T-shirt. The floral bikini she wore underneath revealed a strong, long-legged body nearly six feet tall.

Nina inherited her first name, her golden hair, her slightly roundish face, and a peasant stamina that could put male counterparts to shame from her great-grandmother, a sturdy farm worker who found true love in a Ukrainian cotton field with a Tsarist soldier. From Nina's Georgian mother came the bold, almost Asian eyes of stormy gray, high haughty cheekbones, and lush mouth. By the time the family emigrated to the United States, the genetic airbrush had slimmed the Kirov female silhouette, narrowing thick waists and wide hips, leaving a pleasing width and a healthy bustline.

From the bag Nina took a Nikon digital camera in a custom-built Ikelight plastic housing and checked the strobe light. Next came an air tank and U.S. Divers buoyancy compensator, a black-and-purple Henderson wetsuit, booties, gloves, hood, weight belt, and mask and snorkel. She suited up and on her head attached a Niterider Cyclops light that would keep her hands free, then fastened the quick-release buckles of her BC and snapped on her weight belt. Finally, she strapped a seven-inch Divex titanium knife to her thigh. After clipping a collection bag to a utility hook, she set the time on her latest toy, an Aqualand dive watch with a depth display.

With no dive buddy to check her equipment, Nina went through the routine predive inspection twice. Satisfied with the results, she sat on the stair and worked her feet into her fins, then she slipped off the step before the blistering North African sun cooked her inside the wetsuit. The tepid water seeped between her skin and the neoprene wetsuit and quickly warmed to body temperature. She tested her main and extra regulators, then pushed away from the stairs, turned, and slowly breast-stroked into the pondlike lagoon.

There was virtually no wave motion, and the slimy water was slightly brackish, but even with the surface scum Nina reveled in her freedom. She glided along with gentle fin flutters, pitying the expedition's land archaeologists as they crawled on sore knees wielding trowels and whisk brooms, eyes stinging with sweat-caked dust. Nina could maneuver in comfortable coolness like a plane making an aerial survey.

A low-lying island topped by an anorexic scraggle of stunted pines guarded the entrance. She planned to swim directly toward the island and bisect the lagoon. She would explore each half separately, making a series of parallel runs at right angles to the baseline. The search pattern was similar to that used to find a wreck in the open ocean. Her eyes would take the place of a side-scan sonar or magnetometer. Precision measurements came later. She simply wanted to get a feel for what lay underwater.

Once below the clouded surface, the water was relatively clear, and Nina could see to the bottom, a depth of no more than twenty feet. This meant she could snorkel and conserve air. A series of intersecting straight lines materialized and formed into rectangles created by carefully fitted stone blocks.

The stairway had continued down underwater to an old quay. It was a significant discovery because it indicated the lagoon was once a real port and not a temporary anchorage. The bottom was likely to be covered with layers of civilization over a long period of time instead of junk tossed over the side by transient sailors.

Soon she picked out thicker lines and piles of rubble. Building ruins. Bingo! Storage sheds, housing, or headquarters for a dock and harbormaster. Definitely not an overnight anchorage.

Darkness loomed, and she thought she was at the end of the quay. She passed over a large square opening and wondered if it could be a fish tank, what the ancients called a *piscina*. Far too big. The size of an Olympic swimming pool.

Nina spit out the snorkel, bit down on the regulator mouthpiece, and dove straight down. She moved along one side of the yawning cavity. Coming to a corner, she turned and followed another edge, swimming until she had covered the entire perimeter. It was around one hundred by one hundred fifty feet.

Nina flicked her headlamp on and dove into the opening. The muddy floor was perfectly flat and about eight feet below the quay level. The light's narrow beam picked out broken pottery and debris. Using her knife, she pried potsherds from the mud and put them into the collection bag after carefully marking their positions. She discovered a channel and followed it seaward until it broke out into the lagoon. The opening was easily big enough to allow for the passage of an ancient ship. The space cut into the quay had all the characteristics of an artificial harbor known as a *cothon*. She discovered several slipways, each big enough to accommodate ships more than fifty feet long, and a true *piscina*, which confirmed her theory about the *cothon*.

Leaving the quay, she continued on her baseline course using the land spit to her right as a reference point. She swam between the island and the mainland until she found a submerged mole or breakwater a few yards below the surface, constructed of parallel stone walls filled with rubble. In a drier time it would have connected the mainland and the island.

Coming to the island, she shed her dive gear and walked across thorn-covered slabs of rock to the other side. The island was more than fifty feet wide, almost twice as long, and mostly flat. The trees she had seen from shore barely came up to her chin.

Near the lagoon entrance were piles of stones, probably foundations, and a circle of blocks. It was the perfect spot for a lighthouse or a watchtower, offering a sharp-eyed sentinel a panoramic view of ship traffic. Defenders could be summoned from the mainland whenever a sail was sighted.

Stepping inside the circle, Nina climbed onto a fragmented stair and looked out at the anchored ship she had seen earlier. Again she wondered what would bring an American government vessel to this arid and lonely coast. After a moment she retrieved her scuba equipment. The cooling and weightless environment back in the water was refreshing, and she decided her fishy ancestors had made a big mistake when they crawled from the sea onto dry land.

Nina swam across the lagoon entrance. The other peninsula started low from the land, gradually widening as it rose to a knobby crag. The sheer reddish rocks dropped straight into the water like the ramparts of a fortress. Nina dove until she was at the base of the blank wall, looking for a footpath. Finding none, she continued underwater to the seaward end of the promontory which terminated in a rocky shelf. A perfect defensive position where archers could set up a murderous cross fire to rake the decks of any invader entering the harbor.

A horizontal slab protruded like a Stone Age awning from the rock face near the platform. Beneath the slab was a rectangular opening the size and shape of a doorway. Drifting closer, Nina squinted through her face mask lens and tried to pierce the menacing blackness. She remembered her headlamp and switched it on. The shaft of light fell on a whirl of ghostly movement. She drew back in alarm. Then a laugh bubbled from her regulator. The silver-scaled school of fish that had made the tunnel its home was more startled than she was.

As her pulse returned to normal she recalled Dr. Knox's warning: Don't risk your neck for a nugget of knowledge that would end up in a dusty tome read by a few. With fiendish delight he'd relate in grim detail the fates of scientists who went too far. Furbush was devoured by cannibals. Rozzini was consumed by malaria. O'Neil dropped into a bottomless crevasse.

Nina was convinced Knox made the names up, but she took his point. She was alone, without a lifeline to unreel behind her. Nobody knew where she was. The very element of danger that should have repelled her was seductive in its appeal. She checked her pressure gauge. By snorkeling, she'd used her air supply sparingly and still had time left.

She made a pact with herself to stop just inside the opening and go no farther. The tunnel couldn't be very long. Primitive tools, not diamond drills, had been used to cut through the rock. She shot some pictures of the entrance, then moved forward.

Incredible!

The floor was almost perfectly flat, the walls smooth except for shaggy marine growth.

She went in deeper, forgetting her pact and Knox's sage advice as well. The tunnel was the most beautiful artifact she had ever seen. It was already longer than a similar passageway at the submerged city of Apollonia.

The smooth sides ended abruptly, becoming a rough-sided cave that narrowed and widened, meandering in more or less of a straight line, with smaller passages branching off. Sconces for lamps were set into the carbon-blackened walls. The tunnel borers had extended the natural cave by making an artificial one. Nina marveled at the skill and determination of long dead Bronze Age sandhogs.

The passageway once again became wider and more polished. Nina squeezed over the top of a pile of rubble, encouraged by a greenish glow in the distance. She swam to the light, which became brighter the nearer she came.

In pursuit of knowledge Nina had crawled through piles of bat guano and lairs guarded by bad-tempered scorpions. As wondrous as the tunnel was, she was anxious to be out of it and drew a sigh of relief when the passage ended. She floated up a stairway and through an archway, emerging into an open space surrounded by crumbled foundations.

Nina suspected Dr. Knox had an idea of what she might find in the lagoon, but he couldn't have known the extent of it. *Nobody* could. Hold on, girl. Order your thoughts. Assess the details. Start acting like a scientist, not like Huckleberry Finn.

She sat underwater on a waist-high stone block and pondered her findings. The port was probably a combined military and trading post that kept out foreign traders and guarded commercial shipping. There was a growl in her ear. The dogs of skepticism were hungry for their dinner of solid scientific fact. Before she made her findings definitive, every square foot of the port would have to be explored and evaluated.

She ventured a guess that the port had sunk from a shifting of tectonic plates. Maybe during the big earthquake of A.D. 10. Quakes were not as common here as in the Mediterranean, but it could happen. *Growl.* I know, I know. No conclusion until all the evidence is in. She watched the bubbles from her exhalations rise to the surface, thinking there might be a quicker way to get to the truth.

Nina had a talent that went beyond the ordinary and the explainable. She had discussed it with only a few close friends, and then in forensic terms comparing herself to an FBI criminal scene profiler who reads a crime scene like an eyewitness. Nothing psychic about it, she had convinced herself. Only a superb command of her subject combined with a photographic memory and a vivid imagination. Something like the way dowsers find water veins with a forked twig.

She discovered her talent accidentally on her first trip to Egypt. She had pressed her hands against one of the huge foundation blocks on the Great Pyramid of Kufu. It was a natural gesture, a tactile attempt to comprehend the enormity of the incredible pile of stones, but something strange and frightening happened. Her every sense was assaulted by images. The pyramid was only half as high, its leveled summit crowded with hundreds of dark men in breechcloths hoisting blocks with a primitive scaffolding. The sweat on their skin gleamed in the sun. She could hear shouts. The squeak of pullies. She yanked her hand away as if the rock had turned red hot.

A voice was saying, "Camel ride, missy?"

She blinked her eyes. The pyramid soared in a point toward the sky again. The dark men were gone. In their place was a camel driver. Grinning broadly, he leaned on the pommel of his saddle. "Camel ride, missy? I give you good price."

"*Shukran*. Thank you. Not today." The driver nodded sadly and loped off. Nina pulled herself together and went back to the hotel, where she sketched out the block and pulley arrangement. Later she showed it to an engineer friend. He had stared at her drawing, muttering, "Damned ingenious." He asked if he could steal the idea to use on a crane project he had been working on.

Since Giza there had been similar experiences. It wasn't something she could turn on and off at will. If she got a long-distance call from the past every time she picked up an artifact, she'd be in an insane asylum. She had to be *drawn* to something like an iron filing to a magnet. At a smaller version of the Coliseum, located at an imperial resort outside Rome, the images of pain and terror were so strong, the blood-soaked sand, severed limbs, and cries of the dying so vivid, that she retched. For a while she thought she had lost her mind. She didn't sleep for several nights. Maybe *that's* why she didn't like the Romans.

This was no Roman amphitheater, she rationalized. Before she talked herself out of it, she swam to the edge of the quay, placed her palms on the fitted stones, and closed her eyes. She could picture the longshoremen hauling amphorae filled with wine or oil, and the slap of sails against wooden masts, but these were only imaginings. She breathed a sigh of relief. Served her right for trying to shortcut the scientific process.

Nina shot a few photographs, disappointed only that she hadn't found a shipwreck. She collected more pottery, found a half-buried stone anchor, and was taking a few last shots when she saw the roundish protuberances rising from where the bottom was sandy.

She swam over and brushed the sand away. The lump was part of a larger object. Intrigued, she got down on her knees and cleared more covering from a large stone nose, part of a huge carved face about eight feet from its blunt chin to the top of the scalp. The nose was flat and wide and the mouth broad, with fleshy lips.

The head was covered by a skullcap or close-fitting helmet. The expression could best be described as a glower. She stopped digging and ran her fingers over the black stone.

The fleshy lips seemed to curl as if in speech.

Touch me. I have much to tell you.

Nina drew back and stared at the impassive face. The features were as before. She listened for the voice. *Touch me.* Fainter now, lost in the metallic burble of her breath going through the regulator.

Girl, you've been underwater way too long.

She pressed the valve on her BC. Air hissed into the inflatable vest. Heart still pounding, she ascended slowly back to her own world.

2 THE SWARTHY, THICK-SET MAN SAW

Nina approaching the circle of tents and ran over with his hand extended. In his thick Spanish accent, Raul Gonzalez said, "May I help you carry your bag, Dr. Kirov?"

"I'm fine—" Nina was used to hauling her gear around, and in fact preferred to keep a tight rein on it.

"It would be no trouble," he said gallantly, displaying his painted-on grin to the fullest. Too weary to argue and not wanting to hurt his feelings, Nina handed the load over. He took the heavy bag as if it were full of feathers.

"You had a productive day?" he said.

Nina wiped the sweat out of her eyes and downed a swig from a warm bottle of lime Gatorade. Nina was no absentminded professor. In a field where a bead or a button can be a major discovery, an archaeologist is trained to look for the tiniest of details. She couldn't figure Gonzalez. She had noticed little things about him, especially when he thought nobody was looking. She had caught him studying her, the big-toothed grin absent, the eyes under the fleshy brow as hard as marbles. Nina was an attractive woman and often drew sidelong glances from men. This was more like a lion watching a gazelle. Finally, there was just the way he was always *there,* looking over your shoulder. Not only her. He seemed to be stalking everyone on the expedition.

Nina's elation at her discoveries overcame her normal caution. "Yes, thank you," she said. "It was productive. *Very* productive."

"I would expect no less of such a knowledgeable scientist. I'm very much looking forward to hearing about it." He carried the bag over to her tent and placed it out front, then wandered about the encampment as if he were an inspector-general making his rounds.

Gonzalez told people he had retired early on the money he made selling Southern California real estate and was indulging his lifelong amateur love of archaeology. He looked to be in his mid-forties or early fifties, shorter than Nina by several inches, with a thick, powerful blacksmith's body. His slicked-down hair was as shiny and black as a bowling ball. He had joined the expedition through Time-Quest, an organization that placed paying volunteers on archaeological digs. Anybody with a couple of thousand dollars could get a week's worth of spooning dirt through a sieve with a child's plastic shovel. The third-degree sunburn was thrown in at no extra cost.

Counting herself and Dr. Knox, there were ten people in the party. Gonzalez, of course, and Mr. and Mrs. Bonnell, an older American couple from Iowa who had come in with another pay-as-you-go organization. And to Nina's regret, there was the insufferable Dr. Fisel from the Moroccan Department of Antiquities, who was said to be a cousin of the king. Completing the party were Fisel's young assistant, Kassim, a cook, and two Berber drivers who did double duty working on the dig.

The expedition had assembled from various parts of the world in Tarfaya, an oil port on the southern coast. The Moroccan government arranged for the lease from an oil company of three nine-passenger Renault vans to carry people and equipment. The vehicles had made their way along dusty but serviceable roads, following the coastal plain for a couple of hundred miles.

Even today, much of the country was desolate and uninhabited except for small Berber settlements here and there. The territory had been largely unexplored until Mobil and a few other companies started looking for offshore oil deposits.

The camp was behind the dunes, in a parched field dotted with prickly pear at the edge of a featureless plain that rolled off to a distant high plateau. A few pitiful olive trees sucked enough moisture from the dry soil to maintain their wretched existence. What shade they cast was mostly psychological. The site was close to piles of masonry and fallen columns where the land excavations were being conducted.

Nina made her way to one of the colorful nylon domes pitched in a circle on a flat sandy area. She washed the salt out of her face and changed into clean shorts and T-shirt. Taking her sketch pad to a folding chair, she sat outside the tent and in the afternoon light made drawings of her findings. She had covered several pages when people began straggling in from the dig.

Dr. Knox's khaki shorts and shirt were sweat-stained and caked with dust, and his knees were scraped raw from crawling on hard ground. His nose was shrimp pink and starting to peel. The transformation from the halls of academia was amazing. In the classroom Knox was impeccable in his dress. But in the field he literally *threw* himself into an excavation like a child in a sandbox. With his pith helmet, his baggy shorts, and epaulets on his thin shoulders, he looked as if he had stepped out of an old *National Geographic* magazine.

"What a day," he fumed, slipping his helmet off. "I truly believe we'll have to burrow down another twenty feet before we find anything dating back any earlier than the Rif rebellion! And if you think working with *me* is a bloody trial, I dare you to go a few rounds with that pompous ass Fisel." The glee in his voice at being on a dig belied the grumbling. "Well, *you* certainly look comfortable," he said accusingly. "How did it—? Never mind, I can see it in your eyes. Tell me quickly, Nina, or I'll assign you extra homework."

Knox's use of her first name recalled her days as a student. Nina saw her chance to avenge the gentle taunts she had endured in the classroom. "Wouldn't you like to freshen up first?" she said.

"No, I would *not*. For heaven's sakes don't be a sadist, young lady; it doesn't become you."

"I learned my craft from a good teacher," she said with a smile. "Don't despair, professor. While you drag your chair over, I'll pour us some iced tea and tell you the whole story."

Minutes later Knox sat attentively by her side, head inclined slightly as he listened. She described her explorations from the moment she stepped into the water, omitting only the discovery of the sculpted head. She felt inexplicably uneasy discussing it. Later, maybe.

Knox was silent during the entire account except when Nina paused for breath, when he'd impatiently urge, "I knew it, I knew it. Yes, yes, go on."

"That's the story," she said, finishing her tale.

"Well done. Conclusion."

"I think this was a *very* old port," she said.

"Of *course* it's old," he replied with mock annoyance. "I knew that when I saw the aerial photos of your little pond from an oil company survey. Every bloody thing within a hundred meters of where we're sitting is old. But *how* old?"

"Remember the hungry dogs of skepticism," she reminded him.

Knox rubbed his hands together, enjoying the game. "Let's assume the dogcatcher has captured the annoying creatures and for the time being they languish happily in a pound. What, dear lady, is your educated guess?"

"As long as you put it that way, my guess is that it's a Phoenician military and trading post." She handed over her sketch pad and pieces of the pottery she'd found.

Knox studied the potsherds, lovingly running his fingers along the ragged edges. He put them aside and looked at the sketches, puckering his mouth so that the mustache did a little dance on his lip. "I think," he said with obvious and melodramatic relish, "that we should run your story by the esteemed Dr. Fisel."

Gamiel Fisel sat under a large umbrella. His round body practically hid the chair it was perched on, and with his tan slacks, shirt, and matching complexion, he resembled a large caramel apple. On the table in front of him was a scattering of potsherds from the dig. He was peering through a Sherlock Holmes magnifying glass at one fragment. At his side was his assistant, Kassim, a pleasant young man, supposedly a university student, who served primarily as Fisel's tea boy.

"Good afternoon, Dr. Fisel. Dr. Kirov made some interesting observations today," Knox said with undisguised pride.

Fisel looked up as if an annoying mosquito had just landed on the tip of his nose. He was not unused to women in the workplace. Many Moroccan women worked as professionals. He simply had trouble dealing with a female who was his equal in academic rank, his superior in the number of degrees held, and at least a foot taller. As a nondiver, Fisel was at Nina's mercy on the underwater site, and he didn't like not being totally in control.

Nina cut right to the chase. "I think there was a small but important port here, and that it was Phoenician."

Fisel said, "More tea, Kassim." The young man hurried over to the camp's cooking area. Fisel turned to Knox as if Nina were not there. "Your assistant has a vivid imagination. You've told her, of course, that our excavations at the primary site have produced Greek and Roman artifacts." He had a quick, nervous way of speaking, firing off sentences like bursts from a machine gun.

Nina had deferred to Fisel, but she could ignore his rudeness no longer. "First of all, I'm *not* Dr. Knox's assistant," she said coolly. "I'm his *colleague*. And second, while I have no doubt of Greco-Roman influence, the main center of activity was in the water, not on dry land. And it was Phoenician."

The sketch pad plopped onto the table, and Nina tapped the drawing of the *cothon*. "The Phoenicians were the only ones who cut artificial harbors like this out of dry land. I believe these shards will provide the dating to back me up."

She dumped out her pottery fragments, not caring that they

might be mixed with the others. Taking his time, Fisel picked up a piece, examined it, then studied another one. After a few minutes he looked up. His moist brown eyes boggled behind the thick-lensed glasses, but he was trying hard not to show his excitement.

He cleared his throat and addressed Knox. "Surely you're not going to accept *this* as definitive proof of Dr. Kirov's theory."

"Of *course* not, Dr. Fisel. There's much work to be done, and Dr. Kirov knows that as well as we do. You must admit it's an intriguing beginning, however."

Assuming he had detected a crack in Knox's advocacy, Fisel's putative scowl turned into a fourteen-karat smile. "I am compelled to admit nothing until the case is made."

Kassim arrived with a glass of hot tea. Fisel nodded and picked up his magnifier. The audience with the cousin of the king had ended.

Nina seethed with anger as she and Knox walked away from Fisel's tent. "Imperious little bastard! He knows damned well that I'm right."

Knox gave an avuncular chuckle. "My guess is that Fisel agrees entirely with your findings and will waste no time reporting them."

She grabbed the professor's arm and peered into his dusty face. "I don't understand. Why the act?"

"Oh, it's perfectly clear. He wants to claim the credit for discovering your Phoenician port."

"That's *it!*" She started back toward Fisel's tent. "If he thinks he's going to get away—"

"Hold on, my dear. I promised you'd get credit for all underwater finds, and I meant it. Remember, we hold the important cards. You're the only one on this expedition who knows how to dive."

"He can bring in other divers."

"Yes, he can. Short, plump, bald, and nearsighted though he may be, Fisel swings a lot of weight, figuratively and literally, within his antiquities department. He can bring in all the resources he will need. In the meantime, I want you to finish your sketches, classify what you've found, and continue your survey using scientific methods."

She was still unconvinced. "What if he tries to stop me from diving?"

"This is a joint expedition. I am equal in command to him. He can only go so far until he gets permission. It will take days. If you think *our* red tape is formidable, remember Morocco is heavily influenced by the French, who invented the word *bureaucrat.* I will massage his ego, but I want you to do a very difficult thing. Consider giving Fisel *some* credit for this coup, if it truly turns out to be Phoenician. This *is* his country that we're digging up, after all. He may have some Phoenician forebears."

Nina calmed down and allowed herself a laugh. "You're right. I'm sorry for the outburst. It's been a long day."

"No need for an apology. He *is* a bastard, but I'll remind him that if he doesn't have our cooperation in making this a joint find, he will have the credit taken from him by one of his *own* bastards at a higher level."

Nina thanked the professor, kissed him on the cheek, and returned to her tent. She worked on her sketches until the dinner bell rang. Fisel avoided her eyes at the table. The Iowa couple, who had dug up an intact water jug handle, held center stage. No one paid attention when Nina excused herself and went back to her tent.

After she finished writing a report of her findings on an IBM laptop computer, Nina propped up her notepad and shot some pictures of the sketches with her digital camera. Then she fed images from the camera into the computer. The photos and sketches were razor sharp.

"Okay, Fisel, let me see you try to get a jump on *this.*"

The computer was hooked up to a small suitcase that contained a satellite phone. The solar-powered package cost her an arm and a leg, but it put her in touch with her home base from anywhere in the world. She punched out a number and sent the electronic packet of words and photos winging through the ether until it bounced off a low-orbit Inmarsat global communications satellite, which relayed it to a dish that fed the information at the speed of light into the database at the University of Pennsylvania.

Nina clicked off her computer, satisfied that her reports and pictures were safely in the databank at the university. She was unaware that even on the information highway, there are such things as dangerous detours.

3

ON OFFICIAL BLUEPRINTS THE WIN-
dowless room near the top of the glass office tower overlooking
the peaceful waters of the San Antonio River did not exist. Even
the city inspectors had no idea it was there. The subcontractors
who installed the soundproof walls, the separate electrical conduits, and the voice-activated security locks were paid well to
keep their mouths zipped. If they thought it strange to build a
secret door through the shower stall of a private bathroom, they
kept their opinions to themselves.

The room's decor was as clinically functional as a laboratory.
Uncluttered beige walls. A bank of oversized IBM computer
monitors and hard drives, a document safe, and a center work-
table. A man sat in front of a computer, his hardened face
washed by the cold light from the oversized monitor. He scrolled
down several pages of type and photos and stopped at a series of
line drawings.

With a click of the cursor he enlarged one particular sketch
and zoomed in on a section of the screen, hard blue eyes taking
in every detail. Satisfied he had seen the entire file, he saved it
on a floppy disk and pressed the print command. As the high-
speed printer whirred away, he put the disk in an envelope and
locked it in the safe. He gathered the printed file into a manila
folder, stepped through the shower stall, went through another
door into his office, and switched on an intercom.

"I'll need a few minutes. Right away," he said.

"He has time now," a female voice replied. "Ten minutes in between appointments."

He left his office with the folder and walked through a maze of thickly carpeted hallways. He was tall, at least six feet, no longer young, but the only concession to age was his close-cropped silver hair and a slight stoop to his muscular shoulders. His athletic body was still limber and rock-hard thanks to a Spartan regimen of diet and exercise. Because he rarely smiled or frowned, his face was relatively unlined around the mouth and eyes, as if the skin had been lifted off and stretched over the square jaw and high cheekbones.

The floor held the company's administrative offices and could be entered only by those with hand and voice ID. The work spaces were all on other levels, and he saw nobody until he came to the spacious reception area.

The high-ceiling space was done in burnt red, brown, and green earth colors, repeating a stylized arrow and square Indian pattern on floor and walls. Behind the receptionist was a semi-abstract mural whose brown-skinned figures and giant sprouting quetzal feathers were so intertwined it was hard to tell whether the painting depicted a human sacrifice or a cocktail party. The receptionist sat at a desk that seemed to float on a carpeted sea of burnt orange, unmindful of the painted drama behind her head.

The man stopped in front of the desk and without speaking glanced toward a thick, darkwood door carved with dozens of writhing figures being tormented in a peasant artist's depiction of hell.

"Mr. Halcon will see you," said the receptionist, a middle-aged woman chosen for her blandness, efficiency, and unquestioning loyalty.

The carved door opened into a corner office that was almost as big as the reception area and repeated the Central American theme. Halcon stood at a floor-to-ceiling window, his back to the door.

"Sir, if you have a moment—"

Halcon half-turned, displaying the aquiline nose, set in a pale, narrow face, the profile that had earned him his nickname in the bullring. "Come here, Guzman," he said.

Guzman crossed the room as ordered and stood beside the younger man. Halcon was in his forties, taller than Guzman by an inch or two. He was ascetically lean, almost delicate-looking. Like everything else about Halcon, appearances were deceiving. In a concession to his role as a businessman he had long ago cut off the matador's pigtail, trimmed the Valentino sideburns, and set aside the glittering uniform of the bullring. Yet under his expensive tailored suit still lurked the cruel body of the matador known as the Hawk, who had used his quickness and power to dispatch dozens of brave bulls. If there had been any complaint from the aficionados who followed his brief but illustrious career, it was that the Hawk's kills were coldly efficient and lacked passion. In another age he would have been a deadly swordsman whose blade would have found the beating hearts of men, not bulls.

"Do you know why I chose to build this particular office in this particular location, Guzman?"

"If I would venture a guess, Don Halcon, it offers a good view of many of your company's holdings."

Halcon chuckled at the response. "An honestly blunt answer, as I would expect from my old guardian, but hardly a flattering one. I am not some burgher keeping an eye on his fields."

"My apologies, Don Halcon, I did not mean to offend."

"No offense taken. It was a natural assumption, but an erroneous one." His smile vanished, and his words took on the quiet, steely edge dangerous people give their voices. "I chose this office for one reason: the view it offers of the Mission San Antonio de Valero. It reminds me of what is past, what is present, and what will be." He gestured out at the sprawl of the city visible through the tinted floor-to-ceiling windows. "I often stand here and think of how history can veer off in unexpected directions, drastically changed by the actions of the few. The Alamo was a defeat for its defenders, but it was the beginning of the end for Santa Anna. He was captured at San Jacinto, and in one decisive engagement Texas became independent from Mexico. The lesson of history is clear, is it not?"

"It wouldn't be the first time the death of martyrs brought down the powerful."

"Precisely. Nor will it be the last. What happened once can happen again. The Alamo had one hundred eighty three defenders against six thousand Mexican troops, showing that the determined few can transform the world for the many." He paused, alone with his thoughts, staring out at the sprawling city. After a moment he turned to Guzman like a man emerging from a dream.

"Why did you want to see me?"

"There's a matter of some importance, sir. I just intercepted this transmission from Morocco to the University of Pennsylvania." He handed the file over.

Halcon leafed through the material, finally fastening on the sketch, and murmured, "Astounding." He looked up. "There can be no mistake?"

"Our surveillance system is practically foolproof. As you know, every archaeological expedition in the world sends proposals to our Time-Quest foundation asking for funds and volunteers. Those with serious potential are assigned priority. The computers automatically access all transmissions from the field to their home base and search for preprogrammed keywords, or fax, telex, and e-mail messages."

"Los Hermanos has a watcher on site?"

"Yes. Gonzalez is there."

"Excellent," Halcon said. "He knows what he has to do."

Guzman nodded and clicked his heels softly. As he turned to go his lips seemed to curl in a lopsided smile. But it was only a trick of the light and shadow caused by the white scar that ran from his right cheekbone to the corner of his mouth.

NINA BROUGHT THE CAMERA UP TO
her face mask, framed the foundation wall in the viewfinder, and
squeezed the shutter release on the waterproof housing. The
motor drive whirred softly. The last shot she needed for the
photo-mosaic. *Finally.*

With a quick, sharp expulsion of air she cleared the water
from her snorkel. Using an easy sidestroke, she swam toward the
stairs. Mapping the bottom single-handed had been tedious. She
first laid out a number of small, spherical plastic buoys in a tic-
tac-toe pattern as a guide. Then it was swim, stop, shoot. Again
and again. She carried a mental blueprint of the port in her
head. Had the water miraculously receded, she could have
strolled blindfolded on the old quay and not bumped into a wall
or fallen into a *piscina* or *cothon*.

The task of assembling dozens of photos into a composite
map would be formidable. She had tried to match the photos
using the buoys coupled with distinctive bottom landmarks. A
crude system at best, but fine for now. Nina wasn't looking for
scientific precision, she wanted a *dramatic* package that would
have the tight-fisted bean counters who controlled expeditionary
money dreaming of front-page headlines in *USA Today* and fea-
ture stories in *Time* and on *Unsolved Mysteries.*

She hoisted herself onto the steps and got out of her dive
gear. As she toweled her body dry, she looked out over the

lagoon and decided to put off the buoy removal until the morning. She'd be as wrinkled as a white raisin if she spent any more time in the water. Minutes later she was loping along the path to the camp with a discernible jauntiness in her stride. There was good reason to be pleased. She had accomplished an incredible amount of work in a short time.

People were still working on the excavation, and the camp was deserted. Well, almost. As she neared the tents she saw Gonzalez at the periphery of the campsite talking to someone in a Jeep. As she approached, the Jeep drove off before she got a look at the driver's face.

"Who was that?" she said, watching the dust cloud thrown out by the departing vehicle.

The automatic Gonzalez smile clicked on as if somebody had pressed a switch. "Someone who was lost. I gave him directions."

Lost? What was Gonzalez talking about? This wasn't like taking a wrong turn off a freeway. The camp was miles from anywhere or anything. It was lonely country with nothing to attract anyone except a bunch of crazy bone-diggers. You'd have to *want* to get lost out here. When she first saw the man in the Jeep she thought he might have been called in by Fisel, so while she didn't buy the explanation, she was relieved to hear it.

At breakfast Dr. Fisel had announced the expected arrival of Moroccan divers within a few days. He strongly "advised" Nina to curtail her explorations so as not to disturb the site. Nina leaned over the table and stuck her chin right in his face. A camera was hardly intrusive, she said quietly, but with such cold fury in her gray eyes that Dr. Knox complained after breakfast that icicles had formed on his mustache. Fisel prissily reminded everyone of his responsibility to his cousin the king, then retreated into an unconvincing apology about only wanting to preserve the integrity of the site.

Nina had to admit she was being somewhat devious herself. She was removing artifacts from the site, a big no-no, and had told neither Fisel nor Knox. Nor was Fisel aware that her preliminary findings were sent winging off to UPenn's cybervault. The stone head still remained her secret as well. She rationalized her uncharacteristic behavior. Drastic times call for drastic measures.

Kassim, Fisel's tea boy, gave her a friendly wave. Dumb as a fencepost but not a bad kid when you got to know him. Savoring the tranquility, Nina went into her tent, slipped out of her bathing suit and into dry clothes. She switched on her computer and saw the e-mail icon blinking. The message was from Dr. Elinor Sanford, the faculty member at UPenn to whom she had directed her computer transmission.

Sandy Sanford and Nina had been undergraduate classmates before branching into their own specialties. Sandy went into Mesoamerican studies, explaining that her preferences had more to do with cuisine than with cultures. She preferred burritos to couscous. Her culinary tastes might be open to question, but her scholarship was not. She had just been appointed a faculty curator at the university's museum. Nina scrolled down her message:

Congratulations, Nina! You don't have to bring me Hannibal's head to convince me you've hit a Phoenician port! Wish I could show the fabulous stuff you transmitted to the Jurassic set here in the hidebound halls of archaeological academia. Could start another Punic War. But I'll abide by your wishes to keep things quiet. What does El Grando Professoro think? Can't wait to see you. Stay dry. Love, Sandy.

There was more.

P.S. Re sketch of the big stone head. Some kind of joke, right? I get it, you're just testing me. Check your fax line.

Nina called up her fax function. A photo of a stone face appeared on the screen. At first she thought it was the carving in the lagoon. But next to it for comparison was the sketch she had sent. She stared at the screen. The sculptures were identical. She scrolled some more. Other stone heads came into view. They all could have been carved by the same sculptor. Except for slight details, primarily in their headgear, they shared the same brooding stare, broad nose, and impassive fleshy lips. Below the pictures was another note from Sandy:

Hello again. Welcome to one of the most enduring of all Mesoamerican mysteries. In 1938 the National Geographic Society and the Smithsonian sent an expedition to Mexico to investigate reports of giant basalt heads buried up to their eyebrows. They found eleven African-type rock figures like this at three sites in and around La Venta, sacred center of Olmec culture. Eighteen miles from the Gulf of Mexico. Six to nine feet high, up to forty tons each. Not bad considering the quarry site was ten miles away and they were carried overland without the use of the wheel or draft animals. All had that funny helmet that makes them look like they belong in the NFL. Dating figures at 800 to 700 B.C. Say, what's a nice girl like you doing messing around in Meso?

Nina typed out a quick reply:

Thanks for info. Most interesting! Due home next week. Will fill you in. :-) Love, Nina

She hit the Send key, turned the laptop off, and sat back in her chair, stunned.

A Mexican Olmec head! Calm down, lady. Go over the facts. The figure she found had African characteristics. Big deal. This *is* Africa, after all. Of course, that didn't explain the match with the Mexican figures thousands of miles away. A couple of possibilities could explain the similarities. The La Venta figures might have been carved in Africa and transported to Mexico. Unlikely. Not at forty tons apiece. The alternative theory wasn't much better. That a La Venta figure was carved in Mexico and transported to Africa. With either scenario, there was still the problem with the dating. The heads were carved hundreds of years before Columbus sailed the ocean blue.

Ouch, Nina thought, I'm thinking like a *diffusionist*.

She looked over her shoulder as if someone were eavesdropping on her thoughts. Admitting to an open mind on diffusionism was a one-way ticket to oblivion for a mainstream archaeologist. Diffusionists believe cultures didn't evolve in isolation, that they *diffused* from one place to another. The similarities between the Old and New Worlds had always intrigued Nina. The UFO and Atlantis enthusiasts muddied up the waters, suggesting that the pyramids and Nazca lines were the products of aliens from outer space or beings from lost continents. A female diffusionist was a *double* loser in this business. She had enough problems just being a woman in a man's world.

The diffusionist theory had always faced a major hurdle: the absence of scientifically verified evidence that would prove contact between one hemisphere and another before Columbus. People could yack all they wanted about how Egyptian pyramids and Cambodian temples and Mexican mounds resembled one another. But nobody had discovered the artifact to connect them. Until *now.* And in a Phoenician port. *Oh, Christ.*

This was going to stir up one hell of a mess. It could be the biggest discovery since King Tut's tomb. The archaeological establishment would be turned topsy-turvy. The thing in the lagoon proved a link existed between the Old World and the New *two thousand years* before Christopher Columbus conned the Spanish royals out of three ships. Enough! Nina jammed on her mental brakes before she went over the precipice. She needed to think this through with a clear head. She swatted a couple of flies and lay down on the cot. She tried to put all thoughts out of her mind and concentrate on her breathing. The next thing she knew, she was being awakened by the dinner bell.

Yawning and rubbing her eyes, she stumbled outside. A magnificent purple and gold sunset was in the making. She walked to the mess tent and sat at the opposite end of the table from Fisel, who was holding court. The same old blah-blah. She tuned him out and enjoyed a chat with the Iowa couple. Excusing herself before dessert, she went back to her tent and plunked down in front of her laptop.

Working late into the night, Nina typed up a summary to go with her mosaic photos. By the time she quit, the camp had settled down for the evening. She put on a flannel nightie, congratulating herself for her prescience in packing it. Days were hot and dry, but at night a cool breeze came in off the ocean. She slipped under her blanket and lay there listening to the laughter and Arabic conversation as the mess crew cleaned up after dinner. Before long the voices were silent and the camp was asleep.

Except for Nina. She lay on the cot wishing she hadn't taken a nap. Sandy's fax had wound her up as well. She tossed and turned, finally falling into a light slumber, only to be awakened by the sharp crackling of the fire. Her eyes blinked open, and she stared into space. Sleep wasn't meant to be.

Wide awake once more, Nina wrapped the blanket around her shoulders like a Navajo, pulled on her Teva sandals, and slipped outside. A branch of burning olive tree exploded in little red spark showers on the smoky fire. The only other illumination was from propane-powered lanterns hung outside the tents in case somebody felt the call of nature during the night.

Nina looked up at the black sky. The crystal air was so clear that it seemed she could see distant nebulae with her naked eye. Impulsively, Nina grabbed a flashlight from her knapsack and set off toward the lagoon. The tombs gleamed like pewter in the light of the half moon. Coming to the staircase, she sat down on the top step and gazed out at the moonglade reflection on the lagoon.

Yellow pinpoints glowed on the ocean. The NUMA ship with the turquoise hull must still be offshore. She took a deep breath. The night smelled of stagnant water, rotting vegetation, marsh, and incredible age. She closed her eyes and listened. In her imagination clicking reeds became the slap of hide sails against wooden masts, and frog snorts the grunts of breechcloth-clad sailors hoisting amphorae filled with wine and oil. Before long, slivers of cold air penetrated the blanket. She shivered, realizing she had lost track of time. With a parting glance at the still lagoon, she started back.

As she crested the ridge of dunes a strange noise came from the camp. It sounded like a bird or animal crying out under the attack of a hunting predator. She heard it again. This was no bird or animal. It was *human*. Someone in terrible fear or pain.

She picked up her pace to a trot, emerging from the dunes where she could see the camp.

It was like a scene out of Dante where faceless demons herd new arrivals to their hellish punishment. Expedition members in their night clothes were being prodded and pushed by gun-carrying figures dressed in black. The Iowa couple came into view. The woman stumbled and fell. An intruder grabbed her long white hair, and she was dragged along the ground screaming in terror. Her husband tried to intervene only to be clubbed to the ground, where he lay bloodied and unmoving.

Still in his flannel pajamas, Professor Knox burst from his tent and looked around. Nina was close enough to see the expression on his face. He appeared more bewildered than frightened. Dr. Fisel's unmistakably rotund form appeared, and someone pushed him into Knox. Fisel shouted defiantly, although Nina couldn't hear what he said against the growing background of cries and yells. Most of the expedition people were outside now, crowded into a terrified group. Nina caught a glimpse of the drivers and cook. Gonzalez must have been with the others, but she couldn't see him.

The assailants stopped their brutal attack and moved back from the huddled assembly. Knox had regained his dignity and stood with head high. He seemed frozen in stone; his face looked a thousand years old. Fisel saw what was coming. He shouted in Arabic, but his words were lost in the ugly chatter of gunfire.

The hail of bullets mowed Fisel and the others down like a scythe blade through grass. Incredibly, despite the intensity of the killing fire, pitiful moans came from the pile of bodies. Any hope Nina had of survivors vanished when two intruders stepped over the carnage. Seven shots rang out a few seconds apart. The groaning stopped. The only sound was the faint crackle of the wood fire.

Nina could hardly breathe. Her mouth felt as if it were full of sawdust. Her heart hammered madly. Her dinner rose in her throat, and she gagged as she fought her urge to vomit. She wanted to run. It was only a matter of time before the killers saw her standing at the edge of the clearing. Yet she was rooted to the spot, too scared to save her own life.

A figure broke from the shadows behind a tent and ran in her direction. *Kassim!* He must have been outside when the killers struck. The killers saw him trying to escape and lifted their weapons. They held their fire when one of their number dashed in pursuit of the tea boy.

Mad with fear, Kassim ran directly toward Nina without seeing her. He would have bowled her over if he hadn't tripped on a root and fallen. He tried to scramble to his feet, but his assailant was on him quicker than a falcon on a rabbit. He reached under Kassim's chin and jerked the boy's head back.

Light glinted on cold steel. Like someone cutting a pineapple, he drew the knife across the boy's throat in a swift slashing motion. Kassim's scream died in a wet gargle as his lungs filled and he drowned in his own blood.

His murderous deed accomplished, the killer stood and saw Nina. He was dressed entirely in black. A turban was wrapped around his head covering everything except eyes that burned with a murderous hate. They widened as they saw Nina, then narrowed just before he lunged, the bloodied knife held high above his head.

Nina yanked the heavy blanket from her shoulders and, wielding it in two hands like a great woolen club, she whipped it across the attacker's face. He hesitated and put his left arm up to ward off the blow, not expecting resistance from this helpless victim. Nina brought the blanket down like a hood over the killer's head and, while he was temporary blinded, drove her knee into his crotch.

"Aaaaiiee!"

The scream told her she was on target. She did it again with every intention of driving her knee to his chin. She must have nearly succeeded because he crashed to the ground and writhed in pain.

The other black-clad figures saw their comrade fall and started toward Nina, but the delay gave her an advantage. She bolted like a startled deer and, long legs racing, feet pounding the ground, outdistanced her pursuers.

She could hear shouts behind her. *"La mujer! La mujer!"*

A sandal flew off, and she kicked the other away. Barefoot now, she was through the dune ridge descending the gradual slope to the water. The rise would hide her for a moment. As she sprinted toward the lagoon her bare foot came down on a piece of wood or sharp stone. A dagger of pain stabbed the tender flesh. She went down on one knee for a second, bit her lip until it bled, stifling the urge to yelp, then was up in a limping run.

As she ran past the darkened tombs she thought of hiding inside but quickly discarded the idea as too obvious. She'd be trapped if the killers found her. She decided instead to run along the shore and backtrack on her pursuers. That plan was shredded by the flashlight beams that lanced the darkness behind her. Her pursuers had anticipated her move. Taking their time, they spread out along the dune ridge to cut off her flanks and catch her in a classic pincers movement.

She ran straight to the lagoon. Seconds later she was standing at the top of the stairway. The killers were closing in on all sides. It was only a matter of seconds before they caught up with her.

Nina's brain worked feverishly. She could dive off the steps and swim underwater, but it would only delay the inevitable. When she came up for air the killers would spray the lagoon until their bullets found her. She *had* to stay submerged until she was safely out of range. Impossible. No way.

Fool. Of *course* there's a way. She set off along the rocky shore. Her darting eyes probed the water, searching in the moonlight. She saw the faint gray splotch of a marker buoy.

Lights seemed to be coming from every direction. Soon she'd be caught in the closing net.

Not *this* fish, she vowed. Gathering her strong legs beneath her like springs, Nina leaped off the rocks, her arms reaching straight out. She hit the water in a distance-covering shallow racing dive and swam for the marker buoy with quick hard strokes. The buoy flared into orange brilliance as a light from shore found its reflective surface. The water all around her was covered with shimmering blobs.

A few strokes and she was at the buoy.

A fusillade opened up, and the lagoon's surface erupted in miniature geysers off to her right side.

No time to build up her air supply.

She filled her lungs in a frantic gulp, and her supple body jackknifed in a quick surface dive. Directly under the marker, faintly illuminated by the glow of lights from above, was the stone arch. She wriggled under the arch, reached out until she felt a hard vertical edge, and pulled herself into the the lightless bowels of the tunnel.

As she swam her fingers brushed the smooth wall like a crude, tactile sonar.

Making it to the end of the tunnel was a long shot without air and fins, but even if this damned hole became her tomb, at least she'd have the satisfaction of knowing her pursuers would never learn her fate. She slowed slightly, trying to keep a steady, even pace. Panic would steal oxygen and energy.

She swam deeper. The wall became rough to the touch. She was in the cave. The going would be trickier here. She slowed even more to navigate the twists and turns. Went down a blind alley and had to back out. It felt like hours since she had taken a breath. Her lungs pressed against her ribs as if her chest were going to explode. How long could she hold her breath? A minute? Two? Maybe, if she'd had a chance to hyperventilate and build up capacity. God, how much farther?

Her head slammed into a hard surface. She was sure she felt the plates in her skull shift. She cried out instinctively and lost more air.

Damn. She'd forgotten about the pile of rubble. She groped over the top of the debris and squeezed her way through the opening. She was past the halfway mark!

The wall became smooth again. Good. She was back in the man-made tunnel. Only a few dozen meters. Her lungs were on fire. She let out a small breath as if that would relieve the pressure and started making sounds like a pigeon. God, she didn't want to drown. Not here. She kicked desperately with no attempt to conserve energy.

The lack of oxygen made her dizzy. Next she'd start to black out and swallow water. A painful, excruciating death. Nina stubbornly resisted taking that first fatal breath. She groped for the wall. Nothing. Then felt for the ceiling. Again nothing. Wait! She was out of the tunnel! She arched her body upward, kicked frantically, and broke the surface, where she sucked in great gulps of air.

In time her breathing became almost normal again. She treaded water, looking toward shore, where lights moved like fireflies. Then she struck off around the tip of the promontory and swam parallel to the beach. When she could swim no more, she angled in toward land. Weeds brushed her feet, and her toes felt the cool, mucky bottom. She crawled onto the sand but rested only a few minutes before she got to her feet and walked along the beach. She came to the old riverbed, followed the *wadi* inland a few hundred meters, then climbed the banking and walked across the dunes until she could go no farther. She crawled into a thicket of high grass and lay down.

The horror of the massacre began to play back in her mind. Dr. Knox. Fisel. Kassim. All dead. Why? Who *were* those men? Why were they after her? Bandits who thought the expedition had discovered treasure? No, the concentrated fury of the attack was too organized for bandits. It was *meant* to be a massacre.

Shivering with the cold, Nina removed her flannel nightie, wrung the water from it, and put it back on over her camisole top and underwear. The wet fabric raised goosebumps the size of eggs. She broke off clumps of grass and stuffed them under the nightie until she looked like a scarecrow. The primitive insulation was scratchy, but it helped keep the cold air out. The shivering subsided somewhat, and before long she fell asleep.

Near dawn she was awakened by a murmur of voices coming from the direction of the riverbed. Maybe help had arrived and they were searching for her. She held her breath and listened.

Spanish.

Without a second's delay she slithered into the tall beach grass like a frightened salamander.

5

THE SHARP, BRITTLE GRASS STEMS
were like a fakir's bed of nails that ripped at Nina's nightgown
and tore the skin on her bare arms and legs. Disregarding the
pain, she dug her knees and elbows into the sand and kept moving. She had no other choice. If she stood up to run, she'd be
dead.

The killers had found her too quickly, almost as if they had
followed a map to her hiding place! She cursed in the native
tongue of her grandmother. They *did* have a map. The harbor-
works diagram she had painstakingly drawn lay in plain sight on
her work table. The tunnel had been rendered as two bold lines
and clearly labeled. Once the killers discovered her underwater
escape route, they had only to search the beach for footprints
and follow them into the *wadi.*

The voices rose in pitch and volume, became more excited,
coming from where she had climbed out of the riverbed. The
killers must have found where she'd disturbed the banking. Nina
made a sharp turn and crawled parallel to her original route,
doubling back until she came to the riverbed. She peered from
between blades of grass. No one was in the *wadi.* She slid down
the banking and raced with head low toward the beach. The
riverbed was churned up by footprints which indicated that a
sizable party was tracking her down. Soon she glimpsed the
blue-green of the sea. The turquoise ship was still anchored off-

shore. She paused where the waterway once emptied into the ocean. The empty beach beckoned like a highway in both directions.

Voices and the crunch of footsteps came from behind. Again the killers had spread out like hunters trying to flush a quail. She'd be seen whether she went to the right or the left. As on the previous night, the watery route remained her only choice.

Nina peeled off her ripped and sand-caked nightgown, tossed it aside, and sprinted in camisole and underwear across the hard-packed gravelly delta washed out by centuries of river flow. She hoped the dune ridge would screen her until she reached the water's edge. Still no outcry as she splashed into the shallows. She was aware how vulnerable she was, completely out in the open with no darkness or tunnel to hide her. Any second the killers would crest the dunes, and she'd be an easy target for their bullets.

The knee-deep water covering the salt flats seemed to go on forever, slowing her progress but offering no protection. She pressed on, leaping with long strides, and eventually the water got to waist level. She dove under just as angry lead bees filled the air. The water behind her erupted in a patch of angry foam. Nina dove under and swam off at an angle for as long as she could, surfaced for air, and dove again, porpoise-style. Once beyond the brownish water over the flats and into the deeper blue ocean, she glanced back and saw maybe a dozen figures on shore. Some had waded into the shallows. The gunfire seemed to have stopped.

Pivoting, Nina fixed her eye on the ship, concerned that it would weigh anchor and leave her between the devil and the deep blue sea. A swim to the Canary Islands wasn't in her plans. Rolling onto her back, she looked up at the puffy gilt-edged clouds and caught her breath. At least it was a good day for a swim. She rested only a minute. She had to get the blood moving in her body again.

Pace yourself, rest when necessary, and count your blessings. Calm sea and no wind or currents. No different from the swim phase of a triathlon, except for one thing: if she lost this race, she would die. Taking a bead on the ship's main mast, she threw one arm in front of the other.

Without her wristwatch, there was no telling how long she swam. The water grew colder the deeper it got, and she counted strokes to take her mind off the energy-sapping chill. Waving at the ship would be a waste of time. Her arm would look like the neck of a floating seabird.

She tried singing sea chanteys. The old shipboard work songs helped keep the rhythm of strokes.

Her repertoire was slim, and after she'd sung "Blow the Man Down" for the fiftieth time she simply chopped away at the sea. She drew closer to the ship, but her strokes were becoming sloppy, and she stopped to rest more often. At one point she spun around and was pleased to see she was leaving the low brown shore far behind her. To give herself courage she imagined climbing aboard the ship and washing away the salty dryness of her mouth with a steaming mug of hot coffee.

The deep thrumming sound was so faint she didn't notice it at first. Even when she stopped to listen Nina thought it might be water pressure in her head, or maybe even the noise of a ship generator. She rolled one ear in the water and listened.

The droning was louder.

Nina slowly wheeled around. A dark object was racing in her direction from shore. She thought it was a boat at first, but as it grew quickly in size Nina made out a squat ugly black hull she recognized as that of a large hovercraft, an amphibious vehicle that moves across land and sea on a cushion of air.

It moved back and forth in a series of sharp-angled turns, but Nina sensed this was no rescue boat executing a search pattern. Its course was too determined, too aggressive. All at once it stopped zigzagging and came straight at her like a bullet. She must have been spotted. Rapidly it closed the distance and was practically on top of her when she dove as deep as she could go.

The hovercraft skimmed overhead on its ten-inch cushion, churning the water into a wild frenzy. When she could stay under no longer, Nina surfaced and sucked in air, only to cough as the purple exhaust fumes filled her lungs. The hovercraft spun around and made another pass.

Again she dove. Again she was tossed and buffeted only to fight her way back to the surface, where she bobbed in the wake.

The hovercraft stopped, settling down into the water with its engines purring, facing Nina like a big cat toying with a mouse. A weary and waterlogged mouse. Then the engines came to life, the hovercraft rose up on invisible legs and charged again.

Nina dove and was tumbled like a rock in a polishing machine. Her brain was numb; blood thundered in her ears. She was reacting on pure instinct. The game would end soon. The damned thing could turn on a dime. Each time she surfaced she had less time to take in air, and the craft was closer than before.

The blunt hull was coming at her again, although she could hardly see it with the exhaust cloud and her eyes bleary and stinging from salt water. She was too exhausted to dive and wouldn't have the strength to fight her way up from the sea again. She made a pitiful attempt to swim out of the way, but after a few strokes she turned to face her attacker as if she could beat it back with her fists.

The hovercraft was nearly on top of her, its flatulent roar filling her ears. She clenched her jaw and waited.

The horror of the past several hours was nothing compared to what happened next. The hovercraft was only seconds away when her ankles were clutched in a viselike grip and she was dragged down into the cold depths of the sea.

6

ARMS FLAILING LIKE A WINDMILL IN a gale, Nina struggled to break free, but the iron lock on her ankles never let up even as the maelstrom created by the hovercraft whipped the water around her to a wild frenzy. She emptied her lungs in one last defiant gesture, an angry, frustrated scream that came out as a muted explosion of bubbles.

The grip on her legs relaxed, and a vaguely human form began to take shape in the turbulent cloud of bubbles kicked up by the hovercraft. Like some alien cyclops from a UFO the amorphous shape came closer and solidified until the plexiglass of a diver's mask was only inches from her face. Peering from behind the lens were piercing light blue eyes that projected strength and reassurance rather than menace.

A gloved hand came up, wagged a regulator back and forth in front of her nose, and pressed the purge button so the belching mouthpiece would get her attention. Nina grabbed the regulator and hungrily bit down. No flower-scented breath of summer was ever sweeter than the life-giving compressed air that flowed into her lungs. The leveled hand was moving up and down.

Take it easy. Slow down.

Nina nodded to show she understood the diver's signal and felt a gentle squeeze on her shoulder. She continued to breathe off the "octopus" backup emergency hose until eventually her panic passed and her breathing became more rhythmical.

Another hand signal. The forefinger and thumb formed into a vague O.

Okay?

Nina imitated the gesture.

I'm okay.

Behind the mask a blue eye winked. She didn't know who this aquaman was or where he came from, but at least he was friendly. The diver's head was covered by his close-fitting hood and a combined helmet-mask arrangement. She could see only that he was a big man with wide shoulders.

Nina looked up. The light was shredded in the wake of the hovercraft's violent passage, and engines rumbled through the water. They were still looking for her.

Pressure on her shoulder again. Aquaman pointed toward the surface and clenched his hand in a fist.

Danger.

She nodded vigorously. The thumb pointed downward. She looked below her dangling legs into the gloomy depths. Even the unknown was preferable to the real dangers that lurked above. She nodded again and gave the okay signal. He clasped one hand in the other.

Hold hands.

Nina took his proffered glove, and slowly they began to descend.

The water changed from cobalt to indigo as they continued their measured plunge, becoming so dark that Nina felt the cold bottom muck before she saw it.

From his belt the diver produced a small but powerful high-intensity Tektite strobe-light and held it above his head. She closed her eyes so as not to be blinded by the intense silvery-white flash she knew was coming. When she looked again an undersea firefly was blinking in the distance.

The diver put his forefingers together.

Swim side by side in that direction.

Again holding hands, they swam toward the pulsating light until they neared a second diver. He saw the swimmers coming his way, switched off the strobe he was holding, and his hand went to the microphone button of his Aquacom headset.

"I can't take you anywhere," he said. "I let you out of my sight for a minute, and you show up with a real live mermaid."

The first diver let his eyes travel over Nina's body and decided the description wasn't far off the mark. With her golden tresses, long legs, and minimal covering, Nina easily could have passed for a mythical sea sprite, except for one thing.

"Mermaids are half fish," he said.

"I like the new improved model better. What's her name?"

"Good question. We haven't been formally introduced yet. I bumped into her when I went up top to check on the ship. She was in a bit of trouble, so I gave her a hand. Two hands, actually."

Nina had never used underwater communicators herself, but she recognized the equipment and knew they must be talking about her. As grateful as she was, she wished they would cut their conversation short. She was *freezing!* If she didn't move soon, she'd pass out. She crossed her arms in front of her chest.

I am cold.

The diver she had dubbed Aquaman nodded. With the protection of his drysuit, he had forgotten how cool it must be for an unprotected body.

"Let's get our mermaid back to the ship before she turns into a frozen fish stick."

The other diver checked his compass and led the way. Nina's new friend signaled her once more to swim side by side and gently took her hand. She assumed they were heading for the ship, but in her cold and exhausted condition she wasn't sure she could make it. The diver seemed to sense her struggle to follow with no fins on her feet and squeezed her hand several times in encouragement.

They swam for only a few minutes before they glided down again. A pair of yellow objects sat on the bottom. They were made of plastic and shaped like fat miniature torpedoes with ears. Nina recognized them as DPVs, diver propulsion units, or sea scooters as they were more commonly called.

The divers each picked up a DPV and squeezed the throttles. There were low whines as the battery-driven twin motors in the Stingrays kicked their twin propellers into action. Aquaman pointed to his back. Nina grabbed onto his shoulders, and they ascended to mid-water where it was marginally warmer.

As they glided along Nina's diver called the ship and asked if anyone could see a big hovercraft in the vicinity. He wasn't one to take chances.

"There was a hovercraft around earlier," the message came back. "It headed for land and seems to have disappeared."

"Roger. Please be prepared for a female visitor."

There was a slight pause. "Say again?"

"Never mind. Just be prepared to treat hypothermia."

They surfaced near the ship and swam around to the stern. A welcome party awaited to help Nina aboard and wrap her in towels and blankets. Nina's face was mottled, and her lips were blue. She refused the stretcher but was glad for a helping hand as she walked with wobbly legs, teeth chattering, to the infirmary. She limped on the foot she'd injured escaping the assassins.

The two divers eased out of their gear and lost no time getting to the infirmary. They waited patiently outside the closed door like expectant fathers. Before long the physician's mate, an attractive and trim young woman who served as the ship's doctor, came out into the passageway.

"Is she all right?" the bigger man said.

The mate smiled. "That's one tough lady," she said, admiration in her voice. "I've put antiseptic on her cuts and bruises. She was practically hypothermic, so I just want her to stay warm for now. She can have a cup of bouillon soon."

"Can we see her?"

"Sure. You guys keep her entertained while I see if I can round up some clothes and square away a bunk in my cabin where she can get some rest in privacy."

"What's her name?"

The mate raised an eyebrow. "You don't *know?* You gentlemen must be spending too much time underwater, especially you, Zavala. I thought you'd know her telephone number and what kind of flowers and restaurants she likes by now."

José "Joe" Zavala's reputation had followed him from Washington, which was not surprising, since he had once dated the physician's mate. Always charming with the ladies, he was much in demand by many single women for his young Ricardo Montalban good looks. A slight, almost shy smile played around his lips. "I must be slipping," he said.

"That'll be the day." She smirked and hurried briskly off on her quest.

Nina was sitting on an examination table when the two men stepped into the room. She was wearing a baggy navy sweatsuit, and a thick woolen blanket was wrapped around her shoulders. Although her eyes were red-rimmed from saltwater immersion and her long hair was matted, color had returned to her face, and her lips had lost their bluish tinge. Her hands were cupped around a ceramic coffee mug, enjoying its warmth. She looked up and saw the tall man filling the doorway. With his husky physique and the contrast between his walnut skin and near-white hair color, he looked like a Norse hero from a Wagnerian opera. Yet his voice was quite gentle when he spoke.

"Hope we're not intruding," he said tentatively.

Nina brushed a long wavy strand out of her face. "Not at all. Come on in."

He stepped inside, followed by the dark-complexioned man with a nice smile. "My name is Kurt Austin, and this is Joe Zavala."

"I'm Nina Kirov." Nina recognized the Aquaman's eyes she had seen behind the face mask. They reminded her of the color of a coral reef beneath smooth water. "I think we've already met."

Austin grinned, pleased at the recognition. "How are you feeling?"

"Not bad, thanks. I'll be better after a hot shower." She looked around. "What ship is this?"

"The NUMA research vessel *Nereus.*"

"You're with the National Underwater and Marine Agency?"

"That's right. I'm head of the NUMA Special Assignments Team. Joe is the team's marine engineer."

"I like to think of myself as the team's *propulsionist,*" Zavala said.

"Joe's being modest. He is the one who keeps us moving on, under and above the sea."

Zavala, in fact, was a professional in every kind of propulsion. He could repair, modify, or restore any engine, be it steam, diesel, or electric and whether it was in an automobile, ship, or aircraft. Zavala never hesitated to get his hands greasy when confronted with a mechanical problem. He had designed and directed construction of numerous underwater vehicles, manned and unmanned, including some aboard the research vessel. His talents extended to the sky as well. He had two thousand hours as a pilot in helicopters and small jet and turbo prop aircraft.

"You say you're with a special assignments team."

"That's right. Four of us form the team's nucleus. We've got a deep ocean geologist and a marine biologist, but they're on other assignments. Basically we handle jobs outside the realm of NUMA's ordinary tasks." And outside the realm of government oversight, he might have added.

"What on earth is your ship doing here?"

"We're on a shakedown cruise on our way from the Mediterranean," Austin said. "The Moroccan government is worried offshore oil drilling is affecting its sardine fishery. *Nereus* was going to be in the area, so we said we'd do a quick bottom survey."

"*Nereus,* the Old Man of the Sea," Nina murmured, cocking her head in thought. "There's a quote from Hesiod, the Greek poet: 'A trusty and gentle god who thinks just and kindly thoughts and never lies.' "

Austin glanced at Zavala. Maybe Nina really *was* a mermaid. She was certainly lovely enough. "I don't know if the ship qualifies as the Old Man of the Sea. The *Nereus* was launched only a couple of months ago, but Hesiod was right about not lying. This ship is packed from stern to stem with state-of-the-art survey gear."

"The ship's designer says we scientific types are only on board as ballast," Zavala said.

Nina was having a hard time reconciling the broad-shouldered Austin and his soft-spoken companion with the scholarly scientists she was used to. She sized the two men up with an analytical eye. At six-foot-one and two hundred pounds, none of it fat, the broad-shouldered Austin was built like a professional football player. He had the deeply tanned face of someone who spent most of his time outdoors, with the metallic burnishing look that comes with constant exposure to the sea. Except for the laugh lines around his mouth and eyes, the skin was unwrinkled. Even though he was only pushing forty, Austin's hair was a premature steely gray, almost platinum white.

At five-foot-ten, the darkly handsome Zavala was less powerfully built than Austin, yet his one-hundred-seventy-five-pound frame was flexibly muscular, particularly around the arms and neck, and there were traces of scar tissue around his eyebrows, the legacies of having financed his way through college by boxing professionally as a middleweight. He won twenty-two fights, twelve by knockouts, and lost six. His straight black hair was combed straight back. The humorous, slight smile she had seen when he first came into the examination room hadn't left his lips. Remembering the mate's comment, she could see how a woman could be drawn to the soulful brown eyes.

Their gentlemanly manners couldn't disguise a rough-and-ready quality. The brawnier Austin was positively genial now, but she remembered his fierce determination when he'd yanked her out of the way of the hovercraft. Behind Zavala's gregariousness lurked a flinty hardness, she suspected. The way the two men meshed, like gears in a well-oiled machine, as they got her safely to the ship demonstrated that they were used to working as a team.

"Sorry for being so rude," she said, remembering her rescue. "I haven't thanked you both."

"My apologies for sneaking up on you with the *Jaws* routine," Austin said. "It must have been frightening."

"Not half as frightening as having that ugly boat playing water polo with my head. I can never thank you enough. Please sneak up and pull me out of danger *any* time you want." She paused. "One dumb question, though. Do you *normally* swim around in the Atlantic Ocean waiting for damsels in distress?"

"Dumb luck," he said with a shrug. "Joe and I were puttering around below. I surfaced to get a bearing on the ship and saw you playing dodge 'em with the hovercraft. My turn to ask a question. What was *that* all about?"

Her smile vanished. "Simple. They were trying to kill me."

"I think that was fairly obvious, but why?"

"I don't know," she said in a monotone, her eyes glazed.

Austin sensed she was trying to avoid talking about something. "You haven't told us where you came from," he said gently.

It was like pulling a plug. "Dear God," Nina whispered. "The expedition. Dr. Knox."

"What expedition?" Austin said.

She stared into space as if trying to remember a dream.

"I'm a marine archaeologist. I was with a University of Pennsylvania party working an excavation not far from here."

She related the story of the massacre and her escape. The tale was so fantastic Austin might not have believed it if he hadn't seen the hovercraft attack or the unmitigated fear in Nina's face. When the narrative was finished Austin turned to Zavala.

"What do you think?"

"I think we ought to go take a look for ourselves."

"Me, too. We'll call the Moroccan authorities first. Ms.

Kirov, do you think you can give us directions to your camp?"

Nina had been fighting off the survivor's guilt at being the only one who escaped certain death. She needed to *do* something. She slid off the table and stood on unsteady legs.

"Better than that," she said with a steely edge to her voice. "I'll *show* you."

7

CAPTAIN MOHAMMED MUSTAPHA OF
the Moroccan Royal Gendarmerie leaned against the sun-warmed fender of his Jeep and watched the tall American woman walk slowly back and forth across the sandy clearing, her head bent toward the ground.

Like most of the country's rural policemen, the captain occupied his days chasing down truants among the village schoolchildren, filling out traffic accident reports, or checking papers of strangers, of whom there were pitifully few. The disappearance of a camel he investigated last year stirred up exciting possibilities of rustling before it was determined to be nothing more than a runaway. Yet that was the closest he'd come to tracking down a vanished archaeological expedition.

Mustapha was familiar with the area the Berbers called the Place of the Dead for the old tombs, and he was aware of the nearby ruins. It was far off the beaten track in a patrol territory that covered hundreds of square miles. He had visited the lonely spot once and stayed only long enough to decide he would not come back unless he had to.

The woman stopped and stood for a moment, hands on hips as if she were lost, then she walked over to the Jeep. "I don't understand it," she said, her brow wrinkled in puzzlement. "We were camped right here. The tents, the vans. *Everything* has vanished."

The captain turned to the broad-shouldered man whose hair was the color of the snow on the Atlas Mountains. "Perhaps Mademoiselle is mistaken about the location."

Nina glared at the police officer. "Mademoiselle is *not* mistaken."

He sighed. "These people who attacked you. Bandits?"

She considered the suggestion. "No, I don't think they were bandits."

Mustapha gave a Gallic shrug worthy of a Parisian boulevardier, lit up a Gauloise, and pushed his visor back over his black hair. He was somewhat uncomfortable at being in the presence of a woman who had her legs and arms uncovered, but he was not an insensitive man. He'd have to be blind not to see the lacerations that streaked her skin, and she was clearly distraught. Yet he could observe with his own eyes that there were no tents, no pile of dead bodies, no vehicles. In fact, there was nothing to indicate the story was true.

The officer took a drag from his cigarette and blew the smoke out his nostrils. "I was notified, of course, that an expedition was near the Place of the Dead. Perhaps they left without telling you."

"Great," Nina snapped. "Of all the cops in Morocco, I get a Berber Inspector Clousseau."

Nina's frayed nerves had made her irritable. Austin couldn't blame her for being short-tempered with the policeman's obtuseness after all she'd been through but decided it was time to intervene. "Nina, you said there was a big campfire. Could you show me about where it was?"

With the police officer trailing leisurely after them, Nina led the way to the approximate center of the clearing and drew an *X* in the dirt with the tip of her shoe.

"About here, I'd say."

"Do you have a shovel?" Austin asked the policeman.

"Yes, of course. It is a necessary tool for driving in the desert."

Mustapha sauntered over to his Jeep, and from a tool chest he produced a folding short-handled army-issue spade. Austin took the spade and knelt at Nina's feet, where he began to dig a series of parallel trenches about six inches deep. The first two produced nothing of interest, but the third hit pay dirt, literally.

Austin scooped a handful of blackened earth and smelled it. "Ashes from a fire." He placed his palm on the ground. "Still warm," he said.

Nina was only half-listening. She was staring behind Austin at a patch of ground that seemed to be moving.

"There," she whispered.

The dark blot was formed by thousands of tiny swarming creatures. With the edge of the shovel blade Austin cleared a space in the shiny cluster of ants and started to dig. Half a foot below the surface he turned up a spadeful of dark red-stained earth. He expanded the hole. More reddish stain. The ground was soaked with it. Nina got down on her knees beside him. The cloying smell of dried blood filled her nostrils.

"This is where they were shot," she said, her voice tight with restrained emotion.

Captain Mustapha had been staring dreamily off into space, wondering when he'd be able to get home to his wife and children and a good meal. Sensing the change in atmosphere, he threw his cigarette aside and came over to kneel beside Nina. His nut-brown face turned a shade lighter as he realized the significance of the discolored soil.

"Allah be praised," he murmured. Seconds later he was at his Jeep talking in rapid Arabic into the radio.

Nina was still on her knees, her body rigid, gazing at the earth as if the horrible events of the night before were gushing out of the shallow hole. Austin figured that she would fall apart if he didn't tear her away. He took her arm and helped her to her feet. "I'd be interested in a look around the lagoon, if you don't mind."

She blinked like a sleeper suddenly awakened. "That's a

good idea. Maybe there's something there . . ." She led the way
through the dunes. The Zodiac inflatable that had transported
them from the NUMA ship was pulled up onto the stone stairway.

Nina scanned the lagoon that was so peaceful now. "I can't
believe they even took my *marker* buoys," she said with bitter
humor. With Austin a step behind, she walked along the rocky
shoreline describing the unseen tunnel and *cothon*. Austin pointed out a dozen or so fish floating on the otherwise featureless
surface.

"Probably oxygen deprivation," Nina said. "The lagoon isn't
terribly healthy for living things." She smiled at the unintention-
al irony. "There was something else I didn't mention before."
She briefly described the stone head she found. Austin was
unable to hide his disbelief.

"Olmec! Here?" He chewed his lower lip, trying without success to think of a polite way to express his doubt. "Not a
chance."

"I wouldn't believe it either if I hadn't seen it. I bet you'll
change your mind after a short swim. I'll show you." She kicked
off her borrowed sneakers. Austin wouldn't mind a chance to
cool off, and the swim would take Nina's mind off the grim find
back at the clearing. Their shorts and T-shirts would dry quickly
in the sun.

Nina dove in, and Austin followed. They swam a short distance until Nina stopped to take a bead on a couple of landmarks. She breast-stroked with her head underwater. After a
minute or so, she jackknifed in a surface dive and went straight
down. Near the bottom she swam in a circle, then shot to the
surface, with Austin right behind her.

"It's gone," she shouted breathlessly. "The figure is gone!"

"You're sure this is the right spot?"

"No mistake. I lined up two landmarks when I set a buoy
here. The damned thing has disappeared. C'mon, I'll show you."
Without another word she dove again.

When Austin caught up with her, she was swimming back

and forth near the bottom, pointing at what looked like a moon crater. She picked something from the mud, and they headed up again to face each other, treading water.

"They blew it up," she said, waving a piece of blackened rock in the air. "They blew the stone head to pieces." She began to swim toward land.

Zavala was waiting for them at the stairway. He'd been checking the camp's perimeter.

"The captain says to tell you he called his brigade headquarters," he said. "They're going to get in touch with the Sureté Nationale in Rabat. The Sureté handles the big criminal investigations."

Nina handed her find to Austin. "It's basalt, volcanic. I'm sure it's from the figure."

Austin studied the rock. "The edges are ragged and charred. This piece has been in a recent explosion." He squinted at the lagoon. "That explains those dead fish."

"It doesn't make sense," Nina said with a shake of her head. "They kill everybody, try to kill me. Then, instead of running off, they go to the trouble of blowing up an artifact. Why?"

A silence followed in which nobody offered an answer. Austin suggested they check in with the captain and get back to the ship. They started walking back to the campsite with Nina taking the lead. Zavala purposely lagged behind and walked beside Austin. Speaking in a low tone so Nina wouldn't hear, he said, "I told the captain that maybe he'd like to have someone dig around the excavation."

Austin raised an eyebrow.

"Nina said the expedition had been working for several days," Zavala added. "Yet there was no open excavation. Every trench had been filled in. That suggest anything to you?"

"Afraid it does. It might have been a case of the victims unknowingly digging their own graves."

Zavala handed Austin a pair of wire-rimmed glasses. The round lenses were shattered. "I found these near the dig."

Austin glanced at the eyeglasses and without a word slipped them into his pocket.

As the Zodiac pulled up beside the research vessel, Nina's eyes appreciatively appraised the meld of function and form built into the sleek blue-green hull.

"When I saw the *Nereus* from shore yesterday, I thought it was a magnificent ship. It's even more beautiful up close."

"She's more than beautiful," Austin said, helping Nina onto the stern deck. "She's the most advanced research vessel in the world, two hundred fifty feet from stem to stern, with miles of fiber-optics and high-speed data communications in between. The *Nereus* has bow thrusters so she can turn on a dime or keep steady in a rough sea, and the latest in submersible vehicles. We've even got a hull-mounted sonar system to map the bottom without getting our toes wet."

Austin pointed out the tall cube-shaped structure behind the bridge. "That high superstructure is the science storage area. Inside are wet labs with running seawater. We keep the submersibles, camera sleds, and dive gear there. The ship was built to run with a small crew, around twenty. We can accommodate more than thirty scientists."

With Nina still limping from her foot injury of the night before, they went up three decks into a passageway and stopped at a cabin door. "This is where you'll bunk for the next couple of days."

"I don't want to put anyone out."

"You won't. We've got an odd number of female crew aboard, and there's an empty bunk in the physician's mate cabin. You're conveniently located right next to the library and close to the most important part of ship. C'mon, I'll show you."

He led the way along the passageway to the galley, where Zavala sat at a table drinking espresso and reading a faxed version of *The New York Times*. The air-conditioned sterility was a potent antidote to the desolation at the Place of the Dead. The galley was the standard shipboard decor, Formica and aluminum tables and chairs bolted to the deck. But the aromas coming from the kitchen were not the usual smells of bacon and burger grease that clung to most ships' galleys.

Nina sat down, happy to take the weight off her sore foot. "I must be famished," she said, lifting her chin to inhale. "It smells like a four-star restaurant in here."

Zavala put the paper down. "*Five*-star. We underpaid NUMA types must endure many hardships. The wine list is excellent, but you'll find only California vintages in our cellar."

"This is a U.S. vessel," Austin said in exaggerated apology. "It wouldn't do to have a Bordeaux or Burgundy aboard, though our chef *did* graduate from Cordon Bleu, if that makes you feel better."

"The dinner choices tonight are steak *au poivre* and halibut *au beurre blanc*," Zavala added. "I must apologize for the chef. He's from Provence and tends to go heavy on the basil and olive oil."

Nina looked around at the functional surroundings and shook her head in amazement. "I think I'll survive."

With Nina relaxed, Austin decided it was a good time to bring up an unpleasant subject. First he brought her a tall glass of iced tea. "If you're okay discussing last night again, I'd like to go over what we know in case we missed something," Austin said.

She took a sip of tea as if the brew would fortify her. "I'll be all right," she said, and began to recount again the story of what happened the night before.

Austin listened, eyes half closed in a sleeping lion imitation, absorbing every word and inflection, tumbling the facts over in his mind, looking for inconsistencies with the first account.

When she had finished he said, "I think you're right not going with Captain Mustapha's bandit theory. Bandits might have killed some of your people trying to rob them, but from what you described this was a deliberate massacre."

"What about Muslim fundamentalist terrorists?" Zavala ventured. "They've killed thousands of people in Algiers."

"Maybe, but terrorists usually like to advertise what they've done. This bunch went out of its way to hide evidence. Why would fundamentalists destroy the stone figure? That's another thing that bothers me, by the way. They'd need specialized explosives to do that."

"Which means they would have known about the statue ahead of time," Zavala said.

"That's right. They came prepared for underwater demolition."

"Impossible," Nina responded. Then, less sure, she said, "I don't see how they could have known about it."

"Me neither," Zavala said. "You're certain they spoke Spanish?"

She nodded emphatically.

Austin said, "You can practically walk to Spain across the Strait of Gibraltar from Tangier, and that's not far from here."

Zavala shook his head. "Doesn't mean a thing. I speak Spanish, but I'm a Mexican American who's never been to Spain."

Nina remembered something. "Oh, that reminds me. I forgot about Gonzalez."

"Who is Gonzalez?" Austin said.

"He was a volunteer on the expedition. Actually, he *paid* to be on it through a nonprofit organization called Time-Quest. I saw him talking to a man, a stranger in a Jeep, yesterday afternoon. Gonzalez said the man was lost. At the time I thought it was peculiar."

"You thought right," Austin said. "It could be nothing, but we'll run a check on Time-Quest and see if they have anything on Gonzalez. I assume he was killed with the others."

"I didn't see him, but I don't know how he could have escaped."

"What about the hovercraft that chased Nina?" Zavala asked Austin. "Maybe there's a lead there."

"From what I could see at water level, it looked like a custom model. Maybe a Griffon made in England. I called NUMA earlier and asked them to run a check on the owners of all

Griffon hovercraft. There can't be too many of them in the world. My guess is they bought it through a dummy corporation."

"Which means they've made it hard to trace."

"Maybe even impossible, but it's worth a try." He stared off into space, thinking. "We're still faced with the main question: why would anybody want to wipe out a harmless archaeological expedition?"

Nina had been sitting with her chin resting on her hand. "Maybe it *wasn't* so harmless," she ventured.

"What do you mean?"

"I keep coming back to the Olmec figure. It's at the center of things."

"I'm still having a problem with the Olmec part. Especially since it was turned into a load of gravel."

"It's not just my evaluation. You've got to remember it was Sandy who ID'd it. She's one of the most respected Mesoamerican specialists in the country. Sanford's done papers and field work on all the big sites like Tikal and a lot of lesser-known but important finds."

"Okay, let's say you and Sandy are right. Why is the figure significant?"

"It could shake up the archaeological and historical community. For years people have wondered whether there was contact between the Old and New Worlds before Columbus."

"Like Leif Eriksson and the Vikings? I thought there was pretty conclusive evidence of that," Zavala said.

"There is, but it's been begrudgingly accepted. I'm talking about transatlantic contact hundreds of years *before* the Vikings. The problem has been the lack of any scientifically proven artifact. The Olmec head would have *been* that artifact."

Austin lifted an eyebrow. "Well, so what?"

"Pardon me?" she said, almost affronted.

"Say this figure *does* conclusively prove pre-Columbian contact. Fascinating, and certainly controversial. But how important could it be except to archaeologists, historians, and the Knights of Columbus? What makes it something to kill for, in other words?"

"Oh, I see your point," she said, somewhat mollified, "but I can't answer you, other than to say I think my discovery precipitated the attack in some way."

"No one in the camp knew about your find."

"No. They *would* have known about it in time. Ethically, I should have told Dr. Knox and Fisel the moment I found it. I suspected right away that it was Mexican Olmec, but it seemed so fantastic, I wanted corroboration before I stuck my neck out. That's when I contacted Sandy."

"Except for you, your colleague back at the university was the only other person who had seen evidence of the find?"

"Yes, but Sandy would never tell anybody. Thank goodness the preliminary data are secure in her hands." She paused. "I have to get home as soon as possible."

"We're heading to the Yucatan peninsula to check out the impact area of the asteroid that may have wiped out the dinosaurs. We've got another day of survey here before we leave," Austin said. "We'd love you to be our guest for that time, then we can drop you off at Marrakech, where you can catch a plane to New York. It would give you some time to rest and consolidate your thoughts."

"Thank you," Nina said. "I'm still pretty jittery, but I feel safe here."

"You'll be more than safe, you'll be well fed."

"There is one thing. I've got to notify the university about the expedition and Dr. Knox. The anthropology department will be devastated. Dr. Knox was an institution. Everybody loved him."

"No problem," Zavala said. "I'll take you to the radio room."

Austin got a glass of iced coffee and brought it back to the table. He poured in a dollop of half-and-half and stared at the dark liquid as if the answer to Nina's puzzle lay in the swirling curlicues. None of the story made much sense, and he was no nearer enlightenment when Zavala returned with Nina a few minutes later.

"That was fast," Austin said. "Didn't you get through to the university?"

Zavala was uncharacteristically somber. "We got through immediately, Kurt."

Austin noticed Nina's eyes were moist with tears.

"I talked to the administration," Nina said, her face ashen. "They didn't want to tell me at first, but I knew they were holding back something." She paused. "Good God! What is happening?"

"I don't understand," Austin said, although he suspected what was coming and wasn't totally surprised when Nina said:

"It's Sandy. She's dead."

8

AUSTIN LAY IN HIS BUNK AND
stared at the ceiling, listening with envy to Zavala's soft snores
from across the cabin. As predicted, the chef had gone heavy on
the herbs and oil, but Austin's stomach was fine. It was his brain
keeping him awake. Like a busy file clerk, it was sorting out the
day's events and wasn't about to let him rest.

The shakedown cruise on the *Nereus* was supposed to be a
milk run, a chance to take a break from the NUMA team's more
strenuous probes into the strange and sinister enigmas on and
under the world's oceans. Then Nina appeared with the hounds
of hell snapping at her heels and practically ran into his arms.
Maybe he was really being kept awake by thoughts of the lovely
young woman in the next cabin.

He glanced at the glowing hands of his Chronosport wristwatch. Three o'clock. Austin remembered a doctor telling him
that three A.M. was when most deathly ill people give up the
ghost. *That* got him out of bed. He pulled on a pair of heavy
sweatpants and a nylon windbreaker and slipped into battered
boat shoes that fit like gloves. Quietly leaving Zavala to his
slumber, he stepped into the passageway and went up four decks
to the bridge.

The wheelhouse door was open to admit the night air. Austin
stuck his head inside. A young crewman named Mike Curtis was

on the early morning watch. He sat in a chair with his nose buried in a book.

"Hi, Mike," Austin said. "Couldn't sleep. How would you like some company?"

The crewman grinned and put the book aside. "Wouldn't mind a bit. Things get pretty boring up here. Want some coffee?"

"Thanks. I like mine black."

While Mike poured two steaming mugs Austin picked up the geology book. "Pretty heavy reading for the graveyard shift."

"I was just boning up for the Yucatan survey. Do you really think that a meteor or comet wiped out all the dinosaurs?"

"When an object as big as Manhattan slams into the earth, it's going to shake things up. Whether the big lizards were already on the verge of extinction is another question. This plankton survey should settle a lot of arguments. It's ironic in a way, having little one-celled animals telling us what happened to the biggest life form ever."

They chatted until Mike went to attend to routine duties. Austin drained his mug and walked through the radio shack to the chartroom at the rear of the bridge. With its big wraparound windows the space doubled as an aft control room the crew could use when maneuvering the ship in reverse.

Austin spread a chart of the Moroccan coast on the navigation table and marked an X in pencil to show the ship's present position. Lips pursed in thought, he studied the chart, letting his eyes travel along the occipital bulge in the skull-shaped African continent from Gibraltar to the Sahara. After a few minutes of study he shook his head. The chart told him nothing. A hovercraft could have come from land or sea.

He dragged a chair over, put his feet up on the table, and read the entries in the ship's log from the start of the trip. It had been a picture-perfect cruise up to now. A swift and uneventful voyage across the Atlantic, a brief stopover in London to pick up a batch of European scientists, a pleasant couple of weeks in the Mediterranean testing the submersible, and then the Moroccan stopover two days ago.

Nina's story was bizarre by any measure. The hovercraft attack and the blood-soaked evidence at the campsite had convinced him the tale was true. The terrible news about her colleague's death removed all shreds of doubt. A car accident. Convenient. These assassins had a long reach. They had erased the data Nina sent to UPenn. Now Nina was the only one who had firsthand knowledge of the mysterious Olmec artifact and the veracity to be believed. He was glad she was in her cabin safely asleep, thanks to the mild sedative provided by her roommate.

Austin walked outside and leaned on the rail of a small platform behind the chartroom. The ship was in darkness except for a few floods illuminating sections of the white superstructure and low-level runway lights along the decks. Beyond the range of the lights was a vast velvet blackness. The smell of rotting vegetation that came to his nostrils was the only evidence of the great land mass that lay less than a league away. Africa. He wondered how many expeditions like Nina's had vanished into the heart of darkness. Maybe the truth would never be known.

Enough philosophizing. Austin yawned and pondered whether to go back to the bridge, return to his cabin, or stay where he was and watch the sun come up. He lingered, savoring the beauty of the night. The *Nereus* was like a behemoth at rest. He loved the feel of a sleeping vessel, the hum of idling electrical systems, and the creaks and groans of a ship at anchor.

Tunk.

Austin leaned forward and cocked his ear. The clinking noise had come from below. Metal on metal.

Tunk. There it was again.

Not loud, but out of sync against the background of usual ship sounds. Curious now, Austin quietly descended to the first level and made his way along the deserted deck, his hand running lightly along the damp rail. He paused. His fingers had hit a hard lump. He looked closer and saw the prong of a grappling iron, covered in cloth to muffle sound. Exploring further with his fingers, he felt the bare metal of the shaft, which must have caused the clinking sound when it hit the side of the ship.

He stepped away from the light and peered over the rail. From down at the waterline came the sound of faint rustlings. They could have been caused by ripples of water against the hull. He cupped a hand to his ear.

Whispered voices separated themselves from the sea sounds. He could see moving shadows.

Austin didn't wait to ask if the boarders were friend or foe. The answer was obvious in his mind. He sprinted for the nearest stairway and climbed back to the cabin level. Moments later he was shaking Zavala awake. His roommate slept as if he were drugged, but he had an uncanny ability to snap himself fully alert as if an internal electrical switch were turned on. Zavala knew Austin wouldn't wake him unless it was important. Grunting to let Austin know he was getting ready for action, he rolled out of bed and yanked on a pair of shipboard shorts and a T-shirt.

Austin had thrown back the cover of his foot locker and was rummaging through his belongings. He pulled out a leather holster, and a second later the snake wood grips of a Ruger Redhawk filled his hand. With its fat, four-inch barrel, the .375 Magnum revolver, custom-built by Bowen, was compact yet packed a wallop.

Zavala called the Bowen "Kurt's Cannon" and claimed it used railroad spikes for ammunition. Actually, the gun fired a special load of .50-caliber bullets.

"We've got company," Austin said as he checked the five-shot cylinder chamber. "Starboard side, coming aboard with grapnels. Those are the ones I *know* about. There may be others. We'll need weapons."

Zavala glanced around the cabin and grumbled, "Just my luck. I recall someone telling me this was going to be like a Love Boat cruise. I didn't even bring a cap pistol. I didn't know we'd be repelling Barbary pirates."

Austin slung the holster over his shoulder. "Neither did I.

That's why I didn't bring a reload. I've got five shots and that's it."

Zavala brightened. "What about your London purchase?"

Austin dug into the locker again and lifted out a shiny flat wooden case. "My Joe Manton specials? Hell, why not?"

Zavala took a diver's sheath knife out of a drawer. "This toothpick is it for my arsenal," he said.

"Not exactly what I'd call overwhelming firepower. We'll have to improvise as we go along."

"It wouldn't be the first time," Zavala said with a shake of his head.

Austin started for the door. "My guess is that they're after Nina. I'll get her and wake everyone on this level. You can get below and roust the rest of the crew and scientists. We'll have them squeeze into the bow thruster room forward of the crew quarters."

"That's going to be tight quarters."

"I know, but they can secure the watertight door and buy us some time. We can't have a bunch of unarmed PhDs and deck hands running around where they can be hurt or taken hostage. Unfortunately the *Nereus* is a research vessel, not a warship."

"I'm beginning to wish it *was* a warship," Zavala said. As swiftly as a thought he disappeared down a stairway that led below.

A sleepy-eyed physician's mate answered Austin's knock on the door of the adjoining cabin. Without elaborating, Austin told her to get dressed while he woke Nina. She was still groggy from her medication, but when she saw the intensity in Austin's face her fluttering eyelids snapped open like window shades.

"They're back, aren't they?" she said, her voice hoarse from sleep.

Austin nodded. Moments later he and the two women were in the hallway making their way from cabin to cabin. Soon more than a dozen grumpy people were gathered in the narrow passage. They were dressed in a variety of nightwear or hastily pulled-on mismatches of clothing.

"No questions now," Austin said in a tone that showed he meant it.

He directed the sleepy-faced group down the stairs to the lowest deck level. Zavala was waiting for him with the others. Like cowpokes on a cattle drive, they herded the reluctant throng into the bow section forward of the crew quarters, where crew and scientists jostled for space with the bow thrusters that were used to stabilize the ship in heavy seas.

Austin wasted no time summing up the situation. "I'm got to make this short and sweet. The ship's being boarded by armed attackers. Don't open this door unless you know it's Joe or me."

A researcher piped up: "What are you going to do?"

Damned scientific minds, Austin thought, always asking questions. This wasn't the time for his usual blunt honesty.

"Don't worry. Joe and I have a plan," he said with confidence. "We'll be back." He quickly stepped into the bunkroom and closed the door on the frightened faces.

"You sounded like the Terminator in there," said Zavala, who was right behind him. "It's good to hear *we've* got a plan. Hope you don't mind telling me what it is."

Austin clamped a big hand on Zavala's shoulder. "Simple, Joe. You and I are going to kick these bastards off our ship."

"That's a *plan?*"

"Maybe you'd like to ask them politely to leave."

"Why do it the easy way? Okay, deal me in. Where do we start?"

"We get up to the bridge in a hurry. That's where our uninvited guests will go first. I hope they're not already there."

"How do you know they'll go for the bridge?"

"It's what *I'd* do. They can cut off communications and take control of the ship in one fell swoop." Austin hustled toward the nearest stairway. "Try to stay out of sight. If it's the same gang that wiped out the expedition, my popgun won't stand a chance against automatic weapons."

Using interior stairways they went up the six decks to the bridge. They stopped at each level before proceeding to the next but saw no sign of the intruders. At the deck below the bridge they split up. Zavala went ahead to warn the watch. Austin woke the captain, who was asleep in his cabin under the wheelhouse, gave him a condensed account of the status quo, and suggested he take cover.

Captain Joe Phelan was a craggy-faced, tough-as-barnacles NUMA veteran in his fifties. He answered Austin's suggestion with a snarl.

"I was there when they laid the keel of the *Nereus*," he snapped, anger dancing in his hazel eyes. "I waited thirty years to take the helm of a vessel like this. Damned if I'm going to hide in a closet while these guys have the run of my ship."

Phelan could make the *Nereus* move with the agility of a ballet dancer, but Austin wasn't sure how he'd be at close combat, which was what things might come down to. On the other hand, it might be risky now for the captain to get down to the bow section. The boarders could be swarming all over the ship.

Phelan zipped up the front of a navy jumpsuit and lifted a pump-action shotgun off a wall rack.

"Only a .410," he apologized. "Never know when you're going to have to put down a mutiny." Noting Austin's quizzical frown, he chuckled. "Sometimes I shoot skeet off the deck."

"This time around the skeet will be shooting back," Austin said grimly.

Phelan produced two boxes of shotgun shells and threw them into a canvas bag with the wooden case Austin had been carrying. Then they hurried up to the bridge.

Before they entered the wheelhouse, Austin called out in a low voice, "Joe, it's us."

The warning was well advised because when they stepped through the door they were staring down the barrel of a flare gun.

Zavala lowered the gun. "Mike's sending off an SOS."

The young crewman Austin had coffee with earlier stepped into the wheelhouse from the radio room. "The signal is on automatic and will broadcast our position until someone shuts it off."

Austin didn't have much hope of the cavalry galloping in for a rescue. The ship was many miles from civilization. They would have to do what had to be done without outside help.

"Guess you won't be bored for a while," Austin told the wide-eyed crewman.

"Guess *not*. What should I do?"

"It's too late for you to go below with the others, so I'm going to put you to work. Climb up on top of the bridge where you get a good view of the ship. Captain, when I give you the signal, I want the *Nereus* lit up like Broadway and Forty-second Street, but keep the bridge in darkness."

With a quick nod and no questions Phelan went over to a console and put his hand on a panel of buttons. Austin and Mike went onto the starboard wing, and Zavala took up a position on the port wing.

As Mike started up the ladder to the bridge roof, Austin said, "When the lights go on I want you to count every stranger you see and remember where you saw them. We'll do the same down here. Remember, keep your head low."

As soon as everyone was in place, Austin called in to the captain.

"*Showtime,* skipper."

The ship was equipped with floodlights at every angle, so the crew and scientists could work at night as easily as during the day. Phelan's fingers danced over the console. In an instant the *Nereus* lit up like a Caribbean cruise ship; every deck was bathed in light from one end to another.

Two decks below, Austin saw a trio of figures freeze, then scurry for cover like startled roaches in a pantry.

"*Cut!*" he called.

The lights blinked off.

Mike called down. "I saw three guys on top of the submersible garage. Heading our way. None forward."

"You flatten down and stay put for now." Austin stepped into the wheelhouse as Zavala came in from the other wing.

"Three on my side, three decks below. Dressed like Ninjas."

"Same with me. Mike saw three coming from the aft deck. That makes nine. That we know of. Captain, can Joe borrow your shotgun? He's had a little more experience shooting, ah, skeet."

The captain knew there was a big difference between picking off clay targets and shooting to kill. He handed the shotgun to Zavala. "Safety's off," he said calmly. At Austin's suggestion, he stepped into the radio room where he would be out of the way.

Austin and Zavala stood back-to-back in the middle of the darkened wheelhouse, the guns pointed toward the open doors on each side. They only had to wait a few minutes before their unwelcome company arrived.

9

A PAIR OF SILHOUETTES MATERIALIZED in the starboard doorway, where they were framed against the blue darkness, one behind the other, making no attempt at concealment. It was a fatal mistake. Seizing his opportunity, Austin lined his sights up on the lead intruder and squeezed the trigger. The Bowen's thunderous roar rattled the wheelhouse windows as it sent a heavy .50-caliber slug smashing into the first attacker's sternum, shattering it to bony splinters before the bullet burst from his rib cage and ripped through the heart of the second figure. The force of the impact threw the intruders back, and their bodies crashed over the rail.

The shotgun boomed. Austin spun around with his ears ringing and through the haze of smoke saw another attacker step boldly through the portside door. Zavala's shot had gone off to one side, and the shotgun pellets gouged a head-level chunk from the door jamb. Zavala rapidly pumped another shell into the chamber and got off a second shot. This time the pellets found their mark. The intruder yelped and drew back, but not before squeezing off a quick unaimed burst of machine-gun fire. The rounds went wild except for one.

The bullet grazed Austin's ribs, passing through the flesh under his left armpit. He felt as if he'd been lashed with red-hot barbed wire.

Zavala was shaking his head in disgust and didn't see Austin go down on one knee. "I aimed right at him," he said incredulously. "Point-blank range. I couldn't miss."

The captain came out of the radio room and slammed a fist into his palm.

"*Damn!* I forgot to tell you that old gun pulls right. You've got to aim it an inch left."

Zavala turned and saw that Austin was down. "Kurt," he said with alarm, "are you all right?"

"I've been better," Austin said, clenching his teeth.

Years at sea had given Captain Phelan a hair-trigger reflex in emergencies. He brought over a first-aid kit, and while Zavala kept guard, pacing from one door to the other, the captain fashioned a compress that stemmed the bleeding.

"Looks like your lucky day," he said, rigging a sling. "They missed the bone."

"Too bad I don't have time to play the lottery." With the captain helping, Austin got back on his feet. "I nailed two with one shot. Unfortunately they took their guns over the side with them."

"Showing me up again," Zavala said peevishly. "I think I only wounded my guy."

"My guess is that they figured they'd catch us asleep and unarmed, so they got too cocky for their own good. It won't happen again. They'll test us next time, draw our fire to see what we've got. They'll see real fast that the ship is mostly deserted and will concentrate all they've got on the bridge. We'd better be gone by then."

"We can move around through the ship's conduits," the captain offered. "I know them better than my own living room."

"Good idea. Our guerrilla operation will be a lot more effective if we can pop up where they least expect us. Be careful, these guys are dangerous but not invincible. They fouled up when they let Nina get away, twice, and just now they got a little overanxious and it cost them. So they make mistakes."

"So do we," Zavala said.

"There's one difference. We can't afford *our* mistakes."

They secured the wheelhouse doors and went into the radio shack. The SOS was still broadcasting mindlessly into the night. Austin wondered who would hear it and what they would make of the message. He paused and lifted the Bowen with his good arm. The weight was too much for one hand, and the revolver wavered from side to side.

"My aim's shaky. You'll have to use it."

He passed the revolver to Zavala, who tucked the flare gun into his waistband. Zavala handed the shotgun to the captain and told him to watch the door. "Remember, it pulls to the right." He hefted the revolver. "Two birds with one stone. Good shooting. With four shots left we can take out eight guys."

"We can do it with *one* shot if they all line up, but I wouldn't count on it," Austin said. He picked up the slim darkwood case he'd dug out of his luggage. "All is not lost. We've got the Mantons."

The ends of Zavala's lips twitched. "Poor bastards won't stand a chance against your single-shot dueling pistols," he said with bleak humor.

"Ordinarily I might say you're right, but these aren't just *any* dueling pistols."

A matched pair of antique flintlock dueling pistols lay inside the box snugly cushioned in compartments covered with green baize. The gleaming brownish barrels were octagonal and the highly polished butts rounded like the head of a cane.

During the ship's stopover in London, Austin had gone to a Brompton Street antique dealer whom he'd had good luck with before. The brace of pistols had come into the shop as part of an estate liquidation, said the proprietor, an older man named Mr. Slocum. From their high finish and lack of ornamentation Austin would have known who made the pistols even if he hadn't seen the Joseph Manton label inside the case. Manton and his brother John were the most renowned eighteenth-century gun makers in England, where the best dueling pistols were made. Manton pistols were short on decoration and long on what really counted in matters of honor:

mechanical precision. When Austin heard the astronomical price he balked.

"I do have Mantons in my collection," he said.

Slocum was not to be deterred. "I might point out that these were custom-made by Mr. Manton," he said, using the honorific as if the gunsmith were still living. "These are just the weapons for a *scoundrel.*" Austin took no insult from the statement, understanding exactly what Slocum meant, that the pistols had built-in insurance. Using a creative combination of traveler's checks and American Express, Austin walked out of the shop with the brace of pistols.

When Austin first showed off his acquisition, Zavala held the pistol at arm's length and said, "It feels barrel-heavy."

"It *is,*" Austin had explained. "Gun makers like Manton knew there was something about staring down a .59-caliber muzzle that made a fellow nervous. Duelists tended to shoot high. The barrel was weighted to keep their aim down. The checkering on the grip and the trigger spur for your middle finger will help you keep it steady."

"How accurate is this thing?"

"Duels were supposed to be settled by fortune. Deliberate aiming or barrel rifling were considered unsportsmanlike. Even cause for murder." He removed the other pistol from the case. "This has 'blind rifling.' Manton made it so the grooves stopped a few inches short. You can't see them by looking into the barrel, but it's enough rifling to give you the edge. At three to five yards, it should be right on target for a snap shot."

Standing in the radio room now, Austin brought the gun up quickly and sighted down the ten-inch barrel as if it were an extension of his arm. "Just the thing for a one-armed man."

Earlier Austin had given Zavala a quick lesson in loading, so he had the concept down even if he was lacking in execution. The flat, pear-shaped powder flask had a spring-activated shutoff that measured out the right amount of load. Zavala had no problem tamping the heavy lead ball down the barrel, but he spilled too much primer in the pan. The second pistol took half the time, and the loading was a lot cleaner. Austin told Zavala he'd make an excellent second in a matter of honor. He tucked one pistol in his sling and held the other in his right hand.

Deciding it would be too dangerous to go back through the wheelhouse, they went into the chartroom, and the captain slowly opened the aft door that led outside. With the Bowen at ready Zavala cautiously peered through the crack. All was clear. They slipped out into the night.

Austin softly called up to Mike and told him to lie low, then suggested they go down the exterior ladders and work their way toward the stern to lead the attackers away from where the others were hiding. He and the captain cautiously descended the starboard side, and Zavala went down on the port. They came together on the deck that extended to become the flat roof of the science storage section. The extension of the bridge superstructure was three levels high and nearly the width of the ship's fifty-foot beam. The roof served double duty as a parking lot for the inflatable workboats.

Three attackers had been spotted earlier on the roof. Austin scanned the shadows, thinking that the deck was perfect for an ambush. He worried about the attackers having night-vision goggles. The roof would have been a dangerous place even if their firepower were not laughable.

He whispered to Zavala, "Do you know any insults in Spanish?"

"You're kidding. My father was born in Morales."

"We need something strong enough to draw our visitors out of hiding."

Zavala thought for a second, cupped his hands to his mouth, and let loose with a torrent in Spanish. The only word Austin recognized was *madre,* repeated several times over. Nothing happened.

"I don't understand it," Zavala said. "Hispanics usually go crazy at any insult to their mother. Maybe I'll go to work on their sisters."

He fired off more insults. Louder and with more of a sneer in his voice. The echoes of the last barbs had hardly faded when two figures stepped from behind the workboats and sprayed the deck with gunfire. Austin was crouched with Zavala and the captain behind a large deck winch. The firing stopped suddenly as the shooters exhausted the bullets in their magazines.

"I think they took it the wrong way," Austin said.

"Must be my Mexican accent. What do you figure? AK-74s?" The AK-74 was the newer version of the terrorists' favorite firearm, the venerable AK-47.

"That's my guess, too. Hard to mistake the sound—"

His words were drowned by the ugly chatter of gunfire. The air was filled with the whine of ricocheting bullets being fired at a rate of four hundred rounds a minute. Again the firing stopped abruptly.

Austin and Zavala took advantage of the intermission and rose to move to a position where they might have a clear shot. They heard a shout from the captain.

"Behind you!"

The two men whirled as a shadow dropped noiselessly from the deck immediately above them. Austin saw him first. His good arm came up in a swift motion, and he pulled the trigger. There was a second of delay as the sparks from the flint ignited the powder pan. After what seemed like hours the pistol belched fire like a dragon's mouth. The figure took a step forward and collapsed. The gun he was carrying clattered to the deck.

Zavala made a move to retrieve the gun. It was too risky now that the muzzle flash had revealed their position. With Zavala covering their rear, Austin and the captain moved toward the nearest stairwell and down to the next deck.

Gunfire was coming from every direction. They looked for cover. Too late. The captain cried out, clutched his head, and fell to the deck. Zavala grabbed the captain's arm and pulled him out of harm's way. More shots, and Zavala went down as a bullet plowed through his left buttock.

They had their backs to the science section. Austin opened a bulkhead door and, without checking to see if it was safe, grabbed the captain by the collar and pulled him inside. Zavala was crawling with one leg dragging limply behind him, but with some help he, too, made it through the portal.

Austin bolted the steel door shut and looked around. They were in one of the "wet" labs, so called because of the large sinks and running seawater. He knew the room by heart and easily found a flashlight, then a first-aid kit, inside a storage locker.

He examined Zavala's wound and breathed a sigh of relief when he saw that the bullet had gone in and out of the flesh. As Austin worked to bind up the wound, not an easy task with only one working hand, Zavala kept the Bowen leveled at the door they had just come in.

"How bad is it?" he said finally.

"You won't like sitting for a while, and you might have to explain that you weren't running for the hills when you got hit. Otherwise, you'll be okay. I don't think they knew where we were. Just shooting wild."

Zavala looked at Austin's sling and then at the prone figure of the captain. "I'd hate to be around when they were really aiming."

Austin examined the captain's head. The close-cropped salt-and-pepper hair was matted with blood, but the wound looked to be a graze. The captain groaned as Austin applied antiseptic to the bloodied scalp.

"How do you feel?" Austin asked.

"I've got a hell of a headache, and I'm having a hard time seeing."

"Think of it as a hangover without the taste of booze in your mouth," Austin advised.

His ministrations finished, Austin looked at his bloodstained comrades and shook his head. "So much for guerrilla warfare."

"Sorry I lost the shotgun," the captain said.

Zavala said, "You *should* be. I could be using it for a crutch." He looked around. "See anything in here we can use to make an atomic bomb with?"

Austin squinted at the rows of chemicals and finally picked

up an empty flask. "Maybe we can use these for Molotov cocktails." He glanced at the door they had just come through. "We can't stay here. They're going to figure out what happened to us when they see the blood trail."

Austin helped his partner into the next section, the high-ceiling garage that was home to the submersible when it wasn't plumbing the depths.

"What about those Molotov cocktails?" Zavala said.

Austin's mouth clamped into a tight and not very pleasant smile, and a hard gleam of anger flickered in eyes that had shifted in shade from coral blue to ice water. For all their wisecracks he and Zavala knew that if they failed, Nina and the others on board were as good as dead. The people crowded into the bow would be found, and these black-suited killers would dispatch them with the same cold-bloodedness with which they wiped the archaeological expedition off the face of the earth. Austin vowed that was not going to happen as long as he was able to draw a breath.

"Forget the cocktails," he said with a quiet ferocity. "I've got a better idea."

10

AUSTIN LEANED AGAINST THE METAL
skin of the submersible, and under the unblinking gaze of the vehicle's porthole eyes he outlined his plan. Zavala, who was sitting at the edge of a sea sled to give his wounded haunch a rest, nodded appreciatively.

"A classic Kurt Austin strategy, depending on split-second timing, unsupported assumptions, and lots of luck. Given the fact that we've got our backs against the sea, I say we go for it."

The captain shook his head in unison with Zavala's grin. The man would fall over with a good push, yet he acted as if he had a Fifth Cavalry division behind him. With the butt of the dueling pistol sticking out of his blood-soaked sling, the silver-haired Austin could have passed for a Hollywood buccaneer in an Errol Flynn movie. Phelan decided that if he had to fight for his ship against such lousy odds, he was glad these two lunatics were on *his* side.

Their strategy session done, they crept through a rear door that led from the submersible garage onto the stern deck. Just behind the towering science storage structure, two portable container vans had been lashed to the deck for use as extra lab space. The three men made their way around the vans and across the deck until they were at the very stern of the ship under the massive beams of the aft A-frame that was used to lift the submersible in and out of the ocean.

The deck appeared to be deserted, but Austin knew they wouldn't remain alone for very long, and in fact he was *counting* on having company.

"What do you want me to do?" the captain asked Austin.

Austin regretted that he ever had any doubts about the doughty old sea dog.

"You're the only one with two whole arms and legs. Since brainpower doesn't count with this phase of the operation, you get to do the grunt work."

Under Austin's one-armed direction, the captain transported four of the gasoline tanks used by the workboats from a storage area and strung them evenly spaced in a line across the deck about halfway between the A-frame and the van labs. Each molded red polyethylene tank held nine gallons.

The captain felt dizzy after the work and had to rest. Austin, who was light-headed from the blood he'd lost, couldn't blame him. Zavala had located a short wooden paddle to use as a cane and was thumping about the deck like Long John Silver. He said he was fine, but he clenched his teeth as he eased himself onto a cable drum of a deck winch.

"Guess we won't be giving to a blood bank anytime soon," Austin said. "We'd better get this show moving before we all keel over. It's vital that we make them come to us."

"I can try greeting them in Spanish again. That worked the last time."

Remembering the violent reaction Zavala's taunts provoked on the upper deck, Austin said, "Let 'em have it."

Zavala drew a deep breath and in the loudest voice he could muster let fly a string of insults that called the character of the listeners' families into question in every way imaginable. Fathers, brothers, and sisters, assigning to each an imaginative array of perversions. Austin had no idea what he was saying, but the sarcastic needling tone left no mistake about the meaning of the scornful barbs.

While Zavala threw out the bait, Austin got a tight grip on one of the deck hoses and signaled the captain to turn on the water. The hose jerked as if it were alive. Austin walked across the deck, sweeping the spray back and forth.

The water hit the deck with a spattering hiss that was drowned out by Zavala's insults. Barely visible in the moonlight, a white-foamed ripple began to advance. Austin kept the miniature wave moving until it almost reached the gas tanks.

Zavala's taunts failed to work their scatalogical magic this time. The enemy had become wary after the last episode. Austin grew impatient. He drew the dueling pistol from his sling, pointed it in the air, and fired. If his scheme failed, a single bullet wasn't going to help much anyhow. The ruse worked. Before long, dusky ghosts that were more spectral than real in the faint light of the moon materialized from the shadows around the cargo containers and began to advance slowly toward them.

Austin again had a scary thought that they might have night-vision goggles, but he quickly put it out of his mind. The intruders were moving more cautiously than they did in the earlier attacks, but they showed no sign of being deterred from their task. Austin estimated that it would be only seconds before powerful flashlights clicked on and lethal gunfire sprayed the deck.

The ripple was nearly at the containers.

Red lights glowed in the darkness. Laser sights that would give the gunmen unerring aim.

Austin gave the signal to Zavala.

"Now."

Zavala was sitting in the center of the deck, favoring his good side, his eyes glued on the barely visible line of foam that marked the edge of the advancing water. He lifted the Bowen revolver in both hands, sighted on the tank farthest to his right, and pulled the trigger.

The revolver roared like a miniature howitzer. The tank disintegrated as a fountain of gasoline showered the deck. Zavala quickly moved the leveled pistol to the left. Three more times he fired. Three more tanks were blown to pieces. The thirty-six gallons of gasoline spread out in an expanding puddle.

Austin ordered the captain to turn up the pressure. Floating on the surface of the moving water, the gasoline surged forward and eddied around the prone forms of the attackers who lay belly-down on the deck where they had flattened out at the first roar of Austin's oversized pistol. They got up, and if they thought about the precariousness of wearing gas-soaked clothes as a puddle of waterborne fuel lapped at their shoes, it was too late to do anything about it. All that was needed to turn the deck into an inferno was a spark, and Zavala was glad to provide one.

Zavala put the empty Bowen aside and picked up the flare gun. Austin had been watching the figures get to their feet.

"Now!" he yelled again.

Zavala pulled the trigger. The glowing projectile streaked down at an angle and skipped across the deck in a phosphorescent explosion of streamers. The deck erupted in flames, and Zavala threw his arm up for protection against the hot blast.

A moving wall of yellow flame swept toward the black-clad figures who were thrown into relief as the volatile liquid they were standing in ignited like a napalm bomb. The fire quickly enveloped them as it fed on the gas-soaked clothes and transformed the figures into blazing torches. The intense heat sucked the air out of their lungs. Before they could take a step they crumpled to the deck. Bullets from the useless guns flew in all directions through the cloud of billowing black smoke.

Austin hadn't foreseen this dangerous byproduct of his plan. He yelled out to the captain to grab cover, then helped Zavala. They huddled behind the winch drum until the gunfire ceased.

The blaze used up the fuel and blew itself out almost as quickly as it started. Austin told Zavala and the captain to stay put and walked forward. Five steaming corpses lay in fetal position on the deck.

"Everything okay?" Zavala called.

"Yeah, but it's the last time they'll come to one of our barbecues."

Zavala's voice rang out. "Watch it, Kurt, there's *another* one."

Austin automatically reached for his sling only to realize he had left the useless dueling pistol behind. He froze as a shadow detached itself from behind the base of a crane off to one side. He was out in the open. The Bowen was empty. He was dead. He waited for a fusillade of hot lead to cut him down. He'd be a perfect target against the flames flickering on the water's surface. Zavala and the captain would be next.

Nothing happened. The figure was running away toward the starboard side where Austin had first discovered the grappling hooks.

Austin took a step to follow, then stopped. Unarmed, wounded, and just plain worn out, he could only stand there helplessly as an outboard motor coughed into life. He waited until the motor's buzz faded into the distance, then walked back to Zavala and the captain.

"Guess our head count was off," Zavala said.

"Guess so." Austin let out the breath he'd been holding. He wanted to lie down and take a nap, but there was one more thing he had to do. Mike was still on the roof of the bridge, and the crew and researchers were barricaded in the bow section.

"You wait here. I'll tell the others they can come up for air."

He picked his way around the charred bodies and made his way toward the bow section where the crew and scientists were hiding. Austin was not a cold-blooded man, but he reserved his compassion for those who deserved it. Moments ago the flesh-and-blood entities that had inhabited these smoking charcoal shells were intent on killing him and his friends and colleagues. Something he could not let happen under any circumstances. Particularly to Nina, for whom he was forming a growing attachment. It was as simple as that.

This was obviously the same team that wiped out the archae-ological expedition. They had come to finish the job. Austin and the others had just been in the way. The assassins had been stopped, but Austin knew that as long as Nina Kirov was alive, this wasn't going to be the end of it.

11

THE MONSOONS THAT SWEEP ACROSS
India from the Arabian Sea drop most of their rain on the mountain range known as the Western Ghats. By the time the moist air currents reach the Deccan in southeast India the downpour has diminished to a mere twenty-five inches. As Professor Arthur Irwin stood in the mouth of the cave looking out at the sheets of water pouring down from the slate-colored sky, he found it hard to believe this was supposedly the same amount of rainfall London gets. The afternoon shower that was just ending would by itself have been enough to float the Houses of Parliament.

The cave opening was on a sloping hillside that overlooked a narrow valley choked by lush greenery. The dense forest south of the Ganges River is the most ancient part of India and was once known as a remote and dangerous place haunted by demons.

Irwin was less worried about demons than the welfare and whereabouts of his party. It had been six hours since Professor Mehta had set off for the village with their taciturn guide. The village was about an hour's hike along a muddy road and across a stream. He hoped the bridge hadn't been knocked out in a sudden flash flood. He sighed. Nothing he could do about it; he would simply have to wait. He had plenty of supplies and much to occupy himself. Irwin went back into the cave, walking between a pair of pillars under a horseshoe arch into the cool central hall or chapel.

Poor Mehta. This was *his* expedition, after all. He'd been so excited when he called and said, "I need a middle-aged Cantabrigian ethnologist for a small expedition. Can you come to India? At my expense."

"Has the Indian Museum suddenly become less parsimonious?"

"No, but it's not the museum. I'll explain later."

The Buddhist monks who had carved the cave from sheer rock with pick and ax were following the words of the Master, who advised his followers to take a "rain rest" for meditation and study during the monsoon season.

Doorways on either side of the chapel opened into the spartan monks' cells. The stone couches where Irwin and the other men spread their sleeping bags were not the most comfortable of sleeping platforms, but at least they were dry.

The main hall was built like a Christian basilica. Light from the door reached the far end where the altar would be in a church. Irwin marveled at the artfully sculpted pillars that supported the barrel ceiling. Along the walls were scenes from the life of Buddha and, most interesting to Irwin, court and domestic paintings that portrayed the everyday existence of people and allowed the cave to be dated at about A.D. 500.

The Deccan was famous for its cave monasteries, and as far as anyone knew, all had been discovered. Then this one was found, its entrance hidden behind vegetation. On their first visit Mehta and Irwin were examining the paintings when the guide, who had wandered off, called out to them from an anteroom.

"Come quickly! A *man!*"

They exchanged glances, thinking that the guide had discovered a skeleton. When they entered the cool dark space and flashed their lights on the corner, they saw a stone figure perhaps five feet long. The man reclined, his head turned to one side. On his belly he held a dish-shaped receptacle.

Irwin stared for a moment in disbelief, then went back into the chapel and sat down.

Mehta followed him out. "What is it, Arthur?"

"That figure. Have you ever seen anything like that?"

"No, but obviously you have."

Irwin tugged nervously at his goatee. "I was traveling in Mexico some years ago. We stopped at the Mayan ruins at Chichén Itzá. There's a larger version of this figure there. It's called a *chac mool*. That dishlike receptacle the figure is holding was used to catch blood during sacrifices."

"*Mexico*," Mehta said without conviction.

Irwin nodded. "When I saw it here, it was so out of time and place . . ."

"I understand, of course. But perhaps you're mistaken. There are a great many similarities in cultures."

"Maybe. We've got to get it back for authentication."

Mehta's sad eyes became even sadder. "We haven't even *started* our work."

"There's no reason why we can't still do it, but this is important."

"Of course, Arthur," Mehta said with resignation, remembering how impulsive Irwin was even when they were students at Cambridge.

They trekked back to the village and retrieved their truck, which they drove to the nearest town that had a telephone. Mehta suggested they call Time-Quest, the nonprofit foundation that was funding the original expedition, and ask for more money to pay to remove the artifact. He explained that the only strings attached were that Time-Quest be notified of any significant find.

After a lengthy conversation, Mehta hung up and smiled. "They said we can hire some villagers but to wait until they get someone to us with the money. I told them the monsoon season is almost here. They said forty-eight hours."

They went back to the cave and worked at the site photographing and cataloging. Two days later Mehta and the guide set off for the village to meet the Time-Quest representative. Then the rains came.

Irwin worked on his notes. When the others hadn't arrived by dusk, he cooked curried rice and beans. It grew dark, and it looked as if he would be spending the night alone. So he was pleased when he heard a quiet footfall as he finished washing the dishes with spring water from a cistern.

"At last, my friends," he said over his shoulder. "I'm afraid you've missed dinner, but I might be persuaded to cook more rice."

There was no reply. He turned and saw a figure standing just out of range of the light cast by the lamp. Thinking he might be a villager sent by Mehta, Irwin said, "You startled me. Did Mehta send you with a message?"

In silent reply, the figure took a step forward. Metal gleamed in the stranger's hand, and in the last terrifying moments of his life Irwin realized what had happened to Mehta and the guide, even if he didn't know why.

12

"HOW FAR ARE WE FROM THE SITE, CHIANG?"

The wiry man standing at the riverboat's long tiller held up two fingers.

"Two miles or two *hours?*" Jack Quinn said.

A gap-toothed grin appeared on the steersman's wizened face. He shrugged and pointed to his ear. Either the question had exceeded his meager grasp of English or he simply couldn't hear over the racket generated by an antique Evinrude outboard motor.

Worn valves, defective muffler, and a loose housing that vibrated like a drumhead combined in an uproar that echoed off the riverbanks and drowned out all attempts at verbal communication.

Quinn ran his fingers through thinning black hair and adjusted his stocky body in a vain attempt to locate a more comfortable position for his posterior. It was a lost cause. The low-slung, narrow-beamed craft was shaped vaguely like a surfboard and partially covered by a rough deck whose sun-splintered surface discouraged sitting.

Quinn finally gave up. He hunched his shoulders and stared with glazed eyes at the passing scenery. They had left the rice paddies and tea plantations behind them. Occasionally they passed a fishing village and a grazing water buffalo, but soon only golden fields rolled off to mist-shrouded mountains in the distance. The beauty of China was lost on Quinn. He could think only of Ferguson, his project manager.

The first message from Ferguson had been exciting.

"Found many clay soldiers. This could be bigger than Xi'an."

Quinn knew right away that Ferguson was talking about the seven-thousand-strong army of terra-cotta soldiers discovered in an imperial mausoleum near the Chinese city of Xi'an. It was the sort of news Quinn liked to relay to the governing board of the East Asia Foundation, which he served as executive director.

The foundation was set up by a group of wealthy patrons to promote east-west understanding and atone for the opium trade. It was also a tax write-off so those living comfortably off the fortunes their forebears made hooking hundreds of thousands of Chinese on drugs could enjoy their wealth to the fullest.

As part of its program the foundation sponsored archaeological digs in China. These were popular with the board because they cost the foundation nothing, being largely subsidized by enthusiastic amateurs who paid money to participate, and because they sometimes made the front page of *The New York Times*.

Quinn would visit a site when he could be sure of favorable publicity, but it usually took a lot to pry him from the mahogany and leather comfort of his New York office.

The second message from the field was even better than the first.

"Found exciting artifact. Details to follow."

Quinn had already primed his newspaper and TV contacts when the third message arrived.

"Artifact is *Mayan!*"

Before taking the foundation job, Quinn had run a university museum and had a sketchy knowledge of ancient cultures. He fired off a reply to Ferguson: "Mayan is *not* Chinese. Impossible."

A few days later he heard from Ferguson again. "Impossible but true. No kidding."

That night Quinn packed a bag and took the next flight to

Hong Kong, where he caught a train to the interior. After a bus ride of several hours he arrived at the river just in time to hitch a ride with Chiang. In addition to keeping the expedition supplied, Chiang served as postman, running communications to a telegraph office, which explained why the messages were so agonizingly slow.

Quinn learned that Chiang had visited the site a few days before, which must have been when he picked up Ferguson's last letter. Quinn's anger had been building during the course of his long, hard journey. It was only a question of whether he would fire Ferguson before or after he threw him in the river. As they neared the site, Quinn began to wonder if Ferguson had simply gone raving mad. Maybe it was something in the water.

Quinn still hadn't decided on a course of action when the boat angled in and bumped up against the shore where the banking had been worn down by foot traffic. Chiang tied up at a post stuck in the ground, then he and Quinn both grabbed a couple of boxes with supplies and began to walk inland.

As they followed a path through high yellow grass, Quinn asked, "How far?"

One finger. Quinn figured it to be one hour or one mile. He was wrong on both counts. One minute later they came upon an area where the grass had been tramped down in a more or less circular shape.

Chiang put down his load and gestured at Quinn to do the same.

"Where's the camp?" Quinn said, looking for people or tents.

Chiang's face was creased in a puzzled frown. Tugging at his scraggly beard, he pointed emphatically to the ground.

End of a perfect day, Quinn fumed. He was tired and dirty, his stomach was roiling like a boiled pot, and now his guide was lost. Chiang said something in Chinese and motioned for Quinn to follow. After a few minutes' walk he stopped and pointed to the ground. A couple of acres of dirt had been turned over.

Quinn walked along the perimeter of the disturbed soil until his eye caught a roundish object protruding from the dirt. He dug away at it with his hands and after a few minutes revealed the head and shoulders of a terra-cotta soldier. He dug some more and found other soldiers.

This *must* be the site, but there should be about a dozen people here. Where the hell *was* everybody? Chiang glanced fearfully around him. "Devils," he said, and without another word trotted back toward the river.

The air grew colder as if a cloud had passed over the sun. Quinn realized he was all alone. The only sound was the snake-like rustle of the breeze through the grass. He took one last look around and dashed toward the retreating figure, leaving behind the ranks of silent soldiers entombed in the earth.

13

IN THE SULTRY STILLNESS OF THE
Virginia morning Austin shoved off from the boat ramp,
wrapped his thick fingers around the carbon-fiber oar handles,
and with a long smooth pull sent his arrow-slim racing scull darting into the sparkling waters of the Potomac River.

Sculling on the Potomac was a daily ritual Austin followed
faithfully in between assignments. As the doctor ordered, he had
given his left side a rest. Once the stitches healed he began his
own therapy regimen using the weights and machines in his
exercise room and daily swims in his pool. He had gradually
increased the demands on his body until he considered it safe to
row without tearing newly mended muscle.

The time to test the regimen came on a particularly lovely
day when the siren call of the river became impossible to resist.
He hauled his sleek twenty-one-foot-long Maas Aero racing scull
from the lower level of the boathouse he'd converted into his
home just below the palisades in Fairfax County. Jockeying the
light shell down the ramp and into the water was not difficult.
The real adventure was getting into the slender boat without tip-
ping it over.

His first attempt to row was pure disaster. The Concept II
composite oars were feather-light, but with their nine-foot length
and the weight and pressure of the blades against the water,

Austin took only a few painful strokes before turning back in a cold sweat. His side felt as if a meat hook hung off it. He deliberately capsized the shell near shore, staggered into the house, and stood in front of the medicine cabinet looking at his ashen reflection as he popped painkillers that only slightly dulled the agony. He waited a few days then tried again. He favored his right arm, and the uneven strokes tended to send the scull into an unpretty series of connected arcs, but at least he was moving. Within days he could row without gritting his teeth.

Eventually the stiffness lessened. Today the only reminder of the assassin's lucky shot was the twinge he experienced during his warm-up stretches. He felt good from the moment he slipped into the open cockpit, tucked his feet into the clogs bolted to the foot rests, and pushed the sliding seat back and forth a few times on its twin runners to limber up his abdominal muscles. He adjusted the "buttons," the collars that rest against the outrigger oarlocks, to make sure they were positioned to deliver the maximum power with each stroke.

Leaning forward, Austin dipped the blades into the water and gingerly pulled the oar handles back, letting the weight of his body work for him. The scull skimmed over the surface like a water bug. This was the best day yet. Any residual pain was overwhelmed by his joy at being able to row with a normal rhythm. He sat straight up, hands overlapped for easier pulling. Rowing slowly at first, he used a moderate forward reach and a long pull. At the end of each stroke he feathered the oars, turning them almost horizontal to reduce wind resistance, the blades inches above the water as they came forward. He grunted with satisfaction; he was rowing well.

The scull glided upriver as quietly as a whisper past the stately old mansions that lined the shore. The misty flower-scented river air that filled his lungs was like the perfume of an old love. Which in a way was true. For Austin, rowing was more than his main physical exercise. With its emphasis on technique rather than power this melding of mind and body was like a Zen meditation. Totally focused now, he increased his stroke rate, gradually unleashing more of the power in his broad shoulders, until the dial of the Strokecoach just above his toes showed him rowing at a normal twenty-eight strokes per minute.

Sweat rolled down from under the visor of his turquoise NUMA baseball cap, the back of his rugby shirt was soaked with perspiration, and his butt was numb despite the seat padding of the bike shorts. But his senses were telling him that he was *alive.* The sleek shell flew over the river as if the oars were wings. He planned to row the first leg for forty-five minutes, then reverse and let the lazy current give him an easy ride back. There was no sense pushing his luck.

A blinding flash of light caught his eye from the riverbank. The sun was reflecting off the glass of a tripod-mounted spotting scope. A man sat on a folding chair on the shore peering into the scope's eyepiece. He had on a white cotton hat pulled down low over his brow, and the rest of his face was hidden behind the scope. Austin had seen the same man for the first time several days earlier and had figured him for a bird-watcher. Except for one thing: the scope was always trained on Austin.

Minutes later Austin made the planned turn and started downriver. As he approached the bird-watcher again he shipped his oars, letting the current take him, and waved, hoping the man would lift his head. The eye remained glued to the scope. Austin studied the bird-watcher as the scull glided silently by. Then he grinned and with a shake of his head took up the oars again and pulled for home.

The Victorian-style boathouse had been part of a riverfront estate. With its pale blue clapboards and mansard roof surmounted by a turret, it was a miniature of the main house except for interior modifications. Austin steered the shell toward shore, climbed out onto the ramp, and pulled the scull up and under the boathouse. He maneuvered it onto a rack next to another one of his toys, a small outboard hydroplane. Austin had two other boats, a twenty-two-foot catboat and a full-sized racing hydroplane, tied up at a Chesapeake Bay marina.

He liked the catboat's classic lines and history and the fact that despite its tubby hull and single sail it was fast, especially with the modifications he'd built into it, and could beat the pants off bigger and sleeker craft. The cat was weatherly, too, and he pushed it to extremes of weather and distance just for the thrill of it. While Austin enjoyed the mental challenges of rowing and could sail a boat almost from the time he could walk, he had acquired a taste for speed early in life and raced boats since he was ten. His big love on his time off was still racing boats.

With the scull stowed, he climbed an inside stairway to the main level, then another short flight to the turret bedroom. He tossed his rowing clothes into a hamper and washed away the morning's exertions with a hot shower. As he toweled off in front of the mirror he examined the bullet wound. It had lost its angry redness and turned pinkish. Soon it would join the other pale scars that stood out against his walnut skin. All souvenirs of violent encounters. Sometimes he wondered if his body naturally attracted projectiles and sharp instruments the way a magnet draws metal filings.

Dressed in clean shorts and T-shirt, he went into the kitchen, brewed half a pot of strong Kenyan coffee, and rustled up a pan of bacon and eggs. He carried the plate through a slider to the deck overlooking the Potomac and watched the river go by as he ate breakfast. Still enjoying the cholesterol rush, he refilled a mug of coffee, then went into his combination study-den. He put a Coltrane CD on the stereo, settled into a black leather chair, and listened to Anton Sax's instrument sing in voices its creator could never have dreamed were possible. It was not surprising that Austin favored progressive jazz. In a way the sounds of Coltrane, Oscar Peterson, Keith Jarrett, Bill Evans, and other artists in his extensive music library reflected Austin's own personality: a steely coolness that masked intense energy and drive, the ability to reach deep into his soul when superhuman effort was needed, and a talent for improvisation.

The spacious room was an eclectic collection of the old and the new, authentic darkwood colonial furniture, and white walls hung with contemporary originals. Curiously for a man who was raised in and around the sea and who spent much of his life on or under the water, there were few nautical items. A primitive painting of a sailing clipper done by a Hong Kong Picasso for a China Trade skipper, a nineteenth-century chart of the Pacific, a couple of shipbuilding tools, a photo of his catboat, and a glass-encased scale model of his racing hydroplane.

His bookshelves held the leather-bound sea adventures of Joseph Conrad and Herman Melville and dozens of books of ocean science. But the most hand-worn volumes were those of writers like Plato, Kant, and the other great philosophers he liked to study. Austin was aware of the dichotomy but saw no oddity in it. More than one sea captain had retired inland after a career on the bounding main. Austin wasn't yet ready to move to Kansas, but the sea was a wild and demanding mistress, and he needed this quiet refuge from its crushing embrace.

As he sipped his coffee his eye fell on the brace of Mantons mounted on the wall over the fireplace. Austin had nearly two hundred sets of dueling pistols in his collection. Most of the pairs were stored in a fireproof vault. He kept the more recent acquisitions at the boathouse. He was fascinated not only by the workmanship and deadly beauty of the pistols but by the twists and turns of history that may have been launched by a well-placed ball fired on a quiet morning. He pondered how the republic might have fared if Aaron Burr had not killed Alexander Hamilton. The Mantons brought his mind back to the *Nereus* incident. What a strange night! In the days he'd been home recovering Austin had replayed the attack in his mind again and again, fast-forwarding, freezing action, and rewinding like a VCR.

After the battle the exertion and loss of blood caught up with Austin. He had barely taken a dozen steps before he could go no farther, collapsing in slow-motion and ending up in a sitting position. Captain Phelan had been the one to tell the crew all was safe. They came out of hiding, scraped Austin and Zavala off the deck, and carried them on stretchers to sickbay. On the way they passed the body of the assailant Austin had nailed with a single shot from his dueling pistol. At Austin's direction they stopped, and a crewman with a strong stomach pulled the mask off the dead man. The face was that of a man in his thirties, dark-complexioned, with a thick black mustache, his features otherwise unremarkable except for the round hole in the forehead.

Zavala sat up on his stretcher and let out a low whistle. "Tell me you had a laser sight on that old blunderbuss. A moving target in the dark! If I hadn't seen it I'd say a shot like that was impossible."

"It *is* impossible," Austin said with a rueful smirk. "I was playing it safe with a body shot."

As he explained to Zavala while their wounds were properly bandaged, his uncanny accuracy had nothing to do with his aim or the pistol's disreputable barrel grooving. In his haste Austin had turned the small pressure-adjusting screw next to the trigger in the wrong direction and set the pistol with a hair trigger. Thank goodness for Manton's barrel-weighted idiot-proofing.

A oil-company helicopter summoned by an emergency radio call plucked the wounded men and Nina Kirov from the *Nereus* and dropped them off in Tarfaya. Captain Phelan refused to leave his ship, and after the physician's mate had ascertained he'd be able to function on a limited basis within a few days, he stayed on to take the *Nereus* to the Yucatan. Within hours Austin and Zavala were on a NUMA executive jet that had been diverted to Morocco on its way to the United States from Rome. Nina hitched a ride on the plane to Dulles airport. The painkiller Austin was given knocked him for a loop, and he slept almost the entire flight. His recollections were vague, but he remembered dreaming that a blond angel kissed him lightly on the cheek. When he awoke he was in Washington. Nina was gone, having caught the shuttle for Boston. He wondered whether he'd ever see her again. After spending a couple of days in the hospital he and Zavala were sent home, told to take their medication faithfully and give their bodies a chance to heal.

The jangle of the phone jolted Austin out of his reverie. He picked up the receiver and heard a crisp greeting. "Good morning, Kurt, how are you feeling?"

"I'm coming along quite well, Admiral Sandecker. Thank you for asking. Although I must admit to being a little bored."

"Glad to hear that. Your boredom is about to come to an abrupt end. We're meeting tomorrow at nine to see if we can get to the bottom of this Moroccan business. I'm bringing Zavala in as well. He's been seen around Arlington in his convertible, so I assume he, too, is bored with inactivity."

Zavala, who drove a 1961 Corvette, mostly because it was the last model with a trunk, had used his time to tinker in his basement, where he liked to restore mechanical contrivances and create new technical underwater devices. As soon as he was able to walk without falling over he started working out at a boxing gym. Joe was never bored when there were women around, and he'd been making the most of the sympathetic leverage his wound got him.

Austin had talked to Zavala numerous times on the phone. For all the fun Joe was having, he was itching for action. Austin was telling the truth when he said, "I'm sure he's eager to get back to work, Admiral."

"Splendid. By the way, I understand you're well enough to qualify for a spot on the Olympic crew team."

"As coxswain, maybe. One suggestion, sir. The next time you hire someone to impersonate a bird-watcher, you might make sure he isn't wearing dress shoes and knee socks."

Pause. "I don't have to remind you that NUMA does not have the same pool of clandestine operatives that your Langley neighbors have at their beck and call. I asked Joe McSweeney, one of NUMA's bean counters from accounting, to quietly see how you were coming along. He passes your house commuting to work. Sounds as if a James Bond bug bit him and he took the job more seriously than I imagined. Hope you don't mind."

"No problem, sir. I appreciate your concern. It's better than having daily phone calls from headquarters."

"Thought you might think so. Incidentally, Mac *does* know his birds."

"I'm sure he does," Austin said. "See you tomorrow, Admiral."

Austin hung up, chuckling at Sandecker's paternalism and his disingenuous shot at the CIA whose headquarters were less than a mile from the boathouse. The admiral's agency was primarily scientific, but its operations as the undersea counterpart of NASA were naturally made for intelligence gathering that rivaled or even surpassed the best "the Company" could come up with.

Sandecker envied the CIA's bottomless budget and limited accountability, although he himself was no slouch at prying funding from Congress. He could muster the support of twenty top universities with schools in the marine sciences and a host of large corporations. With its five thousand scientists, engineers, and others; its ongoing studies in deep ocean geology and mining, biological studies of sea life, marine archaeology, and climatology; and its far-flung fleet of research vessels and aircraft, NUMA's reach extended to every part of the globe.

Hiring Austin away from the CIA had been a major Sandecker coup. Austin came to NUMA in a roundabout fashion. He had studied for his master's degree in systems management at the University of Washington and attended a high-rated dive school in Seattle. He'd trained as an underwater jack-of-all-trades, which meant he was proficient in basics such as welding, the commercial application of explosives, and mud diving. He specialized in flotation, lifting heavy objects from the sea, and deep-sea saturation diving in various environments using mixed air and undersea chambers. After working on oil rigs in the North Sea a couple of years, he returned to his father's marine salvage company for six years before being lured into a little-known branch of the CIA that specialized in underwater intelligence gathering. He was assistant director of the secret raising of a Russian submarine and the salvage and investigation of an Iranian container ship carrying nuclear weapons that was sunk clandestinely by an Israeli submarine. He also conducted several investigations into commercial airlines that had been mysteriously shot down over the sea, locating, salvaging, and investigating the incidents.

At the end of the Cold War the CIA closed down the undersea investigation branch. Austin probably would have drifted into another CIA section had he not been hired by Admiral Sandecker for special undersea assignments that often took place outside the realm of government oversight. Sandecker could cry poor mouth and point at Langley all he wanted, but he was well acquainted with cloak-and-dagger operations.

Austin glanced at his watch. Ten o'clock. It would be seven in Seattle. He picked up the phone and punched out a number. A voice with a buzz-saw edge answered.

"Good morning," Austin said. "It's your number one son."

"About time you called."

"I talked to you yesterday, Pop."

"A lot can happen in twenty-four hours," Austin's father replied with good-natured gruffness.

"Oh? Like what?"

"Like landing a multimillion-dollar contract with the Chinese. That's what. Not bad for an old geezer."

It was from his father that Austin inherited his strapping physique and stubbornness. Now in his mid-seventies, the elder Austin had a slight stoop to his wide shoulders, but he regularly put in work days that would kill a younger man. His Seattle-based marine salvage company had made him wealthy. But he still drove himself, especially since the death of Austin's mother a few years earlier. Like many self-made men, it had become the game, not the money, that was important.

"Congratulations, Pop. Can't say I'm surprised. But you're hardly a geezer, and you know it."

"Don't waste your time buttering me up. Talk's cheap. When are you coming out so we can celebrate with a bottle of Jack Daniel's?"

That's all I need, Austin thought. A night out with his hard-drinking father would land him back in the hospital. "Not for a while. I'm going back to work."

"About time. You've gold-bricked long enough." There was disappointment in his voice.

"You must have been talking to the admiral. He said pretty much the same thing."

"Naw, I got better things to do." Austin's father was only half kidding. He had a great deal of respect for Sandecker. At the same time he saw him as a rival for his son and had never abandoned hope that Kurt would come to his senses someday and take over the family business. Austin sometimes thought this hope was what kept his father going.

"Let me see what he wants. I'll get back to you."

Heavy sigh. "Okay, you do what you have to do. Got to go. Call coming in on the other line."

Austin stared at the now dead receiver and shook his head. In more fanciful moments he wondered what would happen if his bearlike father clashed head-to-head with the slightly built but bantam-tough Sandecker. He wouldn't bet on the outcome, but he knew one thing. He didn't want to be around if it happened.

The Coltrane CD was ending. Austin replaced it with a Gerry Mulligan disk and leaned back in his chair with a smile on his face as he prepared to savor the last hours of leisure time he might have for weeks to come. He was glad Sandecker had called and that his vacation was about to end. It went beyond boredom. The admiral wasn't the only one who wanted to get to the bottom of what he called "this Moroccan business."

14

HIRAM YAEGER LEANED BACK IN HIS
chair, hands folded behind his neck, and stared through his wire-rimmed granny glasses at the three-dimensional black-and-white photograph of the buxom Sumatran woman, made even more lifelike by the holographic display, who was projected on the huge monitor beyond his horseshoe-shaped console. He wondered how many millions of young males learned their first lesson in female anatomy from the dusky maidens in the pages of *National Geographic* magazine.

With a sigh of dreamy nostalgia Yaeger said, "Thanks for the treat, Max."

"You're welcome," replied the computer's disembodied female voice. "I thought you'd enjoy a break from your work." The nubile maiden disappeared, sent back to 1937 where she had been frozen in time by a *Geographic* photographer.

"It brought back fond memories," Yaeger said, taking a sip from his coffee.

From his private terminal in a small side room the chief of the agency's communications network could, in a blink of the eye, tap into the vast files of the computer data complex that occupied the entire tenth floor of the NUMA headquarters building. It was NUMA's hardware that usually made world headlines. The exploits of the high-tech research vessels, deep-submergence submarines, and assorted undersea robots were what caught the public's imagination. But one of Sandecker's greatest contributions was NUMA's unseen jewel in the crown, the massive high-speed computer network Yaeger had designed with a free hand and unlimited funding thanks to the admiral.

Sandecker had lured Yaeger to NUMA in a raid on a Silicon Valley computer corporation and assigned him to build what would undeniably be the finest and largest archive of ocean sciences in the world. The vast data library was Yaeger's joy and his passion. It had taken years to put together centuries of human knowledge gleaned from books, articles, and scientific and historical theses. Everything known to have been written about the sea was available not only to NUMA but to ocean science students, professional oceanographers, marine engineers, and underwater archaeologists worldwide.

Yaeger was the only person in NUMA who ignored Sandecker's dress code and got away with it, which spoke eloquently of his talents. With his Levi's jacket and jeans, his long blondish-gray hair tied in a ponytail, and the untamed whiskers that hid the boyish eagerness of his face, the scruffy Yaeger could have come off a sixties hippy commune. In fact, Yaeger did not live in a yurt, but drove to and from a fashionable Maryland suburb in a fully equipped BMW. His attractive wife was an artist, his two teenage daughters were students at a private school, and their main complaint was that Yaeger spent more time with his electronic family than his flesh-and-blood one.

Yaeger was still in awe of the tremendous power at his command. He had given up the keyboard and monitor for spoken commands and the holographic display. His foray into the more revealing aspect of the *Geographic* articles was an excuse to take a break from the demanding assignment he'd been working on at Sandecker's request. On the surface Sandecker's directive had been uncomplicated. Find out if there were any attacks on archaeological expeditions similar to what happened in Morocco. It turned out to be a monumental task. He'd neglected his understanding wife and children even more than usual in his passion to solve the puzzle.

Although the NUMA system was geared to the oceans, Max routinely hacked into other systems, without authorization, to gather information and transfer data among libraries, newspaper morgues, research libraries, universities, and historic archives anywhere on the globe. Yaeger began by compiling a master list of expeditions, divided chronologically by decades and going back fifty years. There were hundreds of names and dates on the list. Then he prepared a computer model based on the facts that were known about the Moroccan incident. He asked Max to compare the model to each expedition, drawing on various sources such as published academic papers, scientific journals, and news reports, cross-checking the accounts to determine if any of these expeditions had come to a similar unscheduled end, always searching for patterns.

The sources were often fragmentary and sometimes dubious. Like a sculptor trying to find a figure in a piece of marble, he chipped the master list down in size. It was still long and complicated enough to daunt the most experienced researcher, but the challenge only whetted his appetite. After several days he had brought together an enormous amount of information. Now he would instruct the computers to sift through the data and refine the results into a palatable serving.

"Max, please print out your findings when you've exhausted your networks," he instructed the computer.

"I will get back to you shortly. Sorry for the delay," the soft monotone voice responded. "Why don't you pour yourself another cup of coffee while you wait?"

Time was irrelevant to a computer, Yaeger reflected as he followed Max's suggestion. It did what it did at unimaginable speeds, but no matter how fast and smart Max was, it had no concept of what it was like to have Sandecker breathing down its circuits. Yaeger had promised Sandecker the results by the following morning. While Max labored, Yaeger could have taken a break, walked to the NUMA cafeteria, or simply left his sanctum sanctorum for a brisk walk. He hated to leave his electronic babies and instead used the time to explore other options.

He stared up at the ceiling and remembered that Nina Kirov had said the killers came in the night, massacred the party, then disposed of the bodies.

"Max, let's take a look at 'assassins.' "

Max was actually a number of computers that, like the human brain, could work on several complicated tasks at the same time.

"That should be no problem." A second later the computer voice said: "Assassins. An English analog of the Arabic *hashshashin,* meaning one who is addicted to hashish. A secret eleventh-century politico-religious Islamic order presided over by an absolute ruler and deputy masters. Unquestioning obedience was demanded of sect members known as 'the devoted ones,' the actual hit men who murdered political leaders and put their skills out for hire. The killers were given hashish and a heavy dose of sensual pleasures and told this was a taste of the paradise that awaited them if they did their job. The sect spread terror for more than two hundred years."

Interesting. But how pertinent? Yaeger tugged at his scraggly beard while Max described other groups of assassins such as the thugs of India and the Japanese ninja. These groups didn't quite fit the profile of the Moroccan killers, but, more important, they had been out of business for centuries. He didn't dismiss them out of hand. If he were forming an assassin squad he'd look toward the past to see how others had operated.

Dr. Kirov said the killers destroyed a stone carving that could be evidence of pre-Columbian contact between the Old and the New World. If he called up everything on pre-Columbian culture, even with Max's speed, it would take ten years to sort things out. Instead, Yaeger had established what he called a "parallel paradigm," basically a set of questions that asked the computer in different ways who would be upset by revelations that Columbus had not been the first Old World representative to set foot in the New World. And vice versa.

A few days ago he started the computers working on the problem but had been too busy until now to call up the findings.

With the machines working on the main question posed by Sandecker, he had some time to review the results.

He said, "Call up 'ParPar,'" the code name he had given the unpronounceable Parallel Paradigm.

"ParPar is ready, Hiram."

"Thanks, Max. Who would be upset at revelations Columbus did not discover America?"

"Some scholars, historians, and writers. Certain ethnic groups. Would you like specifics?"

"Not now. Would this belief be dangerous?"

"No. Would you like me to pursue a link to the past?"

Yaeger had programmed his computers to give short answers so they wouldn't go off on interminable tangents without exact instruction.

"Go ahead," Yaeger said.

"The Spanish Inquisition had made belief in pre-Columbian contact a heresy punishable by burning. The Inquisitors said Columbus was divinely inspired to bring Spanish civilization to the New World. Link to Vespucci?"

"Go ahead."

"When Amerigo Vespucci proved scientifically that Columbus had not reached India but had discovered a new continent, he was threatened with heresy, too."

"Why was this so important?"

"Admitting someone else had discovered the New World would invalidate claims to its riches and weaken power of the Spanish state."

Yaeger pondered the reply. Spain was no longer a world power, and its former lands in the Americas were all independent countries. There was something there he couldn't see. He felt like a child who knows there's a monster lurking in the shadows of his closet, can hear its heavy breathing and see the green eyes, only to have it disappear when he turns the lights on.

The computer softly dinged the Big Ben chimes, and a hologram caricature of himself smiling appeared.

"Processing and printing are complete," his animated doppel-ganger said. "Whew! I'm going out for a beer."

Yaeger spent so much time with this computer it was inevitable that he would program in a few personality traits.

"Thanks, Max, I'm buying," he said.

Wondering what he would do if Max ever took him up on his offer, Yaeger went into an adjoining room and retrieved the lengthy printout he'd requested. As he studied the ParPar report on archaeological expeditions his eyes grew wider, and he began to repeat the word "incredible" under his breath. He was only partially through the report when he picked up the phone and punched out a number. A crisp voice answered.

"If you've got a minute, Admiral," Yaeger said, "I've got something I think you'd like to see."

15

AT EIGHT FORTY-FIVE A.M., AUSTIN
slotted his standard-issue agency turquoise Jeep Cherokee into
the reserved space in the underground parking garage at NUMA
headquarters, the imposing solar glass building in Arlington, Virginia, that housed two thousand NUMA scientists and engineers
and coordinated another three thousand scattered around the
globe. Joe Zavala called Austin's name as he crossed the atrium
lobby with its waterfalls and aquariums and huge globe at the
center of the sea-green marble floor. Austin was glad to see that
Zavala walked with only a slight limp.

The elevator rocketed to the top floor where Admiral
Sandecker had his suite of offices. As they exited the elevator a
pair of men stood waiting to enter. One was a tall, hard-bodied
man standing six-foot-three with an oak-tanned, craggy face. He
had deep opaline green eyes and wavy ebony hair with a touch
of gray at the temples. Not quite as broad-shouldered as Austin,
his body was lean and wiry.

The other man was a contrast. He was only five-feet-four but
built with the massive chest of a bulldog; his arms and legs were
well muscled. His hair was black and curly. The swarthy face and
walnut eyes betrayed his Italian ancestry.

The tall man stuck out his hand. "Kurt, it must have been
three months since we've seen each other."

Dirk Pitt, NUMA's special projects director, and his able

assistant, Al Giordino, were legends within the agency. Their exploits in the many years since NUMA was launched by Admiral Sandecker were the stuff of which adventure novels were written. Though Pitt's and Austin's tracks seldom crossed, they had become good friends and had often gone sport diving together.

Austin matched the firm grip. "When will you two be free for lunch so we can catch up on your latest escapades?"

"Not for a couple of weeks, I'm afraid. We're taking off in an hour from Andrews Air Force Base."

"Where are you headed?" asked Zavala.

"A project the admiral has laid on us in the Antarctic," Giordino answered.

"Did you remember to pack your testicle sock?" Zavala said with a glint in his eyes.

Giordino grinned. "I never leave home without it."

"How about you and Joe?" asked Pitt.

"We're meeting with the admiral to find out what he has in mind for us."

"I hope you're going into tropical waters."

Austin laughed. "So do I."

"Call me when you get back," said Pitt. "We'll all have dinner at my place."

"I'll do that," said Austin. "It's always a pleasure to view your car collection."

The next elevator arrived, and the doors opened. Pitt and Giordino stepped in and turned around. "So long, guys," Giordino said. "Best of luck on wherever you're going." Then the doors closed and they were gone.

"This has to be the first time I haven't seen Dirk and Al limping, bleeding, or covered with bandages," said Austin.

Zavala rolled his eyes. "Thank you for unnecessarily reminding me that working for NUMA can be hazardous."

"Why do you think NUMA has such generous health-care benefits?" Austin said as they entered a large waiting room whose walls were covered by photos of the admiral hobnobbing with presidents and other luminaries from the worlds of politics, science, and the arts. The receptionist told them to go right in.

Sandecker lounged behind the immense desk made from the refinished hatch cover salvaged from a sunken confederate blockade runner. Dressed in razor-creased charcoal-gray slacks and an expensive navy blue blazer with an embroidered gold anchor on the breast pocket, Sandecker would have needed only the addition of a white cap to complete his sporty image. But Sandecker was no yacht club commander. He radiated a force field of natural authority forged by thirty highly decorated years in the navy and tempered in the sometimes bruising job as head of a maritime government empire he had built from scratch. Washington old-timers said Sandecker's commanding presence reminded them of George C. Marshall, general and secretary of state, who could walk into a room and without saying a word make it known that he was in charge. Compared to the burly general, Sandecker was short and slight of build from his daily five-mile jogs and strict exercise regimen.

He leaped up as if he had steel springs for legs and came around to greet the two men.

"Kurt! Joe! How good to see you," he said effusively, grasping their hands in a knuckle-crushing grip. "You're looking well. Glad you both could make the meeting."

Sandecker appeared trim and fit as usual, looking far younger than his mid-sixties. The sharp edges of a Van Dyke beard whose fiery red color matched his hair, and sometimes his temperament, could have been trimmed with a laser.

Austin raised an eyebrow. There was simply never any doubt that he and Joe would show up. The feisty founder and director of NUMA wasn't known to take no for an answer.

Mustering a grim smile, Austin said, "Thanks, Admiral. Joe and I are fast healers."

"Of course you are," Sandecker replied. "Swift recovery is a prerequisite of employment with NUMA. Ask Pitt and Giordino if you don't believe me."

The scary thing, Austin knew, was that Sandecker was only half joking. Even more frightening was the fact that Austin and Zavala were *eager* to take on a new assignment.

"I will be sure to compare contusions with Dirk over tequila on the rocks with lime the next time I see him, sir."

Zavala couldn't resist the opportunity to have a little fun. Keeping a straight face, he said, "A couple of invalids like us can't be of much use to NUMA."

Sandecker chuckled and gave Zavala a hearty slap on the back. "I've always admired your sense of humor, Joe. You could do well as a comic on the nightclub circuit, where, I understand, you've been spending your evenings in the company of young women. I imagine they've been assisting in your recovery?"

"Private duty nurses?" Zavala answered with an angelic expression that didn't quite cut it.

"As I said, Joe, you missed your calling. Bantering aside, how is the, er, backside?"

"I'm not quite ready to run a marathon, but I threw my cane away days ago, sir."

"Glad to hear that. Before we join the others I wanted to congratulate you both on the *Nereus* affair. I read the reports. Job well done."

"Thanks," Austin said. "Captain Phelan deserves a lot of the credit. He was born too late. He would have looked quite at home with a cutlass in his hand, taming the Barbary pirates. I'm afraid we left his ship in a mess."

Sandecker affixed Austin with his cold blue eyes. "Some things have to be done, Kurt. I spoke to the captain yesterday. The vessel is winding up its work in the Yucatan. He feels fine and tells me the *Nereus* is ship-shape and Bristol fashion once again." Sandecker used the old term to describe a tight ship. "He asked me to thank you again for saving his vessel. So, are you both ready to get back to work?"

Zavala swung his hand up in a grand salute worthy of a Gilbert and Sullivan character. "Ship-shape and Bristol fashion," he echoed with a grin.

There was a soft knock, and a side door in the dark-paneled wall opened. A giant of a figure stepped in, ducking his head to clear the door jamb. At six-foot-eight Paul Trout looked as if he'd be more at home on an NBA basketball court than as deep ocean geologist on NUMA's Special Assignments Team. In fact Trout had been offered scholarships at several universities more interested in his height than his brilliant mind.

As befitted his New England heritage Trout was a man of few words, but his Yankee reserve couldn't hide the pleasure in his voice. "Hi, guys. Glad to see you back. We've missed you around here." Turning to Sandecker, he said, "We're ready, Admiral."

"Splendid. I won't waste time with explanations now, gentlemen. The reasons for this meeting will soon be made abundantly clear." Sandecker led the way into a spacious and comfortably appointed conference room adjoining his office.

Austin knew right away something big was in the air. The wiry, narrow-shouldered man seated at the far end of the long mahogany table was Commander Rudi Gunn, deputy director of NUMA and a master of logistics. Next to him was the 1960s throwback and computer whiz Hiram Yaeger. Across the table from the NUMA staffers was a distinguished-looking older man whose craggy profile and bristling white mustache reminded Austin of C. Aubrey Smith, the old movie actor who often played blustering British army officers. The younger man sitting beside him was balding and thick-set and had a pugnacious jut of his jaw.

Austin acknowledged Gunn and Yaeger with a nod of his head. His gaze bounced off the other men like a stone skipped on water and settled on the woman seated at the far end of the table. Her blond hair was braided close to her scalp, an arrangement that emphasized her smoky gray eyes and high cheekbones. Austin went over and extended his hand.

"Dr. Kirov, what a nice surprise," he said with genuine pleasure. "It's good to see you."

Nina was wearing a jacket and matching skirt whose soft periwinkle tones set off her honeyed skin. In the back of his mind Austin was thinking what idiots men are. When he first met Nina she had been beautiful as a lightly clad mermaid. Now, fully clothed, with her hidden curves and contours emphasized under snug-fitting silk, she was absolutely stunning.

Her mouth widened in a bewitching smile. "It's good to see you, too, Mr. Austin. How are you feeling?"

"Wonderful, now," he replied. The formality of the polite exchange couldn't mask its quiet intensity. They held each other's hands seconds longer than they should have, until Sandecker broke the spell with an exaggerated clearing of his throat. Austin turned to see the bemused expressions of his NUMA colleagues, and his face flushed. He realized he was reacting like a dewy-eyed schoolboy caught by his girl-loathing pals.

Sandecker made a round of introductions. The older man was J. Prescott Danvers, executive director of an organization called the World Archaeological Council. The other stranger was Jack Quinn of the East Asia Foundation. Sandecker looked at his watch. "Now that we've dispensed with the formalities, shall we get right down to business? Hiram?"

While Yaeger fiddled with the keyboard of a Macintosh Powerbook, Austin took a seat next to Trout. As usual, Trout's appearance was impeccable. His light brown hair was parted down the middle, as was the style during the Jazz Age, and combed back on the temples. He was wearing a tan poplin suit, Oxford blue shirt, and one of the large, colorfully designed bow ties he was addicted to. In contrast to his sartorial correctness, Trout also favored workboots, an eccentricity some thought was homage to his fisherman father. In reality it was a habit he picked up at the Woods Hole Oceanographic Institution where many scientists wore them.

The son of a Cape Cod fisherman, Trout spent much of his boyhood hanging around the world-famous institution and was offered weekend and summer jobs by scientists who went out of their way to be friendly to a youngster so fascinated by the ocean. His love of the sea later took him to the equally renowned Scripps Institution of Oceanography majoring in deep ocean geology.

"Thought you were down in the Yucatan with Gamay," Austin said. It was unusual to see Trout without his wife. They had met at Scripps, where she was studying for a doctorate in marine biology, and they were married after graduation. Rudi Gunn, an old friend from his high school days, persuaded Paul to come on board as a member of a special team being put together by Admiral Sandecker. Paul accepted, but only on the condition that his wife went with him. Delighted that he was getting two top-notch people, Sandecker readily accepted.

Trout's chin seemed constantly dipped in thought. As was his habit he spoke with his head lowered, and, although he wore contact lenses, he peered upward, as if over glasses.

Speaking in the nasal twang and broad *A* of his native Cape Cod, Trout said, "She'd been trying for weeks to make an appointment with a VIP from the national anthropological museum in Mexico City. Guy couldn't change the date, so I'm here for the two of us."

Sandecker had taken up a post in front of a large rear-projection screen linked to Yaeger's computer. He nodded to Yaeger, and a second later a map of northwest Africa appeared on the screen. Indicating Morocco and using an unlit Managua cigar to point to a blinking red arrow, Sandecker said, "All in this room are aware of the attack on Dr. Kirov and the disappearance of her expedition." He turned to Austin and Zavala. "Kurt, while you and Zavala were recuperating, two more expeditions were reported missing."

Taking the cue, Yaeger projected a map of the world on the screen. He pointed to three red blinking arrows. "Mr. Quinn's organization lost a group here in China. Two scientists and their helper have disappeared from India. This one is Morocco."

"Thank you, Hiram," Sandecker said. "Dr. Danvers, if you could tell us a little about your organization."

"I'd be happy to," Danvers replied, rising. His elegant voice still bore its pseudo-British prep school imprint. "The World Archaeological Council in Washington is a clearinghouse for information having to do with the world archaeological community. At any given moment dozens of projects are under way around the globe," he said with a wave at the map. "They are sponsored by foundations, universities, governmental entities, or combinations of all three. Our job is to collect all this information and dispense it back to them, as needed, in controlled quantities."

"Perhaps you might give us a specific example," Sandecker coached.

Danvers thought for a moment. "One of our members, a university in this case, recently wanted to do some work in Uzbekistan. With one call to our computer banks we could tell them about all past, current, and future work in that country, provide all the papers published in recent years, bibliographies of reference books, and names of experts in the field. We would have maps and charts, information on practical matters, such as local politics, sources of workers, transportation, conditions of roads, weather, and so on."

Sandecker cut to the chase. "Would you also have records of expeditions that have vanished?"

"Well—" Danvers furrowed his frosty brow. "Not as such. It is up to the various members to provide material. As I said, we're collectors and dispensers. Our material is primarily academic. In the Uzbekistan example there would be no mention of a disappearance unless the university provided it. Perhaps warnings that a certain territory might be hazardous. On the other hand, the information might be there, spread throughout the databank, but it would be a question of bringing all that together, and that would be a monumental task."

"I understand," Sandecker said. "Hiram, would you help us out here?"

Yaeger pecked away at the computer. One after another, red blinking arrows appeared on the various continents. He had added about a dozen new sites to the three on the map.

"These are all expeditions that have vanished over the last ten years," he said.

Danvers's nostrils flared as if he smelled a bad odor.

"*Impossible,*" he said. "Where did you get the information to make such a preposterous assertion?"

Yaeger shrugged laconically. "I got it from the files of your organization."

"That can't be," Danvers said. "You have to be a member of the WAC to access our database. And much of the information is privileged. Not even members can move from file to file. They have to be cleared after giving their code name."

This wasn't the first time Yaeger heard somebody suggest his electronic babies could barely walk when in reality they could sprint. He had long ago learned not to argue. He simply smiled.

Scanning the arrows blinking merrily on the map, Sandecker said, "I think we can all agree that this goes beyond the realm of coincidence."

Danvers was still dumbfounded that his database had been violated by someone who looked like a cast member of *Hair*. "*Well* beyond the realm," he said, doing his best to preserve his dignity.

"My sincere apologies, Dr. Danvers," Sandecker said. "When I first heard about the Moroccan incident I asked Hiram to run a survey of similar cases in press reports and to cross-check them with other information available. That he chose your organization to burglarize in cyberspace is testimony to the WAC's importance. I'm afraid, however, that the news is even worse."

Taking the cue Yaeger said, "I ran a scan of archaeological stories in the major publications, compared them with your files, then kept refining the search, separating the wheat from the chaff. The past five years was easy. Things got harder as I got back to the time before people started using computers. This survey isn't complete, but what I have is pretty thoroughly documented. I kicked out all expeditions that didn't have dead bodies or were wiped out by natural disasters."

He clicked his mouse. There was a gasp from Danvers. The

map was lit up like a Times Square neon sign. Dozens of little red arrows winked on every continent.

Quinn's reaction was one of anger. "That's crazy," he said. "This isn't Indiana Jones stuff we're dealing with, for Godsakes! Archaeological digs don't just disappear off the face of the earth without anyone knowing."

Calmly Sandecker said, "Good point, Mr. Quinn. We, too, were astonished at the number of expeditions that had simply vanished into thin air. The public is not indifferent to these events, but the incidents have been spread out over decades, and at one time it was fairly commonplace for explorers to disappear from public view for years. Sometimes permanently. Would we have known what happened to Dr. Livingstone if the intrepid Stanley hadn't gone after him?"

"But what about news reports?" Quinn said.

Sandecker said, "From what Hiram has explained to me, occasionally somebody at a major outlet with resources like *The New York Times* would dig into his morgue and note a similar happening, comparing it to a more recent incident. When there was widespread publicity, such as in the 1936 disappearance of a *National Geographic* expedition into Sardinia, the incident was simply ascribed to bandits or misfortune. We can discount a percentage of them. Floods and volcanoes, for instance." He paused. "What I find disturbing is that the trend is on the increase."

Still unconvinced, Austin leaned forward on his elbows, staring intently at the map. "Communications are a lot more efficient now than they were in Stanley's day," he said. "Could *that* have something to do with these vanishings?"

"I factored that into the equation, Kurt," said Yaeger. "The curve still shows an upswing."

Rudi Gunn removed his horn-rimmed glasses and nibbled thoughtfully on the earpiece. "Reminds me of a movie I saw," he mused. "*Somebody Is Killing the Great Chefs of Europe.*"

"Only in this case it is not chefs, and the incidents aren't confined to a single continent," Sandecker said. "If Dr. Kirov's

experience is any indication, someone is killing the great archaeologists of the world."

Danvers sat back in his seat, his ruddy face now as white as
bread dough. "Good Lord," he said with a hoarse whisper.
"What on earth is happening?"

"What indeed?" Sandecker's blue eyes moved from face to
face. "I asked Hiram to codify similar elements these disappearances had. Nothing presented itself on the surface. The expeditions were incredibly diverse. They varied in size from three
people to more than twenty and took place all over the world.
They were organized by a wide spectrum of groups or individu-
als. There *were* common denominators, however. What the police
call the MO was the same in all cases before Morocco. The expeditions simply vanished. Dr. Kirov's experience was traumatic,
but it may be a stroke of good luck in the long run if it can prevent similar disasters. We know now that these expeditions did
not simply go into thin air. That they were wiped out by teams
of trained assassins."

"Thugee," Gunn said quietly.

"What's that mean?" Quinn said.

"It's where our word *thug* came from. It means 'thief' in
Hindi, what they called followers of the Indian cult of Kali.
They would infiltrate a caravan, strangle people at night, hide
their bodies, and steal goods. The British broke the cult up in
the 1800s, and it went out of business for the most part. One of
these latest disappearances was in India."

Nobody who knew Gunn was surprised when he produced
arcane bits of information. The short, slight Gunn was a sheer
genius. Number one in his graduating class at the Naval Acad-
emy, the former navy commander could be enjoying a top staff
job with the Navy Department. He had advanced degrees in
chemistry, finance, and oceanography but preferred underwater science to warfare. He served in submarines as Sandecker's
chief aide, and when the admiral resigned from the navy to
form NUMA, Gunn followed. In compiling reports and
researching he had absorbed much of the wide-ranging materi-

al from the hundreds of books with which he surrounded himself.

"I checked them out," Yaeger said. "Ninja and *hashshashin*, too. You're right, there are similarities."

Sandecker didn't dismiss the suggestion out of hand. "The idea of a secret society of murderers is certainly interesting," he said. "Let's put it on the back burner for now while I discuss that other common element. As far as could be documented, all expeditions victimized in recent years reported finding pre-Columbian artifacts in unlikely places." He paused for dramatic effect. "And according to Hiram's findings, all were funded to some extent by Time-Quest. Do either of you gentlemen know anything about this organization?"

"Sure," Quinn said. "Our foundation has used them any number of times. Totally respectable as far as I know. You see their ads in all the archaeological magazines. They're known to be pretty generous with grant money. They'll fund your expedition if they like it. Better still, they'll send volunteers, people who pay for the thrill of working a dig. They're tied in with some of the environmental and retired persons organizations. As I say, they're on the up-and-up."

Danvers seemed to snap out of a deep sleep. "Yes, I agree. Many of our clients have used Time-Quest. We have a file on them if that would be helpful."

"I've already checked them out," Yaeger said. "I've pulled info in from other sources, too. Directories of nonprofits, state and federal agencies that regulate nonprofits. Bank statements. Internet. They've got an impressive Web site. They're headquartered in San Antonio. Board of directors is made up of nationally known people."

Austin frowned. "Well-meaning people have unknowingly lent their names to everything from right- and left-wing extremists to organized crime thinking they were pushing a good cause."

"Well put, Kurt," Sandecker agreed. "Hiram, anything to show Time-Quest is a front for extremists?"

Yaeger shook his head. "All the data say Time-Quest is clean."

"So you found nothing out of the ordinary?" Sandecker persisted, his perceptive ear detecting an off-key note in Yaeger's tone.

"I didn't say that, Admiral. There's a ton of information available on the main organization, but most of it is slick press-release fluff that doesn't really tell you anything. When I tried to probe past the PR image, I got nothing."

"They blocked access?"

"That's the thing. Not really. This is more sophisticated. When access is blocked it's like not having the key to get into the room. I had the key, but when I got into the room it was dark, and I couldn't turn on the light switch."

"If your electronic hounds couldn't sniff out the trail, it must be sophisticated indeed. Your work tells us something, though. The organization would not disconnect its light switch unless there were something to hide."

Nina, who had been sitting silently throughout the presentation, suddenly said, "Gonzalez."

"I beg your pardon?" Sandecker said.

"I've been thinking about what Commander Gunn said about *thugee*. There was a man named Gonzalez on our expedition. I mentioned him to Mr. Austin and Mr. Zavala. He had come through Time-Quest. He was . . . he was just strange."

"In what way, Dr. Kirov?"

"It's hard to say. He was terribly obsequious. Always around, looking over your shoulder. Whenever anyone asked about his background he always had the same story. It never varied. He'd get evasive when you pressed him for details. For instance, that last day when I asked him about the stranger he'd been talking to." She paused, her brow furrowed in thought. "I think that had something to do with the attack."

"I read about the incident in your report," Sandecker said. "This Gonzalez was killed with the others?"

"I assume so. There was a lot of confusion. He disappeared with everybody else, so . . ."

"We'll check over the identification of the bodies exhumed from the excavation, and if he's not there Hiram will run a trace on him."

"One question," Austin said. "Time-Quest was connected with every expedition that vanished in recent years, but did some of its expeditions come home perfectly safe?"

"I'll answer that," Sandecker said. "Yes. There have been many expeditions where the most serious injuries were from sunstroke. Again, those that disappeared had all reported unusual finds or, in more specific cases, evidence of pre-Columbian contact. What do you make of that, Dr. Danvers?"

"The archaeological community would certainly scrutinize such claims with the greatest skepticism," Danvers replied. "But to say how they might precipitate murder, well, I'm simply at a loss. Surely it couldn't be a string of coincidences, unlikely as that may be."

Nina shook her head. "Just as unlikely a coincidence as the pre-Columbian artifact I found being destroyed. And evidence of its existence being erased from the university's database." She turned to Yaeger. "How could that happen?"

Yaeger shrugged. "Not a big problem if you know how."

Sandecker checked his watch again. "We've done all we can do here for now. I'd like to thank you for coming, gentlemen and Dr. Kirov. We'll discuss our next step and keep you informed of our progress."

As the meeting broke up, Kurt went over to speak to Nina.

"Will you be staying in the Washington area?"

"I'm afraid not," she said. "I'm leaving right away to start work on a new project."

"Well . . ."

"You never know, we might be working together someday."

Austin inhaled the faint scent of lavender coming from Nina's hair and wondered how much work they would accomplish. "Perhaps we might."

Zavala came over. "Sorry to interrupt. Sandecker wants us in his office."

Austin bid Nina a reluctant good-bye, followed the others into the admiral's aerie, and took up a seat in one of the comfortable leather chairs. Sandecker was behind his desk. He leaned back in his swivel chair and puffed several times on his giant cigar, which he had finally lit. He was about to open discussion when his eye fell on Zavala, who was puffing an identical stogie. There was little in the known universe that Sandecker was unaware of, but one of the most enduring and irritating mysteries in his life had to do with the humidor on his desk. For years he had been trying to figure out how Al Giordino lifted cigars from the box undetected.

Sandecker pinned Zavala with a steely eye. "Have you been talking to Giordino?" he said coolly.

"In the elevator. He and Pitt were leaving for a project in the Antarctic," Zavala replied with cherubic innocence. "We had a brief chat about NUMA business."

Sandecker quietly harrumphed. He had never given in to Giordino, and he was damned if he'd give Zavala the satisfaction of knowing he was irritated or flummoxed.

"Some of you may be wondering why an agency whose precinct is the ocean and what lies under it is in any way involved with a bunch of desert diggers," he said. "The major reason is that NUMA has the best intelligence capacity in the world. Many of these sites were reached by the ocean or rivers that run out to the sea, so technically we have a vested interest. Well, gentlemen, ideas?"

Austin, who had watched the battle of the cigars with interest, turned his mind to Sandecker's question. "Let's go over what we know." Ticking the points off on his fingers, he said, "There is a pattern to the disappearances. People don't simply vanish but are murdered by well-organized and equipped assassins. The expeditions were all linked to an outfit called TimeQuest that seems to have something to hide."

Yaeger interjected, "Could be they're just hiding assets from the IRS and it has nothing to do with the murders?"

"We may well find that's the case," Sandecker said, "which is why I want you to keep digging. Explore every possible angle."

"Did you ever get any leads on the hovercraft that tried a hit-and-run on Dr. Kirov?" Zavala asked.

"Slightly better luck," Yaeger said. "From your description I narrowed the manufacturer to an English outfit called Griffon Hovercraft Ltd. Only so many were built of the model you described. This one is especially interesting. It's called an LCAC type."

"Navy jargon for landing craft air cushion, as I recall," Gunn said.

"That's right. It's a souped-up high-speed over-the-beach version of a commercial model. Eighty-eight feet long. Two props and four gas turbines give her a speed of forty knots with payload. Gun mounts for .50-caliber machine guns, grenade launcher, and M-60 machine gun. We've got a few in the U.S. Navy."

"Why didn't they use their guns to stop Dr. Kirov?" Zavala said.

"My guess is that they were afraid her body would be found. There would have been questions. Have any orders come in from private parties?" Austin asked Yaeger.

"Only one. An outfit in San Antonio."

Austin leaned forward. "That's where Time-Quest has its headquarters."

"Right," Yaeger replied. "Could be coincidence. The hovercraft is owned by an oil exploration corporation, but the company could be one of a series of dummies. It's going to take a while to see if they're linked. Careless of them to allow the chance of a connection."

"Not really," Austin said. "They didn't expect any witnesses. If they'd been successful with their attack on Dr. Kirov, nobody would have known about the killers. Those on the *Nereus* noticed the hovercraft, but it was too far away to see that it was being used for assault and battery."

Sandecker said, "Kurt is right, Hiram. I'd like you to keep

exploring the San Antonio connection. Any proposals on more direct action?"

"Yes, I've been thinking," Austin said. "Maybe we can make them come to us. The trigger in these incidents is the pre-Columbian angle. What if we set up an archaeological expedition and let Time-Quest know we've found something pre-Columbian?"

"Then we put on our Kevlar jackets and see what happens," Zavala said. He puffed on his cigar like Diamond Jim Brady. "A sting. Brilliant."

Sandecker arched an eyebrow. "Zavala's dry wit aside, how would we go about doing that?" Sandecker asked. "It would take weeks, perhaps months, to organize, wouldn't it, Rudi?"

"I'm afraid so, sir. There would be a lot to pull together."

Austin couldn't figure why Gunn looked so amused at his proposal, and the irritation showed in his voice when he said, "Maybe if we really try we can accelerate the process somehow."

"No need to go hell-bent for leather, my friend." Sandecker showed his teeth in his familiar barracuda smile. "While you and Joe were laid up, Rudi, Hiram, and I came up with the same scheme and started things moving. Everything is in place. For reasons of speed and ease of logistics, we've set it up in the American Southwest. The bait will be an Old World 'artifact' found on American soil. *That* should attract someone's attention. Consider this a task for the NUMA Special Assignments Team."

"Assignment accepted," Austin said. "What about Gamay?"

"A marine biologist in the desert might be harder to explain," the admiral said. "I see no need to take her away from her work in the Yucatan. Let her know what we're up to. If we need her, she can be on hand in a few hours. She's been working pretty hard lately. She's probably enjoying the tropic sun on the beaches of Cozumel or Cancun even as we speak."

Zavala took a long puff on his cigar and blew a smoke ring. "Some people have all the luck," he said.

16

THE FOURTH PERMANENT MEMBER OF
the NUMA Special Assignments Team would have been the last
person to describe herself as *lucky*. While her colleagues enjoyed
their air-conditioned comfort, Gamay Morgan-Trout was
drenched with perspiration, and her usual good nature was
ebbing in direct proportion to the rise of the ambient air temperature, which was in the eighties and climbing. She couldn't
believe the humidity was 100 percent without a cloud in the sky.

Arms folded across her chest, she leaned her tall, willowy
body against the Jeep parked on the grassy shoulder of the
asphalt ribbon that slashed through the low-lying rain forest.
Shimmering water puddle mirages danced on the mottled gray
tarmac. The desolate spot reminded her of the lonely highway in
North by Northwest where Cary Grant gets chased by a crop
duster.

Gamay looked up at the pale sky. No crop duster. Only a
couple of turkey vultures making lazy circles. Bad place for hungry buzzards. The roadkill pickings must be slim indeed. One
vehicle had passed in the last hour. She heard the old pickup
coming for miles. It rattled by with its load of half-dead chickens
leaving a trail of white feathers in its wake. The driver hadn't
even slowed down to see if she needed help.

Thinking it was dumb standing out in the sun, Gamay

climbed back into the shade under the Jeep's convertible top and took a slug of cooling water from a thermos. For at least the third time she unfolded the map Professor Chi had faxed her from Mexico City. The paper was damp and limp from her moist hands. Earlier that morning she had driven inland from Ciudad del Carmen where the *Nereus* was anchored, following the map to the letter through the monotonous flat Yucatan landscape, paying strict attention to the neatly written precise mileage notations, pulling over exactly where the arrow indicated. She studied the carefully drawn lines. No mistake. *X* marked the spot. She was exactly where she was supposed to be.

The middle of nowhere.

Gamay was regretting having begged off when she and her husband, Paul, got the call to return to Washington for an important meeting of NUMA's Special Assignments Team. She had been trying to arrange this rendezvous with Professor Chi for days and didn't know if she would ever have another opportunity. She wondered what merited yanking them back to headquarters on such short notice. They had joined the *Nereus* shortly after it arrived in the Yucatan to take part in the meteorite project. Paul would be creating the undersea computer graphics that were his specialty. Gamay would bring in her expertise as a marine biologist. It seemed like a very pleasant assignment indeed. No heavy lifting. Then the call came in from headquarters.

She smiled to herself. Kurt Austin must be back on the scene. Things tended to happen when Austin was around. Like the shoot-out she'd heard about on the *Nereus*. She'd call Paul when she got back to the ship to see if she should hop a plane home.

Good God, she wondered, taking in her surroundings, why had the professor asked to meet her in this dismal place? The only signs of human habitation, past or present, were the faint grass-grown tire tracks that disappeared into the forest. She waved away an insect that strafed the tip of her nose. The Cutter's bug repellent was wearing thin. So was her patience. Maybe she should leave *now*. No, she would wait fifteen more minutes. If Professor Chi didn't show, she would pack it in and head back to the NUMA ship. She would have to admit that the two-hour drive in the rented Jeep had been for nothing.

Damn. She'd never get a chance like this again. She really wanted to meet Chi. He sounded so pleasant on the phone, with his American accent and a Spanish courtliness. Wilted by the heat, a strand of the long dark-red hair swirled up on her head dropped down over her nose. She stuck her lower lip out and tried to blow the wisp out of the way. When that didn't work she brushed it away, checking from habit in the rearview mirror. She saw a speck in the road. The dot grew larger, vibrating in the heat waves. She leaned out the door for a better look. The object materialized into a blue and white bus. Obviously lost, she concluded. She withdrew her head and was taking another swig of water when she heard the hiss of air brakes.

The bus had stopped behind the Jeep. The door opened, and the tomblike silence was shattered by a blare of Mexican music that was heavy on decibels and brass instruments. The local bus systems all had speakers that must have been left over from Woodstock. A lone passenger stepped from the bus. He wore the standard Indian garb, a cotton shirt, baggy white pants, and sandals. On his head was a hard straw hat with a slightly rolled-up brim. Like most Mayan men he was short, barely over five feet tall. There was an exchange of rapid-fire Spanish between the passenger and the bus driver and a waved good-bye. The door clunked shut, and with a grinding of gears the bus took off down the road like a large rolling jukebox.

Ouch!

Gamay bent forward to slap a bug that had sunk its fangs into her calf. When she looked in the mirror again the man had disappeared along with the bus. She checked the side mirror. Only the empty highway. Odd. Wait. Movement to her right. She froze. Eyes like black stones were staring at her from the Jeep's passenger side.

"Dr. Morgan-Trout, I presume."

The man had the same soft-spoken voice with the American accent she had heard on the call from Mexico City. Tentatively, she said, "Professor Chi?"

"At your service." He realized that Gamay was staring at the double-barreled shotgun cradled in his arm and lowered it from sight. "I'm sorry, I didn't mean to startle you. My apologies for being late. I was out hunting and should have allowed more time. Juan, our driver, is a good-hearted but garrulous man who chats with all the female passengers young and old. I hope you weren't waiting long."

"No, that's quite all right." This little brown man with the broad nut-brown face, high cheekbones, and long and slightly curved nose wasn't exactly what she expected. She scolded herself for thinking in stereotypes.

Dr. Chi had lived in the white man's world long enough to recognize the embarrassed reaction. The stony expression didn't change, but the dark eyes sparkled with good humor. "I must have surprised you, a stranger coming up suddenly like that with a gun like a *bandito*. I apologize for my appearance. When I'm home I go native."

"I should apologize for my rudeness, letting you stand out there in the hot sun." She patted the seat beside her. "Please sit in the shade."

"I carry my shade around with me, but I will accept your kind invitation." He removed his hat, revealing gray bangs over a retreating forehead, unslung a canvas game bag, and climbed into the passenger side, carefully resting the shotgun, breech open, between the seats with the muzzle pointing toward the rear. He placed the game bag on his lap.

"From the looks of that bag I'd say you had a successful hunt," Gamay said.

Sighing theatrically, he said, "I must be the laziest hunter in the world. I stand at the roadside. The bus picks me up and drops me off. I walk into the forest. Pop-pop. I walk out to the road and catch the next bus. This way I can enjoy the solitary delights of the hunt and the social rewards of sharing my triumphs and failures with my neighbors. The hardest part is timing the buses. But yes, it went well." He lifted the game bag. "Two plump partridges."

Gamay flashed a dazzling smile that displayed a slight space between her upper front teeth like the actress and model Lauren Hutton. She was an attractive woman, not gorgeous or overly sexy, but lively and vivacious in a tomboy way most men found appealing.

"Good," she said. "May I give you and your birds a lift somewhere?"

"That would be very kind of you. In return I can provide you with some liquid refreshment. You must be very hot from waiting out here."

"It wasn't bad," Gamay said, although her hair was clearly out of control, her T-shirt stuck to the seat, and her chin dripped with perspiration.

Chi nodded, appreciating the polite lie. "If you could back up and then follow that track for a bit."

She started the Jeep, put it in reverse, then shifted into low gear and turned off the road. The tires followed the dried mud ruts through dense forest. After about a quarter of a mile the trees thinned and the ruts gave way to a sunlit clearing dominated by a native shelter. The walls of the hut were fashioned of sticks and the roof thatched with palm leaves. They got out of the Jeep and went inside. The only furniture was a metal folding table, a camp chair, and a woven hammock. A couple of propane gas lanterns hung from the rafters.

"Be it ever so humble there's no *casa* like *mi casa*," Chi said, sounding very much as if he meant every word. Scuffing the dirt floor with his toe, he said, "This land has always been in my family. Dozens of houses have stood on this spot through the centuries, and the design hasn't changed since the first one was built at the beginning of time. My people learned that it was easier to throw a house together every so often than to try to build one that would outlast hurricanes and damp rot. May I get you a drink?"

"Yes," Gamay said, looking around for a cooler. "Thank you. I'd like that."

"Follow me, please." He led the way outside the hut to a well-worn path through the woods. After a minute's walk they came upon a cinderblock building with a corrugated steel roof. The professor opened the unlocked door, and they stepped inside. Chi reached into a dark alcove and rummaged around, muttering in Spanish under his breath. After a few seconds an engine popped into life.

"I turn the generator off when I'm away to save gas," he explained. "The air conditioner should kick in momentarily."

A bare bulb went on overhead. They were in a small entryway. Chi opened another door and hit a wall switch. Fluorescent lighting flickered on to illuminate a large windowless room with two work tables. On the tables were a laptop computer, scanner and laser printer, stacks of paper, a microscope and slides, and assorted plastic bags holding hunks of stone. Larger pieces, carefully tagged, lay here and there. Manila folders were piled everywhere. The bookshelves groaned with the weight of thick texts. On the wall were topographic maps of the Yucatan peninsula, site photographs, and drawings of Mayan carvings.

"My lab," Chi said with obvious pride.

"Impressive." Gamay never expected to see a fully equipped archaeological lab in, well, the middle of nowhere. Dr. Chi was full of surprises.

Chi sensed her astonishment. "People sometimes wonder when they see the contrast between where I live and where I work. Outside Mexico City, I require only the barest essentials to exist. A place to sleep and to eat, a hammock with mosquito netting, a roof to keep the rain out. But it's a different story when you have to work. One must have the tools. And here is the most important tool in conducting scientific inquiry."

He went over to a beat-up but serviceable refrigerator,

stuffed the game bag on a shelf, and took out two Seven-Ups and ice cubes which he put into a couple of all plastic tumblers. With a sweep of his arm he cleared space among some files and brought over two folding chairs. Gamay sat down, took a sip, and let the cool sweet liquid flow down her parched throat. It tasted better than a fine champagne. They sat a few moments quietly enjoying their drinks.

"Thank you, Dr. Chi," Gamay said after accepting a refill, of bottled water this time. "I'm afraid I was more dehydrated than I thought."

"It's not difficult to lose body moisture in this country. Now that our energies are restored, how may I help you?"

"As I said on the phone, I'm a marine biologist. I'm involved in a project off the coast."

"Oh, yes, NUMA's tektites survey near the Chixulub meteor impact site."

Gamay cocked her head. "You *know* of it?"

He nodded solemnly. "Bush telegraph." Seeing her puzzled expression, he chuckled and confessed, "I can't lie. I saw an e-mail to the museum from NUMA headquarters informing us of the survey as a courtesy."

He reached over to a file cabinet, opened a drawer, and pulled out a manila folder.

"Let me see," he said, reading from the file's contents. "Gamay Morgan-Trout. Thirty years old. Resident of Georgetown. Wisconsin-born. Expert diver. Holds degree in marine archaeology from the University of North Carolina. Changed specialties, enrolling in Scripps Institution of Oceanography, where she eventually attained a doctorate as a marine biologist. Puts her talents to work for the world-renowned National Underwater and Marine Agency."

"Not a fact out of place," Gamay said, raising a finely curved eyebrow.

"Thank you," Chi said, replacing the file in the cabinet. "My secretary's work, actually. After you called I asked her to hook onto NUMA's Web site. There's a complete description of ongoing projects with brief biographies of those involved in them. Are you any relation to Paul Trout, the deep ocean geographer whose name was also listed?"

"Yes, Paul is my husband. The site probably didn't mention that we met in Mexico. We were on a field trip to La Paz. Otherwise, I'd say you did your homework."

"It's my strict academic training, I'm afraid."

"I tend to retain details, too. Let's see if I can remember." Gamay closed her eyes. "Dr. José Chi. Born in Quintana Roo, Yucatan peninsula. Father was a farmer. Excelled in his studies, sent by the government to private schools. Undergraduate studies at University of Mexico. Graduate degrees from Harvard University, where he is still affiliated with the prestigious Peabody Museum of Archaeology and Ethnology. Curator at Mexico's National Anthropological Museum. Winner of the MacArthur Award for his work in helping to compile a corpus of Mayan inscriptions. Now working on a dictionary of the Mayan language."

She opened her eyes to see Chi's toothy grin. He clapped his hands lightly. "Brava, Dr. Morgan-Trout."

"Please call me Gamay."

"A beautiful and unusual name."

"My father was a wine connoisseur. The color of my hair reminded him of the grape of Beaujolais."

"Well chosen, Dr. Gamay. I must correct something, though. I'm very proud of my work on the dictionary, but the corpus is actually the work of many talented people. Artists, photographers, cartographers, catalogers, and so on. I contributed my skills as a 'finder.' "

"A finder?"

"*Sí.* I'll explain. I've been hunting since I was eight years old. I've roamed throughout the Yucatan and in Belize and Guatemala. In the course of my wanderings I frequently stumbled across ruins. Some people say I must carry a Ouija board around in my head. I think it's a combination of the alertness to his surroundings a hunter must have, and simple mileage. If you walk long and far enough in these parts, you'll trip over a remnant left by my busy ancestors. Now tell me, what interest does a marine biologist have in the work of a land-bound bone-digger?"

"I have an odd request, Dr. Chi. As you noted in my CV, I was an *underwater* bone-digger before I switched to living things. My two areas of interest have combined through the years. Whenever I'm in new territory, I look for ancient artistic renderings of marine life. An obvious example is the scallop. The Crusaders took it as their emblem. You can find paintings and carvings of scallop shells dating back thousands of years to the Greeks and Romans, and even before."

"An interesting hobby," Chi said.

"It's not really a hobby, although I find it fun and relaxing. It gives me an eye into the past, before the age of scientific drawings. I look at a painting or a carving and get an idea of what a species looked like hundreds or thousands of years ago. By comparing it to the creature as it exists today I can see if there has been genetic evolution or mutation. I'm thinking about doing a book on my collection. Do you know of any archaeological sites that have depictions of marine life? I'm looking for fish, shellfish, coral. Any sea creature that may have caught the eye of a Mayan artisan."

Chi had been listening intently. "What you're doing is fascinating. And worthwhile because it proves that archaeology is not a dead science of use to no one. Too bad you didn't mention exactly what you wanted on the phone. It would have saved you from coming way out here."

"It was no problem, and I wanted to meet you personally."

"I'm glad you did, but the Maya's artistic subjects tended toward birds, jaguars, and serpents. Chances are that any renderings of sea life will be so stylized that you wouldn't recognize them as anything you'd seen in a biology book. Like those parrot carvings that some people say look like elephants."

"That just makes the subject more interesting. I have some time off from the tektites project. If you could point me toward some ruins I'd be grateful."

He thought for a moment. "There's a site perhaps two hours from here. I'll take you there. You can browse around. Maybe you'll find something."

"You're sure it's not too much trouble?"

"Not at all." He looked at a clock. "We'd be there about lunchtime, spend a couple of hours, and be back here by late afternoon. You could drive to the research vessel while it's still daylight."

"That would be fine. We can go in my Jeep."

"No need to," he said. "I have a time machine."

"Pardon?" She wasn't sure she heard him correctly.

"There's a bathroom in there. Why don't you freshen up while I pack lunch?"

Gamay shrugged. She retrieved her rucksack from the Jeep, then came back inside and rinsed her face and combed her hair. Chi was closing an Igloo cooler when she came out of the bathroom.

"Where do I catch the time machine?" she asked, getting into the spirit of things.

"It's in the temporal transport module," he said seriously, leading the way out the door. He took the shotgun with him. "You can never tell when you might run across some birds."

They went around behind the lab building to a path that led to another native shelter. This one had no walls, the roof supported by poles at each corner. Under the palm roof was a blue HumVee four-wheel-drive vehicle.

Gamay let out a whoop. "*This* is your time machine?"

"What else would you call a contrivance that can take you to cities where ancient civilizations once flourished? I'm aware that it looks very much like the civilian version of a military vehicle used in the Persian Gulf War, but that was done on purpose to discourage the curious."

He placed the cooler in the rear and opened the door for Gamay. She got in the passenger seat, recognizing the airplane-like dashboard instrumentation. She and Paul owned a Hummer back in Georgetown. Designed to replace the Jeep, its imposing width made it a formidable force in Washington traffic, and on weekends they weren't remodeling their brick townhouse they liked to drive offroad in rural areas.

"The route we came in with the Jeep is actually the back way," Chi explained. "There's a track here that leads out to the road." He got in and started the engine. His head barely made it above the wheel.

This was going to be some adventure, Gamay thought. She leaned back in her seat and said, "Take it to warp six, Mr. Sulu."

"Warp six it is," he said, putting the Hummer into gear. The vehicle lurched forward. "But if you don't mind, first we'll take a detour through the twelfth century."

17

THE RUGGED PEAK OF MOUNT LEMMON

rising from the Santa Catalina range was visible out Austin's window as the jetliner made its approach to Tucson International Airport. The landing was smooth, and minutes later he and Zavala shouldered their duffel bags, stepped from the terminal into the hard Arizona sunlight, and looked for their ride. A dusty silver Ford F-150 pickup tooted its horn and pulled up to the curb. Austin, who was nearer the truck, opened the passenger door. And blinked. Behind the wheel was the last person he expected to see. Nina Kirov.

Nina had exchanged the dressier outfit of the NUMA meeting for tan cargo shorts and a pale blue shirt. "Can I give you boys a lift?" she said in a deep Southern drawl. "I never paid you back for that exciting sea scooter ride."

Austin laughed, partly to hide his amazement. "I could say we've got to stop meeting like this, but I wouldn't mean it."

Zavala's mouth dropped open when he saw who Austin was talking to.

"Hi, Joe," Nina said. "If you and Kurt throw your bags in the back, we can be on our way."

As the two men tossed their duffels behind the cab Zavala whispered with unveiled admiration, "How'd you arrange *this* one?"

Austin grunted noncommittally and gave Zavala a knowing

wink. They got in the cab, and the truck joined the traffic leaving the airport. As they turned onto Tucson Boulevard heading north Nina said, "I really should explain things. I really do have a new assignment. I'll be working with you and your team on this project."

"I'm pleasantly surprised. I'm just curious why you didn't mention your plans when I saw you in Washington this morning."

"Admiral Sandecker asked me not to say anything."

Zavala chuckled. "Welcome to the weird and wacky world of NUMA."

Nina went on. "He said you had been out of the picture for a while, and he wanted to introduce you to what was going on one brushstroke at a time. Also, he wanted you focused for the meeting and was afraid you might be, uh, distracted if you knew I was going to be working with you."

Austin shook his head. Sandecker could always be expected to do the unexpected. "He's right, I would have been *totally* distracted."

She smiled. "He needed an archaeologist to give the project an authentic ring. He asked me if I would help. I said yes. It was the least I could do." Her voice hardened. "I want to catch these people, whoever they are."

"I can understand your feelings, Nina, but we don't know what we're dealing with. This could be dangerous."

"I considered that possibility very carefully and at great length. The admiral gave me every chance to pull out."

"Please don't take this the wrong way, but did it ever occur to you that the admiral asked you to be part of this for reasons other than your technical expertise?"

Nina glanced at him with serious gray eyes. "He made it very clear from the outset."

"Then you know you're being used as bait."

She nodded. "It's the main reason I'm here, to try to draw the people who killed Dr. Knox, Sandy, and the others. I want them brought to justice whatever the cost. Besides, there's no certainty that they're even interested in me any-more. I've been back in Cambridge for weeks, and the most dangerous thing I've encountered is the traffic around Har-vard Square. Nobody in a black suit has jumped out of a clos-et. I haven't had any bodyguards to protect me, and I'm still alive."

Austin decided not to tell Nina that the bodyguards he'd arranged to keep an eye on her were around; she just hadn't seen them. There was no mistaking the stubborn jut to Nina's chin. She was determined to see this thing through.

"My stern paternal tone may suggest otherwise, but I'm very glad to see you again."

The faint scowl Nina had assumed during Austin's lecture was replaced by a smile.

Before long they turned onto the Pioneer Parkway going toward Oracle Junction. The tract housing started to give way to desert and saguaro cactus. Zavala, who'd been listening patient-ly, knew Austin's mind was working at a couple of levels, his pro-fessional concerns and his personal ones. With his Latin heritage, Joe was a romantic at heart, but he could see that Sandecker was right about possible distractions. He took the pause as an opportunity to kick off the discussion in a more practical direction.

"Now that we've got that matter straightened out, maybe we could discuss the sting."

"Thanks for the reminder," Austin agreed. "Rudi filled us in, but we should go over the details in case he missed some-thing."

"I'll tell you what I know," Nina said. "When we first started talking it quickly became apparent that the obstacles to pulling together an elaborate plan in a short time were substantial."

"Don't know why," Austin said. "All you needed was a promising archaeological site, a dummy expedition that would look credible, people you could count on to dig, an amazing arti-fact to discover, and a way to get word of the find out to friends and enemies alike."

"That about sums it up. It was like putting together an off-Broadway production," Nina said. "Only we were expecting to do it without a stage, actors, or script. The admiral had given Commander Gunn the assignment of organizing the sideshow. He suggested we piggyback on an expedition that was already in place. But this would present its own difficulties."

Austin nodded. "You would have to waltz into a legitimate dig, say 'We're taking over, and oh, by the way, we want to bury a fake artifact because we want to attract a bunch of armed assassins.' Yes, that *could* be a problem."

"A *big* problem. So the commander came up with a proposal that was really a stroke of genius."

"It often is with Rudi," Austin said.

"His idea was to build on a *legend*. The Arizona Romans."

Zavala chuckled. "Sounds like the name of a soccer team."

"It could be, but it isn't. Back in 1924, near an old adobe kiln at the Nine Mile Hole stagecoach stop, some people unearthed what looked like a religious cross made of lead and weighing sixty-two pounds. They thought it might have been left by Jesuit missionaries or Spanish conquistadors. The cross was encrusted in *caliche*, a hard crust of calcium carbonate. When they cleaned off the concretion they found *two* crosses, fastened together with lead rivets. And there was writing on the metal."

"Kilroy was here," Zavala offered.

"Kilroy was writing in Latin. The University of Arizona translated the writing, and it told an incredible story. How in A.D. 775, seven hundred men and women led by Theodorus the Renowned sailed from Rome and were blown across the ocean by storms. They made landfall, abandoned their ships, and continued north on foot until they reached a warm desert. They built a city called Terra Calalus that prospered until the Indians, who had been made slaves, revolted and killed Theodorus. The city was rebuilt, but the Indians revolted again. The Romans' elder, a man named Jacobus, ordered the story inscribed on the cross."

"The Romans had ships big and seaworthy enough to make

the trip," Austin said, "but it sounds more like something out of an old pulp magazine. Conan the Barbarian."

"Or Amalric the Mangod of Thoorana," Zavala added.

"Okay, you two," Nina said with mock irritation. "This is serious stuff. As your reaction so eloquently testifies, the story is fair game for a skeptic, which is what happened back then. But they changed their minds when a Roman head engraved in metal was found near the site of the cross, also covered with *caliche*. An archaeologist at the university organized a dig. They found more crosses, nine ancient swords, and a *labarum*, an imperial Roman standard. Some people became believers. Others said the objects were left by Mormons."

"They came all the way from Utah to bury these things?" Austin said.

Nina shrugged. "There was worldwide controversy. Some experts said that the depth of the objects and the *caliche* crust proved they could not have been a hoax unless it was perpetrated before Columbus. The skeptics found the written phrases were similar to those in Latin grammar books. Someone said the artifacts could have been left by a political exile from the time of Maximilian, whom Napoleon placed on the Mexican throne."

"What happened to the artifacts?"

"The university decided the project had become too commercial. They've been stored in a bank ever since. No money was available to continue excavations."

"I think I see where we're going with this," Austin said. "After all this time, money has been found for the excavation. And my guess is it comes out of the NUMA budget."

"Uh-huh. We're saying that the expedition is being financed by a wealthy backer who wants to remain anonymous. This person has been fascinated by the story since he was a child and would like to see the mystery cleared up once and for all. Magnetometer readings showed some interesting possibilities at an abandoned ranch near the original excavation site. We dug there and found a Roman relic."

"Quite a story," Zavala said. "Think anyone will buy it?"

"We *know* they will. The papers and TV stations have already run articles that have helped to give us credibility. When we got in touch with Time-Quest they knew about the project and were eager to help."

"They gave you money?" Austin said.

"We didn't ask for any. We *did* request volunteers. They sent two of them. In return, they asked, as was their custom, to be notified before the press of any unusual find. Which we've already done."

Austin was thinking ahead. "With all this publicity it's going to be pretty hard to make an expedition disappear off the face of the earth."

"The admiral talked about that. He thinks the public nature of the dig will discourage assassination attempts. They'll try to steal or destroy the relic."

"Maybe they won't come in with guns blazing, but I wouldn't advise standing in their way if that's the case," Zavala said.

"When did you tell Time-Quest about the artifact?" Austin asked.

"Three days ago. They asked us to hold off telling anybody else for seventy-two hours."

"Which means they'll make their move tonight."

Nina briefed them on the excavation. She was the project archaeologist. The NUMA staff's undersea backgrounds were being tweaked to give them more land-oriented credentials. Trout had easily switched into the role of geologist. Austin would be billed vaguely as an engineer, Zavala as a metallurgist.

The truck continued climbing to the high desert country on the fringe of Tucson. It was late afternoon when they left the main highway and bumped down a dirt road past stands of mesquite, chulo, and cactus. They stopped where two Winnebago RVs and several other vehicles were clustered near a crumbling pile of adobe bricks. Austin got out and surveyed the location. Old rock walls more or less defined the abandoned ranch. The rays of the afternoon sun filtering through the buildup of clouds gave the desert a coppery tint.

Trout's lank form came striding over, hand extended. He wore khakis that looked as if they had just come off a clothes rack at the Gap, a button-down pin-striped dress shirt, and a paisley bow tie that was smaller and slightly less flamboyant than his usual neckwear. The only concession to the grunt nature of an archaeological dig were his work boots, although the leather looked as if he had just buffed it with a cloth.

"Got in from DC this morning with Nina," he explained. "C'mon, I'll show you around." He led the way behind the ruins of the old hacienda to a low hill where a patch of ground had been staked out into a grid. An older couple was working at a framework made of wood and wire mesh. The man was shoveling dirt into the screen, and the woman was culling out objects trapped by the wire mesh and placing them in plastic bags. Trout made the introductions. George and Harriet Wingate were a handsome couple who could have been in their late sixties or early seventies but displayed the fitness and energy of younger people. They were from Washington, they said.

"That's the *state* of Washington," Mrs. Wingate corrected with a proud smile.

"Spokane," clarified her husband, a tall man with silver hair and beard.

"Nice town," Austin said.

"Thank you," the husband said. "Thanks, too, for coming by to lend a hand. This archaeology stuff is slightly harder than eighteen holes of golf. Can't believe we're actually *paying* to do this work."

"Oh, listen to him. He wouldn't have missed a chance like this for the world. George, why don't you tell them about the Indian Jones hat you want to buy?"

Her husband pointed to the sun. "That's *Indiana* Jones, dear. Like the state. Just trying to avoid sunstroke," he said with a grin that was almost hidden behind his bushy white whiskers.

After exchanging further pleasantries the new arrivals were led over to the excavation. Two men were on their knees in adjoining shallow rectangular pits scraping the dirt away with garden trowels. Austin recognized them as ex–navy SEALs who had been attached to the NUMA team on previous assignments. Sandecker was taking no chances. These were two of the top men from NUMA's security division. The taller man, whom Austin knew simply by the name of Ned, had the classic broad shoulders and narrow waist of a bodybuilder. The trowel looked like a toothpick in his hand. Carl, his shorter companion, was wirier, but Austin knew from past experience that he was the more deadly of the two.

"How's it going?" Nina said.

Ned laughed. "Okay, but nobody's told me what we do if we actually *find* something."

"I told him to rebury it," Carl said laconically.

"That may not be a bad idea," Austin said. "Beats explaining what a couple of NUMA divers are doing in the middle of the Arizona desert." He'd been going over in his mind what Nina had told him about the Moroccan incident. "Did any strangers drop by today?"

Trout and the other two men exchanged glances, then burst out laughing.

"If you mean strange people, we've had more than our share. It's amazing the type of loonies a project like this attracts."

"Dunno if you're being fair," Carl said. "One guy suggested I look for traces of UFO-Atlantis connections. All seemed quite reasonable to me by the time I got through talking to him."

"About as reasonable as this whole operation," Austin said with a wry grin. "Anyone else?"

"A couple of people showed up with cameras and notepads," Trout said. "Said they were TV reporters or from newspapers."

"Did they have ID?"

"We didn't ask. Seemed like a waste of time. If these guys are as organized as we think they are, they'd have phony credentials. We've had lots of sightseers and volunteers. We've told them we're just doing the preliminary stuff, took their names, and said we'd contact them. Everyone's being videotaped by the remote surveillance camera on top of that cactus."

Austin was thinking about the battle aboard the *Nereus* when they had to fend off the group of well-armed attackers. As defenders they had the element of surprise and luck. But the scars he and Zavala bore testified that events easily could have gone the other way. Even these tough ersatz ditch diggers would be quickly overwhelmed by an attack in force.

"What kind of backup do we have?" he asked.

"We've got six men in that old gas station just before the turnoff," Ned said. "They can be here less than five minutes after they get the signal. We've timed them." He touched the pager at his belt. "I punch a button, and they're on their way."

Austin's eyes swept his surroundings then scanned the distant mountains. Strangely, for a man of the sea, he always felt at home in the desert. There were similarities between the two environments, the endless vistas, the potential for violent weather changes, and the pitiless hostility toward human life.

"What do you think, Joe? What way would you come in if you were attacking?"

Zavala, who had been giving the subject some thought, answered without hesitation. "The road we drove in on offers the easiest access, so the obvious line of attack is from the desert. On the other hand, they might *want* us to think desert so they can come in on the road. Depends on their transportation. I haven't forgotten they used a hovercraft in Morocco."

"Neither have I. A hovercraft might be hard to hide in the open desert."

"Looks can be deceiving," Carl said. "I've scouted the area around the ranch. The terrain out there has got more wrinkles than Sun City. Arroyos, washes, natural basins. You might not be able to hide an army, but you could tuck away a hit team big enough to make life interesting."

"And very *short*," Austin said. "So we'll take the desert. Have the boys in the general store set up posts on the road after dark. Anyone backing them up?"

Ned nodded. "Uh-huh. Chopper and another dozen guys armed to the teeth are camped in a wash about three miles from here. Five-minute ETA for them, too."

Five minutes can be a long time, Austin thought, but overall he felt pretty good about the arrangements. He looked over at where the Spokane couple were hard at work.

"What about our Time-Quest people?"

Trout chuckled. "If they're assassins, it's the best damned disguise I've seen. We did background checks, and they're legitimate."

"I wasn't thinking about that," Austin said. "There should be some plan to protect them if and when trouble starts."

"No problem," Trout replied. "They're staying in a no-tell motel out on the highway."

Austin turned to Nina. "Would I be able to persuade you to get a motel room as well?"

"No," she said emphatically.

"Why does your answer not surprise me? If you insist on staying, I want you close to Joe and me. And do exactly what we tell you to do. Now, where is this incredible artifact that's supposed to provoke the attack?"

Nina smiled. "We've got it in the 'vault.' "

Ned and Carl went back to their work, and Nina led the way to a metal shed that had been thrown up next to an RV. She opened the padlocked door with a key at her belt. There was no electricity, so they lit a gas camp lamp. Two sawhorses had been set up inside with thick planks running crosswise. On the planks was an object covered with a painter's canvas drop cloth.

Trout said, "It's amazing what modern science can do to add years to something's age. The boys at the NUMA lab cooked up a batch of *caliche* that would ordinarily take centuries to accumulate." He paused for dramatic effect, then whipped the cloth off. *"Voilà."*

Austin and Zavala stared for a moment at the object illuminated in the light from the lamp, then moved in for a closer look. Austin reached out and touched the bronze surface. "Is this what I *think* it is?" he said.

Trout cleared his throat. "I believe the term its creators used was *artistic license*. What do you think?"

A broad grin crossed Austin's face. "I think it's *perfect*," he said.

18 GAMAY WAS REGRETTING HER *STAR*

Trek comment. The HumVee hurtled along the narrow two-lane road at warp speed. Chi seemed to navigate with an advanced type of radar. Since he was too short to see over the top of the steering wheel, there could be no other explanation for the ease with which he whipped the wide-framed vehicle around potholes and suicidal armadillos. The woods on both sides were a verdant blur.

Trying a ploy to slow him down, Gamay said, "Dr. Chi, how is your Mayan dictionary coming along?"

The professor attempted to talk over the loud whir of the heavy-treaded tires and the rush of air around the boxy vehicle. Gamay cupped an ear with her hand. Chi nodded his understanding. His lead foot came off the accelerator, and he switched on the AC.

Refreshingly cool air flowed from the vents. "Don't know why I didn't do this before," he said. "Thank you for asking about the dictionary. Unfortunately I've abandoned work on the project for the time being."

"I'm sorry to hear that. You must be busy at the museum."

His response was an amused glance. "My duties at the museum are not what I'd describe as demanding. As the only full-blooded Mayan on the staff I rate a sinecure. I believe they call them 'no-show' jobs in your country. In Mexico these are time-honored positions that command great prestige. I'm actually *encouraged* to be out in the field away from the office."

"I don't understand, then. The dictionary—?"

"—Must play second fiddle to the greater need. I spend most of my time fighting the looters who are stealing our heritage. We are losing our historical artifacts at an alarming rate. A thousand pieces of fine pottery are taken from the Mayan region every month."

"A *thousand*," Gamay said with an uncomprehending shake of her head. "I was aware you had problems, but I had no idea things were quite so bad."

"Not many people do. Unfortunately it is not only the quantity of the stolen goods that is frightening but the *quality*. The traffickers in contraband don't waste their time on inferior work. They take the very best. Codex-style ceramics of the Late Classic period, A.D. 600 to 900, command top dollar. Beautiful pieces. I wouldn't mind having some myself."

She stared out the windshield, lips pursed in anger. "That *is* a tragedy."

"Many of the looters are *chicleros* who work the *chicle* plantations. A very tough breed. *Chicle* is the sap used to make chewing gum. In the past when Americans chewed less, the *chicle* market dropped, the workers turned to looting, and we lost more of our culture. But it's worse now."

"In what way, Dr. Chi?"

"The *chicle* market doesn't make a difference now. Why break your back working in the fields when you can sell a good pot for two hundred to five hundred dollars? They've become used to the money. Looting is organized. Groups of full-time looters are hired by traffickers in Carmelita, in Guatemala. The artifacts are channeled there, loaded on trucks, and taken across the border to Belize. Then by ship or air to the U.S. and Europe. The artifacts bring thousands of dollars in the galleries and auctions. Even more from museums and private collectors. It's not difficult to provide source documentation."

"Still, they must know many of these artifacts are stolen."

"Of course. But even if they suspect this, they say they are preserving the past."

"That's a lame excuse for erasing a culture. But what can you do about it?"

"As I said earlier, I'm a 'finder.' I try to locate sites before they can be looted. I make their location known only when the government can assure me that the sites will be guarded until we get the artifacts out of the ground. At the same time I use my connections in the U.S. and Europe. The governments of the affluent countries are the ones who can bring the traffickers to jail, hit them where it hurts by confiscating their property."

"It seems almost hopeless."

"It is," he said gravely. "And dangerous. With the stakes so high violence has become commonplace. Not long ago a *chiclero* said instead of sending Mayan artifacts out of the country, leave them alone where they are and bring the tourists in to see them. It would mean more money for all."

"Not a bad idea. Did anyone listen to him?"

"Oh yes." His mouth curled in a dark smile. "Someone heard him loud and clear. He was killed. Whoops!"

He hit the brakes. The HumVee decelerated like a fighter jet deploying a drogue chute and swung to the right in a twelve-G turn.

"Sorry!" Chi yelled as they bumped over the shoulder and plunged toward the trees. "I get carried away. Hold on, we're going in!" he shouted over the din of snapping branches and the roar of the engine.

Gamay was sure they were headed for a crash, but Chi's sharp eye had seen what she hadn't, a barely discernible opening in the dense forest. With the professor hanging on to the steering wheel like some mad gnome, the lumbering vehicle crashed through the woods.

They bounced along for nearly an hour. Chi followed a route

that was entirely invisible to Gamay, and she was surprised when he announced they were at the end of the track. The professor maneuvered the vehicle around, taking down at least an acre of vegetation, pointed out, and switched off the motor.

"Time for a stroll in the woods."

Chi exchanged his straw hat for a Harvard baseball cap, worn with the visor facing backward so it wouldn't catch on branches. While he unloaded the packs Gamay changed from shorts into jeans that would protect her legs from thorns and briars. Chi slipped his arms through the straps of the rucksack holding their lunch, slung the shotgun over his shoulder, and hung the machete from a scabbard tucked into his belt. Gamay carried a second pack with the camera and notebooks. With a quick glance at the sun's position to get his bearings, he set off into the woods in a ground-covering scuttle.

Gamay had an athletic figure with long legs, small hips, and medium bust. She was a tomboy as a girl, always running with a gang of boys, building tree houses, playing baseball in the streets of Racine, Wisconsin. As a grown woman she became a fitness nut, deep into holistic medicine, and running and biking and hiking during family four-wheeling trips into the Virginia countryside. At five-ten, Gamay was nearly a foot taller than the professor. As lithe and fit as Gamay was, she had trouble keeping up with Chi. He seemed to melt through branches she had to push aside. His quiet passage through the forest made Gamay imagine she must sound like a cow crashing through the bushes. Only when Chi stopped to hack away with his machete at vines barring the way did she get a chance to catch her breath.

On one such halt, after they had climbed up a small hill, he pointed to broken pieces of limestone layering the ground.

"This is part of an old Mayan road. Raised paved causeways like this run between cities all over the Yucatan. Good as anything the Romans built. Traveling should be easier from now on."

His prediction proved true. Although the grass and bushes were still thick, the solid underpinning made for easier walking.

Before long they stopped again, and Chi indicated a low line of fallen stones that ran through the trees. "Those are the remains of a city wall. We're almost there."

A few minutes later the forest thinned, and they broke out of the trees into the clear. Chi slid the machete into its sheath.

"Welcome to Shangri-la."

They were at the edge of a plain about a half mile in diameter, covered with low bushes and broken here and there by trees. It was unremarkable except for odd-shaped, steep-sided mounds hidden under dense vegetation that rose from the grass between where she and the professor were standing and the tree line on the far side of the field.

Gamay blinked in the abrupt change from shade to bright sunlight. "It's not quite how I pictured utopia," she said, wiping the sweat from her eyes.

"Well, the neighborhood has gone downhill in the last thousand years or so," Dr. Chi lamented. "But you must admit it's quiet."

The only sound was their own breathing and the drone of a million insects. "I think the term is *deathly* quiet."

"What you see is the area immediately around the main one-acre plaza of a fair-sized settlement. Buildings stretched out for three miles on each side with streets in between. Once this place bustled with little brown-skinned people like me. Priests in feathered regalia, soldiers, farmers, and merchants. Wood smoke hung in the air from hundreds of huts no different from my house. The sound of infants crying. Drumbeats. All gone. It makes you think, doesn't it?" Chi's gaze was fixated as if the visions in his mind had come alive. "Well," he said, pulling himself back into the present. "I'll show you why I dragged you into the wilderness. Stay right behind me. There are holes all over the site that drop down to old dome-shaped cisterns. Some of them I've marked. I might have a hard time pulling you out. If you keep to the paths you'll be fine."

Warily eyeing the waist-high grass to either side of the rough trail, Gamay loped after the professor as he made his way across the field. They came to the foot of a mound covered with thick tendrils of vegetation. It was about thirty feet high and sixty feet at the base.

"This is the center of the plaza. Probably a temple to a minor god or king. The summit collapsed, which is what has saved the site from being discovered. The ruins are all below tree line and don't stick up out of the forest. You really can't see this place unless you're standing right on top of it."

"It's lucky you were hunting in the vicinity," Gamay ventured.

"It would be more dramatic if I stumbled out of the woods onto these ruins in pursuit of a partridge, but I cheated. I have a friend who works for NASA. A spy satellite mapping the rain forest saw a vague rectangular spot. I thought it looked interesting and took a closer look. That was nearly two years ago. I've been back a dozen times. On each visit I clear away more paths, and vegetation from the monuments and buildings. There are other ruins in the surrounding woods. I think it might turn out to be an important site. Now if you'll come this way."

Like a guide conducting a museum tour, Chi led Gamay along the path to a cylindrical structure that had been hidden behind a heavily grown mound. "I've devoted my last two visits solely to clearing away this building." They walked around the edifice, which was built of finely fitted brownish-gray stone blocks.

Gamay peered up at the rounded roof that had partially collapsed in on itself.

"Unusual architecture," she said. "Another temple?"

Talking as he worked, Dr. Chi cut away the snaking vines that were boldly trying to reclaim the building. "No, this is actually a Mayan celestial observatory and time clock. Those ledges and window openings are laid out so that the sun and stars would shine in according to the equinoxes and solstices. At the very top was an observatory chamber where astronomers could calculate the angles of stars. But here. This is what I wanted to show you."

He brushed away new vegetation from a frieze about a yard in width that ran around the lower part of the wall, then stepped back and invited Gamay to take a look. The frieze was carved at Mayan eye level, and Gamay had to bend low. It was a nautical scene. She ran her long fingers over a carving of a boat. The vessel had an open deck and a high stern and bow. The stem was elongated into what looked like a pointed battering ram. Billowing from the thick mast was a large square sail. There was no boom, the rope brails holding the top of the sail fastened to a permanent yard, lines sweeping fore and aft to the overhanging stern, a double steering oar. Seabirds flew overhead, and fish leaped from the water near the bow.

The craft bristled with so many spears it resembled the back of a porcupine. The weapons were in the hands of men wearing what looked like football helmets. Other men rowed with long oars that were angled back along the side of the ship. There were twenty-five rowers, which meant there would have been a total of fifty, counting those on the side not visible. What appeared to be a row of shields hung off the rail. She used the human figures to estimate the approximate size of the craft at more than one hundred feet.

Moving along the frieze she saw more warships and what appeared to be merchant vessels with fewer soldiers, the decks crowded with rectangular shapes that could have been boxes for goods. Men she assumed were ship's crew stood in the yardarm hauling on lines to trim the sail. In contrast to the helmeted men, they wore odd, pointed headgear. The motifs were varied, but this was clearly a flotilla of merchants being escorted by armed protectors.

Chi watched her walk around the building, an amused gleam in his dark eyes, and she realized he never intended to show her carvings of marine life. He wanted her to see the ship scene. She stopped at one ship and shook her head. On the bow of the boat was a carving of an animal.

"Dr. Chi, doesn't this look like a horse to you?"

"You asked me to show you sea life."

"Have you dated this?"

He stepped forward and ran his finger along the inscribed border.

"These carved faces are actually numbers. This one represents zero. According to the hieroglyphics that are carved here, these ships were pictured about a hundred and fifty years B.C."

"If that date is even remotely correct, how could this ship be carved with a horse's head? Horses didn't arrive until the fifteen hundreds when the Spanish brought them in."

"Yes, it is certainly a puzzle, isn't it?"

Gamay was looking at a diamond shape in the sky over the ships. Hanging from it was the figure of a man.

"What on earth is this?" she said.

"I'm not sure. I thought it was some kind of sky god when I first saw it, but it's none I recognize. This is a great deal to absorb all at once. Are you hungry? We can come back and look at this again."

"Yes, fine," Gamay said, as if coming out of a daze. She had trouble pulling herself away from the carvings, but thoughts were buzzing around in her head like a swarm of bees.

A few steps away was a round drum-shaped stone about a yard high and a couple of yards across. While Gamay went behind the monument and changed from her jeans to more comfortable shorts she'd brought in her pack, Chi prepared lunch on the stone's flat top. The professor took a small woven mat and cloth napkins from the rucksack and spread them out over the carved figure of a Mayan warrior in full feathered dress.

"Hope you don't mind eating on a blood-stained sacrificial altar," Chi said with a poker face.

Gamay was catching on to the professor's morbid humor. "If the sharp stub I just sat on is any indication, this was once a sundial."

"Of course," he said innocently. "Actually, the sacrificial altar is over there near that temple." He dug into the rucksack. "Spam and tortilla roll-ups."

Handing Gamay her neatly wrapped sandwich, Chi said, "Tell me, what do you know about the Maya?"

She unwrapped the clear plastic and nibbled a bite of tortilla before answering. "I know that they were violent and beautiful at the same time." She swept her hand in the air. "That they were incredible builders. That their civilization collapsed but nobody is certain why."

"It is less of a mystery than some suppose. The Mayan culture went through many changes in the hundreds of years of its existence. Wars, revolutions, crop failures, all contributed. But the invasion of the conquistadors and the genocide that followed put an end to their civilization. While those who followed Columbus were killing our people, others were murdering our culture. Diego de Landa was a monk who came in with the conquistadors and was made bishop of Yucatan. He burned all the Mayan books he could find. 'Lies of the devil' he called them. Can you imagine a similar catastrophe in Europe and the damage it would have done? Even Hitler's storm troopers were not so thorough. Only three books escaped destruction that we know of."

"So sad. Wouldn't it be wonderful if more were found one day?" Gamay surveyed the plain from their perch. "What is this place?"

"I thought at first that it was a center of pure science, where research was conducted away from the bloody rituals of the priests. But the more I uncovered, the more I became convinced that it was actually part of a greater plan. An architectural machine, if you will."

"I don't think I understand."

"I'm not sure I do, either." He produced a bent cigarette from his shirt and lit up, saying, "One is allowed small vices with age." He took a puff. "Let me start with the micro. The frieze and the observatory."

"And the macro?"

"The siting I was talking about. I have found similar structures at other sites. Together with other buildings they remind me of a rather large printed electrical circuit."

Gamay couldn't help smiling. "Are you saying that the Maya could add computer science to their other accomplishments?"

"Yes, in a crude way. We're not looking at an IBM machine with endless gigabytes. More like a code machine perhaps. If we knew how to use it we could decipher the secrets in these stones. Their placement is no accident. The precision is quite remarkable, as a matter of fact."

"Those carvings . . . so strange. The horse's head. Did the hieroglyphics say anything about the inscriptions?"

"They tell of a long voyage many years before with hundreds of men and great riches."

"Have you ever heard the story elsewhere in Mayan lore?"

"Only at the other sites."

"Why here, though, so far from the coast?"

"I've wondered the same thing. Why not at the monuments at Tulum, right on the Gulf? Come, I can show you something that might offer an explanation."

They packed up and walked to the far edge of the plain where the woods resumed, then through the trees and down a gradual slope. The air cooled a few degrees and took on a muddy smell as they descended to the edge of a slow-moving river. Pointing, Chi said, "You can see where the banks are eroded higher up, which means the river was wider at one point."

"Someone on the research ship said there were no streams or rivers in the Yucatan."

"True. The Yucatan is mostly a big limestone slab. Lots of caves and cenotes where there are holes in the limestone. We're more south in Campeche where the terrain is a little different. As you move into the Peten and Guatemala the big Mayan cities are actually located on waterways. That's what I was thinking here, that perhaps the boat was a ferry between settlements."

"You're right, there was a river, but I don't think it was large enough for a vessel of that size. With the high bow and sides, the rugged stem, that vessel was made for the open sea. There was something else. What I first thought were fish are dolphins. Saltwater creatures." She paused. "What's that?"

The sun had glinted off something shiny in the distance. She walked a few paces downstream with Chi coming up behind her. A battered aluminum pram powered by an old Mercury outboard was pulled up onto shore. "This must have drifted in from somewhere."

Chi was less interested in the boat than in the footprints in the mud. His eyes darted into the surrounding woods. "We must go," he said quietly. Taking Gamay's hand in a firm grip, he led her on a zigzag course up the hill, his head moving back and forth like a radar antenna. Near the top of the slope he halted, and his nostrils flared like a hound's.

"I don't like this," he said in a hushed tone, sniffing the air.

"What's going on?" she whispered.

"I smell smoke and sweat. *Chicleros.* We must leave."

They skirted the edge of the woods, then picked up a path that would take them across the plain. They were passing between a pair of square-shaped mounds when a man stepped out from around the corner of one of the hillocks and blocked their way.

Chi's hand flew to his scabbard, whipped the machete out in a blur of metal, and held the long sharp-edged blade cocked menacingly above his head like a Samurai. His jaw jutted forward projecting the defiance that had so amazed the Spanish conquistadors who fought a bloody war of subjugation against his ancestors.

Gamay marveled at how quickly this gentle elf of a man transformed himself into a Mayan warrior. The stranger wasn't impressed. He grinned, showing great gaps in his yellow teeth. He had long greasy black hair and a stubble on his face that didn't quite hide the syphilitic scars of his jaundiced complexion. He wore the standard Mexican *campesino* garb of baggy pants, cotton shirt, and sandals, but in contrast to the immaculate appearance of the poorest Yucatan native, he was dirty and unwashed. He looked to be a *mestizo,* a cross between Spanish and Indian, and flattered neither group. He was unarmed but didn't seem worried about the upraised machete. A second later Gamay learned the reason for his equanimity.

"Buenos días, señor, señora," said a new voice.

Two more men had come around the other side of the mound. The closer one had a barrel-shaped body and short arms and legs. A high Elvis-style black pompadour of thick hair surmounted a face that looked as if it could have come off a Mayan carving. He had slanted eyes, a wide blunt nose, and cruel lips like two pieces of liver. The muzzle of his aged hunting rifle was pointed in their direction.

The third stranger stood behind Elvis. He was bigger than the other two put together. He was clean, and his white pants and shirt looked freshly laundered. His long dark sideburns were as neatly trimmed as was his thick mustache. His belly was round, but the thick arms and legs were muscular. He loosely held an M-16 and carried a holstered pistol on the wide belt that supported his large gut.

Smiling pleasantly, he spoke to Chi in Spanish. The professor's eyes went to the M-16, then he slowly lowered the machete and let it fall to the ground. Next he slipped the shotgun off his shoulder. He put it down next to the machete. Without warning Yellow Teeth stepped forward and struck Chi across the face.

The professor weighed about a hundred pounds, and the blow practically lifted him off the ground and sent him sprawling into the grass. Instinctively Gamay stepped in between the stricken professor and his assailant to ward off the kick she expected would follow. Yellow Teeth froze, staring at her with surprise. Instead of cowering, she skewered him with a warning glance, then turned and bent to help the professor to his feet. She was reaching for his arm when her head was jerked backward as if her hair were caught in a wringer, and for a second she thought her scalp was being ripped off.

She fought for her balance only to be jerked back again. Yellow Teeth had his fingers wrapped in her long hair. He pulled her close to him, so close that when he laughed she practically gagged at his fetid oniony breath. But her white-hot anger drowned out the pain. She relaxed slightly to gain slack and make him think she was no longer resisting. Her head was at an angle, and from the corner of her eye she glimpsed his sandal. Her sneakered foot came down on his instep, and she put her whole weight of one hundred thirty-five pounds into her heel, which she gyrated as if she were grinding out a lighted cigarette butt.

He let out a swinish grunt and loosened his grip. Gamay could see the blur of his face out of the corner of her eye. Her elbow swung back in a short hard arc and caught his nose and cheekbone with a satisfying crunch of cartilage. He yelled shrilly, and she was free. She whirled around, disappointed that he was still standing. He was holding his nose, but anger diffused his pain, too, and he started for her, dirty fingers aimed at her throat. He was a miserable excuse for a human being, but Gamay knew she would still be no match for his weight and male strength. When he grabbed her she would feint a knee to his groin, a streetfighter move he might expect, then she'd drive her knuckles into his eye sockets and see how he liked that. She tensed as he came at her.

"Basta!"

The big man who looked like Pancho Villa had yelled. His mouth was still smiling, but his eyes glittered with anger.

Yellow Teeth stepped back. He rubbed his face where a bruise was forming against the unhealthy skin. He backed off and grabbed at his crotch. The message was clear.

"I got something to give you, too," he said in English.

He retreated when Gamay took a quick step toward him, setting his companions off into gales of dirty laughter.

Pancho Villa was intrigued by the fearless reaction of this slender woman. He moved forward. "Who are you?" he said, his eyes boring into hers.

"I'm Dr. Gamay Trout. This is my guide," she said quickly,

helping Chi off the ground. Chi's knowing expression told her that he understood he might face a bleak future if these men knew his identity. He adopted a groveling servile attitude.

The big man dismissed Chi with a contemptuous glance and concentrated his attention fully on Gamay. "Whatcha doin' here?"

"I'm an American scientist. I heard about the old buildings and came out to see what they were. I got this man to take me here."

He studied her for a moment. "What did you find?"

Gamay shrugged and looked around. "Not much. We just got here. We saw some carvings over there, that's all. I don't think there's much to see."

Pancho Villa laughed and said, "You didn't know where to look. I show you."

He rattled off an order in Spanish. Yellow Teeth nudged Gamay with the shotgun but backed away when she gave him a fierce look. Instead he concentrated his anger on Dr. Chi, knowing she didn't like it. They trekked to the far side of the plain to where the ground was scarred by a dozen or so trenches. Most were empty except for one filled with pottery.

At Pancho's order Elvis retrieved two pots from the trench and stuck first one, then the other, under her nose.

"This whatcha looking for?" the big man said.

She heard a sharp intake of breath from Chi and hoped the others didn't notice.

Taking one pot in her hands, she examined the figures drawn in black lines on the cream-colored surfaces. The scene seemed to represent a historic or legendary event. The ceramics were examples of the Codex-style pottery Dr. Chi had mentioned earlier. She handed the pot back.

"Very nice."

"Very nice," Pancho Villa echoed. "Very nice. Ha-ha. Very nice."

After a short and vocal conference the looters marched their captives for a few more minutes. Pancho Villa led the way. Elvis and Yellow Teeth rode shotgun behind them. They headed toward a grassy mound that was partially exposed to show the stones beneath the vegetation. Pancho walked through a corbeled arch and seemed to disappear. Gamay saw that the building housed a large orifice in the ground. They descended a flight of irregular rough-cut steps into the semidarkness to a dank underground chamber with a lofty roof.

The big man said a few words to Chi. Then they were left alone.

"Are you all right?" Gamay asked the professor, her voice echoing.

He rubbed the side of his face, which was still reddish where he'd been hit.

"I will live, but I can't say the same for the animal who struck me. And you?"

Rubbing her scalp where it hurt, Gamay said, "I needed a perm anyhow."

For the first time a wide grin broke his stony expression.

"Thank you. I might have been dead if it weren't for your intervention."

"Maybe," Gamay said. Remembering the upraised machete she guessed the professor would have cut Yellow Teeth down to size. She looked back toward the stairs they had come down. "What did the big man say?"

"He says he won't bother tying us up. There is only one way out. He will have someone at the entrance, and if we try to get away he will kill us."

"He couldn't have been more direct than that."

"It's my fault," Chi said glumly. "I should not have brought you here. I never dreamed looters had found this place."

"From the looks of that pottery they've been hard at work."

"The artifacts in that ditch are worth hundreds of thousands, perhaps millions, of dollars. The big man is the boss. The other two are just hired men. Pigs." He paused. "It was well that you didn't say who I was."

"I didn't know how far your fame had spread, but I didn't want to take any chances they knew who you were." She looked up at the high roof, which was barely visible in the light coming through the entrance. "Where *are* we?"

"It's a *cenote*. A well where the people who lived here came for their water. I found it on my second trip. Come, I'll show you."

They went in for about a hundred feet. The darkness deepened then lightened as they came to a large pool of water. The light streamed from an opening in the rocky roof she estimated was about sixty feet high. On the far side of the basin was a steep wall that went up to the ghostly glow of the ceiling.

"The water is pure," Dr. Chi said. "The rainfall collects under the limestone and finds its way here and there to the surface through holes like this and underground caves."

Gamay sat on a low ledge. "You know this breed," she said. "What do you think they'll do?"

Dr. Chi was amazed at his companion's calm manner. He shouldn't be surprised, he reminded himself. She had shown no fear defending him and going after the man who attacked him.

"We have some time. They won't do anything until they confer with the traffickers who hired them about what to do with an American."

"Then what?"

He spread his hands. "They have little choice. This is a lucrative excavation that they won't want to abandon. Which is what they will have to do if they let us go."

"So it will be better for them if we disappear from the face of the earth. Nobody knows where we are, although they don't know that. People might think we'd been eaten by a jaguar."

He raised a brow. "They wouldn't have been so free in showing us their loot if they thought we'd be around to tell anybody."

She looked around. "You wouldn't know a secret way out of here?"

"There are passageways off the main chamber. They either end or descend below the water table and are impassable."

Gamay got up and walked over to the edge of the water. "How deep do you suppose this is?"

"It's hard to say."

"You mentioned underwater caves. Any chance that this comes up someplace else?"

"Possible. Yes. There are other water holes in the area."

Gamay stood a minute at the water's edge trying to probe the depths with her eyes.

"What are you doing?" the professor called after her.

"You heard what that creep said. He wants a date with me." She dove in, breast-stroked out into the middle of the basin. "Well, he's not my type," she said, her voice echoing in the chamber. And with a splash she disappeared beneath the still water.

19

FOR A TIME AUSTIN THOUGHT THE thunderstorm would hold off. Festering dark clouds that had been piling up all afternoon in ominous layers had snagged on a jagged peak. As Austin and Nina strolled around the edge of the ranch property they could have been a relaxed couple out for a walk, which was the impression Austin wanted to convey to any unseen watchers. They stopped under the blue-green branches of a *palo verde* tree and looked off into the vast stillness. Rays from the lowering sun cast the wrinkled faces of the mountains in brilliant tones of gold, bronze, and copper.

Austin took Nina gently by the shoulders, encountering no resistance as he pulled her toward him, so close he could feel the heat coming off her body.

"Are you sure I can't persuade you to leave?"

"It would be a waste of time," she said. "I want to see this thing through."

Their lips were almost touching, and at any other time the romance of the setting would have concluded in a kiss. Austin looked into the gray eyes flecked with orange from the setting sun and sensed Nina was far away, her mind with her murdered friends and colleagues.

"I understand," he said.

"Thank you. I appreciate that." She gazed at the darkening desert. "Do you think they will come?" she asked.

"There's no doubt in my mind. How could they resist the bait?"

"I'm not sure they're still interested in me."

"I'm talking about the Roman bust. A stroke of genius."

"It was a collaborative endeavor," Nina said with a smile. "We needed a model who looked like a Roman emperor. Paul's a wonder at computer graphics. He took a file photo, simply removed the beard, thinned the hair, combed it à la Julius Caesar, and substituted a breastplate for the blazer." Suddenly alarmed, she said, "You don't think Admiral Sandecker would be angry if he knew we used his face for a model, do you?"

"My guess is that he'd be quite flattered. He might have something to say about being memorialized as a mere emperor. And the expression is a bit too benign." He glanced at the blackening sky. "Looks like we're in for it after all."

The phalanx of dark clouds had broken free from the mountain peaks and was advancing swiftly in their direction. The mountains were now a deep umber. Faint rumbles echoed across the desert. The sun's rays were frayed and faded.

After stopping to turn on the interior illumination of the two RVs parked near the shed, they made their way in the yellowing light toward the adobe ruins of the ranch house where Trout was manning the command post.

The Wingates, tired from digging and sifting, had returned to their motel early. Ned, Carl, and Zavala had taken up perimeter posts in outbuildings beyond the old corral. Their positions gave them a clear view of the desert stretching out to the horizon. The backup team would move in to secure the road when darkness fell.

A gust of wind kicked up sand, and giant raindrops slapped the ground as Austin and Nina ducked inside the ranch house. Trout was in the kitchen, the only part of the house that still had a roof. Rain leaked in through a few holes and rapidly created rivulets in the dirt floor, but otherwise the interior was relatively dry and sheltered. The ragged opening where the door had been looked out on the RVs. The gaps between the adobe bricks provided views in every direction like the peepholes in a castle wall.

The wind and rain were mere preliminaries. A desert electrical storm doesn't simply sweep in and let loose a few desultory bolts of lightning. It picks a spot and hovers over it, unleashing torrents of rain and crooked bolts of lightning seconds apart, or sometimes in multiples. It will pound away with a malevolence more common to humans, battering the earth like an artillery barrage whose intent is to eliminate the enemy or break his will.

The near-constant stroboscopic light froze the slashing raindrops. While Trout made visual checks, Austin kept in touch with the guards with a hand-held radio. He had to shout to be heard over the thunder boomers and the pounding rain.

The watchdogs had been instructed to call in at regular intervals or immediately if they encountered something unusual. The men on the perimeter identified themselves by their own names. The six men posted at the old gas station called themselves the A Team. The chopper crew, simply known as the B Team, was to listen and maintain silence.

Austin's radio crackled with what sounded like static but was really rainfall.

"Ned to base. Nothing."

"Roger that," Austin replied. "Come in, Carl."

A second later. "Carl. Ditto."

Taking to heart Austin's warning to keep messages brief, Joe answered, "Ditto-ditto."

Then, from the road, "A Team. Negative."

The storm lasted most of an hour, and when it moved on the premature darkness it had brought with it lingered, broken only by lightning flashes in the distance. The fresh-scrubbed air smelled strongly of sagebrush. Patrol reports continued to come in. All was still quiet until a call came in from the road crew.

"A Team to base. Vehicle coming. Taking positions."

The team's plan was to use two men to intercept the vehicle, two to cover them. One would watch the backs of the coverers, and the sixth would keep in touch with the others on the radio.

Austin went to the doorway and squinted toward the road. The headlights were pinpoints in the dark.

A minute later. "Car signaled to stop . . . stopping. Approaching cautiously."

Austin held his breath. There was no reason for anyone to visit the site this time of night. He pictured the men advancing from each side of the car with guns cocked. He hoped it wasn't a diversion while the real thrust came elsewhere. He quickly checked in with the other watchers. All was quiet on the desert side.

The road team reported in after several tense moments. "A Team." The voice sounded more relaxed. "Base, do you know anybody named George Wingate?"

"Yes," Austin said. "What about him?"

"He's operating the car."

"Older man. White hair and beard?"

"Roger that. Says he's working on your dig."

"That's correct. Is his wife with him?"

"Negative. He's by himself."

"What's he doing here?"

"Says his wife forgot her pocketbook. Left it in an RV bathroom. He would have come back earlier except for the storm. Instructions?"

Austin chuckled. "Okay, let him in."

"Roger that. Over and out."

Moments later headlights stabbed the darkness as the car made its way along the road. The Wingates' Buick pulled up between an RV and the shed. The door opened, and a man got out. Wingate's tall figure disappeared around the corner of a Winnebago. A minute later he emerged carrying something under his arm. He stopped and did a curious thing. He turned toward the ranch house and waved. Austin was sure it was no accidental gesture. Then he got into his car and drove off. Austin turned to Nina, who'd found an old butcher block to sit on. She must have seen the puzzled expression on his face.

"Problems?" she said apprehensively.

"No," he said to reassure her. "False alarm."

A minute later the road team called in. "Visitor gone. A Team out."

"Thanks. Good job. Base out."

Trout shrugged. "Maybe tonight's not the night."

Austin was unconvinced. "Maybe," he said, working a muscle in his jaw.

Nobody was surprised when Trout's cell phone rang about fifteen minutes later. He had been trying off and on to make contact with Gamay and had left word for her to call him. He pulled the miniature Motorola flip phone from his pocket.

After a moment he said, "No word? Would you ask the *Nereus* to let me know as soon as they hear from her? Yes, I'd be happy to talk to him. Hi, Rudi." He listened another minute, his brow furrowed. "Okay. I'll brief Kurt and get back to you."

"That's odd," he said after he hung up. "Rudi had set up a dummy corporation that was coordinating this project. Phony name with a telephone number at NUMA headquarters. They got a call not long ago from police in Montana. Seems they picked up an older couple wandering down a highway. Fantastic story of being kidnapped."

Austin was preoccupied with the nonevents of the night, so he was only half listening. "UFOs?" he said.

"I don't think we ought to pass this one off. They said they'd been held a couple of days, that they were on their way to an archaeological dig in Arizona."

Austin's ears perked up. "Do the police have a name?"

"Wingate."

Austin's reflexes had been dulled by a combination of the storm and the boredom of their uneventful watch. An alarm bell started jangling in his skull.

"Damn!" he snapped. "Paul, get that chopper out here in a hurry. And pull the A Team into the site." He bolted out the door. He was halfway between the ranch house and the RVs when the shed went up in a yellowish-red ball of flame. He hit the ground belly-first, covered his head with his hands, and buried his face in the wet sand. The propane tanks on the RVs went off in secondary explosions that rocked the earth and turned night into day. Glowing pieces of metal fell from the sky, but the wind left in the storm's wake carried most of it away, and only a few hot sparks singed the backs of his hands.

The patter of falling debris finally halted. He raised his head and spit out a mouthful of sand. The RVs and the shed had vanished. In their place was a crackling fire. The ground around the blaze was covered with glowing red embers.

When he was sure the explosions had stopped completely, he got up and walked closer to the burning rubble which was all that remained of the RVs and the shed.

Trout and Nina came running up.

"Kurt, are you all right?" Nina said apprehensively.

"I'm okay." Austin looked at the blazing pyre and wiped a few more grains of sand off his tongue. "But I prefer my fireworks on the Fourth of July."

Carl, Ned, and Joe arrived seconds later. Then moving shadows materialized from every direction. The A Team was running in with no attempt to stay out of sight. Their confused yells were drowned out by the *whup-whup* of the helicopter rotors. The chopper pilot saw the rotors fanning the blaze and scattering sparks, so he hauled off and landed near the ranch house.

Circuits were rapidly connecting in Austin's brain. "Paul, do you have the number of the motel where the Wingates are staying?"

"Yes, it's on my cell phone's memory."

"Give the motel a call. See if they're still there."

Trout punched out a number and asked to be connected to the Wingates' room.

He turned to Austin. "I've got the night manager. He says Mr. Wingate paid up, but their car is still there. He'll go down and knock on the door."

The manager came on the phone again after a few moments.

"Calm down, sir," Trout said calmly. "Listen to me. Call the police. Don't touch anything in the room."

Trout clicked off and turned to Austin. "The manager knocked on the Wingates' unit but didn't get an answer. He tried the door. It was unlocked, and he went in. There was a body in the shower. A woman. Mrs. Wingate."

Austin's jaw hardened. "Any sign of Mr. Wingate?"

"No. The manager says he must have hitched a ride with somebody."

"I'll *bet* he did."

"What's going on?" Nina said.

"Can't explain now. We'll be right back."

Leaving Zavala to see if he could create some chaos out of order, Austin and Trout dashed for the helicopter. A minute later the chopper was airborne again. They flew out to the highway, followed it to the bright neon motel sign, and came down in the parking lot.

The police had already arrived and were checking the room. Austin flashed his ID, identifying himself vaguely as being with a federal agency, hoping they would think he was FBI. Explaining what NUMA operatives were doing at a murder scene would have been a long story. The police didn't look too closely at his ID, impressed as they were by his sudden arrival from the heavens flanked by a tough-looking SWAT team.

Mrs. Wingate's body was crumpled in the shower stall. She was wearing a pink terry-cloth robe as if she had just come from the shower when she was killed and shoved back in the stall. Although there was no blood, her head was at an odd angle. Austin went outside where Trout was talking on his phone to NUMA headquarters again.

"The Wingates sent in photos with their original application," Trout said.

"The motel must have a fax," Austin said.

They went to the office, and Trout introduced himself as the one who had originally called him on the phone. The manager said he had a fax, practically brand new, and gave Trout the number. He relayed it to NUMA, and within minutes the pictures came through. The elderly couple in the photos bore no resemblance to either Wingate, dead or alive.

Austin and Trout quizzed the manager, a plump balding man in his fifties. He was still shaken but turned out to be a good witness. Years behind a desk dealing with people had given him a sharp eye for detail.

"Saw the Wingates come back late in the afternoon and go into their room," he said. "Then came the storm. Wingate's car left as the rain was letting up. Then it came back after a while. Wingate went to his room and a short time later dropped by the office and paid. Cash. Almost didn't recognize him," the manager said.

"Why is that?" Austin said.

"Hell, he had shaved off his beard. Don't know why he'd do that. You could see his scar."

"Make believe I don't know what you're talking about," Austin said.

With his finger the manager drew an imaginary line down his cheek from his eye to the corner of his mouth. "A long one, from here to here."

Austin and Trout talked to the manager until the police came in to question him. Then they got into the helicopter, and at Austin's direction the pilot made a sweep of the roads around the excavation site. They saw dozens of headlights, but it would have been impossible to know which vehicle Wingate was riding in. Or even whether he was in a vehicle. They headed back to the ranch, where the glow of the fire could be seen for miles.

Austin filled Nina and Zavala in on the scene back at the motel, Mrs. Wingate's murder, and her husband's disappearance.

"I can't believe Mr. Wingate was one of them," she said.

"That's why he got away with it. It only took him a second to plant the bomb in the shed. Cool customer, whoever he is. He did it right under our noses."

She shuddered. "But who was that poor woman?"

"We won't know for a while. Maybe never." He paused. "I've been thinking about Wingate or whatever his name is. He gave that 'come get me' wave just before the bomb went off. There's something else. He didn't have to shave off that beard right away. He could have left in his disguise and done it later. It was almost as if he were taunting us. Or showing his contempt."

Zavala tried to put the best face on the situation. "At least the admiral won't hear we were playing fast and loose with his noble profile."

"He probably already knows, Joe."

"Yeah, I guess you're right." Zavala put his hands on his hips and surveyed the glowing ashes. "*Now* what?"

"The others can keep an eye on this place. We'll head into Tucson and flop somewhere. Then fly back to Washington in the morning."

"These boys were a lot smarter and more organized than we gave them credit for," Zavala said. "They learned from the bloody nose we gave them on the *Nereus.*"

"Tie score." Austin's eyes gained their glacial coldness. "Let's see who picks up the match point."

20

THE PRESSURE AGAINST GAMAY'S
ears told her internal depth gauge she was more than thirty feet under the black water. She swam back and forth like an aquarium fish foraging for food, moving higher with each zigzag traverse. Her hands explored the slimy surface of the unseen wall, touch substituting for sight.

The previous year she had taken up free diving as a change from scuba. She enjoyed the unfettered feeling of diving without cumbersome scuba gear and had built up her lung capacity to more than two minutes.

The limestone face was pitted with ruts, cracks, and small holes. No opening big enough to offer a way out. She surfaced, swam across the pool, and pulled herself up on the edge to rest and catch her breath.

Chi read the disappointment in her face. "Nothing?"

"Mucho nada. Please pardon my Spanish." She wiped the water from her eyes and looked around the cavern. "You said there are some passages off this chamber."

"Yes. I've explored them. They are all dead ends, except for one which is blocked by water."

"Do you have any idea where the water-filled tunnel leads?"

"My guess is that it is like the others, ending in small basins that fill or not according to the water table. What were you looking for in the pool?"

Gamay pulled her hair back and wrung out a half pint of water. "I hoped to find an opening that might lead to another cave or come out above the water level.

"I'll be right back." She rose and padded to the stairway that led to the cave entrance, quietly climbed the stairs, and disappeared over the top. A few minutes later she returned. "No chance of sneaking up on the guard," she said, chagrin in her voice. "They've blocked up the entrance with boulders. Nothing we couldn't move, but he'd hear us if we tried."

With her hands on her hips, Gamay again inspected their prison, her eyes finally coming to rest on the shaft of light shining through the ceiling hole high above the pool.

Chi followed her gaze. "The ancients dug that hole to lower buckets into the *cenote*. It saved them going up and down the stairs every time they wanted to whip up a bowl of soup."

"It's off-center," she noted, and indeed, the opening was close to one wall.

"*Sí*. They had no way of knowing when they dug from above where the exact center of the pool was. It didn't make any difference as long as they were able to lower a rope and fill their buckets."

Gamay walked to the water's edge and peered up at the opening. Vegetation had grown around the hole and worked its way into the chamber, cutting back on the light.

"That looks like a vine dangling down."

Chi squinted at the dome-shaped ceiling. "There may be more than one vine. My eyesight isn't what it used to be."

It was Gamay's turn to squint. The professor was hardly ready for a white cane, she decided. Even with perfect vision she could barely see the second vine. She lowered her eyes. Much of the wall was in shadow. No reason to assume that it was any different from the underwater wall she had explored.

"It's hard to tell in the poor light, but from here that wall looks easier than some of the rock faces I've climbed in West Virginia. Too bad we don't have some crampons and a pickax." She laughed. "Heck, I'd even settle for a Swiss army knife."

Chi stared thoughtfully into space for a moment.

"Maybe I have something better than a Swiss army knife."

He reached under his shirt, slipped a leather thong over his head, and handed it to Gamay. In the dim light the pendant dangling from the cord looked vaguely like the head of a bird of prey.

Gamay cradled the object in her palm. The green eyes sparkled even in the faint cavern light, and the white beak seemed to glow. "Beautiful. What is it?"

"An amulet. Kukulcan the storm god. He was the Mayan equivalent of the Aztec's Quetzalcoatl, the feathered serpent. The head is made of copper with jadite eyes, the beak of quartz. I carry it for good luck and to cut cigars."

The round base fit her hand. She fingered the short blunt beak.

"Tell me, Dr. Chi, how hard is limestone?"

"It's made of calcium carbonate and ancient seashells. Hard but crumbly as you would expect."

"I was wondering if I could chip hand- and footholds in that wall. Enough to get me within reach of those vines." She wasn't sure what she would do once she escaped from the cave, but she'd think of something.

"It's possible. Quartz is almost as hard as diamond."

"In that case I'd like to borrow this little bird-snake for a while."

"Be my guest," he said. "The power of the gods may be necessary to free us from this dungeon."

Gamay eased back into the water and swam across the pool, then along the wall to a slight bulge in the limestone. Holding on to the ledge with one hand, she reached up and found a hole big enough for her fingers. Using the amulet as a crude adze, she chipped away until the space was big enough to give her fingers a grip. Then she pulled herself up so her knee was balanced on the ledge and chipped another hole somewhat higher.

Once she was able to stand to her full height the work went

quicker. She inched up the face of the wall. Clinging to the sheer rock face with her face pressed against the hard surface gave her an intimate knowledge of the limestone's character. As she suspected, the wall was cracked and gouged. She used natural handholds or simply enlarged existing holes. Her hair was covered with powdery white dust. She had to stop occasionally to wipe her nose on her shoulder. One good sneeze would blast her into space.

How did Spiderman make it look so easy? She would have given anything for a couple of Spidey's web-shooting wrist bands. Hanging on was tough in itself; what exhausted her the most was having to work with her arm extended over her head. Her shoulder ached, and often she had to let her numbed arm dangle until the blood came back into it. She wondered if she would ever work the kink out of her neck.

Halfway up the wall she looked down. The white smudge of Chi's shirt was barely visible in the gloom. He'd been watching her progress.

"Are you all right, Dr. Gamay?" he said, his voice echoing.

She spit out a powdery gob. Unladylike but who cares. "Piece of cake."

Damn, she wished that yellow-fanged cretin hadn't stolen her wristwatch before stuffing them underground. She had lost track of time. The light coming into the cave was more slanted and dimmer than when she started. The sun must be setting. The tropical night fell with the swiftness of a guillotine blade. Soon the cave would be pitch black. Making a grab for the vines would be tough even with light to see them by. In the darkness it would be impossible.

Dr. Chi must have sensed her doubts. Again his encouraging voice came from below, calmly telling her that she was doing fine, that she was almost there. And all at once she *was* there, where the ceiling curved into the domed roof. She swiveled her head slowly and saw she was level with the tips of the vines. She moved higher to give herself the margin of error she needed if her leap was to succeed. Now she was under the curving wall.

The strain was telling on her tired fingers. She had to move fast or not at all.

Another quick glance. The vines hung about six feet out from the wall.

Think your moves through. But be fast! She mentally rehearsed. Spring off the wall, twist her body in midair, grab a vine, and hold on.

As she told the professor. *Pieceacake.*

Her fingers felt as if they were being torn from her hands. She angled her shoulder away from the wall.

No more time. *Now.*

She took a deep breath and leaped.

She spun around as her body described a parabola, her hands reaching hungrily for the vine. Brushed, then caught it. Dry and brittle. She could tell from the stiffness that it wasn't going to hold her weight. Snap! Grabbed with her free hand for the other vine. Felt it break.

And fell.

Still holding the useless pieces of vegetation, she hit the water. No time to move her feet or head around for a clean dive. She landed on her side with a sickening *splat!* When she broke the surface her left arm and thigh stung from the impact. She bit back the pain and swam in an awkward sidestroke to the edge of the pool.

Chi's hand, surprisingly strong, took her by the wrist and helped her out of the water. She sat for a moment trying to rub the sting out of her thigh.

"Are you all right?"

"I'm fine," she said between gasps. The fall had knocked the air out of her. "Phooey, after all that work." She handed the amulet back to Chi. "Guess the gods had other plans for us."

"From what I saw they would have had to give you wings."

"I would settle for a parachute." She broke into laughter. "I must have been quite the sight flying through the air holding on to these things." She tossed aside the useless vine fragments clutched in her hand.

"I don't think Tarzan need fear any competition, Dr. Gamay."

"Nor do I. Tell me again about the passageway, the one with water in it."

The professor took her hand. "Come," he said.

The chamber was almost totally in darkness, and Chi could have been leading her into the jaws of hell for all she knew. At one point he stopped, and a second later the flame from his butane lighter flared and threw grotesque shadows on the rough walls.

"Watch your head," Chi cautioned, leading her into a passageway. "The ceiling gets lower, but we don't have far to go."

After a few minutes the tunnel eventually widened and gave Gamay more headroom. The passageway sloped down slightly, abruptly ending in a blank wall. Below the wall was a small pool.

"The tunnel dips below the water table here," Chi explained. "Whether it goes up or down after that, I don't know."

"But it's not impossible that this tunnel might lead to the surface."

"Sí. The ground of the Yucatan is simply a limestone slab honeycombed with natural caverns and tunnels carved out over the eons by water action."

Gamay shivered, not so much from the cold and damp but at the claustrophobic prospect of swimming into the water-filled earth. She willed her fears away, but some lingered.

"Professor Chi, I know this is a long shot. I'm going to see if this leads anywhere. I can hold my breath for about two minutes, which will give me time to swim a fair distance."

"It is very dangerous."

"Not any more so than waiting for those jokers up above to decide when they're going to wall us permanently into this place. After my dentally challenged friend has some fun, of course."

Chi didn't argue. He knew she was right.

"Well," she said, "time for a dip."

She slid into the pool and started a sequence of noisy hyperventilation exercises to fill her lungs with oxygen. When she had absorbed air to the point of dizziness, she ducked underwater and scoped out the tunnel opening. She rose to the surface and reported her find to Chi. "It angles down, but I don't know how far it goes."

He nodded. "Make sure you allow enough air to return." Chi leaned over and handed her his butane lighter. "You may need this where you're going."

Gamay was already into her deep breathing exercises, so she tucked the lighter into her shorts, gave him the okay sign, and dove into the blackness. Counting seconds off in her head—*one chimpanzee, two chimpanzee*—like a child estimating the closeness of lightning, she swam just below the ceiling. She had decided to push herself to the limit. Swimming forward for nearly two minutes, she could cover thirty or forty yards before having to turn around for a lung-bursting dash back.

As it turned out she didn't have to burst her lungs at all. She was barely past her sixtieth chimpanzee when the ceiling angled up sharply and her extended hand broke out of the water, followed an instant later by her head. She exhaled and took a tentative breath. The air was musty but good.

Gamay couldn't believe her good luck. About *time* they got a break. The tunnel must dip then come up like the water-seal trap under a kitchen sink. She was familiar with plumbing from the almost constant renovation work around her Georgetown house. She laughed at the thought of swimming in an oversized drain, but her mirth was also prompted by relief. The sound of her voice echoed in the darkness, quickly sobering her with the reminder that she wasn't out of this mess yet. Not by a long shot.

She dug Chi's lighter out of her pocket and held it high, Statue of Liberty fashion. After several tries the lighter flint sparked and the flame hissed into life. Treading water, Gamay pirouetted and saw that she was at the bottom of a steep-sided circular hole. She sidestroked around the perimeter, thinking this is what it must feel like to be a kitten down a well. How on earth would she climb these sides? She didn't relish a repeat performance of her Icarus-like plunge into the *cenote*.

She floated over to a shelflike water-level protuberance and raised the lighter. There was another ledge a short distance above the first. Her heart raced with excitement. Steps! There might be a way out of this pit after all. Losing no time she pulled herself out of the water and climbed the steps that spiraled around the inside of the stone cylinder.

Soon she was over the rim of the well. Using the lighter again, she explored her surroundings. She was in a small cave. Her eye fell on the narrow furrow in the stone floor, and she followed it to a low-ceiling passageway. She held the lighter close to the opening and watched the flame flutter. Air was blowing through. Stale and warm. But still air.

Within seconds she was back in the well. She hyperventilated a few times then swam back the way she had come. Surfacing, she blurted, "I think I found a way out."

The professor's voice answered in the hollow darkness. "Dr. Gamay. I was afraid you were gone for good. So much time had passed."

"Sorry to keep you waiting. Wait'll I show you what I found. Can you swim?"

"I used to do laps every day in the Harvard pool." He paused. "How long will I have to hold my breath?"

"Just the other side of the wall. You can do it."

They found each other's hand, and Chi splashed into the basin. With their heads close together, Gamay instructed him in breathing exercises. Between breaths he said, "I wish now my ancestors were Incan rather than Mayan."

"Pardon?"

"Large lung capacity from the thin mountain air. I'm basically a flatlander."

"You'll do fine, even for a flatlander. Ready?"

"I'd prefer to wait until I grow gills, but since that's not possible, *vamanos!*" He squeezed her hand in signal. Gamay sank beneath the surface, quickly found the continuation of the tunnel, and practically yanked the professor through the passageway. The journey took less than half the time of her earlier trip, but the professor was huffing and puffing when they surfaced, and she was glad the distance wasn't any greater.

She flicked the lighter. The professor's head bobbed a few feet away. He was sucking in big gulps of air. Somehow he had managed to keep the baseball cap on his head.

"Steps are over here," Gamay said, towing him behind her. She helped him to the top of the well.

Looking around, Chi said, "My guess is that the inhabitants of the city used this well as an emergency supply when the *cenote* and the river dried up after the rainy season." Chi got down on his knees and peered into the well. "When the water was high they could simply dip into it with their vessels. When the level dropped completely out of their reach they carved the steps. Like that coffee commercial. Good to the last drop."

He stood and traced the track in the floor. "The marks of many feet," he said in wonder.

Gamay was as interested in ancient civilizations as Chi, but the lighter flame was growing smaller and dimmer. When she pointed this out to the professor he picked up several pieces of charred bark from the floor and wove them into a serviceable torch that cast off smoky flames.

"Castor oil plant," he explained. Back on his dry land element, he took the lead. "Well, Dorothy, shall we follow the yellow brick road?" he said with an airy wave of the torch.

Glancing back to make sure Gamay was behind him, Chi ducked through the opening in the wall and into a rough tunnel. Chi's head comfortably cleared the low soot-encrusted ceiling, but Gamay had to bend over as she ascended the crooked and steeply pitched passageway. After only a few minutes the tunnel ended abruptly at the bottom of a narrow shaft. Gamay could stand again.

A crude ladder led up the shaft. Chi tested the rungs, pronounced the ladder rickety but safe, and climbed to the top of the shaft, where he knelt at the rim and held the torch as a beacon for Gamay.

The ladder miraculously held, and Gamay joined him at the

opening of another passageway. This one led to a cavern about twice the size of the cave with the well in it. And like that chamber, there was only one way out. The tunnel was about a yard wide and slightly more than that tall. They navigated the twists and turns of the gradually ascending passageway on their hands and knees. The enclosed space would have been hot and stifling even without the smoke and heat from the torch, and at times Gamay found it hard to breathe. It was difficult to tell length and direction, but she guessed that the tunnel ran for about sixty feet, doubling back on itself at one point.

She had been crawling with her head down, glancing upward from time to time to make sure she didn't get too close to Chi although that was unlikely. He scuttled through the tunnels like a mole rat. The torchlight vanished unexpectedly, and she bumped into the professor's legs. She stood to see what the holdup was.

"Wait," Chi said, and put his arm back for emphasis.

He seemed frozen in place. In the torch's light Gamay quickly saw why. The tunnel had ended at a ledge overlooking a yawning chasm. Three logs had been laid across the abyss. The early engineers who built the span had reinforced it with cross supports and thoughtfully attached a pole for a railing on one side.

"I'll go first," Chi said. Gingerly he put his weight on a log, and when it held he pressed forward. A quick few steps, and he was across.

"It's not exactly the Golden Gate," he said apologetically, "but it seems to be fine."

The word *seems* hung in the air and overshadowed the rest of the reassuring sentence. Gamay balefully eyed the crude span. She really didn't have any choice. Reassuring herself that she only weighed thirty-five pounds more than the professor, she tripped across the bridge like a high-wire walker. It was steadier than she anticipated, and the rough logs didn't roll. Still she was glad when she reached Chi's outstretched hand and put her foot back on solid rock.

"Well done," he said, guiding her to another shaft leading

upward. Gamay almost panicked when she didn't see a ladder, but Chi pointed out the steps worn into the wet and slippery rock. They were barely big enough for her toes and fingers, and she had to use every bit of rock-climbing muscle and skill. The infrastructure around here was made for slightly built Mayans, not tall Anglos, she grumbled to herself.

At the top of the shaft was another low tunnel. Gamay's throat felt like the Sahara desert on a hot day. Her climbing, swimming, and crawling exertions were catching up with her. Her eyes stung from cinders, and her knees were raw from crawling. At one point she and the professor had to squeeze through broken rock. Gamay might have stopped for good had it not been for an exultant shout from the professor.

"Dr. Gamay, we're out!"

Seconds later they stood in a chamber so large the light from the torch wasn't bright enough to illuminate the high ceiling. She rubbed the soot from her eyes. Were those columns? She borrowed the torch only to laugh softly when the light fell not on columns but on huge stalactites. The cavern was irregularly circular. Passages branched off from the chamber. One opening was semicircular in shape and twice as tall as a man. In contrast to the rough opening they had just come through, the portals were smooth and even, the surface of the floor unexpectedly flat.

"You could drive a car through this!" Gamay exclaimed.

"There are legends of underground highways that ran between villages. I always thought they were simply exaggerations, that some of the locals had seen natural tunnels and mistaken them for artificial ones. But this . . ."

They were brought to a halt where a section of fallen roof blocked the way, and turned back to the main chamber, stopping first to explore a side passage. They entered a miniature plaza whose rectangular tiled floor was surrounded by real columns, not stalactites. The vaulted ceiling was smoothed and plastered, as was the wall, which was adorned with murals of red figures in profile.

"Incredible," Gamay said. "Is this some sort of underground temple?"

Chi walked along the walls squinting at the figures whose paint seemed as fresh as if it had been applied the day before.

"The figures are Mayan, but, then again, they are not," the professor whispered.

Pictured was a procession of profiled figures carrying goods on shoulders and heads. Vases, baskets of bread, gold containers, odd shapes that could have been ingots.

"The boats again." Gamay pointed out merchant ships and war vessels similar to those carved into the walls of the structure Chi showed her earlier.

A whole story unfolded as they walked along the walls. Ships coming in. Unloading. The goods being taken off in procession. Even a painting of a man holding a list, obviously a teller. Soldiers standing guard. It was an ancient documentary of some great event or events.

Their attention turned to the center of the room and a large round stone pedestal supported by four heavy columnar legs. On the table was a cut box of purplish crystal-specked stone, similar in appearance to the temple structures on the summits of Mayan pyramids.

Gamay bent low and looked through the square opening in the side of the box.

"There's something inside," she said. She reached in with trembling fingers, lifted out the object, and set it on the mirrored surface of the table. Chi had found more castor branches to replenish the torch, and it burned brighter than ever.

The device, for that is surely what it was, consisted of a boxy wood housing inset with a metal wheel which in turn was strengthened with cross braces. Within the wheel was a large gear that apparently rotated around a central axle, and meshed with its teeth were several smaller gears.

"What is it?" Gamay said.

"A machine of sorts."

"It looks like . . . no, it *can't* be."

"Don't keep me in the dark, Dr. Gamay."

"Well, it resembles something I've seen before, an artifact

taken off an ancient shipwreck, made of bronze as this appears to be but terribly corroded. It was thought to be an astrolabe, a navigational device to determine the attitude of the sun and stars. Someone did a gamma-radiograph. They found gear ratios that related to astronomical and calendar data. It was far more complex than a simple astrolabe. There were thirty gears, all enmeshed, even a differential gear. It was basically a computer."

"A *computer*. Where did you see it?"

She paused. "At the National Museum in Athens."

Chi stared at the machine. *"Impossible."*

"Professor, could you give me a little more light here, where these scratchings are?"

Chi brought the torch so close the flames almost singed Gamay's hair, but she didn't care.

"I don't know much about Mayan writing, but this isn't it."

It was Chi's turn to examine the inscription. "Impossible," he repeated, but with less conviction.

Gamay looked around the chamber. "This whole thing, this cloistered basilica, your underground freeway. *They're* all impossible, too."

"We must get this analyzed as soon as we can."

"I'm with you on that one. There's a slight problem."

"Oh yes," Chi said, remembering where they were. "But I think we're almost out of the caves."

Gamay nodded. "I felt the fresh air, too."

Chi tied the front of his shirt into a makeshift sack to carry the artifact, and they headed back to explore the main chamber. An enormous wooden ladder almost perpendicular in its steepness soared into the darkness above. The ladder was made of bark-covered saplings, logs really, about as thick as a Mayan's thigh and approximately twelve feet wide. The saplings were lashed to tree trunks that were braced horizontally at right angles against the face of the rock. Running up the center of the ladder was a partition that acted as a hand railing.

The ladder was an impressive engineering feat, but time had taken its toll. Some of the round steps had slipped and hung at angles. In places supports had snapped, and the ladder sagged. The wood seemed sturdy enough to Gamay. The fact that the steps and braces were lashed together with vines bothered her. In her sorry experience vines dried, cracked, and broke. Her confidence was not inspired when the bottom step detached itself from the ladder as she put her weight on it.

Chi craned his neck toward the invisible summit of the ladder.

"We'll have to approach this scientifically," he said, examining the construction. "This whole thing could fall at any moment. The support up the middle may give it some stability. It would be something to hang on to. Maybe you should go first. If it holds for you, there should be no problem with me."

Gamay appreciated Chi's gesture, although she didn't agree with it.

"Your chivalry may be misplaced, Dr. Chi. Your chances of making it to the top are better than mine. If I go first and the ladder breaks, you'll never get out of here."

"On the other hand, the ladder could break under my weight, and we'd both be out of luck."

Stubborn Mayan. "Okay. I promise to go on a diet later."

Gamay stepped carefully over the bottom rung to the second sapling and gradually put her weight on it. The rung held. Reaching up for higher rungs so as to spread her weight, she began to climb. She purposely avoided looking at the vines, fearing that they might part from the pressure of her glance.

About six rungs up she stopped. "The air is coming down the ladder," she said brightly. "Once we're at the top we should be home free."

She took another step. The ties snapped on one side, and the end of the sapling came free to hang at a slight angle. Gamay froze, afraid to breathe. Nothing else fell. As slowly and deliberately as a tree sloth she resumed her climb. The ties held until she got midway, where the ladder sagged, putting further stress on the suspension. Another log snapped free and dangled off to one side. One horizontal support came completely loose and crashed to the cave floor. She was sure the ladder was about to collapse. Yet it stayed intact. When the swaying stopped she resumed her climb.

She could have been on the ladder fifteen minutes or fifteen hours. It was hard to tell. But she made steady progress without mishap until she was only a few rungs from the top. Good God, she thought, looking down. The ladder must be almost ninety feet high. She had left the light from Chi's torch behind long ago. From where she was perched it looked like a distant star.

Gamay reached up and to her great relief felt stone instead of tree bark. Even more carefully than before, not wanting to kick a log free, she slithered over the rim to safety. She lay on her back and offered thanks to the Mayan ladder builders, then rolled over on her stomach and called softly down to Chi.

The torch waved back and forth and went out. Chi was on his way up and would need both hands free. She didn't really think he'd have any problem until she heard the noise.

Ca-lunk. Then *clunkity-clunk.*

In her mind's eye she could see the thick loglike saplings break loose and tumble to the bottom of the ladder. She expected that would be the end of it, but then she began to hear more dull clunks. A terrifying sound, because it indicated that the incident hadn't ended with one log. A chain reaction was under way. If she had weakened the vines with her weight it would require only a slight pressure to snap the supports and send the rungs crashing to the floor. More thumps and clunks echoed in the darkness. The noise grew louder. It was evident from the racket that, rung by rung, the ladder was collapsing.

She lit the cigarette lighter and held it over the edge. Maybe the tiny flame would show Chi how close he was to the top. That is, if he weren't buried under a massive log pile.

Chi's voice called out. Hard to tell against the racket how far away.

"Your *hand!*"

She reached over the rim and shouted encouragement.

Something brushed her fingers. She had no idea he was that close.

"Grab hold!" she yelled.

Again she felt a touch, fingers clawing, finding her slim wrist and locking on, her hand doing the same with his wrist. She rolled over, using the leverage provided by her body, pulling Chi up to where he could grab the edge with his free hand. Something was wrong.

"Wait!"

Wait for what?

Chi was fumbling. Finally, after agonizing moments when she thought she was going to lose him, Chi gripped her forearm with both hands and got first one leg, then the other, onto solid rock. A choking cloud of dust rose from the cave. It cleared several minutes later, and they peered over the precipice. Nothing was visible in the inky pit.

"The ladder collapsed below me when I was about halfway up," Chi said. "I was fine as long as I kept ahead of the falling logs, but they started to catch up. It was like climbing a down escalator!"

"Why did you tell me to wait?"

He patted the front of his shirt. "The knot was coming loose. I was afraid I'd lose the artifact." Chi looked with wonder over the edge. "They don't make ladders the way they used to."

Gamay broke into a gale of laughter. "No, I guess they don't."

Cooled by a stream of fresh air they dusted themselves off and followed the apparent source of the breeze, which got stronger as they headed along a well-beaten path through a large winding tunnel. The buzz of insects grew louder. They climbed a short flight of stairs and stepped through a narrow opening into the damp, warm night.

Gamay drew air deep into her lungs and let it out, expelling the dirt and dust. The moonlight cast the old city plaza with its strange slumbering mounds in a pewter light. With Chi leading they set off to work their way toward the path that would take them to where they left the HumVee. Weeks seemed to have gone by since they had arrived here.

The pair moved cautiously from mound to mound. They were near the edge of the woods when they saw what looked like a convention of fireflies. Only these pinpoints were not blinking on and off. They were steady, fanning out across the old city plaza. Gamay and Chi realized simultaneously that their escape had been discovered. And that the threesome who had imprisoned them had been joined by others. They began to run.

A gravelly voice growled in Spanish, and a blinding light flashed in their eyes. Then they heard a nasty laugh that told Gamay she had been reunited with her old friend Yellow Teeth. He sounded highly pleased with himself. He ran the beam slowly down the front of Gamay's body, letting it linger on selected spots, before bringing it back to the leveled barrels of the professor's shotgun, which he held at waist level. Then he yelled in Spanish to attract the attention of his confederates. There was a shouted answer, and beams of light began to move their way.

Gamay couldn't believe it! After all they'd gone through, crawling through the ground like moles, only to be caught within seconds like game panicked by a line of beaters. She was ready simply to walk up to the bastard and twist the gun out of his hands. Chi must have sensed her impetuous mood.

"Do as he says. Don't worry."

Chi stepped off to one side and went along a path. Yellow Teeth barked a command. The professor ignored him and kept walking at a slow, steady pace. Yellow Teeth hesitated. This wasn't supposed to happen. People were supposed to jump to his order when he waved a gun around. With a quick glance at Gamay to make sure she was sufficiently cowed to remain where she was, he started after Chi, yelling in Spanish. Chi stopped, but not before he stepped off the path into the grass, where he got down on his knees in a begging position, arms held high in the air.

This was more like it. Weakness was like fresh blood to a hungry animal. With a snarl, Yellow Teeth lunged through the grass, bringing the gun up so he could crush Chi's skull with the butt. Then he vanished. The flashlight sailed into the air, describing a long arc before it landed in the grass. There was a yelp of surprise, a loud thud, silence.

Chi retrieved the flashlight and directed the beam straight down. When Gamay approached he warned, "Be careful. There's another hole just to your right."

Yellow Teeth had fallen through a circular hole and now lay at the bottom of a dome-shaped chamber with white plaster walls.

"Cisterns," Chi said. "You saw how hard it was to get a drink around here. The city people used to store their water in these things. I've marked them wherever I can. I guess he didn't see this." He fingered a thin orange ribbon tied to a bush.

"Are you going to just leave him?"

Chi looked off to where the fireflies were getting closer.

"We don't have much choice. You don't really care, do you?"

Gamay thought about the long hard climb from the *cenote*.

"I wouldn't mind getting my watch back. But to be perfectly honest, no, I don't give a damn. See how *he* likes being stuck in a gopher hole."

"We'll have to go toward the river. It's the only way."

They sprinted for the woods.

They'd been spotted. Gunfire shattered the night.

They ran faster.

21

JOSÉ "JOE" ZAVALA LIVED IN A SMALL

building that once housed a district library in Arlington, outside Washington. His living quarters on the main floor were decorated in a Southwest flair with much of the furniture built by his father. He liked the decor for its color and warmth, but it was a reminder of how far he had come from his humble origins.

His mother and father, born and raised in Morales, Mexico, waded across the Rio Grande west of El Paso in the late sixties. His mother was seven months pregnant, and José was born and grew up in Santa Fe, New Mexico, where his parents settled, his father being a carpenter who built furniture. The lure of the sea called him from his desert and mountain home. Having graduated from the New York Maritime College as an engineer, Zavala possessed a mechanical mind that bordered on brilliance, and he was recruited right out of college by Admiral Sandecker.

Austin had suggested regrouping at Zavala's place to get away from the overpowering presence of NUMA headquarters and the demands of its director. He had experienced the unpleasant task of calling Sandecker the night before to report the sting's failure. Sandecker advised him to get a good night's sleep and return to Washington as soon as possible. Austin and the others conked out for a few hours in a motel near the airport and were on an early flight that had them back in Washington before noon the next day. Nina, who still had a consulting firm to run, hopped onto a shuttle back to Boston. Austin stopped at his house for a shower and change of clothes and checked in with his office. His secretary said she had a packet of information. Austin asked her to send it by courier to Zavala's house.

Trout was late for the meeting, which was unlike him. While he waited for Paul, Austin sat at a heavy wood dining table and read the file that had come over from NUMA. Zavala emerged from the basement where he'd been tinkering with machinery. Austin handed him a black-and-white photo from the folder. "This came from the FBI."

"Pretty girl," Zavala said. The young blond woman in the photo was not a classic beauty but attractive in a Midwestern corn-fed way, with large innocent eyes and the winning smile she displayed at the Arizona digs.

"Mrs. Wingate?"

Austin nodded. "Mrs. Wingate as she looked forty years ago." He took the picture back. "Her name was Crystal Day. They thought she might become another Doris Day. She had a measure of film success back in the fifties and sixties. Reached her pinnacle doing a clinch scene in a Rock Hudson movie. She might have made it big time if it hadn't been for her expensive alcohol and drug habits and her bad taste in men. The last few years she's been doing bit parts on obscure TV shows, but even those were few and far between."

"What a tragic loss," Zavala said with a shake of his head. "How'd she end up dead in a shower?"

"Her agent says he thought of Crystal when he got a call, supposedly from an independent film company that was looking for a middle-aged woman for a small role. Immediate opening with big money. My guess is that whoever hired Crystal knew she was desperate and would jump at the chance to do the part, even when she found out it wasn't what she expected and she wouldn't be playing before the cameras."

"She was good enough to fool us," Zavala said.

"Yeah, and so was her 'husband,' Mr. Wingate from Spokane."

"The mysterious scar-faced man with the disappearing beard. Has anything turned up on him?"

"He must have worn his gloves to bed," Austin replied with a frown. "The lab boys even checked the handle of the shovel he was using for fingerprints. Nothing."

"Smart move having a mole on the project," Zavala said with unveiled admiration. "It certainly took the stinger out of our sting."

"Look at it as a learning experience," Austin said, his voice gaining an edge. "We've learned not to underestimate these guys. We know they're well organized." He tapped the photo with his finger. "And that they don't like loose ends."

"We've also confirmed the Time-Quest connection. They assign a couple of volunteers to the project, then kidnap them while they send in ringers. Time-Quest comes out clean. Pretty clever."

"Diabolically so. What do you make of Wingate's friendly wave just before the shed blew up and the offhand comment the guards told me he made?"

" 'Nice try'? You have to admit he had a sense of humor for a murderer."

"You don't see me laughing. He was rubbing it in when he didn't have to. Why?"

"He just felt like rubbing it in?"

"Maybe." Austin scratched his chin in thought. "I think it was partly just plain arrogance. He was telling us he knows who we are and that he is part of something so big he can treat us as a joke."

"Bigger than NUMA?"

"I wish I knew, Joe." Austin replaced the publicity photo in the folder. "I wish I knew."

"Any idea where we go next?"

"No more stings. Lucky I was recuperating when *that* scheme was dreamed up. We'll keep looking into the hovercraft link and the murder."

"Not exactly a well-lit highway we're following," Zavala said. "What if I flew down to San Antonio and checked out Time-Quest personally?"

"Might be worth a look-see. I'd be interested in Time-Quest's financial backing."

A soft knock came at the door. Trout entered, ducking his head under the jamb. He had a serious look on his face, but this was standard with Trout.

"Sorry I'm late, guys. I've been talking to the *Nereus* about Gamay."

Clearly worried about his wife, Trout had called NUMA frequently as they flew across the country, to see if Gamay had checked in.

"Any word?" Austin asked.

Trout settled his lanky form into a chair and shook his head. "They confirmed that she got a ride to shore from the ship. That she rented a Jeep. That she left word she was going to meet Professor Chi, the museum anthropologist she's been eager to see. And that she'd be back that evening."

"Did she and this Dr. Chi ever get together?"

Trout shifted uneasily. "I don't know. The folks down there are still trying to get a hold of Chi. Seems he spends a lot of time out in the field, so they said not to worry. But it's not like Gamay to stay out of touch."

"What do you want to do, Paul?"

"I know you need me here," Trout said apologetically, "but I'd like to get back to the Yucatan for a few days to check things out. It's tough trying to follow Gamay's track based on second-or third-hand accounts."

Austin nodded. "Joe's heading down to Texas for a look at Time-Quest. I'll be in Washington working up a report on the Arizona fiasco. Why don't you take forty-eight hours to see what you can learn? If you need more time I'll smooth things with Sandecker."

"Thanks, Kurt," Trout said, brightening. "I've lined up a flight that will get me down there early tonight. I've got a couple of hours before then I can spare for the team."

"Any ideas lurking behind that broad intellectual forehead?"

Trout wrinkled his brow. "The one thing we've solidly established is that the trigger in all of these incidents is the discovery of pre-Columbian artifacts."

"Yes, that's a given," replied Austin, "but we don't know why."

Zavala murmured, "In fourteen hundred and ninety-two, Columbus sailed the ocean blue."

Austin, who'd been deep in thought, looked up with a bemused expression. "What did you say?"

"The first line of a poem from grade school. You probably had to learn the same rhyme."

"I did, and I don't remember the rest of it any better than you do."

"I wasn't trying to get an A in poetry," Zavala said. "I was thinking. Maybe *pre*-Columbian isn't the key. Maybe it's *Columbus*."

"Good point," Trout said.

"It *is?*" Zavala replied. Even he wasn't so sure.

"Paul is right," Austin said. "You can't have pre-Columbian without Columbus."

Zavala grinned. "In fourteen hundred and ninety-two . . ."

"Exactly. That dumb rhyme pretty much sums up what most of us know about Columbus. The date he sailed and the fact we get a three-day weekend in October because of him. But what do we really know about old Chris? Especially as it might apply to these murderous attacks."

Trout's analytical brain was at work. "I think I see where you're headed. We know there's an *indirect* link between Columbus and these incidents. Ergo . . ."

"Keep on *ergoing,*" Zavala encouraged.

"Ergo the question: Is there a *direct* link?"

They exchanged glances.

"Perlmutter," they uttered in unison.

Austin grabbed the phone and punched out a number. In a spacious Georgetown carriage house the private line gave off a ring like a ship's bell. The receiver was plucked from its cradle by a plump hand belonging to a man who was not quite as wide as a barn door. He wore plummy purple pajamas under a red and gold paisley robe. He sat in a chair reading one of the thousands of books that seemed to fill every cubic inch of every room.

"St. Julien Perlmutter here," he said through a magnificent gray beard. "State your business in a brief manner."

"Christopher Columbus," Austin said. "Is that brief enough for you?"

"My God, is that you, Kurt? I heard you've been fighting pirates off the Barbary Coast."

"Just a humble government servant doing my job. Somebody has to keep the seas safe for American shipping."

"Live and learn, my friend. I was unaware that the U.S. Navy had been disbanded in favor of NUMA."

"We've decided to give them another chance to shape up. As you know, pirates aren't NUMA's usual business."

"Ah, yes. So you're interested in the Admiral of the Ocean Sea? You know, it's a wonder he ever made it west of the Canary Islands."

"Bad navigation?"

"Heavens, no. Dead reckoning was adequate for the task at hand. It would have been hard for him to have missed two continents connected by an isthmus even though that's what happened. I'm talking about the crew's *food*. Did you know that the basic ration was a pound a day of hard biscuit, salt meat, salt fish, and olive oil? Beans and chickpeas, of course, with almonds and raisins for dessert," he said with horror in his voice. "The only bright spot was the availability of fresh fish."

Austin sensed Perlmutter was drifting off onto a dissertation on fine food and wines, his burning passion for which was equaled only by his interest in ships and shipwrecks. Perlmutter was the classic gourmand and bon vivant. Weighing in at nearly four hundred pounds, his corpulent figure was a familiar and awe-inspiring sight at the most elegant restaurants, where he often hosted sumptuous dinners.

"Don't forget the weevils that developed in their food," Austin said, trying to move Perlmutter away from his favorite subject.

"I can't imagine what weevils would be like. I've tried locusts and grubs in Africa. Good sources of protein, I'm told, but if I want something that tastes like chicken, I'll eat chicken. You'll have to tell me precisely what you want to know. Why are you so curious about Columbus, if I may ask?"

Perlmutter listened quietly, his encyclopedic mind absorbing every detail, as Austin summarized the story, from the Moroccan murders to the blunted sting.

"I think I see what you need. You want to know why Columbus would inspire anyone to kill. It wouldn't be the first time Columbus excited tempers. He was an incredible survivor. He was wrong about discovering America, yet that is what he is famous for. To his dying day he claimed to have discovered China. He never acknowledged the existence of an entire continent. He started the slave trade in the Americas and brought the terrible glories of the Spanish Inquisition to the New World. He was obsessed with gold. He was either a saint or a scoundrel, depending on your point of view."

"That was *then*. I'm talking about *now*. Why would somebody murder to prevent his discoveries from being discredited? All I need is one link."

"His voyages have produced tons of written material and millions of pages. What has been written about the old boy could fill an entire library."

"I'm aware of that, which is why I called. You're the only one I know who could brush away the dross."

"Flattery will get you nowhere . . ."

"I'll repay your work with dinner at a restaurant of your choice."

". . . But food will. How could any man resist twin seductions of his ego and appetite? I'll start digging right after I have lunch."

22

PERLMUTTER CHEWED OVER AUSTIN'S
request along with succulent breast of duck stuffed with grapes on focaccia, left over from dinner the night before, complemented with a rare Marcassin Chardonnay. Austin would rue the day Perlmutter tempted him with food. There was a new French restaurant in Alexandria he was dying to try. A bit pricey perhaps, but a deal was a deal. His blue eyes danced merrily in his ruddy round face in anticipation. Austin would get his money's worth. Perlmutter knew without turning a page that an ocean of literature had been written on the subject of Christopher Columbus. Too vast to simply jump in and start swimming. He would need a guide, and there was none better he could think of.

After tidying up from lunch he pawed through his card file and dialed an overseas number.

"Buenos días," came a deep voice on the other end.

"Good morning, Juan."

"Ah, Julien! What a pleasant surprise. All goes well with you?"

"Very well. And you, my old friend?"

"Older than the last time we talked," the Spaniard said with a chuckle, "but let us discuss more agreeable subjects. I trust you called to inform me that you have tried my recipe for *cordonices emhoja de parra.*"

"The quail in grape leaves was superb. As you advised I stuffed each quail with a fresh fig instead of the thyme and lemon zest. The results were spectacular. I also used mesquite wood in the grill."

Perlmutter had met Juan Ortega in Madrid at a convocation of rare book collectors. They discovered that in addition to an obsession with antique volumes, they shared a gourmand's fondness for fine dining. They tried to get together at least once a year to indulge their gustatory yearnings and traded recipes in between.

"*Mesquite!* A stroke of genius. I should expect nothing less. I'm glad the recipe pleased you. No doubt you have something for me to try." Perlmutter could almost hear Ortega licking his lips.

"Yes, in a moment. But there is another reason for my call. I must request the use of your skills not as a master chef but as Juan Ortega, the greatest living authority on Christopher Columbus."

"You are too kind, my friend," Ortega clucked. "I am only one of *many* historians who have written books on the subject."

"But you're the only scholar who is astute enough to help me with a most unusual problem. The ghost of Señor Columbus seems to be at the center of some rather odd goings-on. Allow me to explain." Perlmutter outlined the highlights of the situation as Austin had given it to him.

"A strange story," Ortega said at the end of the recitation. "Especially in view of a recent incident. Several weeks ago we had a crime here in Seville that had to do with Columbus. A theft of Columbus papers from the Biblioteca Columbina in the great cathedral of Seville. A coincidence perhaps?"

"Perhaps yes. Perhaps no. What was stolen?"

"A letter pertaining to the fifth voyage of Columbus. It was written to his patrons, King Ferdinand and Queen Isabella. The king, really, the queen having died by then."

"A shame to lose such a valuable document."

"Not really. Columbus did not *take* a fifth voyage."

"Of course, I should have remembered. But I don't understand this letter."

A hearty laugh issued over the phone from three thousand miles away. "A forgery, *amigo*. A fraud. How do you say it? The papers were phony."

"How do you know it was a forgery? From the handwriting?"

"Oh *no*, the handwriting is quite good. So authentic an expert could not tell the difference."

"Then how do you know the writing was forged?"

"Simple. Columbus died May 20, 1506. The log is dated *after* that date."

Perlmutter paused for a moment, thinking. "Could there have been a mistake about the date of his death?"

"The house on Calle de Cristobal Colón, where he expired, has been preserved. There is controversy about where he is buried, however. His remains are said to lie in Seville or Santo Domingo or Havana. At least eight different funeral urns supposedly contain his ashes." Ortega sighed heavily. "When you are dealing with this man, you swim in murky waters."

"I remember in your book *Discoverer or Demon?* you said no one is even certain *where* he was born."

"Yes, that is correct. We don't know for sure whether he was Spanish or Italian. He said he was born in Genoa, but Columbus was not known for his honesty. Some even contend that he came from the Greek island of Chios. The official version says he was an Italian weaver's apprentice. Others maintain this was not so, that he was actually a Spanish mariner named Colón. We know he married the daughter of a Portuguese aristocrat and moved in royal circles, which would have been a difficult feat for the mere son of a weaver. There are no authentic portraits. A true man of mystery. Which is the way he preferred it. He did everything he could to obscure his identification."

"That has always puzzled me."

"Those were turbulent times, Julien. Wars. Intrigue. The Inquisition. Maybe he was on the wrong side of a royal controversy. He may have served a country at war with Spain or one that would be taken over by Spain. There were reasons of heredity as well, evidence he was born the bastard son of a Spanish prince. Hence Cristobol Colón, the name he was known by later in life."

"Truly fascinating, Juan. We must discuss it over glasses of sangria when next we meet. But I'm interested in knowing more about this stolen document."

"You know of the monk Las Casas?"

"Yes, he transcribed parts of the original Columbus log."

"Correct. Columbus presented the log of his first voyage to his patron Queen Isabella. In turn she commissioned an exact replication which she gave to Columbus. Upon the admiral's death, this Barcelona copy, as it was called, was inherited by his son Diego along with charts, books, and manuscripts. These in turn went to Fernando, who was the illegitimate child of Columbus by his mistress. He reminds me very much of you, Julien."

"It's not the first time I've been called a bastard, nor will it be the last."

"I did not mean to sully your birthright, my friend. I meant that he was an archivist and a scholar, a lover of books who assembled one of the finest libraries in Europe. When he died in 1539 his possessions, books, and Columbus papers went to Luis, the son of Diego. His mother removed most of Fernando's possessions to a monastery here in Seville. When she died in 1544 it was a tragedy for the world."

"Why is that, Juan?"

"She had managed for twenty-three years to keep the collection from her son Luis. Now he had everything. It was a disaster. He rifled the collection for papers he could sell to support his debauched lifestyle. The Barcelona copy disappeared and was lost forever, probably sold to the highest bidder."

"It would fetch quite a price now if it were to turn up, I would imagine."

"Indeed, but perhaps not in our lifetime. Fortunately before it disappeared it was seen by a friend of the family, the Dominican friar named Las Casas who produced a handwritten abstract of the log. He was very protective of Columbus, omitting anything that embarrassed him, but overall it is a good synopsis."

"I'm not sure what this has to do with the stolen document."

"Patience, my friend. This document of the so-called *fifth* voyage was also said to have been transcribed by Las Casas. Again it is an abstract, excerpting portions of a long-lost log."

"You've seen it?"

"Oh yes, it was considered a curiosity. I even went so far as to compare it to the original Las Casas manuscript which is in the Biblioteca Nacional in Madrid. It is an excellent forgery. Except for the content, I would be ninety-nine percent certain it was written by Las Casas."

"Do you remember the subject matter?"

"Unforgettable. It read like one of the fantastic stories of long-lost cities that were so popular in Spain in the fifteen hundreds. Columbus had sailed his fourth and final voyage in 1502. It followed a series of disasters, disappointments, and a nervous breakdown. The royals considered him a crank by then but thought he might stumble onto something useful. He was still convinced he had found Asia, that he would discover vast resources of gold and this voyage would restore his tarnished reputation."

"And did it?"

"The *opposite!* His fourth voyage was a disgraceful failure. He lost four ships and was marooned on Jamaica suffering from malaria and arthritis. Yet the account that was stolen says he went back to Spain, secretly outfitted a ship with his own money, and returned to the New World to make that final search for the incredible treasure in gold he had heard about from his very first voyage."

"This log, does it say what happened?"

"The forger used a very clever literary device to keep the reader guessing. At a certain point the narration is taken over by a crewman. Then this narrative ends abruptly. We are never told whether the ship succeeds in its mission. Or if it returned to Spain at all."

"Of course, the ship could have been lost and the log found by other voyagers."

"Yes, so you see what a lovely tale of the imagination it is."

"What if it isn't a made-up story, Juan?"

Again the deep laughter. "What makes you say that?"

"A number of things. Why would somebody make such an excellent forgery?"

"A simple explanation. To use an analogy from your country, if you were to sell someone the Brooklyn Bridge, it would be to your advantage to have a deed with many official seals and signatures on it."

"A persuasive argument, Juan. But if I found an idiot stupid enough to give me money for that which I clearly did not own, I could sign the deed in my own hand and walk away with the cash. Forging official signatures would be unnecessary work."

"This document would be submitted to far more scrutiny than your mythical bridge deal."

"Exactly my point. The document is superbly done, as you say. As a comparison, if you knew the bridge belonged to Brooklyn, no amount of official paperwork would persuade you it was for sale. Similarly you wouldn't have to be an expert to know the document was a fraud if you knew it was dated *after* Columbus's death."

"Another possibility presents itself," Ortega said. "That the hand of Las Casas actually transcribed this document, but the monk did so knowing it was a forgery."

"Why would Las Casas go through all that tedious labor knowing it was a fake? You said Las Casas was very protective of Columbus's ravings. Would someone of that mind-set want to give further circulation to a document that conveys the last words of Columbus as the ravings of a wild man?"

"Perhaps Las Casas never *meant* for anyone to see it. But Luis sold the log to bribe his way out of prison or into the bedroom of one of his women."

"Maybe," Perlmutter replied, "but there is something else. The fact that somebody went through a bit of trouble to steal it."

"As I said, it is a curiosity."

"Enough of a curiosity to risk arrest and imprisonment?"

"I see your point, Julien. I am at a loss to offer an explanation. If I only had the original log which Las Casas copied from. But alas."

"Another Columbus mystery, then?"

"Yes, we must leave it at that." There was a pause. "You can judge for yourself when I send it to you."

"Pardon?"

"The document. I have made a copy and an English translation hoping to present it at a conference. You see, I, too, am fascinated by the odd and bizarre."

"Perhaps there was more to it than that, Juan. Perhaps you have your doubts as to its spuriousness."

"Perhaps, my friend. As I said, it is an extremely good forgery. I still have your fax number. You shall have it this day."

"I'd appreciate that. And in return, and for your magnificent quail recipe, I would like to share with you a shrimp gumbo that a chef in New Orleans passed on to me with the warning that he would split me open and stuff me like a lobster if I shared it with anyone. We must be discreet; my very life is at stake."

"You are a true friend, Julien. Danger will only enhance its delectability. But if you meet such an untimely demise I shall be sure to toast you with a heavenly *bon appétit.*"

"*Bon appétit* to you, *mi amigo.*"

23
THE FAX MACHINE HUMMED, AND THE
first pages of neatly typewritten paper began to come through.
As promised, Ortega sent along copies of the original written in
neat Castilian Spanish. Perlmutter cleared a space on his desk to
accommodate the paperwork. Fortifying himself with a cup of
cappuccino, he began to read the words that may or may not
have been written by Christopher Columbus and transcribed by
Las Casas.

> *23 May, in the year of our Lord 1506*
>
> *Most exalted, excellent and powerful prince, King of the
> Spains and of the islands of the Ocean Sea, our Sovereign. High
> Noble Lord.*
>
> *I sail to the Indies once again, perhaps never to return, for I
> am mortal, old and weakened by illness, and the way is hard
> and fraught with dangers. I make this voyage without the per-
> mission and blessing of Your Highness, but at my own expense,
> having used my meager fortune to fit out a single vessel, the
> Niña, which I know to be suitable to the undertaking for it has
> served me well on many occasions since my first voyage.*
>
> *I go not in my capacity as High Admiral of all the Ocean
> Sea, but as on my first expedition, as a humble sailor, a Cap-
> tain who sailed from Spain to the Indies, to find new lands,
> and gold for Castile, by which the Sovereign may undertake*

the conquest of the Holy Land, which has always been my intention.

But my story must begin four years before this. My Sovereign is well acquainted with the trials of my last voyage, in the year 1502, when, having freed me from chains, and forgiven me for my errors, by your clemency and consolation you and my Queen again granted great favors and ennobled me, sending me forward with four ships. How on this High Voyage our fleet survived a terrible storm and found new lands which I claimed, with the help of God, in the name of the Sovereigns, even though I had fallen ill, often seeming at death's door, commanding the ship from a small cabin I had built on deck.

This was the most unhappy and disappointing of all my voyages. We did not find the strait to the west that we were looking for, the natives greeted us, not with friendliness as before, but with arrows and spears. All was against us, the biscuits maggoty, the weather and wind fearsome, until at last our sinking ships came upon a safe harbor where we were marooned for a year and five days in a place I never expected to leave alive, until that joyful day we were rescued. Then the worst ocean crossing of my life.

But more than any storms, or disease, or the depredations of the natives, was my knowledge that for all my attempt to serve Their Majesties with as much love and diligence as I might have used to win the Gates of Paradise and more, I have failed in matters that were beyond my knowledge and strength. While I charted new lands, I lost four ships and found little gold or other treasure. Even worse, my Queen, who being mortal, left her realm free from heresy and wickedness, to be well received by the Eternal Creator.

I knew of only one way to remedy my sadness and to please my most Serene Prince, and that is to find the goal which had eluded me on my earlier voyages. For in my long stay on that most unhappy of islands, I learned that which I had long sought was within my grasp. I was provided with the key that would open the door to a treasure in gold so fabulous as to make all

*that has come before, which is of no little consequence, appear as
coins for a beggar, and grant for Castile, the Sovereign and your
successors, the greatness you deserve, for all time.*

*I have been well provided for by the gold from my voyages
and my share of the revenue from Hispañola, and had much to
be thankful for, my eldest son Diego employed as a Royal Body-
guard, young Fernando as a page. But still I was saddened by
my failure. The security of hearth is not for a sailor, and I
resolved to go to sea once more, perhaps for a final time, to fulfill
my promise to Your Highnesses, and my obligations as High
Admiral.*

*Thus in this month I made out my will, confirming Diego as
my heir, and using my own monies, in secret, outfitted the ship
Niña, hiring a small crew of fifteen loyal men, left by night,
sailing as in my first and Greatest Voyage of 1492, out of Palos,
altering course after dark to the Canary Islands, to the SW and
south by west.*

Perlmutter paused for a sip of coffee. Interesting. The narrator
knew Columbus favored the *Niña* of all his ships. It was well
known that Columbus was beset by frustration at his failure to
find his way to China. At one point he was brought home in
chains, charged with mismanagement as viceroy of Hispañola,
only to be forgiven by the king, and especially his patron the
queen, and outfitted for his fourth, fateful trip, inaptly named the
"High Voyage." It would have been totally in keeping with Columbus, who in fact had suffered for his hubris, to try to redeem himself. And for his obsession with finding gold to be the engine that
drove him. Only one problem, as Don Ortega pointed out. Columbus started the letter three days after he supposedly died. Oh well.
Perlmutter read on. While the document was written as a
personal letter Columbus the mariner couldn't help making it a
log of his voyage, with observations of wind, direction, and
weather conditions. The trip across the Atlantic was a picture-
postcard repeat of his first voyage. He picked up the northeast
tradewind that begins near Madeira, making the crossing with

day following pleasant day, pushed by gentle breezes, favored by luck. As on his first crossing, the winds were "very gentle, as in April in Seville."

An interesting difference. Perlmutter knew from his reading that on his first trip, Columbus navigated by dead reckoning. In other words he kept tabs of his compass direction and speed and marked his daily position on the chart. The ship's speed was measured with a sand glass known as a "Dutchman's log." The pilot threw a woodchip in the water and counted a rhyme to time its passing.

On his first voyage Columbus didn't need pinpoint navigation because he was mainly concerned with maintaining a westerly heading. He relied on his compass and his long experience at sea and didn't trust an early sextant-like device called a quadrant. Therefore it was of interest to Perlmutter that in several entries Columbus not only noted the miles traveled but made frequent celestial observations as well.

> *May 25, 1506*
> *Took fix on north star, maintaining southwest direction. . . .*
> *May 30, 1506*
> *Stayed on course SW, as calculated by quadrant. . . .*

It was almost as if Columbus wanted to be precise because he *knew* his exact destination. Not as on his first trip, when he thought from earlier charts that he would run into the huge land mass of China or India, and a few degrees of latitude either way wouldn't make a difference.

More evidence that Columbus was apparently following a predetermined course was his frequent reference to the ship's *torleta*.

> *I steered to the WSW more or less, steering first one way and then the other, for the winds are contrary, but still making sixty-six miles and sailing according to the* torleta *of the ancients.*

Perlmutter put the document aside and, with unerring accuracy, navigating by his own kind of dead reckoning, made his way to a wall shelf crammed with books and plucked out a volume on medieval navigation. He knew that *torleta* referred to *torleta del marteloio*, the "table of the bell," the plotting board used to mark each day's position. The bell was rung as the hourglass was turned. The *torleta* went back to the thirteenth century and was actually an analog computer used to solve trigonomic problems. It was made in the form of a grid and kept by the pilot, who drew a line between the start and the end of each day's travel. The pilot factored in his observations of wind and current and leeway and basically took an educated guess.

Perlmutter puzzled over the expression *"torleta* of the ancients." Maybe it was a loose translation, meaning that the plotting board was an old one, which would fit if it were the original on the *Niña*.

He went on with his reading. Columbus had made a smooth Atlantic crossing. By June 26, he was south of Hispañola, one day to become the countries of Haiti and the Dominican Republic with its capital at the settlement of Santo Domingo, which Columbus founded. Perlmutter again saw the problem Ortega had with the document. Columbus was supposedly cruising the Caribbean at a time he had been dead for more than a month. Perlmutter grinned with pleasure. He wasn't going to let a small technicality spoil his enjoyment of this wonderful yarn just as things were getting interesting.

He unrolled a map of the Caribbean next to the letter to trace the ship's course. The *Niña* threaded Hispañola and Cuba and sailed toward Jamaica, where Columbus had been stranded with his crew on his previous voyage. The log jumped back to a description of that unhappy time.

> *My ship headed south and west, bypassing Santo Domingo with a good northeast wind in our sails, for three days. It was on the island here four years before that the people told me of the place called Cigure and its abundance of gold, where the women wear*

*pearls and coral, and the houses are tiled in precious metal. The
natives told me then that the ships of these people are large and the
inhabitants of this land wear rich clothing and are used to a good
living. That there are gold nuggets as big and plentiful as beans.*

*Here was proof that the Lord uses the tiniest of creatures to
carry out His will because it was in this strange land, on my
previous crossing, farther than any has gone before, that the
ships of my High Voyage came apart from the depredations of
the* toredo, *the shipworm. We were marooned for more than a
year. But it was during my confinement on this island prison
that the veil was lifted from my understanding and I saw a clear
path to the riches that I have sought for Castile all these years.*

*Diego Mendez, the brother of one of my captains, set off in a
canoe to seek help in Hispañola, five hundred miles away. In his
absence the Indians he had befriended changed in their hearts
and refused to trade for provisions as agreed. I feared this was
God's retribution, his punishment for my part in the deaths of
the five, for although I did not raise a hand I gave them up to
the Brothers.*

*I got down on my knees and prayed for forgiveness and
vowed to make many pilgrimages to the Holy Land and give up
all that I found in His cause. He heard my prayer, and made
me to remember that from my copy of Regiomantanus that there
would be an eclipse of the moon. I told the Indians and their
chief that my God was displeased with them and would make the
moon die. When the moon disappeared in shadow the Indians
were much afraid and restored our provisions so I would make it
live again. The chief said he was grateful and would make sure
to please my God by showing me the way to gold. He took me to
the east end of the island. Here in a temple as fine as any palace
in Europe he showed me a "talking stone," carved with figures,
which he said showed the way to a great treasure.*

Perlmutter had read in Ortega's book about the eclipse
episode. It showed how resourceful Columbus could be. But
what was this equally odd tale of a talking stone?

The narrator had similar questions.

> *For many weeks I puzzled over the meaning of this strange stone. I perceived it to be a map of the coast I discovered, but the other writings and marks would not yield their secrets. Once back in Spain I took it to learned men who said it was a navigational device but knew not the strange writing. Then it came to me as a simple sailor. That this was a* torleta *used by the ancients to find their way. The stone being unwieldy, I had charts made of its markings and set off as I said above on my fifth voyage, vowing to find some who could understand the strange writing.*

That explained the references to the *torleta* of the ancients. It was apparently a stone tablet, a large and heavy one from the description, carved in a way to indicate it had been used for navigation. Since Columbus couldn't use the stone without explanation, it must not have been a map in the conventional sense. The letter returned to the fifth voyage account.

> *August 10*
> *We continued westerly, favored by good winds as before. And now at last we are anchored off a shore more distant than any man has gone. The native people we have talked to have said that there is more gold nearby than we can ever imagine. I think I am close to the treasure of King Solomon. I am not well, having been made ill and weak once more by the heat and disease, but feel the gold to be near and ask your Majesty that when I return with these mountains of gold and precious jewels I be allowed to make a pilgrimage to Rome and Jerusalem. I will write no more until I have the gold in my possession . . .*

The next entry was dated two days later. The script was written in a firmer hand.

> *The Admiral is gone! When the crew arose at dawn we found that a small boat had disappeared and that the Admiral's*

cabin is empty. Gone too are his maps. I have sent ashore a
party to search for him, and they found the boat, but they were
driven back to the ship by a group of natives who showered them
with arrows. Alas I fear the Admiral is dead, killed by these
ungodly savages! We shall wait safely offshore, but unless we see
a sign that he lives, we must soon weigh anchor and will sail to
Hispañola to seek help. God bless the Admiral of the Ocean Sea.
Signed this day by Alonso Mendez, apprentice pilot.

Perlmutter tapped his plump chin in thought. Columbus was
clearly delirious in his last hours. Solomon's gold indeed! He
wondered off what shore the *Niña* was anchored. He consulted
the map again. Sailing westerly from Jamaica would have put
him into Central America. Anywhere from Mexico's Yucatan
peninsula down to Belize or Honduras if he were a few degrees
off. When he had more time he would go over the daily observations and see if he could plot an exact course to its end.

Columbus took his maps and charts with him, but what
became of the stone? Perlmutter shook his head, amused at how
he had let himself be pulled into the story. He was acting as if
the document he had just finished reading were real when it
might be no more historically meaningful than a challenging
crossword puzzle.

But what if the document *were* the real thing?

What relevance might it have to the modern-day melodrama
Austin had told him about, with black-clad bands of assassins
dashing about killing innocent archaeologists? What was that
odd reference to the "death of the five"? Columbus apparently
felt so guilty about his involvement in this incident that he
thought his marooning was divine punishment. Perlmutter
decided to go through the letter again in case there was something he missed. Then he would start digging into his own
library.

But first a snack was in order.

24

THE MOOD ABOARD THE CANCÚN
flight had been one of joyful expectation since the plane took off
from Washington shortly after the meeting at Zavala's place. As
the pilot made his runway approach vacation-bound travelers
craned their necks to peer down at the luxury beachfront resort
hotels lining the clear blue-green water, and the atmosphere
ratcheted up to one of unbridled excitement. With his conservative gray suit and flamboyant bow tie, and the way his head tow-
ered over the seats, Paul Trout would have stuck out from the
happy crowd even without the gravity of his expression. His
nose was buried in a map of the Yucatan peninsula, his thoughts
on Gamay, and only when he felt the plane bank did he break
his concentration to see where they were.

Within minutes the plane was on the ground. Trout broke off
from the stream of passengers flowing toward the waiting hotel
shuttle buses and headed for the counter of a small charter airline. Minutes later he was buckling into the seat next to the pilot
of a twin-engined Beechcraft Baron. He was the only passenger,
the other seats in the four-passenger aircraft having been converted to cargo space.

As the Beechcraft lifted into the sky Trout silently thanked
the travel experts at NUMA who had done an incredible job
patching together his trip, finding an empty seat on the commercial flight on short notice and hitching him up almost immedi-

ately with the charter. The smaller plane was making a run to Campeche to pick up a party of Texas oil technicians who were meeting their wives and girlfriends in Cancún.

The trip should take about an hour, said the pilot, a talkative Mexican in his thirties who had a good command of English and a firsthand knowledge of the best bars to meet tourist women in Cancún. Before long his voice merged with the drone of the engines. Trout's worry about Gamay had kept him awake during the overnight stay in Tucson. He closed his eyes, to be awakened at one point when the pilot said they were passing over Chichén Itzá. Trout looked down as the pilot pointed out the great four-sided pyramid temple and the ball court.

"About halfway to Ciudad del Carmen," the pilot said. Trout nodded. Mesmerized by the flat green landscape stretching out to the horizon, he closed his eyes again until the pilot nudged him awake. "There's your ship."

The sleek blue-hulled *Nereus* lying at anchor among the other oil tankers and fishing boats in the harbor was a welcome sight. Trout found it hard to believe he had left the ship, and Gamay, only a few days before. He wished now that he had prevailed upon her to come back to Washington. She would never have agreed, he admitted to himself; she was intent on meeting Dr. Chi.

Before leaving Washington Trout had called the Mexican anthropological museum and talked to Dr. Chi's secretary. She checked the professor's calendar and confirmed he was planning to meet Gamay. The professor spent much of his time "out in the field" and called in for messages when he happened to be near a phone, but he had no set schedule. If he were to be found anywhere, she said, it would be at his lab.

As the pilot waited for permission to land, Trout asked him to radio ahead and notify those handling his next ride that he was coming in. He didn't want to waste a minute cooling his heels in an airport lounge. As soon as the Beechcraft taxied to a stop, Trout bolted from the cabin with his one bag, flinging an *"adios"* and a *"gracias"* over his shoulder in New England–accented Spanish.

A stocky man in a police uniform and reflective sunglasses was waiting in the airport lobby.

"Dr. Trout," he said with a toothy smile. "My name is Sergeant Morales. I am with the Mexican federal police. The *federales*. I've been asked to act as your guide."

Trout had called in a marker with the Drug Enforcement Agency. The DEA owed NUMA for some past favors and was happy to oblige when Trout asked to set up a contact with the Mexican national police.

"Nice to meet you," Trout said, glancing at his watch. "I'm ready if you are."

"It is getting late," the policeman said. "I wondered if you would rather go tomorrow."

Trout's answer was soft-spoken, but there was no mistaking the determination in the serious brown eyes. "With all due respect, Sergeant, I took great pains to get here in a hurry so I could start searching for my wife as soon as I arrived."

"Of *course*, Señor Trout," the policeman said, nodding in understanding. "I assure you, this is not a case of *mañana*. Simply common sense. I, too, wish to locate your wife. However, it will be dark before long."

"How much light do we have?"

"One, two hours, maybe."

"Finest kind, Cap," Trout said, answering in fisherman's slang. "We can cover a lot in two hours."

Morales saw there was no use trying to put off the tall American.

"*Bueno*, Dr. Trout. The helicopter is this way."

The Bell 206 JetRanger helicopter was warming up, its rotor and tail blades turning slowly, as Trout eased into the three-passenger backseat and Morales slid in next to the pilot. Seconds later the turbo motor kicked into action and the runners lifted off the tarmac. The helicopter leaped into the air and climbed in two minutes to an altitude of more than three thousand feet. They swung out over the water and headed inland from the coast, following the railroad tracks that snaked into the interior.

Morales gave the pilot directions, frequently consulting from a folded-up map. They left the railroad track and picked up a narrow highway running more or less east-west. The chopper kept its altitude, cruising at a speed of 125 miles per hour until they were well into the interior. The dense woods were broken here and there by a village or occasional town. There were few paved roads. Occasionally they passed over a Mayan ruin. But for the most part the landscape was the same unbroken flatness Trout had noted on the way from Cancún.

The aircraft swung onto a more southerly course. Morales was a competent and sharp-eyed guide, recognizing landmarks and relaying the information to the pilot. Trout anxiously watched the sun lowering in the sky.

"How far?" Trout said with unveiled impatience.

Morales held up five fingers. He jabbed a point on the map for the benefit of the pilot. *"Aquí!"*

The pilot nodded so slightly Trout wasn't sure he heard Morales until the chopper cut speed and described a wide circle that transformed into an ever-tightening spiral.

Morales pressed against the plexiglass and pointed down. Trout caught a glimpse of a clearing and a crude structure before both quickly passed out of view. The chopper came around again, hovered, and began to descend. Their target was directly under them, and Trout couldn't see where they were landing. As the treetops grew closer, the chopper seemed to hang for a second. The pilot suddenly gunned the motor, and they darted off to one side like a startled dragonfly.

The pilot and Morales had a quick conversation in Spanish.

"What's wrong?" Trout strained to see into the forest.

"No room. He's afraid he'll catch the rotors in the trees."

Trout sat back in his seat and crossed his arms, puffing his cheeks out in frustration. The chopper moved out until it was above a lonely stretch of arrow-straight road, then dropped down and landed lightly in a grassy patch at the edge of the blacktop. As the whirling rotors fluttered to a stop, Trout and Morales got out. Nearby a track led into the woods.

"This goes to Professor Chi's house. We must walk."

Trout strode off with the shorter man valiantly trying to keep up without losing his dignity. As they moved into the thick woods Trout noticed that there were deep tracks, made fairly recently by heavy tires set wide apart. Morales said he had called the local *policía* and requested that they ask around. Several locals remembered seeing Chi on a bus. He'd been picked up from hunting and dropped off by the side of the road near where he lived. They remembered a Jeep waiting for him. That fit, Trout thought. Gamay had used a Jeep to drive in from the coast.

"Do you know Dr. Chi?" he asked Morales as they walked.

"*Sí, señor.* I have met him. Sometimes the museum asks me to carry a message to him. He is *muy pacífico*. A gentleman. Always wants to cook tortillas for me."

The canopy of trees was becoming as dark as a subway tunnel. Trout squinted through the branches, trying to catch a glimpse of the sun. He wondered if they would have any problem finding their way out. Maybe Morales was right, they should have waited until morning when they'd have more light.

"Why does Professor Chi have his lab way out here?" Trout asked. "Wouldn't it be more convenient if he had it in a town or village?"

"I ask the doctor the same thing," Morales said with a grin. "He says he was born in this place. 'My roots are here,' he tells me. You understand what he means?"

Trout understood Chi's attachment to his native soil very well. His own family went back more than two hundred years on Cape Cod, spawning several generations of families all tied to the sea, through service as lighthouse keepers, surfmen in the Lifesaving Service, or fishermen. The low-slung silver-shingled Trout homestead was nearly two centuries old, but it had been kept up through the years and looked as if it could have been built yesterday. His was a salty ancestry he wore with pride, but he realized his ties to the past were nothing compared to the Maya, who had inhabited the same country for many centuries before the Spaniards arrived.

They trudged along for about twenty minutes until the forest thinned out into a clearing. The square concrete block building seemed to jump out of the woods, but it was more a case of Trout simply not expecting such a substantial-looking structure in this remote location.

"The professor's laboratory," Morales said. He went over and knocked on the door. No answer. "We come back here after we check the house," Morales suggested.

The thatched-roof hut was similar to those Trout had seen dotting the Yucatan from the air. Trout was more interested in the Jeep parked next to the simple structure. He hurried over and searched the vehicle. Tucked in the sun visor was the diagram indicating how to get to Chi's property and a bottle of bug repellent. He ran his hands over the steering wheel and dashboard and smelled the faint scent of the body lotion Gamay used.

They searched the house, which took about five minutes because of the sparseness of the furnishings. Trout stood in the center of the dirt floor and looked around, hoping to find a clue he had missed on his first round.

"Well, we know from the Jeep that she made it this far."

"I have an idea," Morales said. Trout followed him past the lab building to another simple hut. "This is the professor's garage. Look. His vehicle is gone."

"Those would have been the tracks we saw on the way in. What does he drive?"

"A big car," Morales said. "Like a Jeep, only like this." He held his hands wide.

"A HumVee?"

"*Sí,*" he said with a bright smile. "HumVee. Like the U.S. military uses."

So it was likely they went somewhere in the Hummer. But where?

"Maybe there's a note in the lab," Trout said.

The cinderblock building was pleasantly cooler than outside even without the air-conditioning on. The door was unlocked, and they easily gained entrance. Trout took in the high-tech equipment and shook his head in wonder much as his wife had done the day before. Morales stood nearby at respectful attention, almost as if he were afraid of being caught in forbidden precincts. Except for the general clutter, nothing appeared to have been disturbed.

Paul went over to the sink. There were two glasses in the drying rack.

"Looks they they could have had a drink."

Morales checked the waste basket and found the cans of Seven-Up. Further reconstructing events, Trout surmised that Gamay had been waiting for the professor at the highway, they came in here, drank some soda, then took off. He checked the refrigerator and found the two dead partridges. The birds had yet to be cleaned and gutted. Chi must have planned to return in a short time from wherever he went.

"Is there a village nearby where they could have gone?" Trout asked.

"There is a town, *sí*, but the people there would have seen Dr. Chi in his big blue car. *Nada.*"

Trout examined the maps on the wall. One appeared to be missing. He went over to the table and began looking at the papers on top. It took only a moment to find the map and match the pinholes to those on the wall. Chi could have taken this down to show Gamay. On the other hand, it may have been on the table for weeks. He showed the map to Morales.

"Do you know where this is?"

The police sergeant examined the map and said, "Down south more into Campeche. About a hundred miles. Maybe more."

"What's out there?"

"Nothing. Woods. It's outside the biosphere reserve. No one goes there."

Trout tapped the map. "*Somebody* went there. My guess is it's Dr. Chi. The chopper can get us there in an hour or less."

"I'm sorry, *señor.* By the time we walk back to the helicopter it will be dark."

Morales was right. They were lucky to find their way out of the woods. By the time they returned to the chopper it was pitch black. Trout hated the thought of Gamay having to spend another night wherever she was. As the helicopter lifted above the trees he tried to console himself with other possibilities. That Chi and Gamay had fetched up somewhere. Maybe they were sitting down to a quiet dinner. Less appealing scenarios intruded. An accident. That didn't figure. Gamay was simply not accident-prone. She was too savvy, too sure-footed.

Trout knew that even the most sure-footed person makes a mistake at least once in his or her life. He hoped it wasn't Gamay's turn.

25

SERGEANT MORALES FOUND TROUT A room in a small hotel near the airport. Trout lay on his bed for hours staring at the ceiling fan, wondering what Gamay was doing, before he finally slipped into a few fitful hours of sleep. He awoke at twilight and took a shower that was all the more refreshing because there was no hot water. He was pacing the tarmac when the pilot and sergeant arrived as the sky turned peach pink in the east.

The chopper followed Chi's map in a straight line at its maximum cruising speed, flying at an altitude of fifteen hundred feet. The forest stretched out below like a rough-napped green carpet. Arriving at the area indicated on Chi's map, the pilot slowed the aircraft and dropped it almost to treetop level. The JetRanger admirably fulfilled the purpose of its original design as an army observation helicopter. Trout, who was sitting in the front, noticed a textural difference in the greenery and asked the pilot to circle. Morales picked out the barely distinct edges of the rectangular plain. After a couple more passes for the pilot to acquaint himself with the lay of the land, the JetRanger landed at rough center.

It took Paul less than thirty seconds to decide he didn't like this godforsaken place. Not one damned bit! It went beyond the remoteness and the weird mounds and the darkness of the encroaching forest even in daylight. Something sinister lurked here. As a boy he used to feel the same prickly scalp uneasiness when he walked past the deserted house of a sailor who ate his crewmates while becalmed in the Sargasso Sea.

Maybe Gamay had never been here, he thought, looking around at the desolate spot. All he had was Dr. Chi's map and the supposition that this was their destination. He could be spinning his wheels while Gamay desperately needed his help elsewhere. *No.* He clenched his jaw. This was *definitely* the place. He could feel it in his bones the way his fisherman father sensed a storm brewing.

The police officer suggested that they fan out in three directions, keeping each other in view as much as possible, walk to the edge of the woods, then return to the chopper. A half hour later they straggled back. Morales was about to speak but paused as his ever-searching policeman's eye picked out evidence of an earlier visit.

Squatting for a better look, Morales said, "See where the grass is broken. Here, and here again." He angled his head. "There, when the light is just right, footprints."

Thinking he would never want Morales on his trail, Trout followed the sergeant's example and saw the faint shadows that had caught the police officer's attention. The sergeant instructed the pilot to stay with the helicopter and got no argument. The early morning sun was already hinting at the blast furnace it would be in the hours to come. They set out with Morales taking the lead and had gone only a short distance when they saw a mound that had been cleared so the stone blocks on one side were visible.

At the base of the structure was a reddish patch. In his eagerness for a better look Trout ignored the sergeant's admonishment to stay behind. He dashed past the sergeant to the mound and picked up Gamay's worn maroon L. L. Bean day pack, the same one he had given her as a Christmas gift two years before. With mounting excitement he rummaged inside and found her camera and sketch pads, some plastic lunch bags, empty soda cans, and a bottle of water. Nearby was another pack made of tan canvas. Trout held both packs high over his head for the benefit of Morales, who was walking briskly to catch up.

"This pack belongs to my wife," the NUMA scientist said triumphantly. "The other has Dr. Chi's name on the tag."

Morales inspected the professor's bag. His face was clouded. "This is not good."

"What do you *mean*, not good? This shows they've been here."

"You misunderstand, Señor Trout," Morales said with a quick glance around. "I found a campfire where there were signs of many *chicleros*." Noting Trout's blank expression, he explained, "They are bad men who steal antiquities for sale."

"What's that got to do with my wife and the professor?"

"The coals were warm. And near the river signs of many men. I also find these." He opened his palm to display three spent bullet cartridges.

Trout put a shell to his nose. The bullet had been fired recently.

"Where did you find them?"

Trout's eyes followed the police officer's pointing finger, then looked back to where he had found the rucksacks as if he could draw a line connecting the two points. That's when he noticed the strange carvings on the wall of the structure. He stepped closer and inspected the boats and other figures on the bared stone. His guess was that Gamay and the professor had lunch, then came back to these carvings. Gamay definitely would have been intrigued by the strange etchings, but something must have distracted them.

He turned back to Morales. "You think my wife and the professor ran into these *chicleros*?"

"*Sí,*" Morales said with a shrug. "It is possible. Why else would they leave their sacks?"

"I was thinking the same thing. Sergeant, would you please show me where you found these shells?"

"Come this way," Morales said with a nod. "Be careful where you walk. There are holes all over the field."

They slowly made their way across the plain. There were far more of the mysterious mounds than Trout first assumed. If each one had a stone structure under it, this must have been a good-sized settlement at one time.

"Here," Morales said. "And over there."

Trout saw copper gleaming in the grass and picked up a couple more shells, a combination of pistol and rifle casings. The grass was trampled all around them. His big hand squeezed the hollow copper cylinders as if he would crush them.

"Now can I see the campfire and the river?"

They examined the campsite and found empty tequila bottles and many cigarette stubs. More shells were found in the woods. At the river's edge Trout looked in vain for tracks indicating Gamay's running shoes, but the mud was too messed up. He saw marks indicating boats had been drawn up on shore, as well as more shell casings. This place must have resembled a shooting gallery! But Trout was hopeful. The casings indicated that someone with rifles and pistols had chased somebody to the river. That was the *bad* news. The fact that guns were still blazing from the riverside indicated Gamay and the professor could have made their escape.

Trout suggested that they get into the air and follow the river through the woods. Morales agreed. They walked briskly away from the river and were about halfway back to the chopper when they heard a disembodied groan. They froze, exchanging glances. Morales drew his pistol. They listened, hearing only the drone of insects.

The groan repeated off to the right. With Morales covering him, Trout moved cautiously toward the apparent source. The sound seemed to be coming from practically underfoot. Trout looked down. Partially hidden by the long grass was a black hole. He knelt at the edge but couldn't see anything in the darkness.

Feeling somewhat foolish at talking into the ground, he said, "Who's there?"

Another groan. Followed by a stream of Spanish in a weak voice.

Morales, who had come over to kneel by Trout's side, listened a moment. "It's a man. He says he fell down the hole."

"What's he doing way out here?"

Morales relayed the question, then the answer. "He said he was out walking."

"This is a pretty remote place to be taking a nature stroll," Trout said. "Let's get him out."

Trout went back to the chopper and found a nylon rope in the emergency kit. He dropped a knotted loop into the hole, then he, the pilot, and Morales hauled on their end of the rope. First the head, then the shoulders of a pitiful-looking creature appeared in the opening. The man's scraggly beard and long greasy hair were covered with a gray dust, and the whiteness of his ill-fitting clothes was a distant memory. He sat on the ground, alternately rubbing his arms, legs, and head. His nose was bruised.

The police officer gave him a water bottle. He noisily gurgled the water, slopping half of it onto his chin. Refreshed by the water, the man showed yellow teeth in a cocky grin and tipped the canteen for another guzzle. His sleeve fell as he raised his arm.

Trout kicked the canteen like a punter and sent it flying into the grass. His big hand shot out and gripped the man's hairy wrist. Even Morales was shocked by the unexpected move.

"Señor Trout!"

"This is my wife's watch." Trout slid the expansion-band Swatch off.

"You're sure?"

"I gave it to her." Anger flashed in the normally calm eyes. "Ask him where he got it."

Morales asked the question in Spanish and relayed the answer.

"He says he bought it."

Trout was through playing games. "Tell him that if he doesn't talk we'll throw him back in the hole and leave."

The grin vanished. The threat of being tossed back into the ground unleashed a torrent of Spanish.

Morales listened, nodding. "He's crazy. Name is Ruiz. Keeps talking about the devil woman and the dwarf who made the earth swallow him."

"Devil woman?"

"*Sí.* He says she broke his nose."

"What happened to this woman?"

"He doesn't know. He was down in the hole. He heard a lot of shooting. Then quiet. He says his friends abandoned him. I ask if these *amigos* are *chicleros*. He says no." Morales grinned without mirth. "He's a stinking liar."

"Tell him we're going to take him up in the helicopter and throw him out if he doesn't tell the truth."

The man looked at the granite-hard expression on the face of the giant gringo and decided he wasn't joking.

"No!" he said. "I talk. I talk."

"You understand English."

"*Poco,*" the man said, holding his thumb and finger slightly apart.

In halting English, using Spanish when words escaped him, Ruiz admitted he was with a gang of *chicleros* who came here to steal antiquities. They found the woman and the little old man and locked them in the ground where there was no way they could escape. But they burrowed out of the earth somehow and threw him into the hole. The other *chicleros* gave chase. They never came back to look for him. He didn't know what happened to the man and woman.

Trout pondered the report briefly.

"Okay, get him in the chopper."

Morales handcuffed the man gingerly, trying not to touch him, then used the toe of his shoe to persuade Ruiz to stand. They stuffed him into the rear bench seat, and Morales got in beside him. The man exuded a stench so vile the pilot complained. Morales laughed and said if it got too bad they'd throw Ruiz over the side. Ruiz didn't think it was funny, and his eyes grew wide in fear as the helicopter lifted off the ground. He wouldn't be giving them any trouble. They circled the site a couple of times, then picked up the gleam of the river. It was barely visible through the trees, but with three sets of eyes they were able to trace its course.

Trout couldn't wait to tell Gamay her new sobriquet. *Devil woman.* He hoped that she was still alive to hear it.

26

THE BUZZ OF THE ANCIENT OUT-
board motor was so loud Gamay didn't hear the helicopter until
it was practically overhead. Even then it was Chi's upturned face
that alerted her to the arrival of company. She jammed the tiller
over and aimed the pram toward the shore, bumping into a
grassy bank under a protective canopy of overhanging branches.
From the air the boat would be almost impossible to see through
the thick greenery. Gamay took out extra insurance and nudged
the pram into a huge fern bush. She didn't want the early morning sunlight reflecting off the aluminum hull.

An instant later the air overhead was filled with the slashing
of rotors. Flashes of a shiny red-and-white fuselage came through
openings in the dense foliage as the helicopter skimmed the treetops. It never dawned on Gamay that within hours of learning
she was missing her husband would return to the Yucatan, com-
mandeer a helicopter, and now be hovering a few hundred feet
above her head. Since arriving in this place she'd had her hair
almost pulled out by the roots, been threatened with rape, been
stuffed into a cave to die, crawled through dark and practically
airless tunnels, and been used for target practice. There was no
reason to believe the people who had treated her so badly had
not brought in air support to increase her misery. She breathed a
sigh of relief as the sound of the helicopter receded in the distance, and moments later they headed out into the river again.

After disposing of Yellow Teeth, Gamay and Chi had bolted for the woods, dodging the bullets that whizzed around them, and scrambled down the slope to the river. Finding three battered aluminum prams lined up side by side on shore, they shoved two boats adrift, then piled into the third, got the outboard motor going, and made a dash for safety.

Traveling an entire day without incident, they spent a quiet night pulled over to the side of the river and got an early start the next morning. The helicopter made Gamay realize their smooth escape and peaceful passage had lulled them into a false sense of security. Now they kept a sharp eye on the sky, and Gamay steered close to the river's edge. There was no further sign of the helicopter, but the propeller tangled in vegetation, and she had to angle the boat into shore to clear the blades of weeds. The job should have meant no more than a minute or two of delay. When Gamay went to restart the motor it played hard to get. She couldn't figure it. The antique fifteen-horsepower Mercury didn't look like much with its sand-blasted engine housing. Yet it worked fine before they turned it off. She was trying to figure out what the problem was when they heard voices in Spanish coming from upriver.

Nothing on the face of the earth is more frustrating than a cranky outboard motor, Gamay thought, especially when the recalcitrant hunk of metal is all that stands between you and disaster. Gamay braced her foot against the transom. Hoping to placate the malevolent spirit inhabiting the machine, she smiled prettily, whispered "Please," and pulled the starter cord with all her might.

The motor responded with a soggy *pop-pop*, an asthmatic gasp, a wet sigh, then silence broken by Gamay's cry of pain as she fell back and scraped her knuckles on the hard metal seat. She unleashed a stream of blasphemies that turned the air blue as she called down the furies on dumb, stubborn machines everywhere. Professor Chi was in the bow, clutching an overhanging branch so the pram would not drift out of control with the lazy current while Gamay fussed and fumed over the outboard. Sweat dripped off her chin. With her mouth set in a square of anger, snakelike tendrils of dark red hair framing her features, she could have modeled for an ancient Greek sculpture of Medusa. What's worse, she *knew* how gorgonish she looked. Primping would have to wait.

Their crude attempt to sabotage their pursuers had apparently failed. They couldn't have known that setting the boats adrift wasn't enough, that one pram would catch on a root, that the other would drift back to shore. Now the first of those boats was coming around a bend, emerging from the morning mists, followed seconds later by the second. There were four men in each boat, including the two she had dubbed Pancho and Elvis. Pancho was leading the assault, standing in the bow of the lead boat brandishing a handgun. It was clear from his excited shouts that he had caught sight of the quarry.

The boats were drawing nearer. She willed her eyes back to the motor and discovered the choke had been pushed in. She pulled out the plastic knob and yanked the cord again. The motor stuttered then caught when she adjusted the throttle slightly. They pushed off into the river, aiming for the middle where it was deepest, although it was also where they'd be most vulnerable. She looked back again. The boat in the lead was breaking away from the other. Maybe it had more horsepower, or possibly its motor could be running smoother. It began to inch closer in an agonizing slow-motion pursuit. Before long it would be close enough for the riflemen kneeling in the bow to pick them off.

Smoked puffed from a gun muzzle. Pancho had fired off a couple of quick shots more for show than effect. Either his aim was off or they were out of range, because the bullets never came near. Then she lost sight of their pursuers around a bend. It was only a matter of time, minutes really, before they would be literally dead in the water.

Hack!

Gamay whipped around at the unexpected noise. Chi had found his trusty machete in the bottom of the pram. He was using it to cut down a large branch from the bowers arching low overhead. Another silvery blur of steel. Another branch fell into the river. Chi swung his machete like a madman. More branches fell in a great tangle to either side of the boat, then drifted together in a floating dam of interlocking branches. The improvised floating breastworks fetched up on a midriver sandbar.

The helmsman on the lead boat didn't see the intertwined boughs until it was too late. The pram came around the curve at full tilt. He tried to turn aside. Instead the boat slammed sideways into the blockage. A *chiclero* leaned out to push off and discovered Newton was right when he said every action had a reaction. His body was stretched between the boat and the branches. He splashed into the water. There were loud shouts and confusion as the second boat slammed into the first. A gun went off sending a wild shot into the forest. Startled birds darkened the sky in a chittering, chattering cloud.

"Yes!" Gamay yelped triumphantly. "Nice move, Professor."

From the nascent smile on the Mayan's otherwise poker face, it was clear that he was pleased with both the effect of his labors and the praise. "I knew my Harvard education would come in handy one day," he said modestly.

Gamay grinned and swung the tiller to avoid the shoaling along the sides of the river, but she was far from sanguine. It occurred to her after her momentary elation that she had absolutely no idea where they were going. Or whether they had enough gas to get them there. She checked the tank. Half full. Or half empty if she were thinking like a pessimist. Which might be the more prudent frame of mind in their precarious situation.

After a hurried conference, they decided to go flat out for a time to put as much distance as possible between the pram and their pursuers. Then they would rely on river drift.

"Not to put too fine a point on our predicament, Professor, but do you have any idea where this river goes?"

The professor shook his head. "This stream isn't even on the map. My guess is that we're headed south. Simply because, as you pointed out, there are few rivers in the north."

"They say that when you're lost, following a river will eventually bring you to civilization," Gamay said without conviction.

"I've heard that. Also that moss grows on the north side of trees. It's been my experience that moss grows *all* around a tree. You must have been a Girl Scout."

"I always had more fun playing with boys. Brownie was as far as I got. The only woodcraft I recall is how to cut a stick to toast marshmallows over an open fire."

"You never know when something like that will come in handy. Actually, I'm not too eager to encounter civilization. Especially if it comes in the form of more *chicleros.*"

"Is that a possibility?"

"The ones who are chasing us arrived after we were put in the cave. This means they came from not very far away. Possibly a base camp."

"Or they could have been on their way upriver when we ran into their buddies."

"Either way, I think it's best that we prepare for the worst, that we will be caught between two unfriendly groups."

Gamay's eyes lifted to the patches of blue sky that were beginning to show through holes in the vegetation. "Do you think that helicopter was working with this gang?"

"Possibly, although in my experience these thieves are very much low-tech. It doesn't take sophisticated equipment to dig up antiquities and transport them through the forest. As you saw from the ease by which we escaped the helicopter, the simpler the better."

"We had nature on our side before. We're coming more into the open and might want to think about what to do if it comes back." Gamay switched the motor off. "We'll drift for a while. Maybe we can think up a plan if we don't have this thing buzzing in our ears."

The boat ride was almost idyllic with the outboard silent. There were flashes of bright feathers in the impenetrable greenery that hemmed them in. The high bankings on either side of the river showed that it was an old waterway that had cut its

way through the limestone over a long period. As if mindful of
its advanced years it snaked through the woods at a slow but
steady pace, varying in width, the water bright billiard-table
green where the sun struck it, dark and spinachy in the shadows.
It didn't take long for nature to lose its charm once Gamay's
stomach started to rumble. She realized they hadn't eaten since
the day before and remarked wistfully that it was too bad they
hadn't made more Spam sandwiches. Chi said he would see what
he could do. He had her pull over to the banking and whacked
away at a berry bush with his machete. The berries were tart but
filling. The river was covered with a green algae. Once the scum
was brushed away the water was clear and refreshing.

Their idyll was ended by the whine of approaching outboard
motors.

The boats reappeared a couple of hundred yards behind
them. Again, one was in the lead. Gamay started the motor and
gave it full speed.

They were on a straight, comparatively wide stretch of river
that allowed for no chance at trickery. The chase boat inched
forward, and the distance between them slowly decreased. It
would be only minutes before they were in easy rifle range. The
boats grew closer together, cutting the distance by a third, then
half. Gamay was puzzled. The *chicleros* had not raised their
weapons. They looked like a bunch of guys on a river cruise.

Chi called out, *"Dr. Gamay!"*

Gamay turned and saw the professor in the bow, staring
straight ahead. She heard a low rumble in the distance.

"What is it?" she said.

"Rapids!"

The boat was beginning to pick up speed even though she
hadn't touched the throttle. The air was cooler than before and
damp with haze. Within moments the rumble changed to a roar,
and through the mists hanging over the river she saw white foam
and the sharp points of black shiny rocks. She thought of the
boat's flat bottom and had a vague image of a can opener ripping through thin aluminum. The river had narrowed, and the

tons of water squeezing into this natural funnel spout had essentially transformed a lazy stream into a raging sluiceway.

She looked back. The boats had stopped and were circling in the river. Their pursuers obviously knew about the rapids. *That's* why they hadn't shot at them. Why waste ammunition?

"We'll never make it past those rocks," Gamay yelled over the ear-splitting thunder of rushing water. "I'm going to steer for land. We'll have to make a run for it in the forest."

She pushed the tiller over, and the pram angled toward the shore. Thirty feet from the riverbank the motor coughed and conked out. Gamay tried to start it again, but with no success. She quickly twisted off the gas tank top. All that was left was vapors.

Professor Chi had grabbed a single oar and was trying to scull the boat. The current was too strong and jerked the oar from his hand. The boat's pace accelerated, and it began to spin around. Gamay watched helplessly as the pram was carried like a woodchip toward the toothlike rocks and the boiling white water.

It was Trout's idea to go back along the river. Moments before, the helicopter pilot had tapped the fuel gauge and the dial of his wristwatch, sign language saying they were running low and had to head back.

Trout's thoroughness as a scientist came from working as a youngster with his Uncle Henry, a skilled craftsman who built wooden boats for the local fishermen long after plastic hulls came into style. "Measure twice, cut once," Henry would say between puffs on his overripe pipe. In other words, double-check everything you do. Even years later Trout couldn't start a complicated computer task without hearing his uncle's voice whispering in his ear.

It was a natural reaction to suggest, through Morales, that they go back along the river, slowly this time, in case they had missed something on their first pass. They flew at less than one hundred fifty feet, cruising at a moderate speed, dipping lower when the river opened up. The JetRanger was highly maneuverable, having been designed as a light observation helicopter, and in its military incarnation saw duty as the Kiowa. Before long they came up on the rapids he had seen on the way out.

Trout looked down at the stretch of white water, then beyond it to the calm river just above the cataract, where he saw a curious sight. Two small boats lay close together back from the rapids, apparently sitting there while a third drifted downstream. Someone in the bow was paddling furiously, but the strong current drew the third boat on a path toward the rapids. Trout spotted the flash of dark red in the boat's stern.

Gamay!

There was no mistaking that hair, especially with the sun glinting off it in rusty highlights. There was also no doubt in his mind of what was about to happen. Within seconds the helpless boat would pick up speed and be sucked into the toothy maw and ground to pieces.

Trout yelled at Morales, "Tell the pilot to push them back with the helicopter's downdraft!"

Morales had been watching the unfolding disaster with fascination. Now he tried to relay Trout's statement to the pilot. The translation was beyond his grasp of English. He shot off a few words in Spanish, then shrugged in frustration. Trout pounded the pilot's shoulder. He pointed emphatically at the helpless boat, then twirled his forefinger in a circle and made a shoving gesture. To Trout's surprise the pilot caught on right away to his crude sign language message. He nodded vigorously, nosed the chopper into a glide, and cut speed to a walk until they had positioned themselves between the drifting boat and the crest of the rapids where the river narrowed. The hovering copter descended until the downdraft from the rotors whipped the surface like a giant electric egg beater and created a frothy dish-shaped depression.

Waves rippled out in great concentric circles. The first undulation hit the pram, slowed its speed, then stopped it completely and began to deflect the light boat toward the shore above the

rapids. The long whirling rotor was ill fitted for a surgical operation. Waves produced by the powerful air blast rocked the pram
and threatened to capsize it. Trout, who'd been leaning out the
window, could see what was happening. He yelled at the pilot
and jabbed his thumb upward.

The helicopter began to rise.

Too late. A wave caught the boat and flipped it over. The
craft's occupants disappeared beneath the surface. Trout waited
for their heads to appear. But he was distracted by a sharp rap-
ping noise and a shout from the pilot. He turned to see a spider's
web of shatter lines in the windshield, which had been clear when
he last looked. At the center of the lacy pattern was a hole. They
were being shot at! A bullet must have passed right between them
and hit the bulkhead inches above the head of Ruiz, who was
staring bug-eyed. The *chiclero* began to shout in rapid-fire Spanish
despite the warnings of Morales to shut his mouth. Morales
stopped wasting his breath, leaned over, and crashed his fist into
the man's jaw, knocking him unconscious. Then the Mexican
policeman drew his pistol and fired away at the boats.

Another sharp rap came against the fusclage, as if somebody
were banging the metal skin with a ball-peen hammer. Trout was
torn with indecision. He wanted to wait and see what happened
to Gamay, but he knew the chopper was a sitting duck. The pilot
took matters into his own hands. Cursing angrily in Spanish, he
set his jaw and pushed the throttle ahead. The helicopter surged
forward and homed in on the other boats like a cruise missile.
Trout could see the men below frozen in disbelief until they were
blasted out of the boats by the powerful rotor thrust. The downdraft tossed the empty prams as if they were balsa woodchips. At
the last second the pilot pulled the JetRanger up in a sharp
climb, then banked it around for a second sortie. The maneuver
was unnecessary. The overturned boats were sinking. Heads
bobbed in the water as the men struggled fruitlessly against the
current that was drawing them into the rapids.

Gamay's boat had already started its passage through the
foamy hell, and a chill went up Trout's spine as he thought of

what could have happened. He was still worried about Gamay. There was no sign of her or the other figure, whom he assumed was Professor Chi. The pilot made a couple of quick circles, then pointed to his fuel gauge again. Trout nodded. There was no place to put the chopper down. He reluctantly gave the pilot thumbs up, and they headed away from the river.

Trout was busy formulating plans in his mind and didn't notice how long they were airborne before he heard the engine cough. The chopper lost speed for an instant, then seemed to regain it, only to have the engine cough again. The pilot fiddled with his instruments, then put his finger on the fuel gauge. Empty. He leaned forward, scanning the unbroken jungle for a place to put down. The engine gagged like a cholera victim. The hacking stopped, then came a sputter, followed by the frightening sound of silence as the engine stopped completely and they began to drop out of the sky like a hailstone.

27

"DON'T MOVE, DR. GAMAY." CHI'S
voice, soft yet insistent, penetrated the gauzelike fog. Gamay
slowly lifted her gluey eyelids. She had the odd feeling that she
was swimming in a quivering sea of green Jell-O. The gelatinous
blobs became more sharply defined, the blurs resolving into
leaves and blades of grass. Senses clicked slowly into place. After
sight came taste, a bitterness in her mouth. Then touch, reaching up to the damp stickiness of her scalp, encountering a wet
pulpiness as if her brain were exposed. Her hand jerked back in
reflex.

Fingers dug into her shoulder. "Don't move again or you'll
die. Old Yellow Beard is watching us."

Chi's voice was calm but tense. Her arm froze in midair. She
was lying on her left side, Chi behind her, out of sight but close
enough so she could feel his breath in her ear.

"I don't see anyone," she said. Her tongue felt thick.

"Directly in front of you about fifteen feet. Quite beautiful
in a deadly way. Remember to be still."

Hardly daring to blink, Gamay scanned the grass, letting her
eyes come to rest on a discolored clump that materialized into a
pattern of black-edged triangles set against olive gray that
marked the slender coils of an extremely long snake. The arrow-
shaped head with the yellowish chin and throat was elevated.
She was close enough to see the vertical eye pupils, the heat-

sensing loreal pits that looked liked extra nostrils, even the long black tongue flicking in and out.

"What is it?" she said, scientific curiosity overriding her fear.

"*Barba amarilla.* A big one from the looks of it. What some people call *fer-de-lance.*"

Fer-de-lance! Gamay knew enough about snakes to realize she was face-to-face with a killer. Goosebumps rose on her skin. She felt extremely exposed.

"What should we do?" she whispered, watching the flat head moving back and forth as if in time to unheard music.

"Don't panic. It should move soon to get out of the direct sunlight, probably into that patch of shade. If it comes this way, stay where you are and I'll distract it."

Gamay was leaning on her elbow, a position that had grown uncomfortably painful, and she wondered how long she could remain that way. She wanted the snake to move, but on the other hand, she didn't want it heading in her direction.

The snake made up its mind a few minutes later and began to uncoil to its full length. As Chi said, it was a big one, as long as a man was tall. It slithered silently through the grass to the shade cast by a small tree and took up residence next to Chi's faithful machete, which was leaning against the trunk.

"You can move now. It's sleeping. Sit up slowly." She turned to see Chi on his knees. He put down the boulder he was clutching.

"How long was it there?"

"About a half hour before you woke up. Usually snakes will retreat if you give them a chance, but you can never tell with Yellow Beard, especially if you disturb its sleep. It can be quite aggressive. He can have my machete if he wants it. How do you feel?"

"Okay, except that someone's been using my head as a football. What's this mush where my hair used to be?"

"I made a poultice of medicinal leaves. The pharmacy was closed."

"How long have we been here?" she said, rubbing the arm she'd been leaning on to get the circulation back.

"A few hours. You slept off and on. The bitter taste you have in your mouth is a root-based restorative. You got a nasty bump on a rock when the boat went over."

Vague memories of white roaring water came flooding back. "The rapids! Why aren't we dead?"

Chi pointed to the sky. "You don't remember?"

The *helicopter.* The fragments of memories were jumbled like a boxful of jigsaw puzzle parts. She and the professor were in the pram out of gas. The strong current was pulling them toward the rocks. Then the roar of the deadly water was drowned out by a clatter. The red-and-white chopper they had sighted earlier circled above the river.

Gamay remembered thinking that they were dead, with the armed *chicleros* behind them, the boiling rapids ahead, and the helicopter above. Then the aircraft swooped down like a Valkyrie and hovered just off the water between the pram and the rapids. Downdraft from the spinning rotors chewed up the river in a big circle and created waves that kicked the pram out of the current and sent it in toward shore. But the blast from the chopper dangerously rocked the light aluminum craft. With the grassy shoreline only a few yards away the pram pitched over.

Gamay was catapulted out of the boat like a projectile from a siege machine. Then *bang!* Her head hit something hard. Her vision went squirrely, and her teeth clunked together. A bolt of white lightning. Then blissful darkness.

"The helicopter saved us," she said.

"Apparently so. You would have been fine if you hadn't tried to split a rock with your head. It was only a glancing blow, but enough to knock you out. I dragged you onto shore, then through the bushes to this place. I gathered the roots and leaves to make the poultice. You slept fitfully through the night and may have had some strange dreams. The tonic I gave you is something of a hallucinogen."

Gamay recalled an odd dream. Paul was high above her, calling out her name, the words appearing in a cartoon dialogue balloon, before he disappeared into a vapory cloud.

"Thanks for everything," Gamay said, wondering how the diminutive middle-aged professor managed to haul her from the water and into the forest. "What about the men who were after us?"

The professor shook his head. "I didn't pay much attention to them with all the confusion. I had my hands full getting us to safety. I think I heard some shots. But it's been quiet ever since. Maybe they think we're dead."

"What do we do now?"

"I was pondering the same question when our scaly friend arrived. It depends on how long his nap is. I'd like to retrieve my machete. In this country it could mean the difference between life and death. You rest for a while. If Yellow Beard doesn't wake up we'll discuss another plan. I came across a path, probably what the *chicleros* used to get around the rapids, that we can explore later. In the meantime, we might want to move farther away in case he's grumpy when he awakens."

That was fine with Gamay. With Chi's help she stood. Her legs were shaky, and she felt like a newborn foal. She looked around and saw that they were in a small, sun-dappled clearing protected by trees and bushes. They moved to the far side of the clearing, where Chi removed her poultice and pronounced her bumps and bruises practically gone. He said he would pluck some berries to fill their stomachs while they waited for the snake to finish his power nap. Still tired, Gamay lay back on the grass and shut her eyes. She came awake a moment later. A branch had snapped. Chi would never be so noisy.

She sat up and looked around. The professor stood at the edge of the clearing with a berry-laden branch in his hand. Behind him was the *chiclero* leader Gamay had named Pancho. He was a far cry from the figure who'd ordered them imprisoned in a cave. The slicked-down hair looked like an osprey nest, and his white clothes were dirty and torn. His big pale belly showed through the rips and tears. The sneering smile was gone, too, replaced by a mask of rage. The pistol in his hand was the same one he'd waved around on their first encounter, though, and it was pointed at the back of the professor's head.

The man put down the pack he'd been carrying and snarled at Chi in Spanish. The professor moved next to Gamay. They stood there side by side. The gun barrel shifted from Chi to Gamay, then back again.

"He wants me to tell you that he is going to kill us to avenge his men," Chi said. "First me, then he will have his way with you on my body."

"What is it with these guys?" Gamay snapped. "No offense, Professor, but a lot of your countrymen seem to have their brains between their legs."

The start of a smile started on Pancho's face. Gamay gave the big man a coquettish grin, as if the proposition appealed to her. Maybe she could buy time for the professor and get close enough to this goon to do serious damage to his libido. Chi was a jump ahead of her. He turned his head slightly, stared at the machete against the tree, and leaned his body forward slightly as if he were going to make a dash for it. Gamay knew Chi well enough to see the movement was uncharacteristically clumsy, as if he *wanted* to catch Pancho's attention.

The ploy worked. Pancho followed Chi's gaze to the long knife leaning against the tree, and his mouth widened into its toothy smile. Still keeping his eyes and gun on the professor, he sidestepped across the clearing and leaned over to pick up the machete.

The ground exploded in a blur of black triangles.

Alerted by the heavy footfall, the snake was in striking position when the man reached for the machete. It sank its long fangs into his neck then struck swiftly again, emptying the rest of its venom sac into his arm.

The gun barrel came around, and the stricken man shot the snake several times, turning it into a bloody red-and-green mass. Then he touched the twin puncture wounds next to his carotid artery. His face turned bone-white, his eyes widened in horror, and his mouth opened in a silent scream. He stared, terrified, at Chi and Gamay, then staggered into the bushes.

Chi stepped forward, careful to avoid the fangs that were biting at the air in the snake's death throes, and followed the *chiclero*'s trail. Moments later Gamay heard another shot. When Chi reappeared, the gun in his hand was smoking. He saw the expression of revulsion on her face. Tucking the pistol into his pants, he came over and took Gamay's hand. The stony cast to his features had disappeared, and his eyes had that kind, grandfatherly expression.

"The *chiclero* killed himself," he explained patiently. "He knew death from the *barba*'s bite is very painful. The venom destroys the red blood cells and breaks down vessels. There is bleeding from the mouth and throat, painful swelling, vomiting, and spasms as the body goes into shock. Even with the neck bite, it could have been an hour or two. Remember, before you feel too sorry for him, he wanted us to die in the cave and later in the river."

Gamay shook her head numbly. Chi was right. The *chiclero*'s death was unfortunate but of his own doing. What an extraordinary man the professor was! How the Spaniards ever conquered the Maya was a mystery to her. Her survival reflexes kicked into gear. "We should move," she said, glancing around. "There may be others who heard the shots."

Chi picked up his machete and the dead man's pack. "The river is our only chance. Even if we knew where we were, it would be risky to try a trek over land." He glanced at the bloodied body of the snake. "As you saw, there are creatures in the forest far more deadly than *chicleros.*"

"You lead, I'll follow," Gamay agreed with no argument. They set off through the thick forest, Chi maneuvering with his internal compass until they came to a path about a yard wide that was so beaten down that the white limestone was exposed.

"This is the portage trail I told you about."

"Won't we risk running into someone if we use it?"

"I'm not so sure. Remember what the big man said about avenging his men? I'll play scout. Stay back, and if I signal, get off the trail as quickly as you can."

They set off through the forest, the trail running roughly parallel to the river which sparkled through the trees. Gamay walked behind the professor. Their progress was uneventful. The only sign of life other than the raucous calls of the birds was a tree sloth that looked down with lazy eyes from an overhanging bough.

Chi stopped, signaled her with a wave to come forward, then disappeared around a curve in the trail. When she caught up the professor was standing on a small sandy beach. Three prams identical to the one they had lost were drawn up under a sapling and palm leaf structure that would have kept them hidden from anyone on the river or in the air. In contrast to her last view of the river at its angriest, the surface was back to its calm brownish-green self.

"It looks as if they kept boats on both sides of the rapids," Chi observed. "They could carry the goods along the path around the rough water."

Gamay was only half listening. She had walked back from the river to examine the cold coals of a campfire and noticed a platform built up on stilts. A flat-roofed structure like a child's tree house had been constructed on the platform. She opened the door, which was latched but not locked, and peered inside. She saw several gasoline tanks and a large metal cooler. She pushed back the lid.

"Professor Chi," she called out. "I've found something important."

Chi came trotting over, and when he saw the blue can she was holding, the widest grin she had ever seen crossed his face.

"Spam," he whispered reverently.

There was more than Spam in the cooler chest. There were canned vegetables and juices, bottled water, and tortillas sealed in plastic boxes. Sardines and canned corned beef for variety. The primitive shed had flashlights and tools. The waterproof matches were a real treat, as was a portable camp stove. Soap, too. Each taking a different section of riverside, they washed their bodies and clothes, which dried quickly in the hot sun.

After their bath and a refreshing meal of improvised hash and eggs, Chi explored the area while Gamay consolidated their food and supplies. It was eerily quiet, but they decided not to stay long. They loaded the boat and sabotaged the others, sinking them under rocks then hiding the outboards in the woods after testing to see which motor ran best. Then they got in the boat and pushed out into the river, keeping the motor at low speed, above a quiet idle, using just enough power to stay ahead of the current.

They had gone only less than a mile when the river made a sharp dogleg to the right. Caught in a pocket where the riverbed curved, along with weeds and driftwood, were two overturned aluminum prams whose hulls were dented and ripped open. Scattered among them were the stinking bodies of men, bloating in the broiling sun.

Chi muttered a prayer in Spanish.

"My guess is that this is where we would be if we'd gone through the rapids," Gamay said, putting her hand over her nose.

"They were nowhere near the rapids when we last saw them."

"That's what I thought," she said with a shake of her head. "Something must have happened while we were dealing with an overturned pram."

Conrad's *Heart of Darkness* came to her, the scene where Kurtz, the civilized man turned savage, whispers on his deathbed, "The horror . . . the horror . . ."

With Kurtz's words echoing in her head, Gamay pointed the pram downriver and hiked up the throttle. Gamay wanted to put miles between them and this place of death before night fell, even though she had no idea whether new horrors lay ahead.

28

WHEN PERLMUTTER CALLED AND
asked if they could get together for brunch instead of dinner,
Austin was pleased on two counts. The portly archivist's willing-
ness to settle for a mere lunch at Kinkead's, a popular Washington dining spot on Pennsylvania Avenue, meant Perlmutter's
research had hit pay dirt. And a lunch bill would take a smaller
bite out of Austin's wallet than a six-course dinner. Or so Austin
thought until Perlmutter selected a 1982 Bordeaux and began
picking items off the menu as if he were ordering dim sum in a
Chinese restaurant.

"I wouldn't want you to think you're taking advantage of me
by only having to buy lunch rather than dinner," Perlmutter
said, explaining his extravagance.

"Of *course* not," Austin replied, wondering how he would
sneak the bill for Perlmutter's binge past the keen-eyed NUMA
expense account auditors. He breathed an inward sigh of relief
when Perlmutter put the menu aside.

"Very good. Well, after we chatted on the phone I called my
friend Juan Ortega in Seville. Don Ortega is one of the leading
experts on Columbus, and since you seemed in something of a
hurry I thought he might provide a shortcut through the mass of
information available."

"I appreciate that, Julien. I've read Ortega's books and found
them insightful. Was he of help?"

"Yes and no," Perlmutter said. "He answered some questions and raised others." Perlmutter handed Austin the documents Ortega had faxed from Spain. "Read these at your leisure. In the interests of time I'll recap my conversation with Don Ortega and summarize what you'll find herein."

Perlmutter crystallized his findings, stopping only to nibble now and then at a roll.

"A *fifth* voyage of discovery," Austin mused. "That would certainly shake up the historians and call for an update of the history books. What's your professional opinion? Was the letter a fraud?"

Perlmutter cocked his head in thought, laying a forefinger along his fleshy cheek. "I read it several times, and I still can't give you a definitive answer, Kurt. If it *is* a forgery, it is a damned clever one. I compared it to other, authenticated Columbus documents and Las Casas writings. The style, the syntax, the penmanship are consistent."

"And as you pointed out, why would anybody go through the trouble to steal a phony document?"

"Why indeed?"

The waiter brought the wine to their table. Perlmutter held the glass to the light, swished its contents around, inhaled the bouquet, and finally took a sip. He closed his eyes. "Superb, as I knew it would be," he said with a beatific smile. "Truly a legendary year."

Austin tried the wine. "I'll have to agree with you, Julien." He put the glass aside and said, "You mentioned a reference in the letter about Columbus being contrite over the 'death of the five.' What do you make of that?"

The blue eyes danced with excitement. "I'm surprised you didn't catch that right away. I dug through my library and came across a strange story from a source named Garcilaso de la Vega. It may shed light. He claimed that seven years before Columbus set sail on his historic first voyage, a Spanish ship was caught in a storm off the Canaries and came ashore on a Caribbean island. Of the seventeen-man crew, five survived. They repaired the ship and returned to Spain. Columbus heard of their adventure and invited them to his house, where they were entertained lavishly. As the festivities wore on they naturally poured out the details of their travails."

"Not surprising. Sailors like to swap sea stories even without a few glasses of vino to loosen their tongues."

Perlmutter leaned his great bulk forward. "It was much more than a friendly gam. This was undoubtedly a well-planned intelligence-gathering operation. Those simple sailors had no idea they possessed knowledge of incalculable value. Columbus was trying to organize an expedition and find the funding for it. Here were eyewitness accounts and navigational information that could open the door to vast riches. The crew could provide him with details of current, wind direction, compass readings, latitude, the number of days they sailed. Maybe they had seen the natives wearing gold ornaments. Think of what that meant. Their experience not only proved one could sail to China or India, which is what Columbus thought he'd be doing. It showed how to get there and back! Columbus intended to claim new lands for Spain. He was convinced he'd find gold and at the very least meet the Great Khan and open up a lucrative monopoly trade for spices and other valuable goods. He was well aware of Marco Polo's fame and fortune and figured he could do much better."

"No different from the industrial espionage that goes on today," Austin commented. "Instead of bribes, listening devices, and prostitutes to gather information on corporate rivals, Columbus pumped his sources with food and drink."

"He may have pumped them with more than food and drink."

Austin raised an eyebrow.

"All five men died after dinner," Perlmutter said.

"Overindulgence?"

"I've been at a few meals that nearly killed me, but de la Vega had his own ideas. He implied that the men had been poisoned. He couldn't come right out and say so. Columbus had powerful connections. Consider this, however. It is a historical fact that Columbus had a map of the Indies on his first voyage." He took a sip of wine and paused for dramatic effect. "Is it possible his map was based on what he learned from those unfortunate sailors?"

"Possible. But from what the letter says, Columbus disavowed their deaths."

"Correct. He blamed it on this so-called brotherhood. *Los Hermanos.*"

"Didn't Columbus have a brother?"

"Yes, his name was Bartolomé. But Columbus used the word in the plural. *Brothers.*"

"Okay, suppose you're right. Let's give Chris the benefit of the doubt. He invites these guys to his house to see what information he can get out of them. *Los Hermanos* take the extra precaution of seeing that they will tell nobody else what they've seen. Columbus may be a hustler, but he's no killer. The incident haunts him."

"A plausible scenario."

"Do you have any idea what this brotherhood was, Julien?"

"Not a clue. I'll return to my books after lunch. Speaking of which . . . ah, the Thai fish soup." Perlmutter had spotted the first of many dishes making its way to their table.

"While you're doing that I'll ask Yaeger to see if he has anything on them in his computer files."

"Splendid," Perlmutter said. "Now I have a question. You have a practical rather than a historical knowledge of the sea, as I do. What are your thoughts on this talking stone Columbus mentioned, this *torleta* of the ancients that was described in the letter?"

"Early navigational techniques have always fascinated me," Austin said. "I consider their development to be a huge intellectual leap for mankind. Our ancestors had to bring abstract concepts such as time, space, and distance to bear on the problem of getting from one place to another. I love the idea of punching a button and having a signal bounced off a satellite tell me exactly where I'm standing anywhere on the globe. But I think we rely too much on electronic gadgets. They can break. And we're less inclined to understand the natural order of things, the movement of the stars and sun, the vagaries of the sea."

"Well, then, let's put those electronic gadgets aside," Perlmutter said. "Stand in the shoes of Columbus. How would you go about using your *torleta?*"

Austin thought about the question for a moment. "Let's back up to his earlier voyage. I'm stranded on an island where I'm directed to some kind of stone or tablet with strange inscriptions. The locals tell me it's the key to a great treasure. I take it back to Spain, but nobody can figure out what it is. Only that it is very old. I look at it from a mariner's point of view. The markings are similar in some respects to the kind of plotting board I've used all my sailing life. It's too hefty to haul around, so I do the next best thing. I have charts made based on the inscriptions and set sail. Only problem is, I haven't got it quite right. There's a gap in my knowledge."

"What sort of gap, Kurt?"

Austin pondered the question. "It's hard to know without an idea of what the *torleta* actually looks like, but I'll describe a hypothetical situation. Suppose I'm a sailor from Columbus's time and somebody gives me a NOAA chart. The geographical depictions would help me get around, but the lines with the long-range navigation coordinates wouldn't make sense to me. I'd know nothing of electronic signals sent out by shore stations or receivers that could translate the signals into pinpoint locations. Once I was on the water out of sight of land, I'd have to go back to traditional methods."

"A most lucid analysis. So what you're saying is that once Columbus was at sea, he found that the *torleta* of the ancients was only of limited assistance."

"That's my guess. Ortega's books say Columbus didn't have much faith in the navigational instruments of his day, or maybe he simply wasn't competent in their use. He was a dead reckoning sailor of the old school. It served him fine on his first voyage.

He knew he needed to be precise on this final trip, so he hired someone who could use navigational instruments."

"Interesting, in view of the last passage in the letter, which is written by the *Niña*'s assistant pilot."

"There you go," Austin said. "It's no different from hiring a specialist to do a job today. Now it's my turn to bat a question back to you. What do you suppose happened to the stone?"

"I called Don Ortega again and asked him to chase it down. His guess is that it was part of the estate Luis Columbus squandered to raise money to support his degenerate lifestyle. Ortega will contact museums and universities in Spain, and if he's not successful he will expand his circle of inquiry to surrounding countries."

Austin was thinking about Columbus the sailor, how he went back to the *Niña*, the doughty little vessel that had served him so well on previous journeys. Maybe a modern-day *Niña* could help carry them to a solution of the mystery.

"The tablet originated on this side of the Atlantic," Austin observed. "After brunch I'll call my archaeologist friend Dr. Kirov and ask if she has ever heard about an artifact like it." He chuckled. "Odd, isn't it? We're looking for clues to contemporary murders in events that possibly happened centuries ago."

"Not so unusual. In my experience the past and present are often the same. Wars. Famine. Tidal waves. Revolutions. Plague. Genocide. These happen over and over again. Only the faces change. But enough of such morbid considerations. Let us turn to happier pursuits," Perlmutter said, beaming. "I see another course is on its way."

29

WHILE AUSTIN ENJOYED HIS EXPEN-
sive gourmet lunch, Joe Zavala was sixteen hundred miles away
munching a honey-glazed doughnut at a coffee shop on the
Paseo del Rio, or Riverwalk, the picturesque tourist district on
the banks of the San Antonio River. Zavala checked his watch,
gulped down the last of his coffee, and headed away from the
river to the business district, where he entered the lobby of a tall
office building.

After wrapping up the strategy session, Zavala had packed an
overnight bag and flown to Texas, hitching a ride on an Air Force
flight to Lackland Air Base. From the base he caught a taxi to a
downtown hotel. Yaeger could do wonders with his computer
babies, but even he admitted Time-Quest was a tough nut to
crack. Sometimes a human eye and brain, with their capacity to
sense and analyze nuance, were far more efficient than even the
most sophisticated machine.

Zavala looked up Time-Quest on the lengthy directory of
occupants. Moments later he stepped from the elevator into a
spacious lobby whose walls were covered with oversized sepia
photographs of the archaeological wonders of the world. Directly
in front of a picture of the Great Pyramid was a black enamel
and steel desk that seemed out of time and place in contrast to
the pictorial antiquities. Even more so was the brunette in her
late twenties who sat behind the desk.

Zavala introduced himself, handing the receptionist a business card printed that morning at Kinko's.

"Oh, yes, Mr. Zavala the travel writer," she said. "You called yesterday." She consulted her daybook, punched a button on her phone, and murmured a message. "Ms. Harper will see you in a moment. You're very lucky to get an appointment on such short notice. It would have been impossible if she hadn't had an unexpected cancellation."

"I really appreciate this. As I explained, I would have called earlier, but this was a last-minute thing. I'm out here doing a piece on San Antonio night life and thought I could double it up with another travel piece."

She gave him a friendly smile. "Stop by after you talk to Ms. Harper and I may be able to suggest some hot spots."

The receptionist was young and darkly attractive, and Zavala would have been surprised if she *didn't* know the city's fun places.

"Thank you very much," he said in his most charming manner. "That would be a great help."

The public affairs director of Time-Quest was a handsome and smartly dressed woman in her forties. Phyllis Harper emerged from a corridor and shook Zavala's hand with a firm grip. Then she guided him along thickly carpeted corridors to an office with big windows that offered a panoramic view of the sprawling city and its centerpiece Tower of the Americas. They sat informally on either side of a coffee table.

"Thank you very much for your interest in Time-Quest, Mr. Zavala. I must apologize for only being able to give you a few minutes. Melody probably told you that I had a brief appointment slotted."

"Yes, she did. I appreciate the fact that you were able to give me any time at all. You must be very busy."

"I've got fifteen minutes before my meeting with the executive director." She rolled her eyes. "He's a stickler for promptness. In the interests of brevity, perhaps I can simply rattle on for ten minutes and allow five minutes if you have any questions. The press kit on the organization is quite informative."

From his jacket pocket Zavala extracted a Sony mini-tape recorder he bought at a discount outlet and a notepad picked up that morning in a drugstore.

"Fair enough. Rattle away."

She gave him a dazzling smile that reminded him how a mature woman with class could often be so much sexier than a young unformed beauty like Melody, the receptionist.

"Time-Quest is a nonprofit corporation. We have a number of goals. We wish to promote an understanding of the present and prepare for the future by studying the past. We are educative, in that we support learning about our world, particularly through our in-school programs for the young and our field work. We give the ordinary person a chance at an unusual vacation adventure. Many of our volunteers are retired people, so for them we are the fulfillment of life's dream."

She paused for breath and went on. "In addition we support many archaeological, cultural, and anthropological expeditions. We are known to be a soft touch," she said with her pleasant smile. "Universities are always calling us for support. Usually we are glad to give it. We use money paid by our volunteers, so many of these expeditions are self-sustaining. We provide experts or help pay for them. We have sponsored expeditions to every corner of the globe. In return we ask mainly that we be informed of special discoveries before anyone else. Most people consider it a small demand for what they get. Any questions?"

"How did the organization start?"

She pointed to the ceiling above her head.

"We are a nonprofit subsidiary of the company that occupies the six floors immediately above us."

"Which is . . . ?"

"Halcon Industries."

Halcon. The Spanish word for "falcon" or "bird of prey." He shook his head. "Don't know it."

"It's an umbrella corporation with many divisions. We're one of them. Most of its revenue comes from a diversified portfolio that includes mining, mainly, but also shipping, livestock, oil, and mohair."

"That certainly *is* diversified. Is the company publicly traded?"

"No. It is wholly owned by Mr. Halcon."

"Quite a leap from digging mines to digging in old tombs," Zavala said.

"It is rather an odd juxtaposition, but not really when you think of it. The Ford Foundation has funded esoteric projects that have nothing to do with manufacturing cars. Mr. Halcon is an amateur archaeologist from what I'm told. He would have liked to have been a scholar, but he was much better as an industrialist."

He nodded. "Halcon sounds like an interesting person. Would there ever be a chance of interviewing him, perhaps if I gave you advance notice?"

"You'd have a better chance of interviewing Henry Ford." The dazzling smile again. "I don't mean to be flip, but Mr. Halcon is a very private man."

"I understand."

She looked at her watch. "I'm afraid I have to go." She slid a thick folder across the desk. "This is our press kit. Give it a read, and if you have any more questions, please call me. I'd be glad to put you in touch with volunteers who could give you a first-hand account of their experience."

"That would be very helpful. Maybe I could sign up for an expedition myself. They're not dangerous, are they?"

She gave him an odd look. "We pride ourselves on Time-Quest's safety record. Even in the remotest locations safety is our most important consideration. You remember, I said many retired people participate in our program." She paused. "Those are the expeditions we organize. The ones we support with partial funding are on their own. But overall our record is very good. You're safer on one of our adventures than you are crossing the street in San Antonio."

"I'll remember that," Zavala said, wondering if Ms. Harper were truly aware of all that went on in her organization.

"There's a calendar of events for the upcoming year in that

kit. If something interests you, let me know, and I'll see what can be arranged."

She ushered him back to the lobby, shook hands, and disappeared down a corridor.

Melody smiled. "How was your interview?"

"Short and sweet." He looked after the retreating figure. "She reminds me of that old television commercial where the guy talked like a machine gun."

Melody cocked her head coquettishly. "Well, there are always the night spots."

"Thanks for the reminder. I'm looking for the really out-of-the-way places where the younger, inside group goes. If you don't have other plans, maybe I can buy you lunch and we can talk about the night life in this town."

"There's a great restaurant not far from here. Eclectic and very popular. I could meet you there around noon."

Zavala scribbled the directions and took the elevator down to the lobby. He went over to the directory again and listed the subdivisions of Halcon Industries in his notebook. There were eight in all. Mainly concentrated around mining and shipping, as the PR director had explained. He took the elevator up past Time-Quest and stepped out into a big lobby, with a receptionist and mural-sized wall pictures of ore carriers. Halcon Shipping. He told the receptionist he must have the wrong floor and got back in the elevator.

He repeated his routine at every other company under the Halcon aegis. The offices were all pretty much the same, except for the murals. The receptionists were all young and attractive. He pressed the button for the very highest office in the Halcon tier, but the elevator sped right by it. When he got out he was in the hushed precincts of a law firm.

"Excuse me," he asked the secretary, who was plain and efficient-looking. "I just pressed the button for the floor below and ended up here."

"That happens all the time. The suites below us are for Halcon executives. You need a special code to make the elevator go there."

"Well, if I ever need legal advice, I'll know where to come."

He returned to the lobby, hoping he hadn't stirred the suspicions of security staff in his on-again, off-again elevator rides. After the destruction of the federal office building in Oklahoma City, it would not be wise to be seen casing an office building. He went down to ground level, caught a cab, then another to make sure he wasn't being followed, and hung around a bookstore until it was time to meet Melody.

The restaurant was called the Bomb Shelter, and it was decorated with a 1950s theme. They sat at a booth made with seats from a 1957 DeSoto convertible. Melody was a Texas girl, born and bred in Fort Worth, and had been with Time-Quest about a year.

Over lunch, Zavala said, "Ms. Harper was telling me about the big guy, Mr. Halcon. Have you ever met him?"

"Not in person, but I see him every day. I stay at the office an extra hour after everybody else leaves so I can do some studying. I'm taking law courses." She smiled. "I don't intend to be a receptionist forever. Mr. Halcon stays late, too, and we leave the same time. He comes down in his private elevator, and a limo picks him up."

She'd heard Halcon lived outside the city, but beyond that Melody didn't know much about him.

"What does he look like?" Zavala said.

"Dark, thin, rich. Handsome in a creepy sort of way." She laughed. "Maybe it's just the light down there in the garage."

Melody was intelligent and witty, and Zavala felt like a cad when he took her number to set up a tour of night spots. He made a note to smooth things out with a call when he got back to Washington. After lunch he found a library and used the Internet to read about Halcon Industries holdings. His findings pretty much conformed to the brief description Ms. Harper had given him. Then he went to an auto rental place where he rented an ordinary-looking mid-sized car and picked up a tourist brochure on the Alamo. Might as well absorb some Texas history while he waited for his rendezvous with the mysterious Mr. Halcon.

30

NINA KIROV SMILED AS SHE PLACED the telephone in its cradle, thinking how interesting her life had become since she had met Kurt Austin. When the platinum-haired man with the linebacker's physique and remarkable eyes wasn't plucking her from the Moroccan sea or running sting operations in Arizona, he was popping up with the strangest requests. Like this one. See what she could find out about an artifact, *probably* made of stone, *perhaps* removed by Columbus from Jamaica on one of his expeditions, which *may* have had a navigational function and *might* still be in Spain.

Wait'll Doc hears this, she thought as she dialed the phone. Doc was Dr. J. Linus Orville, a Harvard professor with more letters behind his name than a can of alphabet soup. Orville made his lair behind the ivy-covered walls at Harvard's Peabody Museum. He had gained international repute as an ethnologist specializing in Mesoamerican culture. Among Cambridge academics he was recognized for his brilliance and his reputation as something of a nutty professor.

Zooming around Harvard Square on a chopped antique Harley-Davidson was not something done by most tenured professors. A few years earlier he gained more widespread notoriety by hypnotizing UFO abductees and announcing publicly that he believed they had been kidnapped by aliens. His telephone number had gone into the card file of every freak beat newspaper reporter in the city. Whenever reporters needed a quick quip on any subject in the universe, particularly the weird, they could rely on good old Doc the Harvard professor.

He carefully kept his more esoteric interests separated from his academic specialty. You would never find him claiming that Aztec temples were built by refugees from the lost continents of Atlantis and Mu. The hierarchy at Harvard would tolerate his oddities—every university has its resident fruitcake—but in his own field Doc's credentials had to remain without blemish. Some who had noticed that the gleam in Orville's eye was one not of madness but of intense amusement suggested Doc's eccentricities were well calculated so that he would meet women and be invited to all the right parties.

Doc had forsaken his UFO phase by the time Nina met him at one such gathering. Orville spied her across the room, brushed aside the attractive female grad student he was entertaining, and made a beeline in Nina's direction. She had never met him before but recognized his mop of long red hair, the style referred to by his students as "retro Einstein." Within minutes he was going on about his latest passion: past lives.

Nina listened attentively, then asked, "Why has everyone who has lived a past life been a king or a queen or other royal figure when most people were probably flea-infested farmers trying to scratch a life out of the mud?"

"Aha," he said, eyes practically glowing with glee. "A dangerous woman. A *thinker.* The answer is very simple. These people *choose* whose body they will inhabit in their new life. What do you think of that?"

"I think it's a lot of hooey, and I think I need a refill on my wine. Would you be so kind? I prefer red."

"Charmed," he said, and set off to the bar like an obedient puppy, returning with a full glass and a plateful of shrimp and caviar.

"Let's not talk about past lives," he said. "I only do that to meet fascinating women."

"You *do?*" Nina said, with genuine shock at his frankness.

"And to get invited to parties. It works. Here I am, and here *we* are."

"I'm disappointed. Everyone told me you were pixilated."

"I don't even know how to spell that," he said with a sigh. "You know, we are such a dull gray stuffy bunch, we professors. We take ourselves far too seriously, harrumphing about as if we were truly wise men and not just overeducated nerds. What's wrong with being a little colorful to make oneself stand out from the crowd? There's the added advantage of being shunned by those stodgy old fussbudgets."

"The UFO abductees. That was all a sham?"

"Heavens no. I truly believe *they* believe they were kidnapped. Some of my colleagues do, too; they're just jealous because they weren't. But let's talk about you. I've heard good things about your work."

And talk they did. Behind the nutty professor's mad facade lurked an interesting and interested person. They did not become romantically involved, as he would have liked. Even better, they were friends and colleagues who respected each other.

"Orville," came the voice on the phone. Doc never said hello.

"Hi, Doc. It's Nina." He hated what he called banalities, so she cut right to the chase. "I need your help with an odd request."

"Odd is my middle name. What can I do for you?"

Nina relayed Austin's query.

"You know, that sounds vaguely familiar."

"You're not joking, Doc."

"No-no-no-no. It was something in my Fortean file." Orville considered himself a modern-day version of Charles Fort, the nineteenth-century journalist who collected stories about odd happenings such as red snow, unexplained lights, or frogs falling from the sky.

"Why does that not surprise me?" Nina said.

"I'm always reorganizing the file. You never can tell when someone will call and ask a crazy question." He hung up; Orville was not known for saying good-bye, either.

Nina shrugged and went back to her work. Before long the fax hummed and a single sheet slid out. At the top was a hand-scrawled note: "Ask and ye shall receive. Love, Doc." It was a copy of a newspaper clip from the *Boston Globe* dated March 1956:

MYSTERY ITALIAN ARTIFACT
ON ITS WAY TO AMERICA

Genoa, Italy (AP)—A mysterious stone tablet unearthed in a dusty museum basement may soon yield its ancient secrets.

The massive inscribed stela, carved with life-sized figures and strange writing, was discovered in the Museo Archeologico, Florence, in March of this year.

Preparations are being made to ship it to the United States where it will be examined by experts.

The museum was planning an exhibition entitled "Treasures from the Basement," to bring to light items from its collection that had languished in storage for decades.

The stone artifact is in the shape of a rectangular slab, giving rise to speculation that it might have been part of a wall. It is more than six feet tall, four feet wide, and a foot thick.

What have puzzled scholars who have seen it and stirred up controversy in the scientific community are the carvings on one side.

Some maintain that the figures and writing are without a doubt of Central American, probably Mayan, origin.

"This is not a great mystery," says Dr. Stephano Gallo, head curator at the museum. "Even if it is Mayan it could have been brought back from the Americas during the Spanish Conquest."

Why they transported the stone across the ocean is another question. "The Spanish were primarily interested in gold and slaves, not archaeology. So someone must have seen some value in this artifact to go to the trouble of moving it. It is not like some miniature statue a soldier of Cortez might have picked up as a souvenir."

Efforts to learn where the artifact came from have met with limited success. The museum catalog indicates that the slab was donated by trustees for the Alberti estate. The Alberti family can trace its maternal lineage to the Spanish court during the time of Ferdinand and Isabella.

A spokesman for the estate says the family has no information available, unlike other items in the collection. The Alberti family was originally from Genoa and purchased many Christopher Columbus papers and memorabilia from Luis Columbus, grandson of the explorer.

Historians who have scoured records of the four Columbus voyages can find no mention of the artifact.

The stone will soon be on an ocean voyage of its own. It will be shipped to the Peabody Museum at Harvard University, Cambridge, Mass., for study by Central American experts. This time it will be traveling in style aboard the luxury Italian liner *Andrea Doria.*

Because of its size and weight, it will be shipped in an armored truck that is carrying other valuable items to America.

The article was illustrated with a photo of the slab taken at a distance to include the whole tablet in the frame. An unidentified man stood awkwardly next to the artifact, where he was dwarfed by its mass. The photographer must have grabbed the nearest body to pose beside the object and give it scale. The newspaper was printed back in the days of letterpress, and the photo reproduction wasn't very sharp. Nina could make out faint symbols, glyphs, and figures carved into the stone's surface. She examined the picture using a magnifying glass. No use. The enlarged dot reproduction was even fuzzier than the original. She called Doc.

"Well, what do you think?" he said.

"The important thing is what you think. *You're* the expert in this area."

"Well, you're right, of course." Orville's modesty could be underwhelming. "It's tough without seeing the actual thing, but it looks to me to be similar to the Dresden Codex, one of the few Mayan books that the Spanish didn't burn. I'm thinking about the calendar pages, cycles of the planet Venus, and so on. Venus was very important to the postclassic Maya. The planet represented Kukulcan, the light-skinned bearded god the Toltecs called Quetzalcoatl. The Feathered Serpent. The Maya plotted the travels of Venus practically to the second. Beyond that it's difficult to say without seeing the real thing."

"Nothing else?"

"Not unless I come across a good picture or artistic rendition."

"What about Professor Gallo's comment, about this thing being no great mystery?"

"Oh, he's absolutely right. The fact that a Mayan artifact may have been found in Italy is not a big deal. No more than the fact that you can walk into the British Museum in London and find the Elgin marbles from the Parthenon. The important part of the equation is provenance, as you know. Not just where the artifact was found but how it got there."

"What about the Columbus letter I told you about? It mentions an object similar to this. How does that tie in with the mention of the Alberti family's Columbus collection?"

"You cannot jump to conclusions on the basis of an old newspaper article. You also told me there are doubts as to the authenticity of this letter. Even if the letter were the real McCoy, we'd need more proof that the objects were one and the same. Tantalizing thought, though. It was entirely possible for Columbus to have shipped it home without anyone knowing. He was known as a devious man. Some believe he falsified his mileage readings on his first voyage so the crew wouldn't know how far they were from land. It would have been in character for Columbus to hide something. Unfortunately we have to remember we're scientists, not writers of popular semifictional archaeological claptrap."

Orville was entirely right. It would be unprofessional to jump to conclusions.

"The Italian professor made a good point," Nina pointed out. "The Spanish were interested in plunder, not science."

"True. Cortez was certainly no Napoleon, who brought along the scientists who discovered the Rosetta Stone."

Interesting. She, too, had been thinking about the Rosetta Stone, the pivotal discovery that provided, with the same message in Greek and Egyptian, the key to translating hieroglyphics. "I'd give almost anything to see this thing in the flesh."

"Hmm. I wish I could take you up on your inviting offer. Alas, our artifact is not easily obtainable."

"Of course. How dumb of me. The *Andrea Doria*. It was in a collision with another ship."

"Correct. The *Stockholm*. As a result of that unfortunate incident our artifact lies more than two hundred feet underwater, at the bottom of the Atlantic. We can only hope that the fishes appreciate it. Too bad. Perhaps it could prove the existence of Atlantis, something to make for some catchy headlines. Nutty professor strikes again and that sort of thing."

"I'm sure you'll find something equally controversial," Nina said warmly. "Thanks for your help, Doc."

"I was glad to hear from you. You've been away a lot. How about lunch this week?"

Nina asked him to call in the morning after she had a chance to check her calendar. As soon as she hung up she dialed the number of the *Boston Herald* and asked for an extension in the newsroom. A female voice answered: "K. T. Pritchard."

"Hi, Kay Tee. This is your friendly archaeologist calling for a favor. Do you have a minute?"

"I've always got time for you, Dr. Kirov. You're in luck. I just wrapped up a story, but as long as I look as if I'm working no one will bug me with a new assignment. What can I do for you?"

Pritchard had used Nina as a background source on a prize-winning series she wrote when Boston's patrician Museum of Fine Arts unknowingly bought a stolen Etruscan vase. She was always anxious to pay the favor back. Nina told the reporter she was looking for any mention of an archaeological artifact being transported from Italy on the *Andrea Doria*.

"I'll check out the morgue and call you back."

The phone rang about an hour later. It was Pritchard.

"That was fast," Nina said with amazement.

"Stuff's all on microfilm, so it scans pretty quickly. There were tons of pieces written on the *Andrea Doria* at the time of the accident itself. Then more on the inquiry, but I skipped that. The ship carried piles of valuable cargo. She was apparently a floating art museum. No mention of anything like you described. So I flipped to the anniversary editions. You know how papers like to memorialize disasters so they can write about them ad nauseam on slow news days. I found an article on the thirtieth anniversary. It was about heroes and cowards. Some of the crew bailed while the others should have been given medals. Anyhow, there was an interview with one of them. A waiter. Didn't you tell me this thing was being transported in an armored truck?"

"That's right. According to the Associated Press article."

"Hmm. Well, anyhow, this waiter said he saw an armored truck being robbed as the ship was going down."

"A *robbery!*"

"That's right. A group of armed men. The truck was in the hold of the ship."

"That's incredible! What else did he say?"

"Nothing. The story just slipped out as he was telling the reporter how he went into the hold of the ship looking for a car jack to free one of the victims. I called the guy who interviewed him. Charlie Flynn. A real war horse. He's retired now. He tried to pry more info from the guy. Thought he could make this the lead. The untold story. Sinking ship. Masked men. Drama belowdecks and that sort of thing. But he said the guy clammed up. Wouldn't talk about it. Changed the subject. Got very upset. Asked Charlie not to use this in the story."

"He went ahead and did it anyhow?"

"That's the way it was in the old days. What you said got in the paper. Not like today with libel lawyers breathing down your neck. It was buried, though, way down at the bottom of the story. Copy editor probably thought it was too thin on the facts to use up in the lead but interesting enough as a tidbit. Charlie talked to a few *Doria* survivors to see if he could get the story through another source. Nobody had ever heard anything about it."

"What was the crewman's name?"

"I'll fax you the clip, but hold on. Here it is. He was Italian. His name was Angelo Donatelli."

"Do you have an address for him?"

"He was living in New York at the time. Charlie says he ran a fancy restaurant there. That's all he knew about the guy. Say, Dr. Kirov, is there a story here?"

"I'm not sure, Kay Tee. You'll be the first to know if there is."

"That's all I ask. Call me anytime."

After she hung up Nina stared off into space for a few minutes, trying to connect a massive stone artifact from the time of Columbus with a disaster at sea, an armed robbery, and a Moroccan massacre. It was no use. It would be easier linking Sumerian cuneiform with Minoan Linear B writing. She gave up and called Kurt Austin.

31

ANGELO DONATELLI WAS SURPRISING-
ly easy to trace. Austin simply looked up his name on the Internet and found fifteen references, including a *Business Week* article that described the rags-to-riches rise from lowly cocktail lounge waiter to owner of one of New York's more fashionable restaurants. The picture of Donatelli conferring with his head chef showed a silver-haired and middle-aged man who looked more like a distinguished European diplomat than a restaurateur.

Austin called directory assistance in Manhattan, and a minute later he was talking to the restaurant's friendly assistant manager.

"Mr. Donatelli is not in today," she said.

"When is the best time to get him?"

"He's due back from Nantucket tomorrow. You can try calling here after three P.M."

Nantucket. Austin knew the island off the Massachusetts coast well, having stopped there several times while sailing to Maine. He tried to get a Nantucket phone number for Donatelli. It was unlisted. A few minutes later he was talking to a Lieutenant Coffin at the Nantucket Police Department. Austin identified himself as being with NUMA and said he wanted to get in touch with Angelo Donatelli. He was banking on the fact that small-town police know everything and everybody in their community.

The police officer confirmed that Donatelli had a summer

home on the island, but he was wary. "What's the National Underwater and Marine Agency want with Mr. Donatelli?"

"We're pulling together some historic stuff on collisions at sea. Mr. Donatelli was aboard the *Andrea Doria* when it was hit."

"I've heard that. Met him a couple of times. Nice guy."

"I've tried calling him, but his number is unlisted."

"Yeah, most of the people out where he lives kinda like it that way. They built those big houses so they can have their privacy."

"I may try to get a flight to the island later today and take my chances on hooking up with him."

"Tell you what. When you get on-island drop by the police station on Water Street and ask for me. I can show you where he lives on a map."

Good cop, Austin thought. He wasn't about to dispense information on one of the island's well-to-do property owners without checking Austin out in person.

Austin never dreamed Nina would track down a lead so quickly.

With Zavala in Texas and Trout in the Yucatan, maybe Austin could squeeze in a quick interview with Donatelli. He used his government clout to get a seat with a small commuter airline that ran regular shuttles between Washington and Nantucket. A couple of hours later he was on a puddle-jumper flying northeast.

The flight gave him time to look over the file Yaeger had dropped on his desk as Austin was leaving his NUMA office. Austin had asked the computer whiz to scour his electronic marvels for information on the Brotherhood, the sixteenth-century secret society he and Perlmutter had discussed over lunch. And to run down any links *Los Hermanos* might have had to Christopher Columbus. Austin glanced out the window at the ocean sparkling far below, then opened the file and read Yaeger's note:

Hi, Kurt.

I think I've got it! I've been wading through secret societies up to my eyeballs, but the Columbus angle narrowed it down. I followed up one of those stray facts that go floating across your monitor screen from obscure sources. A one-sentence footnote that Columbus was said to be associated with an outfit called the Brotherhood of the Holy Sword of Truth. (They liked long titles back then.) Can't confirm if he was a member. Probably not.

The Brotherhood was formed in the 1400s during the Spanish Inquisition by an archdeacon named Hernando Perez, head of a powerful monastery known for its extreme beliefs. Heavily into self-flagellation and hair shirts. Perez was slightly to the right of Torquemada, who was the head honcho of the Inquisition. Perez picked the most fanatical of his followers from his monastery. The brothers made up the trusted core of his outfit.

Perez was mad as a hatter, unswerving in his convictions, quite happy to use violence and murder to achieve his ends. He declared absolution for his guys no matter how much blood they shed for his cause, which was to wipe out heretics. And get rich doing it, by the way. They split loot plundered from their victims with the Inquisition. The Brotherhood worked behind the scenes, identifying the unfaithful so they could be fed into the Inquisition's murder machine. Sometimes it sent out its own hit squads. Or for a price it might see that you were spared. As long as they could bleed you of money.

Heresy covered a lot of ground. Which brings in another angle. Back then you could be burned at the stake for saying Columbus discovered America! The Scriptures never said anything about the American continents. It messes with the whole idea of Adam and Eve. So when Columbus claimed that he reached India or China, the powers that be backed him up.

The real reasons were political, though. Church and state were the same thing. When somebody questioned church dogma it threatened the throne. Once doubts set in about the church's teachings on geography the hoi polloi might start asking why they were starving and the bishops and kings were all well fed, and before long the mobs would be marching on the palace.

Millions were at stake as well. Spain wanted the riches of the New World to herself. If other countries could prove Columbus wasn't the first to discover India, rivals of Spain like Portugal might claim the new lands and riches. Gold meant new warships and raising armies, so we're really talking about European domination. That's why the Inquisition, which was the terror instrument of the Spanish state, made it heresy, punishable by burning, to believe there was a continent with separate civilizations and that they had contact with the Old World before Columbus.

To show you how dangerous the idea was, Amerigo Vespucci was sent on a secret mission by the king to check out the Columbus discoveries. When Vespucci demonstrated Columbus had *not* discovered a short route to India, that he'd found a new continent and may not have been the first to go there, he was called a heretic and warned to recant. By making this a capital crime, the Spanish were admitting tacitly that there had *indeed* been prior contact. Torquemada was a sly old devil. He said that even if the Indians *had* received a visitor from the west whom they named Quetzalcoatl, the stranger must have been white and Spanish. That meant Spain had dibs on the new lands even before Columbus was born.

I verified that five sailors died after eating at Columbus's house. Can't prove the Brotherhood had anything to do with it. Could have been food poisoning. I couldn't find anything on the Brotherhood after the 1600s. Maybe they went out of business with the Inquisition. Source material enclosed. Hope this helps.

The rest of the file contained source documents. Austin read through the pile of papers and decided the computer genius had done a good job encapsulating his findings. The account of the Brotherhood was fascinating particularly in its mission to suppress knowledge of contact between the New and the Old Worlds. One problem. The Brotherhood went out of business more than three hundred years ago.

The pilot's voice announced that the plane was passing near Martha's Vineyard. Nantucket's pork-chop shape was visible to the east of the Vineyard. An ocean fog nibbled at the windswept moors and long white strands that edged the island. It was easy to see why the island attracted the peg-legged Captain Ahab and real-life Quaker whaling captains and ship owners who made their fortunes in the whaling trade. Nantucket had at its doorstep a saltwater highway that would take its whaling vessels to all the seven seas on voyages that often lasted years.

Austin rented a car at Tom Nevers Airport and drove into town, past stately brick houses built with riches made from whale oil, the car bumping over the wide main street that was paved with cobblestones once used for ballast in the old sailing ships, then along Water Street bordering the harbor until he came to the police and fire station.

Lieutenant Coffin was a tall stringbean of a man with high cheekbones and a prominent bony nose that had seen too much sun. His mouth dropped open in surprise when Austin identified himself.

"*You* got here in a hurry," he said, sizing up the husky man with the prematurely white hair. "You NUMA guys have private jets?"

"Some of us do. I lucked out in catching a flight. It was a good excuse to get out of Washington."

"Can't blame you for that. The island's awfully pretty this time of year. You're missing the crowds, too." The hazel eyes narrowed. "Just so you'll know, I called NUMA back after I talked to you."

"Can't blame you for that."

Coffin smiled. "Seems like you're on the up-and-up. We're pretty easygoing, but we can't be too careful. Nantucket's got a lot of rich folks who own big houses and pay major taxes. Don't see a burglar asking the police where the house is he plans to rob, but you never know. Good thing you called. People out there kinda look after each other. They'd give you directions to the other side of the island. I'll show you how to get to his house." He slid a tourist map across the counter. "Take the Polpis Road till you get to a sand driveway with a ship on the mailbox." Coffin drew the route with a yellow marker.

Austin thanked the police officer and followed his directions out of town to a narrow winding road that ran through scrub pine forest and past farms and cranberry bogs. At the mailbox, which was surmounted by a metal rendering of a black-and-white ocean liner, Austin turned onto the sand road and drove through stunted forest that turned into rolling heathland. The strong smell of the sea was carried on the ropy tendrils of fog he had seen from the air.

The big house loomed suddenly from the fog. It looked deserted. No vehicles outside, no lights in the windows even though darkness was falling. Austin left the car in the horseshoe-shaped crushed shell driveway, followed a walkway bordered by an expansive and well-manicured lawn to the wide open porch, and rang the front doorbell. Chimes echoed inside. No answer. Maybe the restaurant manager had it wrong. Or perhaps Donatelli changed his plans and went back to New York earlier than expected.

Austin frowned. This could be a time-wasting wild goose chase. He'd known from the start that he was grasping at a straw, trying to connect a robbery at sea decades before with the killings of archaeologists. He wondered if he could catch a flight back to DC. Oh, hell. He'd get home just as fast if he stayed the night and flew out first thing in the morning. With his decision made, Austin decided to explore the grounds. He left the veranda and walked around the house.

Nantucket had become afflicted with a plague of "trophy houses," so big they looked like small hotels, built by wealthy people who saw square footage as a way of one-upping their neighbors. Donatelli's place was large, and the builder had managed to incorporate Italianate architectural features in with the more traditional silver-gray shingles and white trim, but it was all done in good taste.

Behind the house was a fair-sized vegetable garden and a children's swing and slide set. Austin followed the sound of the breaking surf across a wide lawn to the edge of a sandy cliff and stood for a moment at the top of a weather-beaten stairway that led down to the beach. The beach was obscured and ocean sound muffled by the fog, but he could hear distant rollers slapping against the shore. He turned and looked back at the house. In the fog and waning light he could barely see the place.

Figuring he had done all he could, Austin returned to the car and wrote a note that included his telephone number, asking Donatelli to call him as soon as possible. He trudged back to the front door. Low-tech communication, but it might work. He would follow it up with a phone call when he got back to his office.

He climbed onto the broad porch and tucked the rolled-up note under the ornate door knocker, thinking the brass weight would keep the paper from blowing away. He realized he had more important things than the wind to worry about. Hard cold metal pressed against the back of his neck. Then came the unmistakable click of a very large gun being cocked. Until then there had been no sound, not even a footfall.

"Hands up," a harsh voice said. "Don't turn around." The man spoke with an accent.

Austin slowly lifted his hands. "Mr. Donatelli?"

"Don't talk," the man said, emphasizing his order with a hard jab to the neck. A practiced hand frisked Austin, deftly slipping his wallet out of his pocket. Satisfied Austin carried no weapon, the man ordered him to climb the outside stairs leading from the porch to a second-story deck that wrapped around three sides of the house. The fog had closed in with a vengeance, and in the dimming light Austin would not have seen the figure leaning against a railing if his attention had not been caught by the orange glow of a cigarette and the smell of strong tobacco.

"Sit," said the man with the gun. Austin did as he was told, plunking into a deck chair that was damp with moisture. Keeping his gun leveled at Austin, the man spoke in Italian to the smoker. They conferred for a minute.

The figure in the fog spoke. "Who are you?"

"My name is Kurt Austin, and I'm with the National Underwater and Marine Agency."

Pause. "You're consistent, anyhow. That's the same story you gave Lieutenant Coffin." The voice had an accent, but it wasn't as thick as that of the gun carrier.

"You talked to Coffin?"

"Of *course*. The police try to keep their summer residents happy. Especially those who are big contributors to their equipment fund. I've requested that he let me know if anyone ever asks for me. He even offered to come out here with you. I told him I could handle the situation by myself."

"Then you *are* Mr. Donatelli."

"*I* ask the questions." Another sharp jab in the spine. "Who are you really?"

"My wallet has identification."

"Identification can be forged."

Donatelli was going to be a tough sell. "Lieutenant Coffin called NUMA and verified that I am who I said I am."

"I have no doubt you are who you claim. It's what you *really* are that interests me."

Austin's patience was eroding. "Make believe I don't understand what you're talking about, Mr. Donatelli."

"Why would a big government agency like NUMA want to talk to me? I run a restaurant in New York. The only thing I have to do with the ocean is the seafood I buy from Fulton Fish Market."

Reasonable question. "You were on the *Andrea Doria.*"

"Lieutenant Coffin said you mentioned the *Doria.* That's old news, isn't it?"

"We were hoping you might have some information bearing on a case we're working on."

"Tell me about this case, Mr. Austin. You may put your hands down, but remember that my cousin Antonio is from Sicily, and, like most Sicilians, he trusts nobody. He is quite good with the *lupara,* especially at close range."

Lupara was the sawed-off shotgun that used to be the choice of the Sicilian Mafia before they went to automatic weapons and car bombs. An antique but still deadly.

"Before I start," Austin said evenly, "I'd appreciate it if you told Cousin Tony that if he doesn't stop sticking me in the neck, his *lupara* is going to end up where the sun don't shine."

Austin had no way to carry out his threat, but it had been a long day and he was tired of getting jabbed. Donatelli translated for the gunman. Antonio stepped away and stood off to one side, the gun still leveled at Austin. A slit that could have been a mouth opened into what might have been a smile.

A cigarette lighter flared in the darkness, showing Donatelli's deep-set eyes. "Now, tell us your story, Mr. Austin."

So he did. "The whole thing started in Morocco," Austin began. From there he worked his way to the present, explaining how the trail had led to Donatelli. "One of our researchers came across your name in a newspaper article. When I read that you had seen an armored truck robbery on the ship, I wanted to talk to you."

Donatelli was silent for a moment, then he spoke in Italian to his cousin. The stocky figure who'd been standing next to Austin moved silently through the sliders, and a second later a light came on inside the house.

"Let us go inside and be comfortable, Mr. Austin. It's damp out here. Bad for the bones. I must apologize. I thought you were one of *them*. They would never bother to concoct such a fantastic story, so it must be true."

Austin stepped inside. Donatelli gestured to a plush chair next to the large fireplace, eased into an opposite chair, and clicked a remote control. A gas fire huffed on in the hearth. The heat penetrating the glass screen felt good. Austin was covered with moisture that had nothing to do with the dew point.

His eyes rose to the mantel and rested on a minutely detailed scale model of the *Andrea Doria*. The model was only part of the collection of memorabilia, photos, and paintings, even a flotation device, that was sprinkled around the spacious living room. All having to do with the *Doria*.

Donatelli was studying him. The flickering light from the fireplace bathed the still-handsome features of a man in his sixties. The thick head of wavy hair, combed straight back, was grayer than it appeared in the business magazine photo. In general Donatelli had aged well. He was still trim, and in the expensive-looking pale blue running suit and New Balance running shoes he looked as if he worked at keeping fit.

Cousin Antonio was the exact opposite. He was short and squat, with a shaved head and watchful eyes set in a face that looked as if it had been used for a punching bag. The nose was broken, the ears cauliflowered, and the sallow skin covered with a lacework of scars. He was dressed in a black shirt and black slacks. He had reappeared carrying a tray with two brandy glasses and Austin's wallet on it. The waiter image was diminished somehow by the shotgun strapped onto his shoulder.

"*Grappa*," Donatelli said. "It will burn the dampness from our bones."

Austin tucked the billfold back into his pocket and tried the liquor. The Italian firewater seared Austin's throat. It felt good.

Donatelli took a sip and said, "How did you find me here, Mr. Austin? I left strict instructions with my office not to tell anyone where I was."

"They said at the restaurant that you were on the island."

The older man smiled. "So much for my security measures." Donatelli took another sip and stared silently into the fire. After a minute he affixed Austin with his penetrating eyes. "It wasn't a robbery," he said flatly.

"Did the newspaper get it wrong?"

"I called it that for convenience. In a robbery the thieves *take* something. These thieves took nothing except lives." With a sharp memory for detail and touches of humor, Donatelli related the events of that memorable night in 1956. Even after all these years his voice trembled during his description of the shifting of the dying ship as he made his way deeper in the flooded darkness. He told about the murder of the armored truck guards, his flight, and his eventual rescue. "You said the truck carried a stone," he mused. "Why would people kill over a stone, Mr. Austin?"

"Maybe it's not just *any* stone."

He shook his head, uncomprehending.

"Mr. Donatelli, you said earlier that you thought I was one of 'them.' What did you mean?"

The restaurateur considered his words carefully. "In all the years since the ship went down I have said nothing about what happened. The newspaper article was a slip of the tongue. I have known in my heart there was a reason for keeping this secret. After the article appeared someone called and warned me never to say anything about that incident again. A man with a voice like ice. He knew *everything* about me and my family. My wife's hairdresser. The names of my children and grandchildren. Where they lived. He said if I ever mentioned that night to *anyone*, I would be killed. But first I would see my family destroyed." He stared into the fire. "I come from Sicily. I believed him. I gave no more interviews. I asked Antonio to come and live with me. He was in, ah, difficulties with the authorities in his home and was glad to relocate."

From the battered looks of Tony's face and the ease with which he handled his weapon, Austin had a good idea of what Tony's difficulties might have been, but he didn't pursue the matter.

"I assume the man who called didn't tell you his name. Or who he was speaking for."

"Yes and no. That's right. No name. But he indicated that he was not acting alone, that he had many brothers."

"Brothers. Could he have said 'Brotherhood'?"

"Yes. I think that's what he said. You've heard of them?"

"There was an organization called the Brotherhood of the Holy Sword of Truth. They worked with the Spanish Inquisition. But that was hundreds of years ago."

"The Mafia had its start hundreds of years ago," Donatelli replied with an amused glance at his cousin. "Why is this different?"

"The Mafia's continued existence is pretty well established by its continuing activities."

"Yes, that is true, but even though people in the Old Country knew there was such a thing and that the Black Hand had moved with the immigrants to America, the police here never knew about La Cosa Nostra until they found somebody, by accident, who would break the code of *muerto.* Silence or death."

"You are saying that an organization might go on operating in secret for centuries?"

Donatelli spread his hands. "The Mafia had murders, extortion, robbery. Yet the FBI director, Hoover, swore there was no such thing as La Cosa Nostra."

As he pondered Donatelli's words, thinking he had a good point, Austin surveyed the room.

"You've come a long way since your waiter days," he said, taking in the luxurious wood paneling and brass fittings.

"I had help. After the wreck I decided I never wanted to set foot on a boat again." He chuckled. "There is nothing like the unholy terror of being caught in the hold of a sinking ship to take the romance out of the sea. The woman I tried to help unfortunately died of her injuries. When I went to the funeral her husband thanked me again and said he wanted to do something in return. I said it was my dream to have a small restaurant. He gave me seed money for a place in New York on the condition that I take business and English courses which he would also pay for. I named the restaurant Myra, after Mr. Carey's wife. I have opened six more restaurants in large cities across the country. They've made me a millionaire and allowed me to live like this. I married a wonderful woman. She gave me four sons and a daughter, all in the business, and many, many grandchildren." He sipped the last of his grappa and put the glass down on a table. "I built this house here for my family, but also I think because it is near to where the ship went down. On foggy nights like this it brings back memories. You see, Mr. Austin, the accident was bad for many people, like Mr. Carey. But it changed my life for the better."

"Why are you telling me this now? You could have just sent me on my way."

"My wife died last year. After I survived the *Andrea Doria* I thought I would live forever. I saw in her death a reminder that I am mortal like all men. I am not a religious man, but I began to think more about making things right. Those men who were killed in the ship's hold. Maybe the others you told me of. They need somebody to speak for them." His jaw hardened. "I will be the spokesman for the dead." Donatelli looked at the wall clock. "It is getting late, Mr. Austin. Do you have a place to stay?"

"I thought I'd get a room at a bed-and-breakfast."

"Not necessary. You will have your bed here tonight as my guest, and breakfast tomorrow. For dinner I will prepare a special pasta. Tomatoes and zucchini fresh from the garden."

"An invitation like that would be impossible to refuse."

"Good." He poured them more grappa and hoisted his glass high. "Then when we have eaten and drunk our wine, we will find a way to show these people what it means to mess with a Sicilian."

32

AS A MEXICAN AMERICAN, ZAVALA

had mixed feelings about Texas's holiest shrine. He admired the courage of the Alamo's defenders, men like Buck Travis, Jim Bowie, and Davy Crockett, whose names were listed on the cenotaph on Alamo Plaza. At the same time he felt sorry for the 1,550 Mexican troops who died in the siege under the inept command of Santa Anna. The Texans lost 183 men. The Mexicans lost Texas.

He wandered around the chapel that was all that was left of the once-sprawling fort, checked out the museum, and used up the rest of the afternoon watching people at a coffee bar. By six-thirty he was parking his rented car in the garage below the Time-Quest building. He located the parking area marked off for Halcon Industries. Nothing was reserved for the CEO. Zavala's guess was that everybody in the company was well aware the space was forbidden territory and Halcon didn't want to advertise himself.

Zavala parked as near to the Halcon spaces as he could, then walked past two elevators, the public one and another door marked Private, and took up a post nearby in the shadows behind a thick concrete pillar. At five past seven Melody exited the main elevator and walked to her car. Zavala again felt a twinge of regret at not being able to go on a date with the lovely woman, but he had to put those thoughts aside. He wanted a clear head for his first meeting with Señor Halcon.

Zavala's vigil in the underground garage was about to pay off. Shortly after Melody left, a black Lincoln limousine quietly pulled up in front of the elevator door marked Private. Almost on cue the elevator door opened and a man stepped out.

Zavala brought his Nikon to his eye and focused on the tall dark man who exited the elevator and walked with an easy grace to the waiting vehicle. Halcon. He snapped off several shots before Halcon got into the limo, then focused on the driver who was holding the door open for him. The man was wearing a dark suit, and his white hair was cut military short. He was tall and broad-shouldered, his physique muscularly athletic even though he could have been in his sixties at least. Zavala got off a single shot before the white-haired man swept the garage with his eyes as if he had heard the quiet whirr of the motor drive. Zavala melted into the shadows and didn't dare breathe until the car door slammed and the limo moved off.

In the fleeting second he had framed the white-haired man in the viewfinder Zavala had frozen his likeness on his retinas. He leaned against the cold concrete, still not believing the evidence of his eyes. He had just seen the same man in Arizona. He was sure of it, despite the clean-shaven face and the tailored suit. Only then the man with Halcon was wearing work clothes and had long hair and a thick white beard. He had a wife, since deceased. And he went by the name of George Wingate.

Quickly regaining his composure, Zavala dashed for his rental car. He followed the limo onto the street, keeping one or two cars between him and his objective. They headed out of the city on the expressway in a northwest direction. In time the suburbs and shopping malls thinned out. The flat terrain gave way to rolling hills and more forested areas.

Zavala pushed the rental car just to stay in sight of the limo, which flew along well above the speed limit once they were beyond the more heavily congested neighborhoods. They traveled for about an hour, leaving the main highway around dusk to follow a sparsely populated two-lane road. Zavala stayed far back. Before long he saw the flash of brake lights, and the limo disappeared. Zavala slowed until his headlights caught a small plastic reflector nailed to a tree, marking an unpaved road. He kept going to create the illusion he was bound elsewhere, then after a few hundred yards he did a quick U-turn and came back to the reflector.

He switched the car's headlights off as a test and found that he was able to follow the dirt road as long as he kept speed down to a fast walk. He wondered what a big shot like Halcon was doing in the sticks. Maybe he had a hunting lodge. The thick woods quickly enveloped him. Where the trees opened up he could see low craggy hills on either side. He saw no lights ahead, but this didn't surprise him because the road twisted and turned. Not wanting to run into an unpleasant surprise, Zavala stopped every few minutes, got out of the car, and walked ahead, like the point on an infantry patrol, to watch and listen.

On one stop he saw a light ahead. Cautiously he walked toward the glow until he could see that it was a lone spotlight on the gate of a high wire-mesh fence. He pulled the car off the road and made his way toward the fence under the cover of the woods, stopping at the edge of a swath cleared from the perimeter. The fence was about twice the height of a man and topped by coils of razor wire. A white sign with black lettering was attached to the gate warning trespassers to Keep Out. Guard Dogs Trained to Attack. His instincts had served him well. Above the sign was a small box which could serve no other purpose than as a security camera.

The fence was too high to climb, and he had no protection against the wire, or the dogs, but his guess was that the barricade was attached to an alarm. Remembering a low hill a short distance back, he returned to his car and headed away from the fence in reverse so the backup lights wouldn't be seen, then pulled off the road into the bushes. He made his way toward the hill then up its side, no easy task because he had nothing to light his way. He tripped and had to back out of briars a few times but made it to the copse at the hilltop without mishap. He selected a clean-limbed tree and climbed to the highest branch that would support his weight.

The elevation gave him a view over the top of the fence. Except for the lone floodlight on the gate, the area was not illuminated. His eyes had become used to the darkness, and soon several shapes began to materialize. He realized he was looking at a vast complex of buildings, some rectangular, others cylindrical, all dominated by a massive pyramid with a flat top. The structures were built of a whitish stone and seemed to glow in the faint light of the moon.

Some hunting lodge, he muttered. This was crazy! An ancient city in the wilds of the Texas countryside. He tried to call Austin but his cell phone failed to pick up a signal. After several minutes during which he squinted into the darkness in a vain attempt to make out details, he decided he had seen all he was going to see. He was about to climb down the tree when a light flicked on and he saw a strange sight. He got a new grip on the branch and watched, fascinated, as a remarkable scene began to unfold.

33 RAUL GONZALEZ SHIVERED IN THE

darkness and waited for the bullet to smash into his spine, wishing it would happen before he froze to death in the cool night air. Again he cursed that American woman. By thwarting his Moroccan assignment, she was responsible for him being in this place. His angry ruminations were cut short. A spotlight blinked on, and Gonzalez saw before him a fantastic creature, part human, part beast.

From the neck down the figure was a bronze-skinned man of muscular physique. Around his waist was a loincloth of rich green, yellow, and vermilion. The hard growths on either hip proved to be, on closer look, leather padding. The face was hidden behind a mask created in a madman's nightmare. The jade-colored snout was long and scaly, the eyes hungry-looking, and the grinning mouth full of jagged, razor-sharp teeth. Long quetzal plumes streamed from the back of the head. The monster stood as still as a statue, brawny arms folded across a broad hairless chest.

"Madre mia." The pitiful whimper came from off to Gonzalez's left.

"Silencio," Gonzalez growled at the hydrofoil captain.

They'd been ordered to remain silent or be shot. Gonzalez wasn't about to be killed because a sniveling coward couldn't keep his mouth shut. The man standing quietly on his right was more to his liking. Lean and snakelike in his movements, an assassin like himself. At another time Gonzalez would have talked shop with the man about the murderous skills he learned as a skinny sore-plagued orphan in the squalid alleys of Buenos Aires, where he'd dodged death squads hired by local businessmen. The businessmen considered the street boys as vermin. Gonzalez was barely a teenager when he approached the shopkeepers and offered to infiltrate the packs he knew so well and quietly dispatch his sleeping peers with knife or garrote. As he grew older he obtained bigger jobs. Competitors. Politicians. Unfaithful spouses. All sent to an early grave. Gun. Knife. Torture. Gonzalez earned a reputation for delivering exactly what his employer wanted.

Blink.

A second circle of light revealed another muscular figure with a different mask, the snarling mouth and blood-red tongue of a jaguar.

Gonzalez again swore under his breath. Standing in the cold while some idiot puts on a costume pageant! It wasn't fair. All because he'd botched a few jobs. Business had been going to younger killers when the Brotherhood's emissary approached him. He didn't know the group even existed, but they knew everything about him. They wanted him for special assignments, and the aging hit man signed on eagerly. The money was good. The work wasn't difficult. Just like his street days. Wait for a call. Infiltrate and kill. Easy assignments. Like the one in Morocco.

Morocco. He wished he'd never heard the name.

A simple job, said the caller from Madrid. Unarmed, unsuspecting scientists. Infiltrate the expedition. Set up the ambush. Roust the victims from their beds, slaughter them like sheep, and quickly bury the bodies without a trace. If it hadn't been for that bitch with the Russian name! Jesus Mary, he'd had sweet plans for her. He would study that slim body, hungrily watching as she sat in front of her tent combing hair the color of golden wheat in the afternoon sun. When they talked she was politely rude. Brushing him off as if he were an ant crawling up one of those slender legs. He was going to enjoy making her beg for her life with the only thing she could offer, that gorgeous body.

But she hadn't been sleeping when he burst into her tent, and when he and the others gave chase she ran like the wind. Three times the Brotherhood had her in its grasp only to fail in its attempts to bring her down. The hovercraft failed to drown her. The hit squad sent to finish the job on the NUMA ship was either shot or incinerated, its only survivor the lone commando by his side.

The order to come to Texas wasn't a total surprise. Gonzalez assumed he'd get a sharp reprimand, have his pay docked, and be reassigned. Instead men with machine pistols had herded him with the others. After dark they were escorted out into the night and told to stand at attention. Warned they would be shot if they made a move or uttered a peep. So they had waited, listening to the howl of coyotes in the desert night air. Until now.

Blink. A third figure stood in relief. He wore the death's head with its staring empty eyes and dead grin.

A voice came out of the night, amplified by loudspeakers. "Greetings, my brothers," it said in aristocratic Castilian Spanish.

"Greetings, Lord Halcon," echoed the murmured response from unseen voices.

"We know why we are here. Three of our number were given tasks to further our noble cause, and they have failed us." The voice paused. "The punishment for failure is death."

Here comes the bullet, Gonzalez thought. Oh, hell, it's been a good life. He braced himself for the hail of lead that must soon come smashing into his body, hoping that it would be quick. His feet hurt from the unaccustomed standing. He was surprised by a round object that flew out of the darkness and hit the ground with a bounce. Gonzalez thought the black-and-white sphere was a soccer ball until it rolled to a stop about midway between the two facing lines of men and he saw that its markings were images of skulls.

The voice again. "You will be given a chance to win your lives. The ball game will determine whether you live or die."

The spotlights blinked off. The three figures vanished. But only for a moment. A battery of bright lights came on, and Gonzalez saw that he and the others were standing between two parallel stone walls. The three costumed men had removed their masks and stood at the far end of the alley. Halfway down from the top of each wall was a ring carved with the face of what looked like a macaw. In the semidarkness on top of the wall he sensed people moving, hundreds from the sound of their voices.

"The ball represents fate," boomed the loudspeaker. "The court is the cosmos. The alligator, the jaguar, and the death's head symbolize the lords of the underworld, your opponents. The rules are as they have been for two thousand years. The lords will use their feet. You may use your hands *and* feet. Your goal will be to move the ball to the other end of the playing field. If any team moves the ball through a ring, that side wins. The losers will be vanquished."

Gonzalez was dumbfounded. *Soccer,* for Godsakes. They were going to play a game of kickball for their lives! Gonzalez had played as a street youth and later in an organized amateur team, and he had not been bad at it. He was dreadfully out of shape from the excesses of booze, drugs, and women. His swarthy body was still powerful, but he'd grown flabby around the gut and short of wind.

"You've played before?" he said out of the corner of his mouth.

"A little," said the assassin. "Forward."

"I was a goalie," the hovercraft operator said tentatively.

"We're playing for our lives," Gonzalez warned. "There will be no rules. Anything goes. Do you understand?"

Both men nodded.

The trio at the far end of the court awaited their move.

"I'll kick off," Gonzalez said. His eyes focused entirely on the ball, he got a running start, brought his foot back, then swung it forward. The ball was heavier than he expected. Probably solid rubber. The kick sent a painful shock up his leg. He got the full power of his body behind the blow, but his aim was off, and the ball skittered along the wall and back into the court in front of their opponents.

The point man was on the ball like lightning, quickly moving it forward to halfcourt with short skillful steps. His teammates flanked him on either side. The three men could have been triplets, all with the same bronze-hard bodies, the black hair cut in bowl-like bangs just above dark, uncaring eyes.

The ball handler saw Gonzalez loping in his direction and snapped the ball off to the man at his left. Gonzalez was unwavering. He had no interest in the ball; he wanted to *maim*. He had done the simple arithmetic in his head. Injure only one man, and his opponents would lose thirty percent of their team. He lowered his head and charged the man who had passed off the ball. His target coolly waited until Gonzalez was a hair's breadth away, then deftly sidestepped and stuck his foot out. Gonzalez tried to stop, couldn't, tripped over the extended leg, and slammed against the ground so hard it rattled his teeth.

Ignoring the pain in his cracked ribs, he scrambled to his feet and tried vainly to catch up with the fast-moving play. His teammate, the assassin, lunged in an unsuccessful attempt to steal the ball, but he jabbed his elbow into the ball handler's sternum, eliciting a satisfactory grunt of pain.

Gonzalez followed up, slamming into the man with a body block from behind. The player went forward onto his knees, which is where most men would have stayed, but he was up again in an instant, hurrying to run interference with the teammate, who was moving the ball toward the end zone. Gonzalez looked on in dismay.

So soon.

Three-on-one.

Only the hovercraft man stood in the way of a goal.

The ball handler saw his opponent, underestimated him, and decided to take the ball through instead of passing it off to the side for an easy kick goal. He was moving too fast to take a sharp turn without losing the ball, so he feinted with the eyes to his left but moved to his right.

The hovercraft man saw the ploy and moved forward with his forearm lifted. His elbow drove into the man's jaw with the force of their combined speed and lifted him off the ground. There was a resounding crack as the ball handler's jaw broke, and he crumpled to the ground with blood gushing from his mouth. Gonzalez gasped for air with every breath he took, but his teammate's skillful move gave him new strength.

Gonzalez got the ball under his heel and kicked it between the two opponents who were double-teaming him without a glance at their fallen comrade. With a hoarse yell of triumph he followed up on his kick and barreled into the pair like a bowling ball, intent on knocking them to either side. One man straight-armed Gonzalez and might have broken his neck if the palm hadn't been absorbed by the fleshy jowls. Gonzalez realized that the rule was no hands for moving the ball, not for defending it.

The assassin had the loose ball, but it was quickly stolen and was being moved in Gonzalez's direction. The player saw the hovercraft operator running in to stop him and chose to get past the slower Gonzalez. Again Gonzalez concentrated not on the ball but on the man, aiming his sharp toe at the man's groin.

The player side-slipped him, turning so the blow glanced off his leather padding, then moved the ball toward the end zone again. The assassin dashed in from the side, reached in with a swipe of his foot, and stole the ball away, then kicked it back to midcourt. Before anyone could stop him he scooped the ball up with his hands and tossed it toward the ring.

The shot might have been true, but just before the ball left his hand he was slammed between the shoulder blades, and his aim went off. The ball struck the top of the ring in a vertical rim shot and thudded back into the court.

Showing its partiality, the crowd roared its approval in the darkness.

It was a new game. Three-on-two. Gonzalez was huffing and puffing but tasting victory.

His opponents stared at them, their wide, high-cheekboned faces as unemotional as granite sculptures. The sphere designated as fate rested between them. Gonzalez was tiring and knew he wouldn't last more than a few minutes at this pace.

"Get them!" he barked.

Newly honed into a team by desperation, the two men on the outside went directly for their opponents while Gonzalez charged up the middle to take control of the ball. Taking his time, he cocked his foot for a long slam shot that would send the ball high. The feel of his foot making contact with the ball was satisfyingly solid. The sphere lifted off with seemingly nothing to stop it. As the ball left the ground the man being guarded by the assassin side-slipped the attack and did a leaping ballet midair twist, turning so that his hip padding deflected the ball. It bounced off with a loud thud to the man's teammate, who fell to the ground.

Gonzalez thought the man had tripped, but the move was deliberate. The man picked up the ball in his ankles and, using his legs for leverage, looped the ball in the air. His teammate gave it a boost with his head, and the ball flew toward the ring. For an instant it looked as if there wasn't enough force to send the ball through the ring, but the aim was true, and the ball slipped through the opening then bounced onto the court again.

The game was over.

There was a wild burst of screaming from the spectators on top of the walls.

Then silence.

Gonzalez and his teammates stood there panting, sweat-drenched clothes caked with dirt and grass. The ball had been sent through the goal with practiced ease. They'd been toyed with, Gonzalez realized; their opponents had truly played like gods, and there was never a chance of winning.

The interior wall of the courtyard was carved with a series of pictures. Gonzalez had paid little attention to the artwork before, but now he followed the eyes of his opponents. The carvings showed a series of players facing each other over a ball marked with skulls. In one a victor held a knife in one hand and a head in the other. A decapitated victim knelt before him. Blood flowed from his neck in the form of serpents.

The crowd closed in, forced him and his companions to their knees. His hair was grabbed roughly, exposing his neck, and Gonzalez knew his fate. Three swordlike knives flashed in the air, and three heads thumped to the ground almost simultaneously, eyes blinking frenetically, as they rolled to a stop near the ball that had sealed their fate.

High in his treetop observation post Zavala whispered hoarsely, "My *God!*" He couldn't believe his eyes. Zavala had watched the ball game, more curious than concerned, actually enjoying the play. Even at his distance he could see it was a rough game indeed. But it was only at the last minute that he saw how lethal it was for the losers. He scrambled down the tree and ran through the chaparral toward his car.

The room within the pyramid was immense, its stone block walls lined with glass display cases holding dozens of priceless jade masks. On one wall was a huge screen. Halcon watched as Gonzalez and his teammates played out the last bloody moments of their life, then turned to the scar-faced man who sat in a leather chair puffing on a cigar.

"Would you like to watch the instant replay, Guzman?"

"I'll catch it later on sports highlights if you don't mind, sir," the scar-faced man replied.

Halcon waved at a hidden sensor, and the screen went blank.

"Don't tell me you're losing your appreciation of the ball game."

"I'm not ready for cricket matches yet, sir," Guzman replied, taking a sip from his brandy glass. "But the games are far too short and lack skill and finesse."

Halcon plucked a cigar from a gold-embossed humidor of fine leather, lit up, and surveyed Guzman contemplatively through a curtain of smoke, unsurprised at the bluntness of the answer. He had known Guzman from the day he was born, when Halcon's father appointed his trusted henchman as his son's official protector. The man was totally without guile, which is why he was so refreshing to a Machiavellian schemer like Halcon. He glanced at the screen. "You're right," he said with disgust. "A brawl like that demeans the goals of the game, to instill fear and obedience in my followers while giving them a pride in their cultural past."

His hand went to his phone console. "Have the winning ball team line up for their awards where I can see them," he ordered with a curt command, then went over to a glass cabinet that held several rifles and handguns. He pulled a rifle with a telescopic scope off its rack and said, "Come, Guzman."

Halcon led the way through a door onto a darkened balcony that overlooked the complex. The winning ball players stood in a line on the bright green of the ball court. Halcon brought the rifle butt to his shoulder and squinted through the telescopic sight. The rifle cracked three times with Halcon smoothly working the bolt. When the echoes of gunfire faded three still figures lay on the grass.

"I know you prefer the Austrian rifle for your assignments," Halcon said, surveying the deadly result of his handiwork with satisfaction, "but I've always had good luck with this English L42A1."

Guzman gazed out at the ball court and curled his lips in a sardonic smile. "I suppose you've just terminated their contracts."

Halcon laughed, and they went back inside. He carefully replaced the rifle in its case and turned to the scar-faced man.

"My apologies, Guzman. I should have known better than to suggest that the man who single-handedly sank the most beautiful ocean liner in the world was losing his taste for blood sport. I must apologize, too, for keeping you in the dark about my plans for so long. I didn't ask you to my sanctum sanctorum tonight simply to watch that pitiful performance on the ball court. You will be the first to hear the details of my grand vision for the future."

"I am honored, Don Halcon," Guzman said with a slight bow of his head.

Halcon lifted his brandy snifter to a huge gilt-framed portrait over the massive walk-in fireplace. "To my distinguished ancestor, the founder of the Brotherhood, I dedicate my fondest dream."

The oil was done in the El Greco style, except in this painting the subject's long face and pointed ears were not exaggerated. The saturnine tonsured man in the simple dark brown monk's cassock had pale, almost translucent skin in stark contrast to the red voluptuary's lips. Diamond-hard pale gray eyes glittered as if reflecting flames. The background was in shadow except for a glow in one corner, where a struggling figure was being burned at the stake. Guzman first saw the painting of Hernando Perez as a young initiate into the Brotherhood. Halcon's father had explained with an ironic grin that Perez had the artist put to death as a heretic because he wanted his portrait to be the man's last.

Guzman was the first and only non-Latin member of the order. He was the illegitimate son of a German Stuka pilot stationed in Spain and a Danish nursemaid in the Halcon household. The pilot died in the war, and the maid committed suicide. The old master raised the boy in his house and provided for his upbringing. His motive was not altruistic. He recognized that one unquestionable loyal follower was more valuable than a platoon bound only by self-interest. He gave him a new name and sent Guzman to the finest schools, where he learned to speak several languages, and to more specialized tutors who versed him in the martial arts and use of weapons. Guzman killed his first man during the saber duel that gave him his hideous scar. The old master's vision was justified. Guzman grew into a devoted aide whose natural skills for murder and mayhem proved to be a bonus.

"I remember your father saying that Perez was basically a simple man," Guzman said.

"He was a fanatical nihilist. The good archdeacon formed the Brotherhood of the Sacred Sword of Truth because he felt Torquemada was too soft on heretics. Fortunately," he said with a smile, "his priestly vows didn't prevent him from enjoyments of the flesh with the female novitiates. Otherwise the Halcon family would not be here. Nor did his religious zeal stop him from stealing the property of those he condemned. His beliefs resulted in the Brotherhood's prime directive."

Guzman recited the directive like a recording machine. "The Brotherhood's prime duty is to erase all evidence of prior contact between the Old and the New World before Columbus."

"It is still our duty, but I am about to make some changes."

"Changes, sir?" The directive was holy writ in the Brotherhood.

"Don't be surprised. The Brotherhood has shifted direction before. We evolved from a religious group to a terrorist organization to protect the Spanish crown. We did our work well. The Brotherhood stamped out suggestions of pre-Columbian contact that questioned church dogma and hence the infallibility of royal decisions. By defending the belief that Columbus was the first European to travel to the New World, we kept other countries from claiming our riches. That's why doubting his deeds was a capital crime. As a youth I remember asking my father, 'Why does that still matter? King Ferdinand and Queen Isabella are dead. Spain is no longer a great power.' "

"It is not the idea itself," Guzman murmured, "it is the *purity* of the idea."

"My father taught you well. He drummed the same thing into my head. Only by obeying our sacred vow to carry out our original mandate can we remain an elite priesthood united in a sacred cause. Under the Brotherhood, Columbus has achieved near sainthood. Even today modern scholars who deviate from the premise laid down by our medieval brothers risk their careers. The world wonders how Generalissimo Franco was able to remain in power to his deathbed. It was because of the alliances he had forged with the Brotherhood. The greatest threat to our fraternity was averted, thanks to you."

"Your father told me the object on board the ship could destroy the Brotherhood. But he also wanted to show his followers

that he was willing to go to any lengths to preserve the raison
d'être of *Los Hermanos.*"

"Yes, he compared that event with Cortez burning his ships
so his followers had no choice but to stay by his side."

"Your father was a wise man."

"Wise, yes, but his obsession with the past would have led to
the demise of the Brotherhood. We were becoming nothing more
than a Spanish Mafia when I took control. If the Brotherhood is
to go on for another five hundred years, we must do as Cortez,
burn our ships. We no longer work to protect a nonexistent
Spanish sovereignty but to lay the foundations for a new empire.
Our inspiration will be Quetzalcoatl, the plumed serpent of the
Maya, who will return in different forms to begin a new era.
This time Quetzalcoatl will be reborn as a hawk."

"I don't understand."

"The reason we continue to conceal pre-Columbian contact
is to give Hispanics greater pride in their own heritage. If claims
were blasted in the media that all the great cultures of
Mesoamerica came from Europe and China or Japan, it would
greatly dim the accomplishments of our people and send them
to the backwaters of history. Thanks to another lusty ancestor, I
carry the blood of the Maya in my veins. I am not just a
Spaniard but an Indio. I embody the heritage of two great civilizations. To suggest that my people's glorious culture was
imported from foreign civilizations across the seas is repugnant.
To imply that the Olmecs, the Mayans, and the Incas were little
more than savage peoples who created architectural wonders,
ingenious astronomical science, and beautiful art only after
being influenced and taught by Asians and European intruders
cannot be endured. The children of Latin America and their children must believe their ancestors achieved grandeur and greatness entirely from their own inventiveness. This is vital so that
we can produce a resurgence of our former glory and take our
place as the leading civilization of the twentieth century."

"That's a pretty tall order."

"Hear me out," said Halcon. "In less time than you can

imagine, the southern third of the United States will secede and become a Latin American nation."

"With all due respect, Don Halcon, America fought a civil war the last time someone suggested secession."

"The situation is completely different," Halcon declared flatly. "What I propose would happen if I lived or died. In fifty years non-Latins will be a minority in the U.S. It is already the case in the border states like New Mexico. I simply propose to accelerate the process by leading a mushrooming Hispanic movement for independence, with your help."

"I will do my best as always, Don Halcon."

"It will not be as hard as you might think." Halcon spun an antique globe on its axis. "See how different the world has become. The USSR. East Germany. Vanished." He placed his finger on the globe to stop its spinning. "It is not Halcon but the geographers who say Belgium one day will split into Flanders and Wallonia. Australia will become four separate countries. China will break up into a series of autonomous zones like Hong Kong. Italy will separate into the prosperous north and the poor south. Most important are what scientists are saying about North America."

He guided Guzman to a heavy mahogany table where there was a large map laid out and tapped a word covering the southwestern part of the United States.

"Angelica?" Guzman read.

"The blending of borders is inevitable, even the governments know North America must change. The blueprint is being drawn as we speak. When Canada loses Quebec the landlocked maritimes will join the U.S. Alaska merges with British Columbia and the northwestern states to create Pacifica, an entity whose common interest lies in the Pacific Rim. Mexico's northern state will join with the Southwest U.S. states." He swept his hand over the map. "I will unify those of Indian and Spanish heritage in a new wave that will sweep over territory once owned by Mexico."

"How can you go up against the armed might of a superpower?"

"The same way Cortez and a handful of followers defeated

the great empire of the Aztecs with its millions, by creating alliances, pitting one group against another. The lines are already being drawn for a military confrontation. The border towns will be engulfed in blood. None will be spared. The greater the atrocities, the stronger the reaction, the faster it will spread. When the violence starts, the U.S. will *beg* me to end it. I will take my place as a leader, and we will instill the old values and the old ways." He chuckled. "One day the ball game will be as popular as bullfighting and the NFL. The bloody rebellion we fomented in Chiapas proved it can be done."

Guzman smiled. "That was as easy as tossing a match into a pail of gasoline."

"Exactly. The government reacted by massacring Indians. The Mayan Zapatista rebels showed the same ferocity as their ancestors in forcing concessions from the government. In the United States, Californians are arming themselves against illegal crossings by immigrants that we are encouraging."

"Ranchers want a bigger military role to fight the drug lords whose drug operations we are supervising along the border," Guzman said.

"All according to plan. The U.S. will lose patience. The violence will unite the millions of Hispanics and Latinos throughout the Southwest. This is why we cannot afford to have our glorious past rewritten. I have spent a fortune to buy territory, voting, and political influence. Halcon Industries is stretched to the limit. I built this new Chichén Itzá to be the capital of the new country. But even the vast resources of our cartel can't equip an army to defend itself against a United States that might not recognize the trend of the future. This is why it is vital that we find the vast riches that will enable us to carry out our plan. It will not succeed without the treasure."

"We are close to assembling all the pieces of the puzzle. Our agents have acquired documents from a number of sources in Spain and other countries."

"Has there been any outcry?"

"Not yet. The *International Herald-Tribune* reported the unexplainable theft of Columbian memorabilia from auction houses and museums, but nobody has put it together yet."

"Not until now," Halcon said with a sly smile.

Guzman raised a frosty eyebrow.

"Our experts have analyzed the old documents," Halcon went on. "They have located the key that will open the secret that has baffled us for so long."

"Congratulations, Don Halcon. I'm most pleased."

"You won't be when you hear the details. You see, the key we seek lies on the bottom of the ocean in the hold of the *Andrea Doria.*"

Guzman was stunned. "Not the artifact? How could that be? Your father ordered me to sink the ship."

"As I said, my father was not infallible. He thought the artifact could destroy us."

"There's no mistake?"

"I've had the documents checked again and again. I have read them myself. No, my friend, I'm afraid there is no doubt. The artifact that my father once thought would end the Brotherhood will show the way to greater glory. I want you to fit out a salvage project right away. You will have all the resources of Halcon Industries at your command. This should be done as quickly as possible."

"I'll start work as soon as we are through here, sir."

"Excellent. Are there any more archaeological expeditions that could derail our plans in the meantime?"

"There seems to be a freeze on activities around the world. Except for the short-lived NUMA project in Arizona, of course."

"My compliments for cauterizing that infection so quickly. How much of a threat is NUMA?"

"I wouldn't underestimate them. You saw what happened in Morocco."

"I agree. I think it best that you remain in charge of all operations where NUMA is concerned. Use all force necessary."

Guzman's cell phone rang, and he excused himself to listen.

"Yes. Immediately. Patch it into Don Halcon's closed circuit."

A moment later the television screen blinked into life and showed a wooded scene in black and pale green.

"What is it?" Halcon snapped impatiently.

"This was taken with a surveillance camera in the small rise on the north of the complex."

As they watched the colors were manipulated so that the face of a man running through the woods was enlarged to fill the screen.

Guzman swore under his breath.

"Do you know him?" Halcon asked.

"Yes. His name is Zavala, and he was with the NUMA team on the Arizona project."

"You're correct about NUMA not being a toothless dog." Halcon stared at the screen, thinking. "You said there was another man, the leader of the team."

"Kurt Austin. He was running the project."

"They'll do for a start. Have him and this man killed. Put the salvage plans off if you have to."

"As you say, Don Halcon."

Halcon dismissed Guzman and went back to his map.

Guzman had no illusions about Halcon. He had known him since he was a boy, hovering over him like a guardian angel. He thought Halcon's megalomaniacal scheme had more to do with his selfish pursuit of power and riches than restoring the lost grandeur of those he called his people. He was using those of Indian blood toward his own ends and would enslave them much as his conquistador ancestors had. What he was proposing would mean civil war, certain bloodshed, possibly the death of thousands.

Guzman knew all this and didn't care. When the old master took the young blond boy under his wing, he created a being of undiminished loyalty. Killing highly placed NUMA operatives could be a big mistake, Guzman thought as he left the room. But he had become bored with his work in recent years, and what had become important was the game. The NUMA men would be worthy opponents. His mind began to work on an assassination plan.

34

THE YUCATAN HAMMOCK WAS NEVER
meant for a man as long as Paul Trout. The handwoven fiber
sling was designed with the diminutive Mayan stature in mind.
When he wasn't swatting mosquitoes Trout was trying to find a
place for the arms and legs that dangled to the dirt floor of the
Indian hut. Dawn's first gray light was a welcome relief. He
extricated himself from the sack, smoothed the wrinkles out of
his suit as best he could, decided he could do nothing about his
morning beard, and with a bemused glance at Morales, who lay
snoring in another hammock, emerged into the morning mists.
He trekked across a cornfield to the edge of woods where the
helicopter lay on its side resembling a big dead dragonfly.

The pilot had tried to land in the field as the helicopter used
up the fuel vapors powering its engine. The aircraft plunged into
the canopy of foliage that was so deceivingly soft-looking from
above. The fuselage crashed through the treetops accompanied
by a horrendous racket of snapping branches and the screech of
tortured metal.

Trout had the wind knocked out of him. The pilot hit his
head and was knocked cold. Morales was dazed. Ruiz, who'd
been awakened by the racket, sat there in bewilderment with
drool on his whiskered chin. Morales and Trout dragged the pilot
out of the chopper, and he came around in the fresh air. Everyone had bruised knees and elbows, but no serious injuries were

noted. Trout was glad Ruiz had survived; he might prove a valuable source of information in finding Gamay.

With his hands on his hips Trout surveyed the damage and shook his head in amazement. The trees had cushioned the copter's momentum. The runners had collapsed, and the main and tail rotors were history, but the body remained miraculously intact. Trout rapped on the mangled fuselage. There was a stirring inside. The pilot, who had chosen to spend the night in the copter, crawled out, stretched his arms, and opened his mouth in a bellowlike yawn. The noise awoke Ruiz, who was on the ground with his hands cuffed to the useless runners. He blinked sleepily when he saw Trout. The mosquitoes didn't seem to have bothered him. Smelling like a swine pen had its advantages, Trout guessed. He walked around the chopper and thought again that it was a miracle they'd got down in one piece. He had counted seven bullet holes in the helicopter including the lucky fuel tank shot.

Minutes after the JetRanger hit the ground a figure had approached from across the cornfield. An Indian farmer who lived nearby had seen the crash. He greeted them with a friendly grin from under his straw hat. He was unperturbed, as if strange men dropped out of the sky every day. The pilot did a quick damage assessment and found that the radio was useless. They followed the farmer to his hut, where his wife offered food and water and four young children eyed them warily from a distance.

Morales questioned the farmer at length, then turned to Trout.

"I asked him if there is a village or town near here with a telephone. He says a priest in a nearby village has a radio. He will go there to tell him about us and ask to send help."

"How far is the village?"

Morales shook his head. "It's a ways. He will spend the night and come back tomorrow."

Thinking of Gamay, Trout chafed at the delay, but there was nothing he could do. The farmer's wife packed food in a cotton sack, and her husband climbed onto a grizzled burro, waved good-bye to his family, and set off on his grand adventure. Trout watched the burro plod down a trail and prayed the unsteady animal would last the trip. The farmer's wife offered the use of her home and said she would stay the night with relatives. She was back by the time Trout and the pilot returned to the hut to see if Morales was awake. Then she prepared tortillas and beans for everyone.

After breakfast Trout took some tortillas out to Ruiz. Morales unlocked the *chiclero*'s cuffs but kept his legs bound. Ruiz noisily devoured the tortillas, and Morales gave him a cigarette. He puffed on it gratefully. The crash had wiped the cocky sneer off his face, and he was more than cooperative when Morales asked a series of questions.

"He started working with this gang of looters about six months ago," Morales translated. "He says he used to gather *chicle* sap before that, but I don't believe him." He quizzed the man again, more forcefully this time. "*Sí,*" he said, laughing. "It is as I thought. He is a thief. He used to steal from the tourists coming to Merida. A friend told him he could make more money smuggling artifacts. The work is harder, but the pay is better and there is less risk."·

"Ask him who he works for," Trout suggested.

Ruiz shrugged when the question was presented to him. Morales said, "He worked for a man who used to be a policeman guarding the ruins. There is a small gang, maybe a dozen. They find a place and dig trenches. The jades and the pots with the black lines are the best, he says. Maybe two hundred to five hundred dollars for one pot. His boss takes his cut and arranges transport."

"Transport to where?" Trout said.

"He's not sure," Morales translated. "He thinks his boss was connected with people operating out of the Petan, just over the border in Guatemala."

"How does he get the artifacts there?"

"He says they would move the goods down the river in the small boats to a place where trucks come in. Then maybe they go to Carmelita or probably across the border to Belize. I have heard what happens then. The artifacts go on planes or ships to Belgium or to the States where people pay big money for them." He glanced, almost with pity, at Ruiz. "If this toothless idiot only knew these people make hundreds of thousands of dollars and he takes all the risks." He chuckled. Ruiz, sensing a joke but not understanding with his limited English that he was the butt of it, grinned his toothless grin.

Trout turned the information over in his mind. Gamay and Chi must have stumbled onto a smuggling operation. They escaped on the river, using the same route as the smugglers, and were trying to get away when the helicopter found them. He asked Morales to find out how far the truck-loading spot was from the rapids.

"Couple of nights on the river, he says. He doesn't know the distance in miles. He says the river goes dry in places sometimes, and they work it after the rainy season."

At Trout's request, the pilot dug a map out of the helicopter. No river was depicted, confirming the information from Ruiz. There was no way to trace the course Gamay would take.

The interrogation was interrupted by a commotion. A boy of about ten was running across the cornfield, shouting in his high-pitched voice. He rushed up to the helicopter and announced breathlessly that his father was home. They retied Ruiz and went back to the hut.

The farmer said he would have been home sooner, but he took the opportunity to visit his brother who lived near the village. Oh, yes, he said after a long description of his family reunion, he had talked to the priest, who no longer had the radio. Trout's heart fell. Then rose again a minute later when the farmer said the priest used a cell phone that he kept for emergencies, mostly medical. The priest had called for help and asked the farmer to relay the following message, which he wrote on sheet of paper: "Tell the men in the helicopter that someone will be sent to find them."

With rescue imminent Trout was even more impatient. He

paced the edge of the cornfield, frequently glancing at the cloud-less blue sky. Before long he heard a faint *wugh-wugh* sound. He cocked his ear. The noise became louder until he could actually feel the vibration of whiplashed air.

A Huey painted in greenish brown flashed into view above the trees with another right behind it. Trout waved his arms. The helicopters made a tight circle around the field, then touched down at the perimeter of the corn rows. The doors opened even before the rotors stopped, and men dressed in camouflage uni-forms spilled from the choppers. Morales, the pilot, and the farmer and his family went to greet the new arrivals. There were six of them, including a captain in the lead helicopter and a medical technician in the second. The med tech examined every-one and gave them clean bills of health except for superficial injuries.

Trout and Morales went to the downed helicopter, but Ruiz was gone. The *chiclero* had squirmed out of his hastily tied bonds. After a quick parley they decided against a time-consuming search. Trout would have liked to see if Ruiz had more informa-tion to offer, although from what the *chiclero* recounted he was at the bottom of the smuggling totem pole. Looking at the escape optimistically, maybe Ruiz would be eaten by a jaguar. He would pity the jaguar. They thanked the farmer and his family for their hospitality and got into the Hueys. Within minutes they were skimming a few hundred yards over the treetops.

Less than an hour later they set down at an army base. The captain said the base had been established near Chiapas at the time of the Indian uprising a year earlier. The captain asked if they would like food and a bath and a change of clothes. A shower could wait. Trout had other priorities. He asked to use a phone.

Austin was in his office at NUMA headquarters examining the photos Zavala had taken in Halcon's underground garage when the phone rang. Zavala had just described the trip to Halcon's complex and the bloody ball game, and Austin was bringing him up to speed on his Nantucket encounter with Angelo Donatelli. A broad smile crossed his face when he heard Trout's voice. "Paul, good to hear from you. Joe and I were talking about you a few minutes ago. Did you find Gamay?"

"Yes and no." Trout told Austin about the near miss on the river, the helicopter crash and rescue.

"What do you want to do, Paul?" Austin said quietly.

A heavy sigh came from Trout's end of the line. "I hate to let you down, Kurt, but I can't come back. Not until I find Gamay."

Austin had already made his decision. "You don't have to come back. We'll come down to you."

"What about the job we've been working on? The archaeology thing?"

"Gunn and Yaeger can work up an operational plan while we're gone. You stay put until we get there."

"What about the admiral?"

"Don't worry. I'll handle things with Sandecker."

"I really appreciate this, Kurt. More than you know." The statement was as far as Trout's Yankee reserve would let him go.

Austin dialed Sandecker and told him the story.

Sandecker had a reputation for carrying out a project once started, but his loyalty to his staff was equally legendary. "It took me years to put this Special Assignments Team together. I'm not going to have one of its key members kidnapped by a bunch of damned Mexican bandits. Go get her! You'll have every resource NUMA can offer."

It was the reaction Austin expected, but one never knew with the unpredictable admiral. "Thank you, sir. I'll start right off with a request for quick transportation to Mexico."

"When do you want to leave?"

"I want to put together a specialized gear package. Say two hours?"

"You and Zavala be at Andrews Air Force Base with your toothbrushes. A jet will be waiting for you."

Austin hung up. "Gamay's in trouble, and Paul needs our help." He sketched out the details. "Sandecker's given the okay.

We'll be leaving from Andrews in about two hours. Can you handle that?"

Zavala was up and heading for the door. "On my way."

A minute later Austin was on the phone again. After a quick conversation he was out of the office as well and on his way to the boathouse, where he threw some gear and clothes into a duffel bag and headed to the airport. Sandecker was true to his word. A swept-wing Cessna Citation X executive jet painted in NUMA turquoise blue was warming up its engines on the tarmac. He and Zavala were tossing their bags to the copilot when an army pickup truck rolled up. Two husky Special Forces men got out and supervised while a fork-lift hoisted a large wooden box from the truck and into the cargo section of the plane.

Zavala raised an eyebrow. "Glad to see you brought beer for the trip."

"I thought the basic Austin Rescue Kit might come in handy." Austin signed a receipt for one of the Special Forces men. Minutes later he and Zavala were buckling into their seats in the plush twelve-passenger cabin, and the plane was in line for takeoff.

The pilot's voice came over the speaker.

"We're cleared for takeoff. We'll be flying at a cruising speed of Mach .88, which should put us in the Yucatan in less than two hours easy. Just sit back and enjoy the ride. You'll find the scotch in the liquor cabinet and soda and ice cubes in the refrigerator."

Minutes later the plane was in the air, climbing to its cruising altitude at four thousand feet per minute. As soon as they leveled off Zavala was out of his seat. "This is the fastest commercial jet except for the Concorde," said a misty-eyed Zavala, who had flown everything under the sun. "I'm going to chat with the guys in the cockpit."

Austin told him to go ahead. It would give him the chance to think. He put his seat back, closed his eyes, and tried to imagine the events Trout had described in their phone conversation. By the time Zavala came back and relayed the pilot's message that they were about to land, Austin was erecting a mental framework the way a bridge builder extends steel girders into thin air.

Trout was waiting for them as the Citation taxied to a stop. He'd bathed and shaved and had borrowed a camouflage uniform to wear while his suit was being cleaned. The uniform was made for the smaller-framed Mexican GI and emphasized Trout's long arms and legs, giving him a spidery aspect.

"Thanks for coming so quickly, guys," he said, taking their hands.

"We wouldn't have missed seeing you in that uniform for the world," Austin said with a grin.

"Suit's being laundered," Trout replied with some discomfort.

"You look quite fetching in cami," Austin said. "Sort of a distinguished Rambo, wouldn't you say, Joe?"

Zavala shook his head slowly. "Dunno. I think maybe Paul is more the Steven Seagal type. Jean-Claude Van Damme, maybe."

"I'm so glad you rushed down here at NUMA expense to evaluate my sartorial splendor."

"No problem at all. It's the least we could do for a pal."

Trout's face grew somber. "Kidding aside, it's great to see your ugly faces. Thanks for coming so quickly. Gamay needs backup in the worst way."

"She'll get more than backup," Austin replied. "I've got a plan."

Zavala glanced over at the Special Forces boxes being unloaded from the plane. "Uh-oh," he said.

The greatest asset for a sniper is not aim, Guzman mused, but patience. He sat on a blanket in the bushes on the shore of the Potomac River, his cold eyes fixed on the Victorian boathouse exactly opposite. He had been there for hours, lapsing into a detached yet alert zombielike state that allowed him to ignore the numbness in his buttocks and the biting insects. He had watched the sun go down, aware of the beauty of the river but not connecting with the changing reflections and shadows in any emotional way.

He knew Austin was not coming even before the automatic nightlight flicked on in the living room of the darkened house. He lifted the Austrian Steyr SSG 69 sniper's rifle from his lap and sighted through the Kahles ZF69 telescopic sight on the picture of a boat hanging on the wall. A squeeze of the trigger would send a bullet winging across the river at 2,821 feet per second. He made a click sound with his tongue, then lowered the rifle, picked up a cell phone, and dialed a number at NUMA headquarters.

The answering machine's recorded message said Mr. Austin would be away from his office for a few days, gave NUMA's office hours and asked Guzman to leave a message. He smiled. There was only one message he wanted to give Mr. Austin. He punched another number. The phone rang in a car parked outside Zavala's house in Arlington.

"It's off," Guzman said, and hung up. The two men in the car looked at each other and shrugged, then started the engine and drove off.

Back along the Potomac, Guzman carefully wrapped the rifle in the blanket and set off through the woods as silently as a ghost.

35

THE PRAM GLIDED THROUGH THE
eerie mists as if in a dream. Moist exhalations rising off the river
materialized into ectoplasmic wraiths that waved their spectral
arms as if in warning. *Go back.*

Gamay steered while Chi sat in the bow like a carved
mahogany figurehead, his sharp eyes probing the gauzy haze for
obstacles human and otherwise. They had been on the move
since dawn after overnighting on a small midstream islet. Chi
slept ashore on the oversized hummock. The encounter with Old
Yellow Beard still gave Gamay the shivers. Chi assured her there
was no danger from snakes. Even a worm would have been
unwelcome company, she said. She preferred the discomfort but
relative security of the pram. A loud hiss startled her awake, and
she was relieved to see it was only the camp stove. Chi was
preparing coffee. They had a quick breakfast of trail mix and got
an early start on the river.

The *chicleros'* larder would keep them well supplied for days.
With little room in their pram, they had filled another boat with
food, bottled water, and fuel and towed it behind them. The
added burden slowed their progress, but the supplies were vital if
they expected to survive.

The mid-morning sun burned the fog phantoms away, and
visibility was clear once more even though the tradeoff was a suffocating humidity. Gamay had found a battered straw hat that

helped prevent sunstroke and shaded her eyes from the blinding tropical light.

The river twisted and turned. As they approached each bend, Chi raised his hand and Gamay reduced the throttle to an idle. For a few minutes they would float with the current and cock their ears, listening for voices or the buzz of motors. No longer fearful of attack from behind, they were wary of surprises from ahead. They didn't want to round a bend and bump into a boat-load of brigands. The jury was still out on the helicopter. They still weren't sure whether it was friend or foe. The chopper had saved them from the rapids. Yet they hadn't forgotten that it also dumped them into the river.

Sometimes a fish jumped out of the water, and the splash was like a gunshot in a barrel. Otherwise, aside from the metallic gurgle past the aluminum hull, they heard only the chatter and squawk of birds gossiping in the trees and the drone and whine of insects. Gamay was grateful for the generous supply of Cutter's. The bug repellent had to be reapplied frequently to replace the goop washed away by sweat or the occasional rain shower. Chi didn't seem to be bothered by bugs. Natural selection, Gamay surmised. Any Mayan susceptible to malaria or other insect-borne ailments would have been weeded out of the pack long ago.

The river's character changed as the hours passed. The waterway was reduced to half its original size. Squeezing the same amount of river into fifty percent less space made for a strong, smooth current. The flat countryside had become more rolling, the banks steeper and higher, covered with impenetrable growth.

Gamay had chafed at their steady but slow *African Queen* pace. She wasn't sure she liked the toboggan run aspect any better. As their speed picked up there was less margin for error. "I wonder where we are," she murmured, eyeing the vine-covered limestone walls that closed in from each side.

"I've been thinking the same thing." Chi scanned the sky. "We know that must be east because it's where the sun rose. We have need of your Girl Scout training."

She laughed. "What we *really* need is a hand-held GPS receiver."

Chi reached into his pack and extracted the ancient instrument they'd found in the cave temple. The sun glinted off the burnished metal. He handed the instrument to Gamay. "Know how to work one of these gadgets?"

"As a marine biologist I spend most of my time under the water and leave it to others to get me there. I've taken a couple of navigational courses, though."

Chi took the tiller while Gamay examined the instrument. It was the first chance for a close look at the device since they discovered it. Again she marveled at the workmanship of the boxlike wooden case and the circular interlocking gears. The lettering was definitely ancient Greek, spelling out the names of various gods.

She applied pressure with her forefinger to the largest wheel, but like the other moving parts it was stuck fast by corrosion. Engraved in the largest wheel were depictions of animals. Sheep. Goats. Bear. Even a lion. From their positioning Gamay concluded that they represented star constellations. It reminded her of the cardboard star charts with the rotating dials that show the night sky at a given time of the year. Clever.

"Whoever put this device together was a genius," she said. "I've only figured out part of its function. It tells you what the night sky looks like at a given time of year. More important, it could tell you from the sky what time of year it was."

"In other words, a celestial calendar that would be invaluable in knowing when to expect the rainy season, when to plant and harvest."

"And when to sail, too. Also *where* you are. You can use the backside as a sextant that gives you an approximate but fairly accurate sun's azimuth."

"What are the other wheels used for?"

"They could be a can opener for all I know. You'll have to ask someone with technical expertise," Gamay said with a shake of her head. "Too bad the mechanism is corroded. I wouldn't mind knowing where we are."

Chi rummaged in his rucksack and pulled out a map which he spread on his knees. "This river isn't shown," he said, tracing their approximate route with his finger. "My guess is it's only this big after rainy season. When we factor in our direction and speed, I'd venture that if we haven't gone over the border to Guatemala, we're very close to it. Which would make sense. The looted artifacts are smuggled through Guatemala to Belize and points beyond."

"I wasn't planning on a trip to Guatemala when I came down here for NUMA, but I guess I don't have much choice."

"Look on the bright side," Chi said. "We have the chance to put a stop to this terrible business of smuggling antiquities."

Gamay cocked an eyebrow. She hoped some of Chi's optimism would rub off. Given the precarious state of their minute-to-minute existence, she hadn't thought of them as a smuggler-busting duo. Her main goal was *survival.* She was getting tired of playing the *Perils of Pauline.* The fact that they weren't dead was probably mostly a result of dumb luck.

She indicated several penciled *X*'s on the map. "Any idea what these are?"

After a moment's study Chi said, "They could be anything. Dig sites, places they stockpiled artifacts or supplies, distribution."

"And we're heading right into the middle of things from what this handy-dandy device tells us." She hefted the instrument and gave it back to Chi.

"Interesting," Chi said thoughtfully as he carefully stuffed the ancient instrument into his pack. "In our zeal to put this to practical use we have forgotten its archaeological significance."

"I'll leave it to others to hash that out. I'm a marine biologist now."

"Yet you can't deny that finding an ancient Greek artifact in a pre-Columbian setting raises questions."

"Questions I'm not prepared to answer."

"Nor am I. Not yet. But I know that I will bring the wrath of the archaeological establishment down on my head at the slightest hint of pre-Columbian contact with Europe. This instrument did not get here by itself. It was either delivered by Europeans to America or transported by Americans who went to Europe."

"Maybe it's a good thing we don't have anybody to tell," Gamay said.

The strengthening current ended their discussion. The river had become even narrower and gorgelike, the walls steeper and higher. Chi was having trouble controlling the boat, and Gamay took over. There was no noisy rushing of water that would indicate they were near rapids, not yet, but Gamay stayed alert.

"Our speed is picking up," she told Chi.

"Can you slow us down?"

"I've got the motor practically on idle to maintain steering control. Keep a sharp eye and ear out. If it looks like rough water ahead I'll steer for shore, and we'll figure out what to do."

At the foot of the wall-like bankings was a muddy beach a couple of yards wide. Enough space to pull off the river for a breather. She was buoyed by another consideration. This was the only way the *chicleros* could have come. Which meant the river was navigable for a small boat. Controlling the towed boat was a problem. Time to pull up on shore, transfer supplies, and cut loose.

The river suddenly narrowed considerably, and the water speed doubled.

She and Chi exchanged puzzled glances. Still no sound of rapids. They were rounding a long curve, the bankings closing in so that it seemed that they could almost touch them. Gamay planned to go wide on the turn and simply run the boat onto the narrow beach. The supply boat whipsawed, then jerked in the other direction to throw her steering off. She knew from experience that when things go wrong on a boat they *really* go wrong. Drastic action is the only way to avoid disaster.

"Cut her loose!" she shouted.

Chi stared at her, uncomprehending.

She made a knifing motion with the edge of her hand. "Cut the supply boat line, or it will tangle in our propeller."

Once Chi understood he acted quickly. He severed the tow-line with a quick swipe of his machete. The loaded pram went into a slow spin and headed right at them. Gamay and Chi were both watching the boat, hoping it would pass them. A collision in the narrow canyon would be a disaster. She was glancing over her shoulder, trying to steer so as to avoid a crash, and didn't see the wall of limestone that loomed directly in their path until the last second.

Gamay ducked so she wouldn't hit her head as the pram shot through an opening in the wall. Within seconds the swift-moving river had sucked them deep into the maw, and the vestiges of daylight disappeared.

"We need a flashlight, Professor," she said, her voice echoing in the inky darkness.

The flashlight flicked on, and the shaft of light fell on wet rocks that glistened only yards away. She swung the tiller to avoid a crash, oversteering in her haste, and was turned sideways by the current. After a few dicey moments she had the boat under control again and was moving with the river flow.

Chi played the flashlight beam ahead and above on rough wet walls and ceilings. The underground river reminded Gamay of a fun house, only she wasn't having any fun. Especially after the beam picked up what looked like clusters of black leaves covering the ceiling. The light reflected on thousands of burning-red pinpoints of light. She held her breath not so much out of fear but to block out the overpowering ammonia stench.

"I *hate* bats," she muttered, gritting her teeth.

"Keep still, and you'll be all right," Chi cautioned.

No need for that warning. Gamay was frozen in place by the thought of leathery wings and sharp pointed teeth.

The creatures stayed where they were, however, and in time the bat population thinned out to nothing.

"Fascinating," Chi said. "I've never seen a river go underground so abruptly."

"Excuse me for saying so, Professor Chi, but your country has too many caves and holes in the ground for my taste."

"*Sí*, Dr. Gamay. It's like Swiss cheese, I'm afraid."

Gamay tried to look on the bright side, then realized there wasn't one. They had been sucked into the bowels of the earth, and there was no assurance they would ever come out. At best, this was the route the *chicleros* used, which meant they might bump into more of the smugglers. Gamay lifted the propeller out of the water, and they used a paddle to steer, fending off with their hands and feet when the pram bumped noisily into the sides of the cave.

Gamay grabbed on to a small stalagmite and wrapped a few turns of their severed tow line around it. The makeshift cleat held. They crawled up onto a rock shelf and lit a camp light. Gamay expected their errant supply boat to come barreling by, but it must have been caught up. Chi mourned the loss of his Spam. Gamay said maybe they would catch up with it later. She wouldn't miss the canned meat, but the fuel and water would come in handy.

Over lunch of jerky and cold tortillas they discussed their options and agreed that there was only one: they had to go on. Neither expressed the unspoken fear that the river would come to a dead end. Or no end at all. But the possibility hung over their heads like a black cloud.

They got back in the boat, restarted the motor so they'd have control and traveled another half hour, often bending over with fits of coughing from the damp musty air. Gamay felt as if her lung linings were becoming as mildewed as the rest of her. The current seemed to diminish. Chi, who'd been lighting the way ahead, announced that the river was almost back to its original width above the rapids. Chi had placed the camp light in the prow of the boat, and its yellow glow illuminated what looked like a large cave.

"Stop!" Chi shouted over the suddenly echoing sound of the motor.

Gamay cut power and jerked the tiller around, narrowly avoiding a collision with the black wall in their way. The river had disappeared again. It must have gone even deeper, she surmised.

They were in a large pool. A narrow tributary extended off the main waterway. For want of a better course, Gamay pointed the pram into what looked like a man-made canal.

Chi shut off the lantern and leaned forward, staring into the darkness at a faint orange glow which grew larger and brighter as they neared, finally materializing into a flickering kerosene lantern on the piling of a small pier. Gamay slid the boat in next to two identical prams tied up at the dock and cut the motor. They listened intently but heard no sound louder than their own nervous breathing.

"Guess this is the end of the ride," Gamay said.

They packed Chi's rucksack with their remaining supplies and made their way cautiously along the pier which was built against a level limestone shelf about as wide as a sidewalk. The walkway widened, and the rough walls gave way to smooth ones. They followed a trail of lights, moving from one lantern to another, until they were in a large chamber. The walls and ceiling were smooth and square-cut.

Chi took in his surroundings. "This was a quarry. Probably used by the ancients to cut limestone for their temples and houses. We're in the middle of Mayan activity."

"I don't think the ancients used kerosene lanterns."

"Nor do I. The good news for us is that there must be an entrance somewhere."

They explored further and came upon dozens of wooden boxes stacked on pallets. Chi walked down the row and peered into the boxes. "Incredible," he whispered. "There must be hundreds of Mayan artifacts here. They're using this quarry to store stolen antiquities."

"Makes sense," Gamay agreed. "The loot is brought in via the river and shipped out from here." A light bulb went off in her head. "They'd need land transportation to move the artifacts out of here."

Chi wasn't listening. He was standing in front of a set of wide shelving built against the chamber wall. The beam of his flashlight went back and forth over a number of large stone blocks lined up on the shelves like a display at a tombstone store. "The boats again," he whispered.

Gamay stepped closer and saw carvings in the stone. "These are similar to the carvings we saw back at the ruins."

"Yes, it seems the looting is far more extensive than I imagined. They must have hit other archaeological sites similar to the one we visited. They used a diamond-edged power saw to cut these sections from the wall." He sighed heavily. "This is a tragedy."

Intellectual curiosity momentarily overwhelmed their survival instinct. They might have stayed there all day comparing notes if Gamay hadn't noticed a whitish glow at the far end of the quarry. *Daylight*. At last, a way out of this creepy place. Since they'd climbed out of the boat she'd been dogged by the feeling that they were not alone. With a quick glance over her shoulder she grabbed Chi by the arm and practically dragged him away from the stone artifacts.

The light was coming through an opening about as wide as a garage door topped with the typical Mayan corbeled arch. They stepped outside. The sudden change from dark coolness to dazzling heat was a shock, and they blinked their eyes against the bright sunlight. In front of the opening was a crude loading platform and a winch hanging from a crane. The earth around the platform was soaked with motor oil and churned up by tire treads.

Gamay stepped forward for a closer look only to stop as she saw something in her peripheral vision. She turned to the right, then to the left, and didn't like what she saw. On either side of the quarry entrance, which was cut into a hill, was a man. One had a rifle trained on her, the other a shotgun leveled at Chi. They had pistols tucked in their belts as well. Gamay and Chi agreed with their eyes not to make a precipitous move. Their only escape route was back the way they'd come, and that was blocked a second later when a third armed man stepped from the quarry. Her instincts about being followed were right on the mark, Gamay thought ruefully.

All three men had the dirty, unshaven look that she had come to expect from the locals, but these *chicleros* had a harder, more disciplined aspect about them than the men who had chased them downriver. That would make sense. The men back at the excavation site would have been at the bottom of the pecking order, the laborers who dug up the antiquities and the mules who transported them. These must be the guards. The third man issued a curt order to the others. They gestured with their weapons for Gamay and Chi to move along a dirt road that led away from the quarry.

They followed it for several minutes through the forest until they came to where the trees and brush had been cut away to make a parking space for a dented and mud-spattered four-wheel-drive GMC pickup truck. The door of a small shed was open, revealing the greasy tools hanging inside. A man was working on the engine. He backed out from under the upraised hood when he heard the others approaching. He was a skinny, waxen-skinned man whose scraggly narrow beard made him look like a poor man's Satan. He and the head guard talked. Even without knowing Spanish, Gamay could tell that the mechanic was the one in authority.

He directed a question at Chi, who had slipped back into his humble peon mode. They talked a minute, then the man frowned and shook his head in a this-is-all-I-need expression. Gamay noted with relief that there was none of the leering rape threat of her earlier encounters, but she wasn't reassured by seeing that the man kept his hand on his pistol grip the whole time he talked with Chi. After a moment's thought he got in the truck's cab and talked in low tones to a squawking radio voice. The conversation was heated at times, but the mechanic was smirking when he came back and issued an order to the guards. They grabbed Gamay and Chi and roughly plunked them on the ground behind the truck, then bound their feet and tied their arms to the bumper.

"What did he say?" Gamay whispered when they were left alone.

"I told him we were lost, that you are a scientist and I am your guide, that we were drawn into the cave by accident."

"Did he buy the story?"

"It didn't matter. He said he has orders to shoot anyone he finds here. But he checked with his bosses on the radio and they told him to bring us in."

"He looked pretty pleased with himself for passing the buck. How long do we have?"

"The truck has an engine problem. When he gets it fixed, we *vamanos.*"

Gamay took a deep breath and let it out. She wasn't afraid. Just weary and somewhat discouraged that they had been captured so close to freedom after the last few days struggling down the river. For all their efforts they were no better off now than when they'd been stuffed underground. Looking on the bright side, these *chicleros* didn't leer at her body and make unveiled threats of rape. And they wouldn't have to walk out of the forest. She focused her thoughts on the truck. It could be their ticket out of here if they could figure out how to wrest the ignition keys from four armed men. She leaned her head back against the bumper and sorted through their options. She realized quickly that as things now stood only one thing could get them out of this bind. A miracle. She closed her eyes. It was going to be a long night.

36

ZAVALA SAW THE BODIES IN THE
dawn light from the lead helicopter. The Huey was flying above
treetop level following the serpentine twists and turns of the
river when Zavala noticed the human flotsam caught in a sharp
bend. He asked the pilot to go in for a closer look. The Huey
banked over the water and hovered. Zavala leaned out its big
door and inspected the bloated corpses. Then he radioed the second helicopter, which was making a wide lazy circle above.

"Paul and Kurt, from what I can see there's nothing to worry
about. All the bodies appear to be male." In other words, Gamay
wasn't among the dead.

"Are you certain?" Trout replied.

"As sure as I can be from up here."

Austin's voice cut in. "Thanks. This is a good place to make
our insertion. Is our limo ready?"

"All gassed up and set to go."

"Good. Let's do it."

The two helicopters on loan from the Mexican army had
overflown the old ruins where Gamay had first been captured.
Trout wanted his NUMA teammates to have a total picture of
Gamay and Chi's flight from start to finish. Trout flew over the
rapids and continued downriver until the bodies were sighted.

Zavala relayed Austin's command to the pilot. The Huey
drifted out over the widest part of the river, then slowly descended

until the large object slung under its belly touched the water. Zavala hit a release switch, and the helicopter lurched upward, relieved of the weight it had been carrying. The Huey moved out of the way, and the aircraft carrying Austin and Trout darted in to take its place.

Austin was out the door first, quickly rappelling down a line into what looked like an oversized, vaguely banana-shaped bathtub. He released the rappel line and punched a starter button, then maneuvered the strange craft to keep it under Trout, who was descending the rope.

A waterproof bag was lowered next. Trout guided it down. It was tricky going directly under the wash of air from the rotor. Trout's height gave him a first-baseman's edge as he reached for the package holding their vital supplies. Although his dignified manner reflected his academic background and his lean frame suggested a frail physique, Trout had built up muscular shoulders and arms from his days as a commercial fisherman. He easily hoisted the swinging package off its hook, and the Huey moved away.

"I don't usually pick up hitchhikers, but you have an honest face," Austin yelled over the engine racket.

Trout smiled. Despite his worry about Gamay, he was happy to be *doing* something at last. He unclipped the hand-held radio from his belt and talked into it.

"Thanks for bringing the limo around, Joe."

"No problem. Better give it a test run before you take it for a spin."

The "limo" was a two-person Seal, one of the smallest hovercraft made. The foam and fiberglass grass-green hull, with its rounded stern and sharp pointed nose, was only fifteen feet long. With the combined kick from its thrust propeller and lift fan, the Seal could plane along on an air cushion, on water or land, with its payload, at a speed of up to twenty-five miles per hour. Recalling Nina Kirov's experience with the giant hovercraft, Austin had reasoned that the bad guys weren't the only ones who should be driving fun boats. The Seal was designed for hunters and wildlife people who wanted to get into otherwise inaccessible locations. The Special Forces had modified the civilian model, adding brackets for a light machine gun, spotlight, and infrared night sensors.

Austin goosed the twenty-horsepower Briggs and Stratton engine and felt the craft rise out of the water on its air cushion. He tried some circles and loops, planing at high speeds and low. Satisfied that he had the hang of it, he turned the controls over to Trout. While Trout got accustomed to the feel of the little craft, Austin dug through their supply bag and pulled out his pistol and two CAR-15s, the shortened carbine version of the M-16. In addition to a rate of up to 950 rounds per minute on automatic, the weapon could be used as a grenade launcher.

Austin would have been satisfied if no shot had to be fired, but he wasn't optimistic. He was no longer laughing at Trout's cami uniform and had borrowed one of his own and covered his stark white hair with a matching fatigue cap.

Nothing could have prepared them for the powerful stench as they approached the floating bodies. The NUMA men dipped their neckerchiefs in the river and tied them over their noses before moving in closer. The bodies looked as if somebody had pumped air into them. Trout's mouth was clamped in a tight line as he made himself inspect each corpse one by one.

When he was sure of what he had seen he clicked the radio. "We're okay, Joe. Gamay isn't here."

"Glad to hear it, pal."

"My guess is these are the guys who tried to shoot us out of the sky." He shivered, remembering Gamay's close call with the rapids.

"We'll make a quick sweep down the river. She could be waiting just ahead for you and Kurt to rescue her."

"Thanks again for giving up your seat."

"No problemo, *amigo.*"

There had been a brief discussion the night before over who would accompany Austin. Zavala was eager to go in, but he knew Trout should be there when they found Gamay, dead or alive. For a more practical reason, they needed someone in the command post who could speak Spanish and act as liaison with the Mexicans.

An instant later both Hueys disappeared over the treetops. Austin pointed the Seal downriver and cranked her up. The hovercraft lifted above the water and leaped forward as if out of a slingshot. When he asked his Special Forces pals if they had anything that would get them in and out of tight places, Austin knew air reconnaissance could cover a lot of ground in a short time, but the lowland rain forest would hide anything as small as a human being.

They took turns at the controls, keeping the Seal at twenty miles per hour. For all their time on the river, Gamay and Chi had barely covered fifty miles since leaving the rapids. With the hovercraft's superior speed and no overnight stops, they would cover the same distance in a fraction of that time. Trout's sharp eye caught the glint of sunlight ahead in midstream. They pulled up to the tiny islet, and Trout stepped out. Chi had been scrupulous about not littering the island, but he had dropped a trail mix wrapper. Without a word Trout stepped back into the boat and showed his find to Austin, who nodded, gunned the throttle, and notched their speed up to the limit. The game was afoot!

The radio crackled, and Zavala's voice came on. "Kurt, this is crazy!"

"We hear you, Joe. What's going on?"

"I'm not sure. We were following the river ahead of you. It twists back and forth, then narrows after a while into sort of a canyon. No sign of Gamay or Chi, but we're tooling along, and all at once the river disappears."

"Say again?"

"The river just *stopped*. One second it was flowing along. The next it was gone."

"Where are you now?"

"We're conducting a search pattern to see if we can pick it up again. If not, we'll come upriver and meet you."

The mini-hovercraft continued to skim along. They, too, noticed the narrowing of the river and the increasing steepness of the walls.

Zavala came on the radio again. "Nothing, Kurt. We're going to have to head back. The choppers are running low on gas."

They had brought extra fuel and left it back at the ruins. It wouldn't take them long at their speed to get back, fuel up, and return to the river search. Austin said he and Trout would go as far downriver as they could and rendezvous with the Hueys. They waved as helicopters flashed overhead on their way back to refuel, and the hovercraft continued on its way.

They were in the gorge, moving even faster with a kick from the current, when they saw the pram. It was jammed into the mud along the shore. Austin pulled the hovercraft onto the beach, and he and Paul jumped out. The pram was loaded with cartons, and it was probably their weight that kept the current from dislodging the boat and pulling it back into the river.

"What do you think, Paul?"

"I'd say they were never in this pram. My guess is that they were towing it. Look, it's so full there isn't room for anyone to sit. The outboard's in its up position. This bow line has been cut."

Austin pulled at a thin rubber hose. "You're right. Look, the motor's fuel hose isn't even connected to the gas tank."

They shoved the pram farther onto the shore and moments later were back in the hovercraft. They were only moving for a few minutes when the river ended. Austin gave the hovercraft more power to hold it in one place.

"That's the answer to Joe's disappearing river," Trout said. "No mystery. It just runs underground." He tried to reach Zavala on the radio but got no answer and assumed they were out of range or the transmission was blocked by the high rocky walls. They decided without hesitation to push ahead. They went in slowly, coming down from their air cushion, Trout illuminating the way with his hand-held spotlight.

The vibration and noise created by the thrust propeller unnerved the bats. They came off the roof as if blown by a gust of wind, a squeaking mass of flapping membranous wings and sharp claws. Austin doubled their speed. The hovercraft was on its air cushion again. Both men crouched low in the open cockpit, hardly able to see through the flying swarm of black furry bodies. The craft bounced off the rocky shores several times, but as long as he was able to go forward, Austin kept the pedal to the metal.

Then they were through it and into the clear.

Austin brought the engine down to an idle, and the current moved them ahead.

"Are you okay?" he asked.

"My hair will probably go as white as yours, but other than that I'm fine. Let's keep moving."

The sound of the motor was horrendous in the close confines, echoing and reechoing off the rough walls. Austin could only hope that any adversaries they met were stone deaf, because their arrival would have been announced for miles. They moved at a steady clip, throwing up waves on either side, and before long they emerged into the larger cavern. They made a quick circle of the pool to get their bearings and saw that the river ended again but that there was a canal leading off from it.

The canal ended at a small pier illuminated by a lantern. They tied up next to three prams and left the hovercraft. With their weapons at ready they proceeded along the walkway into the quarry. They stopped to inspect the contents of the boxes, then pressed on. Sunlight was shining faintly in the distance.

37

AUSTIN STOPPED UNDER THE COR-
beled archway and listened to the music playing faintly in the
distance. A Latin beat. With his back to the wall he edged his
way around the corner, CAR-15 held at ready, finger on the trigger. He stuck his head out, scanned the area around the loading
platform, and, seeing no one, stepped cautiously into the glare of
daylight. He signaled Trout to follow. With Austin still at point
they moved silently along the narrow dirt road, staying close to
the foliage on the side.

Near where a rutted track into the woods left the main road
they melted into the bushes and got down on their hands and
knees. They crawled parallel to the track, then dropped to their
bellies and slithered to the edge of a cleared area. Austin inched
forward and peered through the tall grass. Trout's hand gripped
his shoulder, but Austin had already seen the mop of hair that
was the hue of fine red wine. Gamay. She was tied to the rear
bumper of a battered GMC truck. Her face was the color of
boiled lobster, skin peeled off her sunburned nose, and her
crowning glory was a tangle of greasy curls, but otherwise she
seemed all right. Next to her was an Indian man who must be
Dr. Chi. Gamay had her eyes closed, but she opened them and
looked cautiously around as if she sensed their presence.

Austin quickly took in the rest of the scene. The source of
the music was a portable boom box perched on the bed of the

truck. Sitting on the ground behind the truck were three men engrossed in a game of cards. Their weapons lay within arm's reach, and all three men wore pistols. Austin's eye traveled to the front of the truck to where a fourth man was working on the engine. He, too, wore a pistol, but more worrisome was the AK-47 leaning up against a tire. Austin signaled Trout to back up. Paul nodded, understanding the need to reconnoiter, but the disappointment in his face was obvious.

Minutes later they leaned up against a tree and assessed the situation.

"We've got four armed men who would ordinarily be no problem up against the weapons we're carrying," Austin said. "But Gamay and Dr. Chi are directly in the line of fire. I don't like the idea of the fourth man separated from the others. He's got an AK right at hand. He could still cause damage. Any suggestions?"

"We could call in reinforcements," Trout said, patting the walkie-talkie at his belt. "But even if they got here soon, that would mean more shooting, more chance of someone getting hurt."

"My sentiments exactly." Austin scratched the stubble on his chin. "Gamay and Chi seem to be okay, which means someone wants them kept alive, for now at least."

"My guess is that they'll move out as soon as they fix their mechanical problem."

"That's when the situation will get fluid. The card game will break up, and the guards may move out of the line of fire. Or maybe we will get our chance when they put Gamay and Chi in the truck. Once they're out of the way we can make our move."

"There's another possibility," Trout said. "More of these guys could show up."

"I know that we'd be trading a known situation for an unknown, and I don't like it any more than you do, but I don't think there's anything else we can do except wait."

Trout nodded in reluctant agreement. They crawled back to the edge of the clearing. The card game was still in progress, and the mechanic continued to fiddle around with the engine. Austin was glad to see that Gamay and Chi both had their eyes open. He suppressed the surge of anger he felt at their plight.

Long after Austin had decided he never wanted to hear Latin music again, the mechanic backed out from under the hood, wiped his hand on a greasy rag, and got into the cab. The engine started on the first try, filling the air with an unmuffled rumbling. A cloud of purple smoke poured out of the exhaust pipe and enveloped Gamay and Chi, who turned their heads from side to side in a vain attempt to escape the fumes.

The card game was cut short. The players grabbed their money, scrambled to their feet, and with hands over their mouths and noses moved away from the rear of the truck. And their weapons, Austin noted with pleasure. They started yelling at the mechanic, who had just hopped out of the cab. When he saw that the guards were not showing the proper enthusiasm for his accomplishment, he went over and grabbed the nearest one by his collar, angrily dragged him to the front of the truck, and exhorted him to listen to the motor. The remaining guards broke out in laughter and joined the others.

"Show time," Austin said.

The essentials for a successful ambush are surprise and concealment. They could have mowed the *chicleros* down with a single sweep of their carbines, but Austin was into rescue, not murder. He and Trout stood up and strode casually into the clearing. Trout let off short bursts of fire in the air, while Austin kept the *chicleros* covered. The object was intimidation. The gunfire had the desired effect. At least partly. The three guards saw the two terminators walking toward them, glanced at their useless weapons, then back at the hard-eyed white-haired man and his towering companion, and scattered into the forest like leaves before a wind.

The mechanic dove into the cab, threw the truck into gear, and mashed the accelerator. The spinning tires gouged trenches in the ground and threw out twin showers of dirt. With a roar of the engine the truck started out of the clearing, dragging Gamay and Chi behind like tin cans on a honeymoon-bound car. Music still blasted from the boom box on the truck's bed.

Austin shouted for Trout to cover the departing *chicleros* and drew the Bowen from his hip with the speed of a Dodge City gunfighter. Holding it in both hands, he coolly sighted on the rear of the cab. The barrel belched fire five times, and the cab window disintegrated in an explosion of glass. The last shots were unnecessary because the first bullet had taken off the back of the driver's head.

The truck went on for another few yards as if it were on auto pilot, but it finally lurched to a stop as the engine stalled. Austin ran for the truck. But Trout got there ahead of him, quickly sliced through Gamay's bonds with a hunting knife, and took his wife in his arms.

38

A WEEK LATER A TAXI DROVE PAST
the black cast-iron fence that surrounded the shaded lawns of
Harvard Yard, turned onto a quiet grass-lined street, and pulled
up to a five-story Georgian-style brick edifice that seemed out
of place next to the more modern science buildings keeping it
company. Zavala emerged from the cab and surveyed the sign
for the Peabody Museum of Archaeology and Ethnology. Turning to Austin and Gamay, he said reverentially, "This is a great
day for the Zavala family. My mother always hoped I'd go to
Harvard."

"Your mother has my husband, Paul, to thank for her little
boy's success," Gamay said, "but congratulations anyhow."

"Thank you. My mother thanks you, too. Shall we enter the
hallowed precincts?" he said with a gallant sweep of the hand
that was entirely in keeping with his character.

For indeed it was Trout's summons to his NUMA colleagues
that brought them to Cambridge that morning. Trout had
arrived at the museum by a roundabout route that started in the
Yucatan jungle. After the reunion with his wife Trout and the
others hitched a ride back to the *Nereus* aboard a Mexican helicopter. While they waited for the choppers to arrive they took a
closer look at the looted antiquities stored in the cave.

Chi had led the way, moving down the line of crates and
shelves, sadly shaking his head as he explained the significance

of the artifacts and the damage that had been done by their random exhumation. Pausing in front of the inscribed stone panels, Chi lamented, "I know these stones tell a story, an important one. But because of the way they were carelessly dug up and thrown into this place, it could be months, maybe years, before we will know what it is."

Chi's words echoed in Trout's ears as the helicopter flew him and the others to the *Nereus*. Gamay was checked out and found to be run-down but otherwise in good health. With his wife in a real bunk and enjoying the gourmet treats of the vessel's galley, Paul hitched a ride back to the *chicleros'* camp, bringing with him a case of photographic equipment.

The army had established a camp to guard the artifacts and mop up stray looters. Chi had stayed on to inventory the stolen goods. When Trout outlined what he had in mind the professor gave him an enthusiastic go-ahead. Trout made hundreds of digital photographs of the stones and their inscriptions. Then he packed up and returned to the research vessel to rendezvous with Gamay and fly home. Back in Washington, Paul worked the data into his computers.

As a deep ocean geologist Trout had developed a high degree of skill using computer graphics for his undersea projects. His work went beyond simply probing the ocean bottom with electronic eyes and ears. His arcane findings on strata or thermal vents had to be presented so that a PhD wasn't needed to understand them. Archaeology was already using computer imaging to reconstruct everything from ancient cities to skeletal remains. He conferred frequently by phone with Dr. Chi, who had returned to Mexico City. After his analysis he called Austin and said, "I know this sounds crazy, but this stuff I've been doing for Dr. Chi may tie in with the assignment we've been working on."

Austin didn't need any coaxing. He gave Nina Kirov a brief telephone rundown on Trout's findings and asked if she could match Paul with a Mayanist. Nina immediately recommended Dr. Orville. Trout took his computer disks to Cambridge and set up shop at the Peabody.

The museum's small reception area was dominated by an Eskimo totem pole whose grotesque faces looked down at the young college woman at the front desk. Austin gave their names to the receptionist, who punched the intercom button on her telephone. An equally attractive guide appeared and led them up the metal staircase, past the scowling sculpture of a seated Mayan warrior, to the fifth level.

Their guide kept up a running commentary. "The Peabody is one of the oldest museums in the world devoted to anthropology," she said. "It was established in 1866 with a $150,000 gift from George Peabody. Construction on the five-story main building began in 1877. The museum has fifteen million items within its walls, but we're giving much of the material back, particularly artifacts from E. H. Thompson's work at the sacred *cenote* of Chichén Itzá where they used to sacrifice virgins."

"I can think of better things to do with a virgin," Zavala murmured.

Fortunately the guide didn't hear his comment. She ushered them through a door into a lecture hall. Nina stood next to the lectern talking to a thin man with wild red hair. She smiled brightly when she saw the others, especially Austin, he was pleased to note, and quickly came over to take his hand. Austin felt his blood quicken whenever he set eyes on Nina's lush mouth and the bold curves of her supermodel's body. He vowed to himself that he would take her where they weren't surrounded by their friends and colleagues.

Nina introduced the new arrivals to Dr. Orville. Austin had learned long ago that looks didn't count, but he wasn't sure in this case. The Mayanist wore a rumpled high-button tweed suit even though the day was warm. His widely unfashionable thrift-shop tie was decorated with old food stains. The manic gleam in the hazel eyes was magnified to incredible proportions by the thick glasses, but a burning intelligence kept the creeping shadow of madness at bay. Just barely. Austin expected the orbs to spin around at any moment like those of a crazed cartoon character. He decided to contemplate the thin line between genius and derangement another time.

"Paul is putting the final touches on the presentation and should be with us in a few minutes," Nina announced.

The door opened. Gamay had expected her husband's usual head-ducking entry. Her mouth gaped in surprise, then widened in a smile. Extending her hand to the short, slight figure, she said, "I hardly recognized you without your machete, Professor."

The professor's change in appearance went beyond a simple sugar cane knife. He had on a custom-tailored Armani suit of bullet gray and a yellow power tie which he wore as naturally as he had his peasant's clothes.

Chi's classic Indian face was as stony as a gargoyle, but his dark eyes danced with amusement.

"When in Rome . . ." he said with a shrug.

"This is a wonderful surprise, Professor. You look well," she said.

"And you, too, Dr. Gamay."

The last time she saw the professor he was waving from the ground as she ascended into the skies in a helicopter. Chi appeared none the worse for their river adventure. Gamay by contrast didn't feel her normal self until she got back to Washington. The assault by the blistering Yucatan sun had taken its toll on her fair skin. The trail mix diet and sleepless nights haunted by snake dreams hadn't helped.

The lecture hall began to resemble a fashion spread from *GQ* when Trout stepped through the door. Befitting his Ivy League surroundings, Trout was in a pseudo-English mode, wearing a hound's-tooth custom sports jacket tailored in London to fit his tall frame, razor-creased olive slacks, and the inevitable bow tie. He apologized for the delay, and while the professor took over the lectern Trout went to the table and slipped a floppy disk into a laptop computer connected to the projection screen. The setup was similar to that used at NUMA headquarters by Hiram Yaeger. Nina sat at the table, and the rest of the NUMA team settled into the front row of seats like eager freshmen on the first day of class.

Orville opened the meeting. "Thank you all for coming. Nina will tell you that I have a reputation for making wild assertions in the local press." His mouth stretched into a strange lopsided grin. "But I'll have to admit even *my* fertile imagination would be hard put to come up with a story more fantastic than the one you are about to hear. So without further ado I will turn the meeting over to my esteemed colleague and dear friend, Dr. José Chi."

The lectern dwarfed Chi as he stood beside it with his hands behind his back.

"I would like to thank Dr. Orville for arranging this meeting and allowing us to use space at this institution where I spent many happy hours as a graduate student," Dr. Chi said in a voice as crisp as dry leaves. "As you know, Dr. Gamay and I discovered a horde of hundreds of stolen antiquities. The artifacts included some intriguing carved stone blocks and stelae cut from temples and buildings with no regard to origin, and many were damaged. While I would have preferred for the antiquities to have lain undisturbed in the ground and cataloged *in situ*, the people who removed them may have inadvertently been helpful in resolving what I understand from my friends at NUMA to be a situation of some urgency."

Chi raised his finger, and Trout punched a computer key. An aerial photograph filled the screen.

"This is the looted site," Chi said. "The mounds you see are the remnants of buildings clustered around what was once the central square of a Mayan city. Next, please."

Another picture came on the screen.

"This is an observatory. Please note the details on the frieze. Next. Construction wasn't confined to the ground level. This is a subterranean temple. It is only one of the features that make this a highly unusual site."

Austin leaned forward in his chair as if he were trying to put himself into the scene. "Unusual in what other ways, Dr. Chi?"

Gesturing toward the image behind him, the professor said, "Most Mayan cities are combinations of administrative, religious, and residential uses. *This* center was devoted entirely to science. Primarily the study of time and astronomy. Ultimately Mayan science tied in with religion in much the same way as religion was tied to political power. But I have the feeling that more pure science was practiced here than usual. Its Mayan name is Sky Place. For our purposes I am calling it MIT."

"Like the Massachusetts Institute of Technology?" Zavala said. The world-renowned research and teaching institution was only a few miles from where they sat.

"Yes," Chi replied, "but in this case MIT stands for the *Mayan* Institute of Technology."

Like a standup comedian in a Borscht Belt hotel, Chi waited for the laughter to die down, then turned the meeting over to Trout and took his place at the table.

In contrast to the professor, Trout had to lean onto the lectern to use it.

"From the start Dr. Chi was convinced that the pictures and glyphs inscribed on the stones described a narrative," Trout said. "Our problem was that everything was jumbled up. It's as if you tore the pages out of a novel and shuffled them. Actually several novels, because the stones came from different sources. This was even tougher because the 'pages' were heavy stones. So we made dozens of photographic images and fed the data into a computer where we could rearrange the pictures on a monitor. We used common sense and information provided by the Mayan writings, which Dr. Chi and Dr. Orville translated. Then we organized the stones into a sequence, similar to the story board used for a television commercial. The tale they tell, as Dr. Orville implied, is indeed a strange and unbelievable one."

Trout went back to the projection controls, and Orville took his place. "It was fairly easy to categorize the images. We simply concentrated on pictures of boats like those on the MIT observatory you saw earlier and went from there. This is the first one in the chronology."

Austin studied the busy scene for a moment. "It looks like the Spanish armada setting off to sea."

"Yes, from the number of boats it is definitely a fleet rather than random shipping activity at a port. The activity is frenetic but organized. Here you see boats lining up, being loaded, then standing by with cargo aboard."

The photo was replaced by a series of scenes showing the fleet at sea.

"Here we have a rather fanciful voyage with all sorts of strange sea creatures," Orville continued. "Many of these scenes differ only slightly in detail. Probably an artistic device to give a feeling of time passing."

"Any idea how much time?" Gamay said.

"The Mayan writings say the voyage lasted one moon cycle. About thirty days. The Maya were precise timekeepers. Here is the last in the series. The boats have arrived at their destination. They are being greeted as they unload. There is an easy familiarity to the operation which suggests they were known to the inhabitants of this land." He turned to Trout and said, "It is time, my friend, to perform your computer magic."

Trout nodded. The blinking computer cursor selected three figures from the scene, framed their faces in a heavy white outline, then enlarged them. One face was that of a bearded man with an aquiline profile and a conical hat. The next was wide with full lips and a close-fitting skullcap or helmet. The third was a man with high cheekbones and elaborate feathered headdress.

Trout moved the images to the left of the screen, arranging them top to bottom. Three new faces appeared to the right.

"Looks like they were separated at birth," Zavala observed of the pairings.

"The similarity is pretty obvious, isn't it?" Orville noted. "Let's go back to the full scene again. Dr. Kirov, as our marine archaeologist, we would be pleased to have your opinion."

Using a laser pointer Nina highlighted first one ship then another. "What we have here is basically the same vessel used for dual purposes. The features are identical. The long and straight flat-bottomed hull. The absence of a boom; the brails or ropes used to lower and raise sail hang from a fixed yard. The lines sweep back to an overhanging stern. Three decks. Fore and aft stays. The carved bow." The red dot lingered for a second. "Here is the double steering oar. The protrusion at this other end is a ram. This is a row of shields along the deck."

"So it's a warship?" Zavala said.

"Yes and no," Nina said. "On the top deck of one of these ships are men with spears. Obviously soldiers or marines. There are lookouts in the bows and space for lots of rowers." The laser flicked to another ship. "But here the deck is reserved for a person of quality. See this figure of a man reclining in the sunshine. The staff has a crescent on top, indicating the admiral's flagship. This thing hanging off the stern could be a decoration, a rich carpet maybe, that indicates the admiral is in authority."

"How long would this ship be?" Austin asked.

"My guess is that they're somewhere in the range of one to two hundred feet. Maybe longer. That would put them at around a thousand tons."

Orville interjected. "Nina, could you mention that comparison you used with us landlubbers?"

"I'd be glad to. This ship is much longer than an English ship of the seventeenth century. The *Mayflower*, for example, was only one hundred eighty tons."

Orville asked, "So in your opinion, Nina, what are we looking at?"

Nina stared at the images, as if she were reluctant to vocalize what was in her brain. The scientist won out, however, and she said, "In my opinion as a nautical archaeologist, the ships shown in this rendering reflect the characteristics of Phoenician ocean-going vessels. If that sounds a little vague, yes, I am hedging my bets until I have more evidence."

"What sort of evidence would you need, Nina?" Austin said.

"An actual ship, for one thing. What we know about Phoenician ships we learned mainly from their pictures on coins. There have been some reports that they were as long as three hundred feet. I'd take that with a grain of salt, but even if you cut that length down by half you still have a substantial vessel for its day."

"Substantial enough to cross the Atlantic?"

"Without a doubt," she replied. "These vessels were a lot bigger and more seaworthy than some of the minuscule sailboats that have made the crossing. People have rowed across the ocean in a dory, for heaven sakes. This vessel would have been ideal. You can't beat the square sail for an ocean passage. With a fore-and-aft rig you've always got the possibility of a dangerous jibe, the boom swinging violently over with a shift of the wind. With the brails they could shorten sail in a brisk wind. They'd get a roll with that shallow keel, but the rowers could help keep her steady, and the length of the ship would help. A trireme like this could sail more than a hundred miles a day under ideal circumstances."

"Short of an actual ship, what would you need to convince you this is Phoenician?"

"I'm not talking about convincing me," Gamay said. "I'm already convinced. Could we go back to those faces again, Paul?" The six carved heads came up on the screen again. The laser dot touched on one depiction of the bearded man, then flicked to his twin. "The pointed hat on these gentlemen is consistent with those worn by Phoenician mariners."

"Which should come as no surprise," Orville interjected, "because the picture on the right came from a Phoenician stela discovered near Tunisia. The gentleman below him is identical to African-type faces found at La Venta, Mexico. The third physical type is from the Mayan ruins at Uxmal."

"I hear a conclusion lurking in there," Austin said.

Orville sat back in his chair and made a tent with his fingertips. "Basing conclusions on pictorial matching is fine if you're a pseudo-scientist trying to sell a paperback book, but it's not good archaeology," Orville said. He took a deep breath. "My colleagues would drag what's left of my tattered reputation from one end of Harvard Yard to the other if they heard me say this. Marine archaeology is not my forte, so I can't assess Nina's statements. What I do know is that the inscriptions on these rocks show Phoenicians, Africans, and Mayans together in one place. Furthermore, Dr. Chi and I have translated the glyphs together and independently, and we've come up with the same results each time. The stones say that those ships arrived in Maya country after fleeing a disaster in their homeland. What's more, they were greeted not as strangers but as old acquaintances."

"Did the glyphs indicate a date?"

"Knowing the Maya's obsession with timekeeping, I'd be surprised if there weren't one. The ships arrived in what would be 146 B.C. in our calendar."

Nina stared at the projection and whispered in Latin.

Seeing all eyes turned in her direction she explained, "It's something you learn in first-year Latin. *'Delenda est Carthago.'* Carthage must be destroyed! Cato the Elder ended every speech he made in the Roman senate with the phrase. He was trying to whip up public sentiment in favor of a war against the Phoenician city of Carthage."

"It worked, as I recall. Carthage *was* destroyed," Austin said.

"Yes. In 146 B.C."

"Which means these ships could have been escaping the Romans."

"A date is a date," Nina said, digging in her heels before she got dragged too far into Austin's theory. "I simply pointed out the coincidence. I made no conclusion. As a scientist I'd be irresponsible to make a statement like that," she added, but she couldn't hide the excitement building in her gray eyes.

Austin said, "I understand why as scientists you can't come out and say what you're thinking without more solid evidence. But from what I've seen here today I'm convinced the inscriptions on these stones suggest that ancient voyagers arrived in America long before Columbus. You know the Phoenicians were capable of making the crossing."

"I know they were the world's greatest explorers up until the fifteenth or sixteenth century. They circumnavigated Africa and went as far as Cornwall on the English coast and Cape Verde. On one voyage they supposedly took thousands of people on sixty ships."

"I rest my case," Austin said with exaggerated smugness.

"Not so fast, Perry Mason. The doubters will say these inscriptions are interesting, but who's to say they are authentic? Years ago inscriptions in Brazil supposedly described a Phoenician expedition in 531 B.C. The consensus was that they were forged. It sounds crazy, but you'll get people saying the antiquities looters could have been carving this stuff to sell to gullible collectors. Sure, you could make a case that the 'ships of Tarshish' undertook transatlantic voyages, but you need more substantial and substantiated proof to get anyone in the scientific community to accept it."

"What about the astrolabe you and the professor found?"

"Even that wouldn't do it, Kurt. They would say someone with Cortez or a Spanish hidalgo brought this thing in, an Indian stole it and stuck it in an old temple. Close but no cigar until you know for sure how it got there."

"Did the writing indicate what the ships were carrying?"

"We've been saving that for last," Orville said, giggling like a schoolboy.

"Oh, yes. We *know* what their cargo was," Chi said. "The Mayan writing says it was mainly copper, jewels, gold, and silver."

Austin looked like someone shaking off a head punch. "You're saying the ships were loaded with *treasure?*"

Chi nodded.

"This wasn't a routine trading expedition," Austin said, his green eyes flashing. "Carthage was under siege by the Romans. The Carthaginians would have done everything they could to make sure the Romans didn't get their hands on the royal treasury."

"Any idea what happened to the treasure?" Zavala asked.

"Unfortunately none of the carvings goes beyond the one you saw of the safe arrival of the ships," Chi said.

Nina frowned. "All this talk of treasure is exciting," she said with impatience, "but the dazzle of gold and jewels should not keep us from trying to find the answer to the question of why my expedition was massacred in Morocco."

"Nina's right," Austin said. "Let's concentrate on the thread that connects these inscriptions to the other discoveries overseas. Christopher Columbus. We know that hundreds of years after these stones were carved Columbus heard tales of a great treasure." He pointed at the screen. "Could this be what he was looking for?"

"I hate to throw cold water on your theory," Orville countered. "The rumors Columbus was following could have had their basis in the real riches held by the Aztecs. As we know the Spaniards hit the jackpot later." He paused. "You say Columbus was sailing a definite course. Do I understand he was following a map?"

"Not exactly," Austin said. "You remember that news clip Nina asked you to dig out of your files?"

"Oh, yes, the article from my Fortean file about the stone artifact."

"Columbus mentioned that he was being guided by a 'talking stone.' "

"Now I remember. The carved monolith they found in Italy. It was being shipped in an armored truck. Headed right here to the Peabody, in fact."

Austin said, "That stone could be the key to this whole mess. Treasure and assassinations."

"What a shame we can't take a look at it."

"Who says we can't? NUMA has tackled deeper and more difficult projects."

"Let me see if I follow your line of thinking," Orville said with disbelief. "You're planning on diving more than two hundred feet into a wrecked ocean liner in God knows what condition to retrieve a massive stone artifact from a locked armored car?"

Zavala winked at Austin. "With any luck we can do it between breakfast and lunch and celebrate at dinner."

"Hmm," Orville said with a smirk. He leaned forward and pointed his finger at the two NUMA men. "And they say *I'm* a nutcake."

39

THE MINI-SUBMERSIBLE WAS BARELY
a few fathoms below Nantucket Sound's blue-green waters, and
Austin was already having second thoughts about diving with
Zavala. His misgivings had nothing to do with Zavala's skill as a
pilot. There was hardly a craft in, on, or above the water Joe
couldn't operate. It was his off-key singing. As the crane lifted
the two-passenger craft off the deck and into the water Zavala
had broken into a Spanish rendition of "Yellow Submarine."

Austin barked into his microphone, "Do you know any other
songs?"

"I'm taking audience requests."

"How about singing 'Far Far Away'?"

Zavala's quiet laughter came over the earphones. "Gee, I
haven't heard that one since I was a *muchacho.*"

"Desperate times call for desperate measures."

"*No problema.* It sounds better with a guitar anyway. Where
do you want to go, *amigo?*"

"How about *down* for starters?"

Zavala's wave of acknowledgment was visible through the
observation bubble that was so close Austin could have reached
out and touched his colleague on the shoulder if not for the
plexiglass that enclosed their heads. The twin domes were
mounted at the front of the mini-sub, jutting at an angle from its
flat green ceramic surface like the bulbous eyes of a frog.

The Deep Flight II was unlike most deep ocean submersibles and bathyscaphes which tended to be shaped like a fat man, rotund and thick around the waist. It looked more like a futuristic fighter plane than an undersea vehicle. The fuselage was rectangular and flat, with the leading and trailing edges tapering like the business end of a chisel. The sides were perpendicular to the flat top and bottom with sharp edges as if canvas had been stretched over a frame. The wings were stubby and squared off and equipped with fixed running lights. Thruster fans were mounted behind the wings and observation domes. At the front were a pair of manipulator arms and a movable spotlight.

Unlike the crew of a traditional submersible, who sat upright as if at a desk, Austin and Zavala lay prone, Sphinx-like, face forward, strapped into form-fitting pans, elbows set into padded receptacles. They had dual controls, including a joystick for elevation and another for speed. Zavala handled the sub while Austin took care of the other systems such as lights, video, and the manipulator arms. He kept an eye on the heads-up digital display that contained compass, speedometer, and odometer and controls for depth gauge, air-conditioning, strobe unit, and sonar. The craft was slightly buoyant and dove by moving through the water and adjusting the elevators in its tail section like an airplane.

Their bodies were elevated at a thirty-degree angle to simulate the natural position of a person swimming. This attitude also made rapid descents and ascents less frightening. The space was adequate for Austin's six-foot-one height but snug around his broad shoulders. Still, he had to admit, even with Zavala's serenade it was a pleasant way to scout out a wrecked ocean liner.

The wreck was marked by a red spherical buoy. Zavala put the sub into a slow series of descending circles around the buoy line which ran down one hundred eighty feet from the surface to a length of chain attached to the third portside lifeboat davit. Normal descent to the highest part of the wreck took three to four minutes. With its five-knot speed the mini-sub could make the trip in a fraction of that time, but Austin wanted to get a feel for the environment they would be working in. He asked Zavala to ease them to the bottom.

The deepening water filtered the colors out of the sunlight streaming down from the surface. The red tints disappeared first, then on through the spectrum. At five fathoms all hues had been lost except for a cold bluish green. In compensation for the artificial dusk, the water became as clear as fine crystal as the sub broke through the warmer layers of thermocline where particles of vegetation were held in suspension. The sub corkscrewed lazily into the sea around the anchor line. A huge dark mass loomed from the pale bottom sand and filled their vision.

With the excellent visibility the sub had been running without lights. At a depth of one hundred twenty feet Zavala flattened their trajectory, slowed the mini-sub's speed to a crawl, and switched on the craft's belly light. The ship lay on its side. The large circle of illumination transformed a section of the hull below them from black to a cadaverish grayish green broken here and there with leprous splotches of yellow and rust stains like dried blood. The patina of marine growth, made up of millions of sea anemones, stretched off into the dimness beyond the reach of the light.

Austin found it difficult to imagine that this huge dead leviathan was once one of the fastest and most beautiful ships afloat. It is possible to stand before a building as tall as the *Doria* was long and not be awed by its size. But if that same seven-hundred-foot tower is turned horizontally and placed by itself on a flat empty plain, its immensity becomes breathtaking.

Lying on its starboard or right side, hiding the fatal gash from the *Stockholm*'s sharp beak, the *Doria* looked like a monstrous sea creature that had simply lain down to rest, had fallen asleep, and was now being reclaimed by the sea. The mini-sub switched on its video camera and glided toward the stern, staying a short distance above the rows of portholes. Dwarfed by the massive hull, the craft resembled a little bug-eyed crustacean checking out a whale. Near the sixteen-ton portside propeller

Zavala made a sharp turn and passed over the sharply etched black rectangles that once served as windows to the promenade deck. When open water appeared he dropped the sub down to a depth of two hundred feet and pointed the craft back toward the bow on a path parallel to their earlier course. The multitiered decks were a ninety-foot-high vertical wall off to their left. They moved past the three swimming pools that had once cooled passengers according to class on their transatlantic passage, scudding along the lifeboat deck whose davits didn't work any better now than they did in 1956.

Dozens of fishing nets had become snagged on the hooklike davits. The nets veiled the decks like great shrouds draped over an immense bier. The mesh was coated with a hoary cloak of marine growth. Some nets, held aloft from the wreck by their buoys, were still snaring fish from the schools of large pollock and cod that darted dangerously close. Noting the rotting bones caught in the mesh, Zavala wisely kept the mini-sub at a respectful distance from the still dangerous nets.

The ship's great red-and-white smokestack had fallen off, leaving an immense square shaft down to the engine room. Other openings marked uncovered staircase wells. The superstructure had slipped off and lay in a jumble of disintegrating debris on the sea bottom. With its distinctive stack and superstructure gone the *Andrea Doria* looked more like a barge than a ship. Only when they glided by the remnants of the wheelhouse and saw the massive booms, winch heads, and bollards intact on the foredeck did they began to get the sense that this was a huge passenger liner. It was hard to believe a vessel this big could ever sink, but that's what they said about the *Titanic,* Austin reminded himself.

They had been as reverent as mourners at a funeral, but now Austin broke the silence. "That's what thirty million dollars looks like after a few decades at the bottom of the sea."

"Hell of a lot of money to pay for an oversized fish catcher," Zavala said.

"That's just for the hull. I didn't count the millions in furnishings and artwork and four hundred tons of freight. The pride of the Italian navy."

"I can't figure it," Zavala said. "I know all about the thick fog, but both these ships had radar and lookouts. How in all of those millions of square miles of ocean did they happen to occupy the same space at the same time?"

"Plain lucky, I guess."

"They couldn't have done better if they planned out a collision course in advance."

"Fifty-two people dead. A twenty-nine-thousand-ton ocean liner on the bottom. The *Stockholm* heavily damaged. Millions in cargo lost. That's some planning."

"I think you're telling me it's one of those unsolved mysteries of the sea."

"Do you have a better answer?"

"Not one that makes any sense," he replied with a sigh that was audible over the mike. "Where to now?"

"Let's go up to Gimbel's Hole for a look-see," Austin said.

The mini-sub banked around as gracefully as a manta ray and headed back toward the bow, then cruised evenly about halfway down the length of the port side until it came to a jagged four-sided opening.

Gimbel's Hole.

The eight-by-twenty-foot hole was the legacy of Peter Gimbel. Less than twenty-eight hours after the *Doria* went under, Gimbel and another photographer named Joseph Fox dove on the liner and spent thirteen minutes exploring the wreck. It was the start of Gimbel's fascination with the ship. In 1981 he led an expedition that used a diving bell and saturation diving techniques. The divers cut away the entrance doors into the First Class Foyer Lounge to get at a safe reported to hold a million dollars in valuables. Amid great hoopla the safe was opened on TV, but it yielded only a few hundred dollars.

"Looks like a barn door," Zavala quipped.

"This barn door took two weeks to open with magnesium rods," Austin said. "We don't have that long."

"Might be easier to raise the whole thing. If NUMA could raise the *Titanic*, the *Doria* should be a cinch."

"You're not the first one to suggest that. There have been a pile of schemes to bring her up. Compressed air. Helium-filled balloons. A coffer dam. Plastic bubbles. Even Ping-Pong balls."

"The Ping-Pong guy must have had some *cojones*." Zavala whistled.

Austin groaned at the Spanish double entendre. "Aside from that astute observation, from what you've seen, what do you think?"

"I think we've got our work cut out for us."

"I agree. Let's go topside and see what the others say."

Zavala gave him a thumbs up, tweaked the motor, and lifted the nose of the sub. As they quickly ascended with the power from four thrusters, Austin glanced at the gray ghost receding in the gloom. Somewhere in that huge hull was the key to the bizarre series of murders. He put his grim thoughts aside as Zavala broke into a Spanish chorus of "Octopus's Garden." Austin thanked his lucky stars that the trip was short.

The Deep Flight broke the surface in an explosion of froth and foam. Through the water-streaked observation bubbles a gray-hulled boat with a white superstructure was visible about a hundred fifty feet away. The mini-sub was as agile as a minnow underwater. On the surface its flat planes were susceptible to the wave motion, and it rocked in the slight chop being kicked up by a freshening breeze. Austin didn't normally get seasick, but he was starting to feel green around the gills and was happy when the boat got under way and rapidly covered the distance between them.

The boat's design was typical of many salvage and survey ships whose main function is to serve as a platform for lowering, towing, and hauling various instruments and vehicles. It had a snub tugboat's bow and a high forecastle, but most of the sixty-five-foot length was open deck. At either side of the deck was an elbow crane. An A-frame spanned most of the twenty-two-foot beam at the stern where a ramp slanted down to the sea. Two men in wetsuits pushed an inflatable down the ramp into the water, jumped into it, and skimmed over the wave tops to the mini-sub. While one man manned the tiller the other secured the sturdy hook to a grommet at the front of the submersible.

The line led to a deck winch that pulled the mini-sub closer, the boat maneuvering until the Deep Flight was on its starboard. A crane swung over and lowered tackle that was attached by the men in the inflatable to cleats on the sub. The cable went taut. The sub and its passengers were lifted dripping from the sea, swung over the deck, and lowered onto a steel cradle. The operation was handled with Swiss-watch precision and dispatch. Austin would have expected nothing less than perfection from one of his father's boats.

After the revealing session at the Peabody, Austin had called Rudi Gunn to fill him in and request a salvage vessel. NUMA had dozens of ships involved in its far-flung operations. That was the problem, Gunn explained. The agency's boats were flung all around the globe. Most carried scientists who had stood in line for a spot on board. The nearest ship was the *Nereus,* still in Mexico. Austin said he didn't need a full-blown salvage ship, but Gunn said the quickest he could get something to Austin was a week. Austin told him to make a reservation and hung up. After a moment's thought he dialed again.

The voice like a bear coughing in the woods came on the line. Austin told his father what he needed.

"Hah!" the older man guffawed. "Chrissakes, I thought NUMA had more ships than the U.S. Navy. Can't the admiral spare you one dinky boat from his fleet?"

Austin let his father enjoy his gloat. "Not in the time I need it. I could really use your help, Pop."

"Hmm. Help comes with a price tag, lad," the old man said slyly.

"NUMA will reimburse you for any expenses, Pop."

"I could give a rat's ass about money," he growled. My accountant will find a way to put it down as a charitable donation if he doesn't get sent to Alcatraz before then. If I get you something that floats, does that mean you'll wrap up whatever nonsense Sandecker's got you involved in and get out here to see me before I'm so damned senile I don't recognize you?"

"Can't promise anything. There's a good chance of it."

"Humph. Finding a boat for you isn't like hailing a cab, you know. I'll see what I can do." He hung up.

Austin laughed softly. His father knew exactly where every vessel he owned was and what it was doing, down to the smallest rowboat. Dad wanted to let him wriggle on the hook. Austin wasn't surprised when the phone rang a few minutes later.

The gruff voice said, "You're in luck. Got you an old scow. We've got a salvage vessel doing some work for the navy off Sandy Hook, New Jersey. Not one of your big research vessels, but she'll do fine. She'll put into Nantucket Harbor tomorrow and wait for you."

"Thanks, Pop, I really appreciate it."

"I had to twist the captain's arm, and I'll lose money on this job," he said, his tone softening, "but I guess it's worth it to get my son out here in my declining years."

What an actor! Austin thought. His father could whup his weight in wildcats. True to his word the senior Austin had the boat in Nantucket the next day. The *Monkfish* was hardly a scow. It was, in fact, a medium-sized, state-of-the-art salvage vessel less than two years old. An added bonus was Captain John McGinty, a hard-boned, ruddy-faced Irishman from South Boston. The captain had dived on the *Andrea Doria* years before and was delighted to work on her again.

Austin was removing the cassette from the mini-sub's video camera when McGinty strode over. "Well, don't keep me in suspense," he said with excitement in his voice. "How's the old gal look?"

"She's showing her age, but you can see for yourself." Austin handed over the cassette. The captain glanced at the mini-sub and chuckled. "That's some hot rod," he said, and led the way to his quarters. He set Austin and Zavala up with soft chairs and hard drinks, then popped the video into his VCR. McGinty sat in uncharacteristic silence, taking in every detail as the swept-back hull and its patina of anemones rolled across the TV screen. When the video ended he punched the rewind button.

"You boys did good work. She looks pretty much the way she did when I last dove on her in 'eighty-seven. Except there are more trawler nets. And like you said," he sighed, "she's getting a little worn around the edges. It's what you *can't* see that's the problem. I've heard the ship's interior bulkheads are rotting away. Won't be long before the whole thing collapses in on itself."

"Could you give us an idea what we'll be dealing with down there?"

"I'll do my best. Want a refill?" Not waiting for an answer he poured the equivalent of a double shot of Jack Daniel's into each glass and dropped in a couple of token ice cubes. He took a sip, staring at the blank TV screen. "One thing you can't forget. The *Doria* may look pretty, even with all that scum mucking up her hull, but she's a man-killer. They don't call her the Mount Everest of divers for nothing. She hasn't killed as many as Everest, around ten last time I got counting, but the guys who dive on the *Doria* are looking for that same adrenaline rush from the danger that mountain climbers get."

"Every wreck has its own character," Austin said. "What are the major hazards on this ship?"

"Well, she's got all sorts of tricks up her sleeve. First of all there's the depth. With a two-hour decompression. You need a drysuit because of the cold. Sharks come to feed on the fish. Mostly blues. Not supposed to be dangerous, but when you're hanging on the anchor line decompressing you just hope some nearsighted shark doesn't mistake you for a fat pollock."

"When I first started diving my father told me to remember that in the water you are no longer the top of the food chain," Austin said.

McGinty grunted in agreement. "None of that stuff would be major except for the other problems. There's always a wicked current. It can be bad all the way down and even runs through the boat. Sometimes it seems like it will pull you right off the anchor line."

"I felt it pushing against the mini-sub," Zavala said.

McGinty nodded. "You saw what the visibility was like."

"We could see pretty well today. We found the wreck without our lights," Austin said.

"You were lucky. Sun was shining, sea wasn't stirred up much. On a cloudy or foggy day you can be practically on the wreck without seeing it. That's *nothing* compared to inside. Black as Hades, silt all over the place. Just touch it and you're surrounded by a cloud so thick your light won't penetrate it. Real easy to get confused and lost. But the biggest problem is entanglement. You can get into real trouble with all the wires and cables hanging down from the ceilings. That's if you get past those nets and ropes all over the hull and the monofilament from the party boats that fish the wreck. It's invisible. You don't know it's there until it's grabbed on to your tank. With scuba you've got twenty minutes max to get yourself out of trouble."

"That's not much time to explore a huge ship."

"That's one of the reasons it's so damned dangerous. Fellows want that piece of pottery or dish with the Italia crest on it. Figure they've spent all that time training and money to get out there. They forget. They get tired real fast, especially if they're fighting the current and breathing tri-mix. Make mistakes. Get lost. Forget the plans they memorized. Equipment's got to be working perfectly. One guy died because he had the wrong mix in his tanks. On my last dive I had five tanks, weight belt, lights, knives. I was carrying two hundred twenty-eight pounds. It takes a lifetime of experience to dive the ship. Even so, it's easy to become disoriented. You've got the ship lying on its side, so the deck and floors are overhead, the bulkheads between the decks are vertical."

"The *Andrea Doria* sounds like just our kind of place, doesn't it, Joe?"

"Only if the bar still serves tequila."

McGinty furrowed his brow. Ordinarily this kind of cockiness before a *Doria* dive was a one-way ticket to a body bag. He wasn't sure about these two. The big man with the hair that didn't match the unlined face and the soft-spoken dark man with the bedroom eyes exuded an unusual confidence. The captain's worried expression disappeared, and he grinned like an old hound dog. No, it wouldn't surprise him to see them belly up to the *Doria*'s first-class bar and order a drink from a ghostly bartender.

Austin said, "What's the weather going to be like, Captain?"

"Weather tends to be cantankerous as hell out here on the shoals. Calm one day, howling gale the next. Fog is notorious. The guys who were aboard the *Doria* and the *Stockholm* could tell you how thick it gets. Wind's blowing southeast now, but it will come around more westerly, and my guess is you'll have flat seas. Don't know how many days that will last out here."

"That's okay, we're in something of a hurry to get the job done," Austin said. "We don't have days."

McGinty grinned. Yup, damned cocky. "We'll see. Still, I've got to admit you boys have got brass. What's this you're looking for, an armored truck in the hold? That's going to require some doing. Especially where you don't know the wreck." He shook his head. "Wish I could help you, but my diving days are over. You could use a guide."

Austin saw a blue hull come into view through a porthole. The name *Myra* was painted on the bow.

"Excuse me, Captain," he said. "I think our guide has just arrived."

40

"GAMAY, DO YOU HAVE A MINUTE?"
Trout called out from his study. He was bent over the monitor of
his computer, staring intently at the oversized screen he used for
developing graphics for his various undersea projects.

"Yrrph," Gamay answered with a muffled grunt from the
next room. She lay on her back, suspended horizontally above
the floor like a yogi in a trance, balanced on a narrow plank scaffolding supported by two ladders. She and Paul were constantly
remodeling the interior of their Georgetown brick townhouse.
Rudi Gunn ordered her to take a few days off to rest before
reporting to NUMA headquarters. But the second she got back
home she picked up on a project she had left undone, painting
lifelike flower garlands on the ceiling of their sunroom.

She walked into the study wiping her hands on a rag. She
was wearing old jeans and a chambray work shirt. Her dark red
hair was stuffed under a white cap with the words Tru-Test Paint
on it. Her face was smudged with green and red splatters except
for a racoonish area around her eyes where she'd worn protective
goggles.

"You look like a Jackson Pollock painting," Trout said.

She wiped a gob of crimson from her mouth. "How
Michelangelo painted the ceiling of the Sistine Chapel is
beyond me. I've only been at it an hour, and I've got a bad case
of painter's elbow."

Trout peered upward over nonexistent glasses and broke into an easy grin.

"What's with the wolfish smile?" Gamay said warily.

He put his hand around her slim waist and pulled her closer. He'd touched her at every opportunity since they had returned home, as if he feared she would disappear into the jungle again. The days she was missing were a nightmare for him, but his Yankee upbringing would never allow him to come out and say so.

"Just thinking about how sexy you look with paint splattered on your face."

Gamay gently tousled his fine hair and brushed it down over his forehead. "You perverts really know how to sweet-talk a gal." Her eye caught the images on the screen. "Is that why you called me?"

"So much for sudden impetuous romantic gestures." He indicated the screen. "Yes. Tell me what you see."

She leaned on Paul's shoulder and squinted at the monitor. "No-brainer. I see beautifully detailed sketches of eight fantastic-looking heads." Her voice lapsed into the scientific mode, like the monotone of a pathologist conducting an autopsy. "At first glance the profiles appear identical, but upon further examination I detect subtle differences, mostly around the jaw and mouth but on the cranium as well. How am I doing, Sherlock?"

"You not only see but you also observe, my dear Watson."

"Elementary, my dear fellow. Who drew these sketches? They are works of art in themselves."

"The esteemed Dr. Chi. A man of varied talents."

"I saw enough of the good professor not to be surprised at anything he does. How do you happen to have them?"

"Chi showed them to me when I was at Harvard. He asked me to run them by you. He remembered your background in archaeology before you switched to biology. But mostly he wanted a fresh eye." Trout leaned his long body back and laced his fingers behind his head. "I'm an ocean geologist. I can take this stuff and make all the pretty pictures I want to, but it doesn't make any sense to me."

Gamay pulled a chair up beside her husband.

"Look at it this way, Paul. It's no different from somebody handing you a rock from the bottom of the ocean. What's the first thing you'd ask?"

"Easy. Where they got it."

"Bravo." She pecked him on the cheek. "The same thing applies in archaeology. Mayan studies wasn't my area of expertise before I switched to marine biology, but here's my first question to you. Where did these glyphs come from?"

Trout tapped the screen. "This one here is from the site Chi calls MIT. Where you first ran into the *chicleros*."

Gamay felt a frisson along her spine at the reminder of beating sun, jungle rot, and unshaven, unfriendly men. "What about the others?"

"All from different locations Chi has visited."

"What made him pick these, aside from the fact that they are almost identical?"

"Location. Each face was from an observatory carved with the frieze showing the boats that may or may not be Phoenician."

"Intriguing."

"Uh-huh. The professor thought so. The boat theme tied them together."

"What's it all mean?"

"I don't know," he said with a shrug. "I'm afraid that's the extent of my Mesoamerican expertise."

"Why don't we call Professor Chi?"

"Just tried. He wasn't in his Mexico City office. They said he was there earlier but would be unavailable."

"Don't tell me. They said he was in the field."

Trout nodded. "I left a message."

"Don't hold your breath now that he's got his HumVee back. What about Orville?"

"The nutty professor? Exactly what I had in mind. First I wanted to run this stuff by you in case you had any inspiration."

"Call Linus Orville. That's *my* inspiration."

Trout flipped through his card file and punched out a number. When Orville answered Trout put him on the speaker phone.

"Ah, Mulder and Scully," Orville said, referring to the FBI characters in the popular TV program. "How are things with the *X-Files*?"

In the most serious tone he could muster, Trout said, "We've uncovered solid proof that those mysterious carved boats are from the lost continent of Mu."

"You're *kidding!*" Orville replied breathlessly.

"Yeah, I'm kidding. I just like to say the word *Mu.*"

"Well, moo to you, too, Mulder. Now please tell me the *real* reason you called."

"We need your opinion on those sketches Professor Chi left with Paul," Gamay said.

"Oh, the Venus glyphs."

"Venus?"

"Yes, the series of eight. Each figure represents an incarnation of the god Venus."

Gamay looked at the grotesque profiles with their protruding jaws and foreheads. "Ugh. I've always thought of the goddess of love as a delicate maiden drifting out of the sea foam on a scallop shell."

"That's because you've been brainwashed by Botticelli's vision and wasted your time on classical studies before you got out of the Temple of Doom game. The Mayan Venus was a *male.*"

"How chauvinistic."

"Only to a point. The Maya were firm believers in equal opportunity when it came to human sacrifice. Venus symbolized Quetzalcoatl or Kukulcan. The feathered serpent. It's all tied in. The analogy of birth and rebirth. Like Quetzalcoatl, Venus disappears for part of its cycle only to reappear."

"I get it," Trout said. "The Maya decorated their temples with representations of the god to make him happy so he'd come back."

"There was some of that, yeah, toadying up to the big guy. You have to understand how architecture was worked into their religion. Mayan buildings were often fixed on key points like the solstice and equinox or where Venus appears and disappears. A celestial calculator, in other words."

Gamay said, "Professor Chi compared the observatory tower at the MIT site to a computer's hardware, the inscriptions on its side to software. He felt that it was only part of the whole picture, the way one circuit is part of a computer."

"Yes, he ran that theory by me, but your carved tower has a long way to go before it becomes an IBM clone."

"Still, it's possible that the tower and the others were part of a unified plan?" Gamay persisted.

"Don't get me wrong. The Maya were incredibly sophisticated and always manage to surprise. They often lined up palace doorways and streets to point to the sun and stars at various times of the year. You see, predicting the movements of Venus would give the priests tremendous power. The Venus god told the farmers about important dates like planting, harvest, and rainy season. The Caracol at Chichén Itzá has windows that line up with Venus at various points on the horizon."

"There are no boat inscriptions on the Caracol, as far as I know," Gamay said.

"Only on those eight temples the glyphs came from. Venus disappears for eight days during its cycle. A scary thing if you were depending on the planet for important decisions. So the priests tossed a few maidens into a well, did some creative bloodletting, and everything was peachy again. Speaking of bloodletting, I've got a class in five minutes. Can we resume this fascinating discussion later?"

Gamay wasn't through. "You say Venus disappears for eight days and that there are eight temples we know of with the boat carvings. Coincidence?"

"Chi didn't think so. Got to go. Can't wait to tell the class about the Mu-sters."

The phone clicked off. Paul picked up a yellow legal pad.

"That was edifying. Let's go over what we have. We've got eight temple observatories. Each one was built to chart the movements of Venus." Trout made a note. "These structures were also dedicated toward a single theme, the arrival of boats that could have been Phoenician, bearing great treasure. A wild guess. The observatories and Venus have something to do with the treasure."

Gamay agreed. She took the notebook and drew eight circles at random. "Say these are the temples." She drew lines connecting the circles and stared at her doodles for a moment. "There's something here," she said.

Paul looked at the scribbles and shook his head. "Looks like a flat-footed spider."

"That's because we're thinking in earth-bound terms. Look." She drew two stars near the edge of the page. "Rise above the earth. Let's say this is Venus at its extreme points on the horizon. That temple I saw at MIT had two slotlike openings like an archer's port in a castle. Here's what you would see if you drew a line from the window to one extreme of Venus. Now I'll do it out the other window." Satisfied with her artwork, she drew lines from each observatory to the Venus points.

She stuck the rough grid she'd produced under Paul's nose.

"Now it looks like the mouth of an alligator about ready to have dinner," he said.

"Maybe. Or a hungry serpent."

"Still thinking about that snake?"

"Yes and no. Dr. Chi wore an amulet around his neck. He called it the feathered serpent. That's what this reminds me of, the jaws of Kukulcan."

"You need the exact locations of the observatories, even admitting it's possible to make sense from this. Too bad Chi is in the field."

Gamay was half listening. "I just thought of something. That talking stone Kurt and Joe are out looking for. Wasn't it supposed to show some kind of grid?"

"That's right. I wonder if there's a connection."

Trout picked up the phone. "I'll call and leave a message for Chi to get in touch with us as soon as possible. Then we'll give Kurt a ring to tell him you may have something."

She examined her doodle-bug sketches again. "Yes, but *what?*"

41

THE CABIN CRUISER THAT HAD BEEN
circling the salvage boat pulled alongside within hailing distance
and cut its engine to an idle. The white, red, and green tricolor
of Italy fluttered on the signal mast under the American flag.
The slim, silver-haired figure of Angelo Donatelli stepped out of
the pilothouse and waved.

"Hallo, Mr. Austin, I've come on a rescue mission. I understand you are running out of *grappa*. May we make a delivery?"

"Hallo, Mr. Donatelli," Austin yelled back. "Thank you for
the resupply. Until now we've had to drink battery acid."

Captain McGinty cupped his hands around his mouth, an
entirely unnecessary gesture because his normal voice was a bel-
low. "Skipper thanks you, too, and invites you to come aboard
on your mission of mercy."

Donatelli saluted in acknowledgment and went back into the
pilothouse. The anchor dropped into the water with a rattle and
a splash, and the engine died. Donatelli and his cousin Antonio
stepped into an outboard launch the yacht had been towing,
buzzed the short distance to the salvage ship, and climbed
aboard.

Donatelli handed the captain a bottle of the fiery Italian
liquor. "With my compliments," he said, then turned to Austin
and swept his hand toward the cabin cruiser.

"How do you like my blue beauty, Mr. Austin?"

Donatelli's continued use of the honorific was Old World habit or simply the practiced good manners of a restaurateur used to dealing with a high-class clientele, Austin figured. It was a refreshing change from the phony first-name, "Hi, my name is Bud" informality that was one of Austin's favorite gripes.

Austin's eyes swept the cruiser stem to stern and took in its navy hull and creamy superstructure as if he were studying the curves of a lovely woman. "She's got classically beautiful lines," he said. "How does she handle?"

"Like a dream. I fell in love the first time I saw her abandoned in a boatyard in Bristol, Rhode Island. I've spent thousands restoring her. She's forty-five feet, but the sweep of her bow makes her look even longer. A very stable boat, perfect for taking the grandchildren out." He laughed. "And a way to escape the family when I need peace and quiet. My clever accountant has made the boat part of the business, so I have to catch a fish now and again for the restaurants." He paused and looked misty-eyed at the sea where a flock of gulls speckled the dark water like snowflakes. "So this is where it happened."

Austin pointed to the red plastic bubble bobbing in the slight chop. "The top of the ship lies thirty fathoms under that marker. We're directly over her." There was no need to use the *Doria*'s name; they both knew what vessel he was talking about.

"I have cruised the waters all around the island," Donatelli said, "but I have never, never been to this spot." He chuckled softly. "We Sicilians are superstitious people who believe in ghosts."

"All the more reason to thank you for helping with this project."

Donatelli affixed Austin with piercing deep-set eyes. "I wouldn't have missed this for the world. Where do we start?"

"We've got a set of plans in the captain's cabin."

"*Bene.* Come, Antonio," he said to his cousin, who'd been imitating a fire plug. "Let us see what we can do for these gentlemen."

Captain McGinty unrolled a sheet of heavy white paper onto a table in his cabin. The paper was labeled Italian Line *"plano delle sistemazioni passeggeri,"* or plan of passenger accommodation. At the top was a photo of the liner cutting its way through the waves in better days. Below the photo were diagrams of nine decks.

Donatelli tapped the area that showed the Belvedere Lounge at the front of the boat deck. "I was working here when the *Stockholm* hit us. Boom! I landed on the floor." His finger moved to the promenade deck. "All the passengers are here waiting for rescue. A big mess," he said, shaking his head in disgust. "Mr. Carey finds me, and we go down to their cabin. Here. On the starboard side of the upper deck. Poor Mrs. Carey is trapped. Off I go like a scared rabbit to find a car jack. Down here." His finger retraced his route of that night. "Past the shops on the foyer deck, but the way is blocked, so I go way back here to the stern, then down to A Deck."

Donatelli halted his straightforward account, remembering the terror that gripped him as he descended into the dark bowels of the sinking ship. "Excuse me," he apologized, a catch in his voice. "Even now, after all these years . . ." He took a deep breath and let it out. "That night I found out what Dante went through in his descent to Hades." He puffed his cheeks and continued. "So finally I make it to B Deck, where the garage is. Everyone knows the rest of the story?"

The others gathered around the table nodded.

"Good," Donatelli said with obvious relief. Although the cabin was cool his brow glistened with perspiration, and a vein throbbed on the side of his head.

"Could you tell us exactly where in the garage you saw the armored truck?" Austin said.

"Sure, it was up here in this corner." He borrowed a pencil and made an X. "I heard there were nine cars in the garage, including the fancy one the Italians built for Chrysler." He compressed his lips in a tight smile. "I never found the jack I was looking for."

"Our plan is to go in through the garage doors," Austin explained.

Donatelli nodded. "The cars could drive right into the garage from the pier. I think it's a good plan, but I know little of these things," he said with a shrug.

Captain McGinty was less equivocal. A few minutes earlier he'd been diverted by a call on the ship's phone. Now he was back at the table shaking his head. "Hope you boys aren't going on a fool's errand. I see a big problem staring me in the face."

"That may be an understatement. I'd be surprised if the problems weren't jumping up and down on our backs like an eight-hundred-pound gorilla," Austin said.

"This one is a pisser. I know guys who've gotten into that hold, coming down through the decks." He indicated the starboard wall of the garage. "Everything in that space—cars, trucks, cargo—would have fallen onto this side that's lying in the bottom sand. Your armored truck could be buried under tons of junk. Guys who've been in that hold saw that future car Chrysler was shipping over, but they couldn't get at it because the space is full of twisted beams and busted bulkheads. You go in with gym suits like you're planning, there's the danger you could get caught up."

Austin was well aware this could be one of the toughest assignments in his varied career. More difficult in its own way than raising that Iranian container ship or the Russian sub.

"Thanks for the warning, Captain. My idea is to approach this as if we were looking for a target where the bottom's been littered with wrecks. Like the East River, for example. You may be right, that the job is impossible. But I think it's worth taking a look." He grinned. "Maybe we'll even find Mr. Donatelli's car jack."

McGinty let out a whooping laugh. "Well, if it's a fool's errand, you're my kind of fool. What say we offer a toast to our success?"

Donatelli opened the *grappa* and poured drinks all around using a waiter's flourish that hadn't deserted him.

"By the way, that was the boys down below calling from the bell," McGinty said. "They've just about cut through the hull. I told them to get things ready for tomorrow, then take a rest. You'd be down first thing in the morning to do the job."

Austin raised his glass. "Here's to lost causes and impossible missions."

The quiet laughter was cut short as Donatelli solemnly raised his glass high. "And here's to the *Andrea Doria* and the souls of all those who have died on her."

When they tossed their drinks down, it was done in silence.

42

LIFE IS NEVER DULL AROUND THE *Andrea Doria* for the schools of silver-scaled fish that claim squatter's rights in luxurious cabins that cost their previous occupants thousands of lira. But nothing could have prepared the denizens of the blue twilight world for the arrival of two creatures more bizarre than any inhabitant of the depths. Their plump bodies were covered with shiny yellow skin, their backsides protected by a black carapace. In the center of their bulbous heads was a single eye. Twin stumps protruded from the bottoms of their rotund bodies. Near the top were similar, shorter appendages, each ending in a claw. Most curious were the softly whirring fins on each side.

The creatures hung in the water like balloons in the Macy's Thanksgiving parade. The soft laughter of Zavala's voice cackled in Austin's headset.

"Have I ever told you how much you resemble the Michelin man?"

"After the meal with McGinty last night I wouldn't be surprised at anything. My gym suit is a little tight around the gut."

The Ceanic Hard Suit must have been nicknamed by someone with a vision problem. The so-called gym suit was actually a body-fitting submarine. The forged aluminum skin was technically a hull. Vertical and lateral propulsion thrusters on each side were activated by foot controls. With its oxygen recirculation and carbon dioxide scrubbing capability, the suit was good for six to eight hours of dive time with forty-eight hours of emergency life support. It topped the scales at nearly half a ton, yet in water the suit weighed less than eight pounds. The Hard Suit provided mobility, long dive time, and no decompression. The suit's major disadvantage was its bulkiness. Penetrating the interior following Donatelli's route would be suicide. They would become ensnared on wires or lines within minutes.

In formulating a dive plan, Austin reviewed all past dives on the *Doria,* successful or not. Austin thought the Gimbel expeditions had the right idea. The 1975 attempt tried to use a submersible for reconnaissance, but the craft lacked the power to fight the current. The diving bell intended for use as an elevator and work station was improperly ballasted and went dangerously out of control. What impressed Austin was the fact that saturation divers working from the surface with umbilical hoses managed to accomplish a great deal against formidable odds. They actually got into the garage. The 1981 Gimbel expedition was better prepared. The bell system worked well. Although it ran into all sorts of problems, including nasty weather and a current that tangled the umbilicals, divers managed to find the safe and hook it up to a crane.

In the end, Austin chose a combination of Hard Suits and saturation divers. He patched together an expedition relatively well equipped for the task. His father provided the *Monkfish* and crew. Gunn combed through the NUMA expedition and ship schedule and pulled together the diving bell and a decompression chamber on the deck that was equipped with showers and bunks. The borrowed mini-sub, with its recon capabilities, was an unexpected bonus. Most important were NUMA's six experienced saturation divers who were flown in from Virginia. Since their arrival on the *Monkfish* they had been worked in round-the-clock shifts to cut a hole in the liner's hull.

The weather on Nantucket Shoals lived up to its reputation for changeability. When Austin and Zavala crawled out of their bunks that morning the air was transparent. The lumpy sea of the previous day had vanished, and the ocean was mirror calm, reflecting like polished glass the images of the seabirds dotting the surface. A pair of black fins cut the water. Dolphins. McGinty said they were a sign of good luck and would keep the sharks away. The surface current was about one knot. He predicted that a thick fog would later work its way onto the shoals, and the current might come up, but they could deal with that.

Encased in their heavy suits, the NUMA men were lowered by crane into the water. They spent several minutes just under the surface checking out their gear while the crane again swung out over the water and dropped a Kevlar cable that was ganged into four short lines ending in sturdy metal clips. They gripped the line firmly in their mechanical claws. With a hum of vertical thrusters they descended into the indigo sea. The *Monkfish* was locked in place exactly over the wreck by four anchor lines, two at the bow, two at the stern, one hundred meters in each direction. Stability was crucial. Otherwise the diving bell would swing at the end of its tether like a pendulum.

Although the Hard Suits were equipped with lights and they brought portable lamps with them, no illumination was needed. The visibility was at least thirty feet, and the shadowy outline of the ship stood out in relief against the paler bottom. They headed toward where a section of the hull was illuminated by a cold pulsating glow.

At the center of the eddying bluish corona two saturation divers clung to the upended port side of the ship like insects on a log. One diver knelt on the hull with a cutting torch in his gloved hand while the other tended the Kerry cable that conveyed the fuel and kept an eye on things in general. They had been transported down earlier by the diving bell, which served as an elevator and underwater habitat for the dive team.

Suspended by a thick cable that ran to a winch on the deck of the *Monkfish*, the bell hung a few meters above the hull. It was shaped like a gas-powered camp lantern. The four sides were rounded slightly at the corners, the roof sloped down from the hole for the hoisting cable. Another cable containing communications and power entered the bell from a lower point on the roof. Fastened to the outside were tanks holding breathing gases and torch fuel. The bottom of the bell was open to the sea, which was held in abeyance by air pressure. From the opening umbilicals snaked to the divers, carrying the breathing mixture and hot water to body-warming tubing in their Divex Armadillo suits. In addition each diver carried an emergency breathing tank on his back.

The divers were working on a section of steel plating that had been scraped clear of anemones to expose the black hull paint. The heat discoloration from the magnesium rods in the high-pressure feed oxy-arc cutting torch outlined a large rectangle around the garage doors. The saturation diver who'd been tending the torchman became aware of the twin yellow blimps approaching. Using the slow-motion movement that comes with working in deep water, the diver reached up to take the cable from Austin and Zavala. The NUMA men could communicate directly with themselves and with the salvage boat, but there was no direct link to the saturation divers except through the bell. Austin was unconcerned because everyone had gone over the plan many times, and hand signals were adequate for all but the most complicated message.

The kneeling diver snapped off his torch when he saw the new arrivals. He pointed to each corner of the rectangle where he had cut double holes and gave the thumbs-up signal. Then he and his companion attached the clips from the surface line to the holes. The divers moved several meters away, and one made a jerking motion with his hand like a locomotive engineer pulling the whistle cord.

Austin radioed the deck crew. "All clear. Start hauling."

The deck crew relayed the message to the crane operator, and the Kevlar line went as taut as a bow string. Seconds passed. Nothing happened. The framework around the door had been cut like a dotted line on cardboard. Austin was wondering if more cutting was needed when there was an explosion of bubbles from the deck. The section pulled free with a muffled boom.

Austin directed the surface crew to move the crane over and let the doors drop onto the hull.

A huge gaping rectangular hole had been opened in the side of the ship at the B Deck level. The tourist-class cabins had been stuffed into fore and aft sections of this deck and C Deck, the level below it. The forward section of deck was where the cabins were split by the *autorimessa*, the deck that housed nine cars and an armored truck.

Zavala powered his suit so he was directly above the newly created opening.

"You could drive a HumVee through this thing."

"Why do things halfway? Think of it. Everyone who dives on the wreck from now on will think of this as Zavala's Hole."

"I'll pass that honor on to you. How about naming it Austin's Aperture?"

"How about scouting things out?"

"No time like the present."

"I'll take the point. We'll go nice and slow. Watch out for ceiling cables and collapsed bulkheads. Remember to keep a safe distance apart."

Zavala didn't need to be warned. The Hard Suits resembled space suits worn by the astronauts. As with astronauts floating in free fall, motions had to be deliberate and unexaggerated. Even at slow speed a collision between the thousand-pound suits would rattle their teeth.

Austin moved in under Zavala so that the light from his suit pointed straight into the ship. The powerful beam was swallowed by the darkness. He gave his vertical thrusters a short blast, descended feet-first into the garage, then stopped and rotated the suit three hundred sixty degrees. The water was free of loose ends and projections. He gave Zavala the all-clear and watched the bloated yellow figure sink through the blue-green hole and come to a hovering stop.

"This reminds me of the Baja Cantina in Tijuana," Zavala said. "Actually it's not as dark."

"We'll stop for shots of Cuervo on the way back," Austin

replied. "The ship is ninety feet wide. The cargo would have slid down to the bottom like Captain McGinty said. Everything is at a ninety-degree angle, so the floor of the garage is actually that vertical wall right behind you. We'll stick close to the wall so as not to become disoriented."

As they descended Austin went down a mental checklist, anticipating obstacles and reactions. While he worked on practical problems and solutions his brain was busy on another, irrational level, probably the survival mechanism that raised the hackles on the unshaven necks of his ancestors. He was hearing Donatelli's voice describing his terrifying descent into the innards of the ship. The old man was wrong, Austin concluded. This was worse than *anything* Dante could have imagined. Austin would take the fire and brimstone of the Inferno any day. At least Dante could *see* something. Even if it was only demons and the damned.

It was hard to believe now that the decks of this vast empty hulk once throbbed with the diesel power of fifty thousand horses, and more than twelve hundred passengers basked in the ship's sensuous beauty, their needs served by a crew of nearly six hundred. The first person to dive on the *Andrea Doria* after she slid beneath the Atlantic said the ship seemed still alive, producing an eerie cacophony of groans and creaks, the banging of loose debris, water rushing in and out of doorways. Austin saw only decay, emptiness, and silence, except for the sound of their rebreathers. This huge metal cairn was a haunted place where a man who lingered too long could go mad.

The ship seemed to close in on them, and Austin kept checking his depth gauge. Although they were only about two hundred feet from the surface, it seemed deeper because of the darkness. He looked upward. The blue-green rectangle that marked the opening was diffused in the murk and eventually might have become invisible if the saturation divers hadn't placed a strobe light on the edge as a beacon. Austin glanced at the blinking pinpoint and felt reassured, then turned his focus to what lay below.

Under their feet solid objects were looming out of the darkness into the circle of illumination cast by their lights. Straight lines and edges. Mysterious rounded shapes. Tons of debris were jammed into the horizontal space that had once been the starboard bulkhead of the *Doria*. When the ship was level the garage was covered with heavy metal mesh and catwalks. Now these were vertical as well. Austin and Zavala started a search pattern, moving in parallel lines, back and forth, between the vertical partitions formed by the old floor and ceiling of the garage, the type of search they would execute if they were on the surface looking for a shipwreck. They encountered dangling wires from the old light fixtures but not enough to be dangerous and they were easily avoided.

Their lights caught the glint of metal and glass and vague forms that occasionally resolved into familiar shapes.

"Hey, Kurt, is that a Rolls-Royce I see down there?"

Austin directed his light at the distinctive heavy grille sticking out of the debris.

"Probably. According to the liner's manifest a guy from Miami was shipping his Rolls back from Europe."

"Goes to show it pays to have a Rolls on every continent."

Austin glided over the Rolls and saw part of another car with unconventional sweeping lines.

"That looks like the Chrysler experimental car built by Ghia. Too bad Pitt isn't here. He'd go through hell and high water to add a one-of-a-kind to his collection."

"He'd have to go through a lot of mud, too."

The cars had tumbled on top of one another and now were largely covered by debris and silt. Austin had briefly entertained thoughts of a plan to excavate the debris, but it was an intellectual exercise only. Too dangerous, costly, and time-consuming. Any effort to dig through the cover would stir up a cloud so thick it would take days to settle.

From what Donatelli said of the truck's position, the vehicle should have fallen onto the top of the heap. It should have been visible. Could the old man have been wrong? He was under tremendous stress that night. Maybe the car was in another cargo hold. Austin groaned. It had taken a tremendous effort to cut into the garage. They had neither the time nor resources to try again. His expeditionary force was made up of assets borrowed for only a few days.

Doubts grew the longer they searched. They went over every square yard of visible debris.

"Whatever happened to the plan to refloat this thing with Ping-Pong balls?" Zavala said.

"I don't think there are enough Ping-Pong balls in China for the job. What's your take?"

"I think Angelo Donatelli was one gutsy guy. This must be the biggest sensory deprivation tank in the world. Hard to believe we're still on planet Earth. I feel like a fly in a molasses jar."

"I'm beginning to wonder if the truck is in here at all."

"Where would it be?"

"I wish I knew," Austin replied.

"Nina is going to be disappointed."

"I know. What say we go topside and deliver the bad news?"

"Fine with me. My bladder is telling me I drank too much coffee this morning."

They powered the vertical thrusters, keeping a slow but steady pace, homing in on the flashing beacon above. As they ascended they flashed their lights ahead and above to make sure they weren't coming up on unseen obstructions. The beam from Zavala's light stabbed the blackness in a corner of the garage, moved away for a second, then came back.

"Kurt," he called out excitedly. "There's something in the corner."

They stopped their ascent. Austin saw two red eyes glowing in the inky darkness.

Having spent more than an hour in this otherworldly environment his first reaction was that they were looking at a huge sea creature who'd made the ship its lair. He pointed his light at the twin orbs, and his pulse rate ratcheted up a few beats. It *couldn't* be. Both men moved in for a closer look and put the full force of their lights on the corner.

"Well, I'll be damned," they said in unison.

43

DECADES BEFORE AUSTIN AND ZA-
vala cut their way into the *Andrea Doria*'s garage a ship's officer presciently pictured the dire consequences of an armored truck weighing several tons crashing around in the hold during a storm at sea. To head off that possibility the vehicle was lashed by strong cables passed over the truck's body and bolted to the floor. More than fifty years later the cables still held the truck in place at a right angle to the vertical wall that had once been the garage floor.

The black body was mottled with rust, and the tire rubber had softened into an evil-looking mush. The chrome still held a dull shine, though, and the truck itself was in one piece. After as thorough an inspection as they could make, Austin and Zavala left the hull and went back into the open sea. The saturation divers had retreated to the dry comfort of the pressurized bell. Austin didn't blame them. Saturated tri-mix is eight times as difficult to breathe as air from a scuba tank.

Austin called McGinty. "Tell Mr. Donatelli we've located the truck."

"Goddamn! Knew you could do it. Is it accessible for salvage?"

"With a little luck and the right equipment. I've got a shopping list."

Austin quickly laid out the gear he wanted.

"No problem. There's a fresh crew coming down. They'll bring the stuff with them."

The bell rose to the surface, and the divers inside exchanged places with a team living in the decompression chamber. When the bell returned, the equipment Austin ordered was secured to its exterior. Austin had talked by radio to the replacement divers before they left the ship and outlined the plan. The divers popped from the bottom of the bell and swam over to the hole in the hull. Austin and Zavala reentered the ship first. The saturation divers followed with their umbilical life-support hoses trailing behind. One of them carried an oxygen cutting torch.

Austin regretted not having direct contact with the divers. He would have liked to hear their comments when they saw the truck hanging from the wall at a right angle. Their animated arm waving was almost as enjoyable. After their initial reaction they got right to work on the truck's rear doors. They wouldn't yield to a crowbar or the mechanical claws of the Hard Suits.

Donatelli had said the assassins who killed the armored truck guards simply slammed the doors. They were probably rusted shut rather than locked, Austin guessed. The torch blazed to life, and the diver drew its scalpel-like flame along the lock and hinges, the rust exploding in a shower of sparks. They tried the crowbar again, both saturation divers putting their backs to it. The doors fell off, and a brownish cloud of rotting debris, flushed out by the intruding seawater, enveloped the four men. When it settled and the water was somewhat clear again, Austin edged forward and probed the truck's interior with his light.

The space was piled with metal strongboxes that had fallen off shelves. The swirling water had cleaned away the clothing, hair and remnants of tissue so that the grinning skulls caught in the beam of the light looked freshly scrubbed, not green with algae as they might otherwise have been. The bones had all tumbled in a heap onto one side of the truck with the other debris. Austin moved aside to make room for his partner.

Zavala was silent for a moment. "Looks like the charnel house you see under the old churches in Mexico and Spain."

"It's more of a *slaughter*house," Austin said grimly. "Angelo Donatelli's memory is pretty good. Those strongboxes are probably for the jewels that were being shipped." He willed himself to avoid the sightless eyes. "We'll deal with that stuff later."

He gestured to the saturation divers, and they swam closer to inspect the inside of the truck. In telling the divers about the stone slab earlier, Austin had warned, "You'll also come across some human bones. I can tell you later how they got there. Hope you're not superstitious."

The divers stared into the truck and shook their heads, but their stunned reaction was temporary. The NUMA divers were pros. They swam into the truck without further hesitation and started moving the boxes and bones aside. Within minutes they had exposed a solid-looking corner of a blackish-gray object.

The long-lost talking stone.

While the divers tidied up the interior, Austin and Zavala scudded back to the diving bell and returned with a block and tackle attached to the Kevlar tow line that went up to the ship. The bones had been respectfully placed in a neat pile. The strongboxes were stacked out of the way except for one the divers had set aside. With great ceremony a diver opened the box to display its contents. Light glittered off a breathtaking fortune in diamonds, sapphires, and other precious stones.

Austin heard Zavala's sharp intake of breath. "That stuff must be worth millions."

"Maybe *billions* if the other boxes are as full. This confirms that the motive was murder, not robbery." He signaled the saturation divers to move the box, and he set the double block and tackle he was carrying just inside the door. Zavala had been carrying a metal loop. The saturation divers attached this wire collar around a protruding end of the slab, then affixed the line to the pulley.

Austin knew that the center of lift should be maintained directly above the center of gravity. He also knew this ideal seldom occurred. It was like telling someone to lift with his legs, not his back. Good advice, but of little use when the load is in the back of a closet or under the cellar stairs. The Kevlar cable went through the hull, then angled to the truck. The block and tackle would translate its force into a more lateral pull while doubling the pulling capacity.

Austin was dealing with a number of unknowns. One was the weight of the slab. An object is buoyed up by the water it displaces. Austin knew the slab would be lighter in water, but since he could only guess at its original weight, this didn't do much good. He'd asked McGinty for two tackles rigged with a continuous fall, which can lift twice as much as a single tackle. It was reeved for a right-angle luff. Technical jargon meaning that they'd done everything they could to compensate for the awkward pulling system.

The next problem, after they'd yanked the slab out like a dentist extracting a tooth, was preventing it from plummeting to the bottom. The solution was ocean salvage tubes, a fairly new concept. The elongated bags of nylon fabric were designed for salvaging boats. With a lifting capacity up to one and a half tons each they might be able to hoist the entire armored truck to the surface.

The saturation divers used the block and tackle to move the slab to where they could lash an uninflated bag to each side of the stone. Austin went through and inspected the whole crazy setup, especially the fragile cables holding the truck to the wall, then gave the signal. Using a hose coming from the bell, the saturation divers pumped air into the tubes, which plumped out as quickly as sausages on a skillet. They fed the air in gradually to build up positive buoyancy. The slab lifted like a magician's assistant floating in midair. Keeping the lift line attached in case of an emergency, the divers nudged the slab out of the truck until it floated through the door.

Austin thought this was one of the strangest sights he had ever seen. It was like a painting by Dali, where everything is askew. The black slab floating in space over the abyss like a magic carpet in the immense ink-dark chamber. The divers dangling like newborn salamanders from their umbilicals. The seaworn armored truck hanging off the wall at a right angle.

Flanked by Austin and Zavala, who illuminated the way with

their lights, the divers swam the slab toward the opening. It was delicate work, especially with the current running through the wreck, but at last the slab was directly under the hole they'd cut in the hull.

"Wish I could talk to these guys and tell them what a great job they're doing," Zavala said. He tried to signal a "well done" with his mechanical claw, but it didn't quite make it. "Guess we'd better not high-five until we get out of these suits. Which I hope will be damned soon."

"Shouldn't be more than a few minutes before we can turn the rest of the job over to McGinty. Hear that, Cap?"

The conversations between the Hard Suits were communicated to the deck so the men on the topside could keep tabs on what was going on below.

"Bet your ass," McGinty barked. "I heard the whole skinny. Got a case of Bud on ice. Get that thing out of the wreck, and we'll do the rest."

The saturation divers had to stay at depth or they'd come down with the bends. Once the load was out of the wreck, Austin and Zavala would take over and guide it to the surface. When the slab was near the surface they'd tend it until the crane could finish the job.

"What's the weather like up there?" Austin asked.

"Sea's still flat calm, but the Nantucket fog factory has been going full tilt. Fog bank is rolling in with stuff so thick you could fry it up like dough."

Both Austin and the captain would have been even more concerned if they knew what the fog hid. While Austin and the others had struggled to pull the stone slab from the armored truck and haul it to the surface, a large ship whose gray hull made it practically invisible was approaching the *Monkfish*, traveling just fast enough to keep pace with the moving wall of fog. The oddly shaped vessel was six hundred feet long, with a deep V-shaped bow and wide back, and it was powered by six water jets that could send it skimming over the sea at forty-five knots, an amazing speed for a ship that size.

Austin responded to McGinty's weather report with a "Finest kind, Cap," borrowing one of Trout's expressions from his fishing days. He signaled the saturation divers to put more air into the lift tubes. Slowly the load began to rise through the hole. The saturation divers stayed with the stone, making sure it didn't oscillate when it hit the stronger current flowing over the wreck. Austin and Zavala remained just inside the wreck, off to one side so they wouldn't be under the slab if it came down in a hurry. They had a clear view of both divers, one on either side of the slab, keeping pace with its ascent with slight flutters of their fins. A picture-perfect operation. One for the books.

Until all hell broke loose.

One of the divers jerked in a wild ungraceful dance, his arms and legs flailing like an epileptic in a *grand mal.* Then he doubled over, clawing at his umbilical. Just as suddenly he regained control of his body, floated in place for a moment, then jackknifed in a dive that took him back through the hole into the innards of the *Andrea Doria.*

The whole mad sequence took only a few seconds. Austin had no time to react. But as the diver swam closer, Austin saw what had happened. The man's umbilical trailed uselessly behind his suit. The diver had switched to his emergency tank. What the hell happened? The hose couldn't have been cut on the ragged edge of the hole. Austin had been watching the whole time. The diver swam toward him, the exposed part of his face white as marble. Austin cursed himself for not insisting on total underwater communication. The man jabbed the water above his head.

Zavala, who had been moving in a slow circle, yelled over the intercom, "Kurt, what's going on?"

"Damned if I know," Austin said. He squinted up at where the slab was suspended over the opening. "We've got to get this guy into the bell. He's okay on his spare tank, but he'll freeze to death without the hot water feed. I'll give him a ride up and take a look at the same time."

Austin held out his thick metal arm as if he were escorting a prom date. The diver got the hint and grabbed on to his elbow. Austin activated the vertical thrusters, and they levitated from the wreck. The second diver was nowhere to be seen.

While Austin scoured the sea for him, something stirred in the murky gloom. A fantastic figure moved into the range of the light cast by the diving bell. It was a diver wearing a Hard Suit of burnished metal that reminded Austin of the armor made to accommodate Henry VIII's porcine bulk.

Austin suspected that the stranger had something to do with the saturation diver's problems. That suspicion was reinforced a second later when the newcomer raised an object in his hand. There was an explosion of bubbles and the blurred glint of metal. A projectile rocketed past Austin's right shoulder, barely missing him.

The saturation diver took off and swam toward the bell with wild kicks of his flippers. Austin watched him disappear through the bottom hatch, then turned his attention to more pressing matters.

Other silvery figures had materialized and were heading in his direction. Austin counted five of them before he nailed the down control on his vertical thruster and plunged back into the *Doria*.

MCGINTY WAS ANXIOUSLY SHOUTING
over the radio.

"What the hell's going on? Someone get back to me, or I'll come down there and see for myself!"

"Wouldn't advise it," Austin shot back. "Six guys in Hard Suits just showed up for tea, and they're not very friendly. One just took a shot at me."

McGinty erupted like a volcano. "Jesus Mary Joseph and all the saints at sea!"

Another voice cut in. Near hysteria. "Those sonsofbitches cut Jack's line!" The missing diver was talking from inside the bell. Austin recognized his Texas drawl.

"Is he okay?"

"Yeah, he's in here with me. Scared brainless, but he's fine."

"You and Jack sit tight," Austin advised. "McGinty, how soon can you yank the bell to the surface?"

"I've got my hand on the switch."

"Then start hauling."

"It's on its way. D'you want me to call the Coast Guard?"

"A squad of navy SEALs would come in handy, but you can call in the Bengal Lancers for all the good it will do. This thing will be over before help gets here. We'll have to deal with it ourselves."

"Austin, you watch your ass! Haven't been in a donnybrook in ages. Wish I could get down there and break a few heads."

"So do I. Don't mean to be rude, Cap, but I gotta go. *Ciao.*"

Behind the dark plexiglass shielding Austin's face the pale blue-green eyes were as hard as turquoise stones. Most mortals placed in Austin's situation would have reacted with alarm. Austin wasn't fearless. He could make a good case that his hair had turned platinum white from the healthy scares he'd received in his career. Had he seen six white sharks bearing down he would have been wishing he'd renewed his life insurance. The forces of nature were unthinking and relentless. Despite the fearsome picture the intruders presented, Austin knew that under their aluminum skins were men, with all their frailties.

A replay flashed through his eyes of the attacks in Morocco. The only difference was the underwater setting. They wanted the talking stone, and the NUMA divers were in the way. Further intellectualizing was dangerous. Thoughts could be like slippery banana peels. What was needed was cunning rather than intelligence. A wolf doesn't think about its prey before it pounces. Austin let his mind slip into its survival mode, letting instincts dictate his moves. A spreading warmth chased away the cold chill that had gripped his body when he'd first seen the attackers. His breathing became regular, almost slow, his heart beat at an even pace. At the same time he wasn't kidding himself. A wolf had claws and teeth.

Zavala had heard the radio exchange with McGinty. "What's the game plan, Kurt?" The words were measured but edged with anxiety.

"We'll let them come to us. We know the territory. They don't. We'll need weapons."

"My specialty. I'll see what I can dig up."

Zavala glided toward the back of the armored truck. "Cable cutters. What do those guys have?"

"I don't know. I thought it was a spear gun. Now I'm not so sure."

Zavala brandished the loppers. "If we can get close enough I can cut a few zippers."

Austin's mind, which had been working at Mach speed, came

to a screeching halt. He'd been staring past Zavala at the open door of the armored truck, mesmerized by the bright rectangle of light standing out against the inky blackness. He moved closer. The portable halogen lamps they had used during the slab removal brightly lit up the interior.

"I may have a better idea," Austin said. "The Venus flytrap."

Keeping an eye on the hull opening, Austin outlined his plan for Zavala.

"Simple yet audacious," Zavala replied. "That takes care of one. What about the others?"

"Improvise."

Zavala raised the loppers like an Indian brave armed with a tomahawk about to do battle with the rifles of the cavalry and melted into the darkness on the far side of the truck, just beyond the engine compartment. Austin pried the lid open on two more jewelry chests.

It was like opening boxes full of stars. Even underwater the glitter of diamonds, sapphires, and rubies was blinding. He arranged the strongboxes neatly in a row just inside the truck where they would be in plain view, propping up their backs. He added a few skulls for dramatic effect, then moved away from the truck until he, too, was cloaked by the artificial night within the great ship. He hovered in the vast empty space, glancing back and forth between the truck and the hull opening above. Although the interior of the Hard Suit was dry and cool, he was sweating.

There was a glow near the hull opening, then a pair of divers came into the ship like ferrets entering a rabbit burrow, their twin flashlight beams stabbing the murkiness, probing this way and that. Watching their cautious entry Austin recalled the tentativeness with which he and Zavala had first entered the wreck, their nervousness at the unknown, and the adjustment to a disorienting topsy-turvy world where up and down were no longer useful referents. He was counting on that initial confusion. And on the natural tendency of the eye to focus on the only visible object in the empty void. The armored truck, looking out of place and time.

The divers moved back and forth, probably debating a course of action, whether they were walking into a trap. They approached the truck, staying close to each other, adjusting to the current, drawing nearer until their burnished suits were semi-silhouetted in the doorway.

Austin cursed. They were shoulder-to-shoulder. As long as they stayed that way his plan was dead, and maybe so were he and Zavala. Then human nature intervened. One diver muscled the other aside. He was framed directly in the truck's doorway, body at a forward slight angle, head bent into the truck. Austin's lips curled in a fierce grin. Pushiness doesn't pay, pal.

He alerted Zavala. "Assuming ram speed."

"Cutting started," Zavala shot back.

Austin kicked both thrusters into lateral full speed and aimed for the back of the truck. The suit accelerated slowly, then gathered momentum as its half-ton weight overcame the forces of inertia and water resistance.

He flew directly toward the truck like a bowling ball trying to pick off the last pin, praying that the diver would stay put. He didn't want an eternity with Zavala reminding him how he spent his last earthly moments imitating an accordion.

His luck held. The diver remained transfixed by the jewels, probably trying to figure out how he could carry them off.

Austin focused on the suit's wide metal butt, just below the hard plastic shell covering the air tanks like a tortoise shell. Damn. He was coming in too low. He gave himself a slight vertical lift.

Back on target.

"Now!" Austin yelled, knowing there was no need to raise his voice.

As he hurtled forward he brought his feet up like a boy making a cannonball dive, trying to imagine himself on an invisible bobsled, but the best he could do with the metal joints that restricted his movement was to elevate his knees.

Zavala was working feverishly. The pincher jaws had nibbled away at some of the strands of the front cable holding the truck.

He was afraid of cutting through too soon. At Austin's shouted command he put all the power of his shoulders, built up over many hours punching a body bag in his boxing days, into the lopper's long handles. The center of the cable had some life in it, and there was slight resistance at first. Then the beaklike blades cut through the remaining strands as easily as a raptor ripping apart its prey.

Austin fought to extend his feet straight out, but his metal knees slammed into the metal posterior of the diver ogling the jewels. Without the suit Austin would have popped his knee joints like a skier taking a backward spill, but the stiffness of the suit saved him. The diver was launched forward as if he had been tossed by a Brahma bull and flew head-first into the truck. Austin bounced back and spun out of control.

The other frantically tried to back out of the truck, but his thrusters were caught on a shelf frame. Austin had his own problems. He tumbled through space trying to figure out the thruster combination that would stabilize him.

He heard Zavala call out: "Bombs away!"

With one cable cut the armored truck had dropped down at its front end and hung precariously off the wall at an angle, its headlights pointing almost straight down. For an instant it seemed to Zavala, who had moved a safe distance away, as if the vehicle would stay that way. Then the full weight of the truck proved too much for the remaining cable. The restraint snapped, and the truck dropped away from the wall. It plunged into the darkness, joining the automotive graveyard in a big explosion of silt, taking with it the bones of its defenders, the jewels, and the struggling diver.

The whole sequence involved only a few seconds. The surviving diver had glimpsed Austin's attack and watched with astonishment as the truck disappeared, but he recovered quickly from his shock. Austin had finally regained stability and was fighting off the dizziness when the bright light from the diver's flash exploded in his face. He nailed his down thruster, knowing that in the time it took to drop a few yards he'd be an easy target. He gritted his teeth and braced himself against the searing pain he knew would come. The blinding light stayed on him, then shot off at an angle, and he saw the other diver struggling wildly.

Zavala!

Seeing Austin's predicament Joe had come from behind and hooked his arm behind the diver's weapon arm, throwing him off balance. They wrestled in slow motion like two monstrous robots. In his left claw Zavala clutched the lopper, but it soon became clear to him that his opponent was not going to stay still long enough for Zavala to cut a zipper as intended. The half-baked arm lock was slipping, and Zavala was just plain weary from his morning's exertions.

Improvise, Zavala remembered.

He jammed the loppers into the gym suit's lateral thruster. The wire cutters were wrenched from his grip. The spinning propeller disintegrated in its housing. Zavala backed off. The diver hit both thrusters to get away, but the unequal thrust of one propeller sent him into an undesired spin. He whirled off into the darkness on a wobbling crash course.

Weighted for neutral buoyancy, the diver's weapon floated until Austin grabbed it in his claw. The device was primitive in design but made of contemporary metals, a deadly instrument of death underwater where firearms were useless. Attached was a cradlelike magazine with room for six bolts. The short bolts had fins at one end and, at the other, four razor-sharp blades that could have sliced through his aluminum suit like a can opener. The oversized controls were simplified so that even a mechanical claw could string a bolt in place for firing.

Zavala glided closer. "What *is* that thing?" he said, panting from his wrestling match.

"Looks like a modern version of an old crossbow."

"A *crossbow!* Last time it was dueling pistols," Zavala said with a combination of wonder and disgust. "Next we'll be throwing stones at the bad guys."

"Beggars can't be choosers, Joe. Wonder if this thing really works." Austin held the weapon's butt against his chest and aimed. "Lethal, but my guess is it's not terribly accurate except at close range."

"You're about to get your chance to find out. We've got bogies at one o'clock."

Twin gossamer lights floated through the open hull and into the ship. Two more divers, both armed and less prone to ambush than their predecessors.

"I don't think we can sneak up on these guys as easily," Austin said. "They would have been talking to the others on their radios so they'll have an idea what to expect."

"We've got a couple of points in our favor. They don't know we're armed. And for now they don't know where we are."

Austin sorted through the options. They could run and hide, but eventually as they became more exhausted they'd screw up. The Hard Suits weren't made for the kind of demands being placed on them, and eventually they would run out of power or air.

"Okay, let's *show* them where we are. I'd flip to see who gets to be bait, but I don't have a coin. How are you at imitating a firefly?"

"You just get your little crossbow ready, Robin Hood."

The intruders had paused, distracted by their spinning comrade who was bouncing erratically around the cargo space. Zavala turned on every light on his suit and flashed them on and off for effect. For a moment he hung suspended in the darkness like a bizarre road sign. Then he disappeared. *That* caught their attention. The attackers moved toward his last sighting. Only he wasn't there. He moved several meters off to the right. *Flash. Click-click.* The chest and head lamps came on and off. He shifted again. Lights on. Lights off.

The effect was startling even to Austin, who knew what was going on. Zavala clones seemed to be popping up all over the place.

"Never thought I'd end up as a flasher," Zavala said.

"Your mother would be proud of you, Joe. It's working. They're coming closer."

It would be only a matter of time before they were on top of Zavala.

"One more time, Joe," said Austin. "I'm right behind you."

Zavala again blinked on and off like a Christmas tree. The attackers picked up speed and headed for the last place they had seen him. Directly toward Austin.

He brought the weapon up to his shoulder. "Five seconds to get out of the line of fire, Joe," he said evenly. "Beat feet."

"Going *down*," Zavala said in a parody of an elevator operator. He dropped several yards. Austin counted slowly, his sights transfixing the darkness behind the nearest approaching light. When he was sure Zavala was in the clear he squeezed the trigger mechanism and felt the crossbow kick slightly as it loosed the bolt. It was impossible to see the missile, but the shot must have been true because the light beam on the right jerked crazily.

Austin levered the bowstring back for another shot, reloading a new bolt in its cradle, swearing at the clumsiness of the mechanism especially in the dark. By the time he brought the crossbow to his shoulder for another shot, the second attacker had figured out what was going on and snapped off his light. Austin let off a bolt anyhow but knew just from the feel of things that it had missed.

"I nailed one of them, Joe. Missed the other guy. Let's see if we can find him. I've got the weapon, so I'll take the lead."

He stared into the darkness. *Useless!* He'd have to take a chance. He flicked the lights on the front of his suit and his head lamp and saw a reflection. He headed for it.

"He's making a break for the hole."

"I see him," Zavala said. "I'm right behind you."

They started after their quarry like two blimps on an attack run. Austin was pumped up with excitement, but even as he flew through the water with Zavala keeping pace, he couldn't help think that this must be one of the strangest battles of all time. Men encased in metal skins fighting to the death with ancient weapons in the massive cargo space of a mortally wounded ship.

A shadow flitted through the opening and was gone.

Damn. "Too late, Joe." Austin powered down. "He's in the open."

"You said there were six. One went down with the truck. You nailed another, and the third is imitating a whirlagig. That leaves three."

"That's my guess, but I wouldn't swear to it. You'll recall my miscount on the *Nereus.*"

"How could I forget it? Close enough for government work, as they say. Let's wrap this thing up," he said wearily. "I'm tired as hell, I have to take a leak, and I've got a date this Saturday with a beautiful agricultural lobbyist. She's got cactus-flower eyes that are blue like you've never seen, Kurt."

One day scientists would tap into Zavala's libido and unleash one of the strongest forces in the universe, Austin reflected.

"I wouldn't want to stand between you and your sex drive, Joe. It might be dangerous. You're the weapons officer. Got anything up your sleeve?"

"I think I see the torch hose." Zavala rose several yards and grabbed the dangling torch. "Got it. Don't know what use it is. Hey, the slab is gone."

Austin rose until they were both almost directly under the huge hole in the ship's side. Where the stone slab had floated earlier on its air-filled pontoons, the blue-green of water was impeded only by nosy fish.

"They hijacked it while we were busy." Austin pictured the theft in his mind. "They'd need at least two guys to swim that load through the water. They'll have their hands full. They'll never expect us to go for them."

"What are we waiting for?" Zavala shot back. He threw the useless torch aside, and they both hit their vertical thrusters. They popped out of the ship into the open ocean. They were still deep beneath the cold dark Atlantic, but Austin was happy to escape the claustrophobic darkness inside the *Doria*'s corpse.

The diving bell was gone, and the only illumination was the filtered shimmer from the surface. The giant hull of the *Andrea*

Doria stretched out in both directions, grayish near them and black beyond their immediate proximity. Austin saw a metallic glint in the distance, but it could have been a fish. He wished he could reach up and rub his eyes. The best he could do was squeeze them shut, then open them. No good. Only the unbroken bluish monotone.

Wait.

There it was again. He was sure of it.

"I think I see them near the bow."

They moved higher, then leveled out and glided toward the bow in fighter plane formation. Zavala saw a movement and called Austin's attention to it. The slab was being pushed along, floating on the pontoons. Two divers, one on either side. A tow line stretched off into the gloom ahead, probably being pulled by an unseen diver.

"We'll try to bluff them. Give them a light show. I'll take a shot."

The beams washed the slab and the divers on either side.

The divers accelerated, as if they thought they could outrun their pursuers. Austin loosed a bolt, trying not to puncture a pontoon. He thought he saw the projectile bounce off the slab. The attackers shot off into the murk. The tow line went loose. The slab came to a slow stop above the old bridge wing of the *Doria.*

"Let them go, Joe. We've got to tend to this thing."

They swooped down and started to swim the stone back toward the hull opening where McGinty could find them with the bell. It was slow going because they were pushing against the current flowing over the ship.

A voice crackled in Austin's earphones. "It's McGinty. Are you okay?"

"We're both fine. Got the stone. We're moving it back to the work area. You can drop the bell anytime."

There was a pause followed by a faint snort. "That might be a problem," the captain said, his voice burred with irritation. "We've lost the bow anchors. From the looks of the lines, they've been cut. Surface current's pushing us around. If we drop the bell, it'll swing like a big pendulum. Could knock us over."

"Looks like our pals covered their escape, Joe."

"I heard. Any chance of reattaching the anchor lines?"

Austin and Zavala were dangerously tired. The Hard Suits were not designed for hand-to-hand combat, and the metal skins with all their paraphernalia had become personal prisons.

"It's doable, but not by us. It'll be easier just to wrassle this thing up on our own. And *that's* not going to be easy." He asked the captain if he could get the boat roughly into the same position and hold it there.

"Not exactly, but close enough," McGinty said.

They were approaching the hull opening. The *Monkfish* should be right above them.

McGinty did a skillful job. The line they had used to lift the hull section dangled a short distance above the wreck. They attached the line to the slab, not easy without the fingers of the saturation divers to do the detailed work, then gave the captain the go-ahead.

"Okay, Cap," Austin said. "We're coming up."

45

AUSTIN HAD A GOOD VIEW OF THE
impenetrable wall of fog bearing down on the *Monkfish* as he
dangled like a hooked flounder over the ocean. The crane pivot-
ed and lowered him onto the deck, where crewmen helped him
out of the dripping gym suit like pages attending to an armored
knight.

Hauled aboard a few minutes earlier, Zavala looked strangely
shrunken without the benefit of his form-fitting hull. Like those
of an astronaut coming out of free fall, Austin's first steps were
wobbly. Zavala handed him a mug of hot coffee. A few sips of
the strong brew got his blood circulating. Then they dealt with
their top priority, a stiff-legged race for the nearest head. They
came out smiling, After changing into warm dry clothes they
went back on deck.

The trip up from the *Andrea Doria* wreck had been uneventful but tense, especially during the first few moments as the
winch eased the strain with slow stop-and-go pulls and at the
surface where the load lost its buoyancy. The skilled *Monkfish*
crew attached more floats to make sure they didn't lose the
stone, got it into a sling, then winched it aboard using the stern
A-frame.

Austin gazed at the innocuous-looking block, now lying on a
wooden pallet, and found it hard to believe it had caused so
much trouble and cost so many lives. The slab was shaped

vaguely like an oversized headstone, which was appropriate given all the people who'd been killed for its sake. The object was a little longer than a tall man, almost as wide and as thick. Austin knelt on the deck and ran his hand over the surface, which was going from black to dark gray as it dried. He traced the hieroglyphics, but they made no sense to him. Nothing about this case made sense.

Crew members covered the slab with a quilted protective material, then wrapped it in a plastic tarp. A small forklift transported the slab to a storage space at deck level. It didn't seem fragile, having weathered nearly half a century in a submerged armored truck and a ride to the surface, but he didn't want to take the chance that it would break into a thousand brittle pieces.

With sad eyes, Donatelli watched the stone being taken away. "So that's what all those men died for."

"The killing still hasn't stopped," Austin answered grimly as he squinted at the fog, which now encased the salvage ship in a yellow-gray tomb that muffled sound and light. The temperature had dropped at least ten degrees. He shivered as he remembered Angelo's description of a similar fog bank that hid the *Andrea Doria* from eyes on the *Stockholm.*

"Let's check in with the captain," he suggested, and they climbed to the bridge.

Inside the wheelhouse McGinty motioned for them to come over to the radar screen and pointed to a white blip against the green backdrop. Austin blinked. Maybe he'd been underwater too long. The blip's rapid progress across the screen was more like that of an aircraft than a boat.

"Is that vessel moving as fast as I think it is?" Zavala said.

"Goin' like a banshee," McGinty growled.

Austin tapped the screen with his finger. "Could be our bad boys."

McGinty's eyes sparkled. "When I was growing up in Southie the cops would swing the cruiser through the housing project and you'd see guys running in every direction. Cops always found someone wanted for *some*thing. If you had a guilty conscience all you had to do was see that blue bubble atop the cruiser to get your legs moving. Same thing here, I'll bet."

"The guilty flee when none pursueth," Austin said. The blip passed other craft moving in the same direction as if they were stationary. "My guess is that those folks fleeth at about fifty knots."

McGinty let out a low whistle. "This looks like a big ship to me. I don't know of any vessels of size that can move like that."

"I do. It's called a Fast Ship. It's a new design. Company called Thornycroft and Giles makes them. They use a semi-planing monohull with water jets that eliminate propeller cavitation. Even a Fast Ship container vessel can cruise at forty-five knots. The newer versions might even be faster. Cap, did you see any big boats around the wreck just before the attack?"

"This is a busy place." McGinty pushed his cap back on his forehead as if it would help his memory. "Lots of boats, fishermen mostly, coming or going. Did we actually *see* this ship? Maybe. There was a good-sized craft hunkering a mile or so away, but we lost it in the fog bank. I was busy with dive operations."

"My guess is that if we could cut through the corporate red tape, we'd find it was owned by Halcon Industries."

"Can we get air surveillance?" McGinty asked.

"Impossible in this fog. But what if we do find it? We'd need a warrant to go aboard."

Zavala had been listening silently, his mouth in an uncharacteristic frown. "Something's been bothering me," he said. "Those guys knew where we were and what we were doing. How did they know? We just decided to go after this thing a few days ago. We didn't exactly advertise our plans."

Austin and McGinty exchanged glances. "This operation involved a lot of people. Any one of them could have dropped enough of a hint to let the cat out of the bag." It was an explanation Austin didn't believe himself. His attackers were too well prepared.

Before long the wind shifted, blowing away the fog, Donatelli bid good-bye to the NUMA men and the *Monkfish* captain, and he and Antonio set off in the yacht. Austin promised to update the *Doria* survivor on NUMA's every move.

The *Monkfish* plowed through the fog and rounded Cape Cod, and before long they could see the lights of planes taking off and landing at Logan Airport. They steamed past the Boston Harbor Islands and tied up at a dock near the aquarium. Austin called an excited Dr. Orville and asked him to arrange for a truck to pick up the stone. Austin and Zavala followed the truck to Harvard and saw it safely under lock and key. Orville said he would work through the night to discipher the inscriptions if he had to and invited them to stay. Austin declined the invitation. He and Zavala were exhausted from the day's events and wanted to catch an early flight to Washington. After a light dinner they had a nightcap of Irish whiskey with McGinty, then crawled into their bunks and fell asleep almost immediately.

The tubular green-glassed tower of NUMA headquarters was like the welcome beacon of a lighthouse as the taxi navigated the unpredictable seas of Washington traffic. Austin and Zavala had caught the water shuttle to Logan Airport and were back in Washington by late morning. McGinty bid him adieu with a lung-shaking slap on the back and the highest of praise. Austin, he proclaimed, was a chip off his old man's block.

"Wonder what the Trouts are up to." Zavala's musings cut into his thoughts.

Austin had called their team colleagues from the salvage ship the night before to tell them about the fight in the *Doria* and the retrieval of the stone. Gamay said she and Paul had new information they'd share with them the next day. Austin was too tired to ask what it was. The Trouts were waiting with Hiram Yaeger in the private conference room where they held their first meeting. Rudi Gunn showed up a minute later and said Sandecker was having brunch at the White House. The vice president the admiral would have blown off, but not the president.

Gamay opened the meeting. "You've all been briefed so I won't go into the details of my Yucatan jungle adventure with Dr. Chi. As you know we discovered a stash of stolen Mayan artifacts awaiting shipment out of the country. The storage was centrally located with respect to roads and water routes. We found hundreds of objects taken from a number of important sites, known and unknown to legitimate excavators. When Dr. Chi inventoried the goods, in addition to ceramics he found a number of stone carvings, apparently removed from Mayan buildings with a diamond-edged saw. The unusual boat motif on them must have caught the eye of the *chicleros*. His guess was that the carvings were taken from temple observatories similar to a structure he showed me at the Mayan site called MIT. There was only one problem: the carvings were not identified as to location."

She paused as Trout passed the pile of folders he'd been guarding to the others at the table. Gamay waited until the rustling of papers died down, then continued.

"The paper you see on top has eight sketches drawn by Dr. Chi. These profiles are glyphs that represent the Mayan god Quetzalcoatl, who also went by the name Kukulcan. At first glance the drawings appear identical, but if you look closer you'll see subtle differences."

Yaeger brought his quick eye for detail to the task. "Jaw's a little more prominent on this one," he said. "This one's got a thicker eyebrow."

Gunn squinted at the sketches. "This guy's nose looks as if it ran into a right cross."

Gamay smiled like a proud schoolmarm. "You catch on fast, gentlemen. These facial differences indicate a particular *place*. Each city or urban center interpreted the god in a way that was peculiar to it."

"Like the owl was the symbol of ancient Athens?" Austin ventured.

"Correct. In this case the god also represents the planet Venus."

Austin stirred impatiently in his seat, his eyes glazing over.

He was expecting to hear information with a direct bearing on the case, not a lecture on Mayan theology.

"Gamay, this is all very interesting," he said, making no effort to hide his impatience, "but I'm not sure where you're going with it."

She flashed her disarming tomboy grin. "These glyphs were all incorporated into carvings of the boat motif."

Austin's interest was piqued. He leaned forward. "The *Phoenician* boat?"

"We don't know yet for sure whether it was Phoenician or not. But, yes, the inscriptions apparently marked the event we saw, strange boats and strange people being received by Mayans."

Paul Trout chipped in. "Dr. Chi had already guessed that the carvings came from temple observatories. Dr. Chi used the city glyphs to pinpoint the location of the observatories. Mayan observatories are scattered all over Central America. But only eight, as far as he knew, have that particular boat theme."

Austin said, "You've got eight identical observatories at separate locations, dedicated to Venus, keyed into its cycles, and all having something to do with a mysterious fleet of boats."

"That's right," Gamay said, resuming her explanation. "And the number eight goes to the heart of the matter." Noting the blank expressions, she said, "Quetzalcoatl and Kukulcan were incarnations of the Maya's most important god, Venus. The Maya plotted the planet's course with incredible accuracy. They knew there were eight days in the Venus cycle when the planet disappeared. The Mayans believed Venus went to the underworld during that time. They used architectural features to keep track of Venus and other celestial objects. Doorways, sculptures, pillars. The placement of streets. Professor Chi thinks these observatories were part of a greater plan. A map. Chart. Even a crude computer meant to solve a problem."

"Like the problem of the Phoenician, excuse me, the as-yet-unidentified boats?" Austin said.

"Exactly," Paul replied. "Page two in your folder is a map showing the locations."

Another rustle of papers.

Gamay said, "We tried connecting the temples, drawing parallel lines from them. Nothing made sense. While we were tearing our hair out we got a call from Dr. Chi. He had come in from the field for supplies and heard we were trying to get in touch. We told him we were groping in the dark for something we were sure was there and needed his help."

Paul announced, "Page three in your folder, gentlemen. Dr. Chi had this faxed from the national museum. The Spanish destroyed all but a few of the Mayan books. This is one of the few that survived. The Dresden Codex. It has detailed observation tables for Venus. The data were collected from observatories."

"What bearing does it have on our mystery?" Gunn inquired.

"Mainly as an example of the type of information that was so important to the Maya," Gamay replied. "Try to imagine the Mayan priests night after night gazing at the stars. They collect the information on the movement of the stars, then, using architectural features built into these same temples, forecast what the stars and planets would do."

"I've *got* it," blurted Yaeger. "Sometimes it helps to be a nerd. You're saying that these eight temples and the carvings are the *hardware.* The Codex would be the software that tells the hardware what to do." Yaeger blinked rapidly behind his wire-rimmed glasses. "Carrying the analogy forward, the physical form of software can be soft, like the floppy disk that contains the program, or hard, like the hard drive."

"Or for our purposes, hard as *stone,*" Austin said.

"Bingo!" Gamay said. "What geniuses we have at NUMA."

Galvanized now, Austin ticked the points off on his fingertips. *"One.* We have eight temples dedicated to the temple Venus. *Two.* The temples are set up in a way that will help us solve a puzzle having to do with those mysterious boats and their cargo. *Three.* The talking stone tells us how to operate it."

"I wasn't positive until Dr. Orville called this morning. He found the same eight glyphs on the stone. There's a fax of the tablet in your folder. The inscription is composed of three main elements. The glyphs and a condensed rendition of the boat landings are the first and second elements."

"Any idea why the ship is about to be eaten by the big snake?" Zavala asked, looking at the fax.

"That's element number three," Gamay explained. "The feathered serpent is the earthly embodiment of Quetzalcoatl-Kukulcan."

"Ah," Zavala said. "*That* certainly clears things up."

"Look at it this way," Gamay said. "The glyphs tell you *where.* The boat inscription tells you *what.* The serpent tells you *how.* Look at the Kukulcan. Tell me what you see."

"Feathers mostly," Gunn said after a moment.

"No," Yeager said. "There's something else. The feathers are confusing. Look at the jaws. It's some sort of grid."

"*Bravo.*" Gamay clapped, clearly delighted. "Our computer guru goes to the head of the class."

"I don't know why," Yaeger said with a shrug. "Damned if I know what I'm talking about."

"Check out the next picture in your folder. This shows one of those eight temples. Pretty typical. Cylindrical, balcony around the top, frieze on the bottom part. Take a close look at those two vertical slit windows. We assumed they were used for some sort of astronomical calculation. We made an educated guess that the windows lined up with Venus at the extremes of its position in the sky. It still didn't make sense until Paul had the idea of looking *down* on the temples, as if we were in an airplane."

Picking up the explanation, Paul held up the last sheet in the folder. "We extended the lines from each window and found that they intersected."

"I'll be damned," Yaeger said. "It's the same grid as in the feathered serpent."

Gamay nodded. "I started thinking about it when I noticed the grid reminded me of an amulet I once borrowed from Dr. Chi. The jaws of Kukulcan."

Gunn said, "Weren't we talking about Columbus depending on some kind of grid?"

"That's right," Paul said. "Orville's theory is that Columbus tried to use this stone but was at a disadvantage to start with. He knew there was treasure but couldn't decipher the glyphs. He had drawings made from the stone to take on the *Niña*, probably hoping to find someone who would translate for him."

Austin had been staring at the diagram. "Back when Columbus sailed the ocean blue, navigators had maps with straight lines called rhumbs on them. Someone sailing from Spain to Hispañola chose the line giving him the most direct route and set a compass course. You'd end up where you were supposed to be, as long as you weren't messed up by current and winds. Columbus may have wrongly thought these lines were rhumbs. The Maya were a lot more sophisticated than he knew. Were you able to work this out on a map?"

"It didn't make sense at first," Paul said. "Venus would have been in a different position in the sky a couple of thousand years ago. We had to do some recomputing. Our guess is that the V-shaped intersection of the jaws, here where you see the boat, is where *something* is located."

Austin had another question. "How long do you think it will take Halcon to figure this out?"

The Trouts exchanged glances. Paul said, "There have been reports of Columbus papers and Mayan documents being stolen from various museums. I suspect Mr. Halcon has been trying to piece things together, but we've got the stone, and now we know how to use it."

"We'd better get moving on this in case Halcon's smarter than we think," Austin said.

Gunn cleared his throat and squared the edges of his papers. "With all due respect, Kurt, maybe before we go jumping into the jaws of Kukulcan we had better figure out what all this is about. Starting with Halcon and why he is causing so much trouble."

"I see your point. Okay, I'll start the ball rolling. Here's my theory. Like Columbus, Halcon is after the Phoenician treasure that was removed from Carthage. The key to finding the stuff lies in pre-Columbian evidence. He doesn't want anyone else to step on his turf so he destroys the evidence and those who have found it."

"I've considered that theory and think it's on the mark," Gunn said, "but it's only part of the picture. I asked Yaeger to compile a detailed dossier on Halcon. Tell us about his finances, Hiram."

Yaeger glanced at a computer printout in front of him. "Between his family fortune and widespread holdings, he's worth billions, and that's a conservative guess."

"Thanks, Hiram. That's what bothers me, Kurt. Why would Halcon go through all this trouble of killing people, attacking you on the *Andrea Doria* and trying to steal the so-called talking stone, just so he can find a treasure, however fabulous? He has more money than any normal person could ever want."

"You may have answered your own question," Austin countered. "You said a *normal* person. From what Zavala told us about the ball court executions, Halcon sounds like a madman."

"I've considered that possibility, too. But I think Señor Halcon is a lot more complicated than a bored rich eccentric who takes up treasure hunting for a hobby. Hiram, would you run through the other material you picked up on the gentleman?"

Adjusting his granny glasses, Yaeger said, "Francisco Halcon was born in Spain of a family that goes back centuries. *Halcón*, which means 'falcon,' was apparently not the real family name, which I was unable to determine. He went to expensive private schools in Switzerland and attended college in England. Oxford man," Yaeger said with a smirk. "He became a bullfighter known as El Halcon and didn't do too badly but left the *toro* business under a cloud of scandal. He was said to have put poison on the tip of his killing sword, so even if he didn't hit the bull's vitals it would die."

"Hardly seems sporting for an Oxford man," Austin said in a stage British accent.

"Cambridge maybe, but not Oxford," Zavala said.

Yaeger shrugged. "From the bullring he went into one of the family businesses. The Halcons were very thick with the dictator Franco and the Spanish military before and during the war and made a lot of money on armaments. After Franco died and the king returned and restored democracy. Halcon's business activities came under suspicion. Interpol says he was suspected of being tied to a Spanish Murder Inc. He left the country and came to Mexico where a branch of his family that goes back to the Spanish conquest owned a number of businesses. Halcon took over the U.S. operations, used his money and influence to cultivate political connections, and in short time became an American citizen."

"He's done pretty well from what I saw of the companies under his aegis in San Antonio," Zavala said.

"The American dream personified," Gunn added, not attempting to conceal his sarcasm.

"In more ways than one," said Yaeger. "His legitimate businesses were just a cover for shady operations on both sides of the border. He's suspected of large-scale drug and immigrant smuggling from Mexico."

"That would mean he is close to the ruling party in Mexico," Zavala said. "No big business, legal or illegal, escapes their attention."

"Fits in with the way the family operated in Spain and the United States," Austin said. "Has anyone ever mentioned the Brotherhood?"

"As I say, he was supposedly tied to a Spanish Mafia organization," Yaeger replied. "They could be one and the same, although I don't have confirmation."

"What about that complex I saw outside San Antonio?" Zavala asked. "What's the story on that?"

"Owned by one of his corporations. Perfectly legal, according to the local licensing authorities. He's considered something of a nut, but a rich nut, so if he wanted to build his own personal theme park, who's to stop him? By the way, the plans for the complex show the ball court as a soccer field."

"That wasn't like any game of soccer I ever saw," Zavala said soberly.

"The locals have heard explosions from time to time and

report an unusual amount of traffic, but other than that he's a good neighbor who pays his taxes."

"Hiram has saved the best for last," Gunn said.

"It took time, because of the front companies and interlocking corporations and foundations, but Halcon Industries has been spreading all over the Southwest and California. Halcon controls banks, real estate, political figures, newspapers, anything that's for sale."

"Evidently he's trying to increase his power as well as his wealth," Austin said. "No different from any other corporation with its armies of lobbyists."

"Interesting that you should use the word *army,*" Gunn said. "On a whim I ran some of Hiram's findings by the ATF. They immediately caught a whiff of something that smelled very bad. They recognized the name of one of Halcon's companies as an outfit that has been buying arms from the Czech Republic and China."

"What sort of arms?"

"You name it. Everything from infantry rifles to tanks. Lots of missiles, too. SAMs. Antitank. That sort of stuff. The ATF got a search warrant for the company that was handling the shipments. It was an empty office."

"Where has all this stuff been going?"

"Specifically? Nobody knows. Generally, northern Mexico, the Southwest states, and California."

"Arms purchases like the ones you've described cost money, *big* money."

Gunn nodded. "Even a billionaire might become strapped spending enough on arms to start a revolution."

The room became silent as the last word in Gunn's statement hung in the air.

"*Madre mia,*" Zavala whispered. "The treasure. He needs the treasure to do what he wants to do."

"That was my take," Gunn said quietly. "It sounds loony, but he seems to be planning some sort of combined military and political takeover."

"Any indication when this is supposed to happen?" Austin said.

"Soon is my guess. Hiram's sources have detected a lot of money being moved around Europe through Swiss bank accounts to arms dealers. He's going to have to replace that in a hurry if he wants to stay off the bad credit report. Which means he'll be desperate to find the treasure."

"What about our armed forces?"

"On alert. Even if he is stopped militarily a lot of innocent blood will be shed."

"There's another way to stop him. No treasure, no revolution," Zavala said.

"Thanks, Paul and Gamay, you and Dr. Orville have done a great job of pointing us in the right direction," Austin said. He rose from his seat and glanced at the faces around the table. "Now it's our turn," he said with a grim smile.

The elegant dining room was largely in darkness except for the center table where Angelo Donatelli sat going over the next day's menu. Donatelli's restaurant was done in a Nantucket motif, but unlike other places with a nautical theme, the decorations did not come from a mail-order house. The harpoons and flensing irons had actually pierced whale flesh, and the primitive paintings of sailing ships were all originals. Antonio sat opposite Donatelli, an Italian newspaper spread out on the spotless white tablecloth. Occasionally they sipped at a glass of amaretto. Neither was aware they were no longer alone until they heard the quiet voice say, "Mr. Donatelli?"

Angelo looked up and saw two figures standing just beyond the circle of illumination. How the devil did these people get in? He had locked the front door himself. The after-hours visit itself didn't surprise him. The waiting period was weeks for a reservation, and people tried all sorts of stunts to shortcut the process. The voice was vaguely familiar, too, which persuaded him that it might be one of his clientele.

"I'm Angelo Donatelli," he said with his unfailing politeness.

"I'm afraid you've come too late, the restaurant is closed. If you would call tomorrow the mâitre d' will do what he can to accommodate you."

"You can accommodate me by telling your man to place his gun on the table."

From his lap, Antonio lifted the revolver he had slipped out of his shoulder holster and slowly placed it on the table.

"If you've come to rob us, you're too late for that, too," Donatelli said. "All our cash has been deposited at the bank."

"We haven't come to rob you. We've come to kill you."

"*Kill* us. We don't even know who you are."

In answer, the figure stepped forward into the light, revealing a dark-complexioned slender man who took Antonio's gun and tucked it into the belt of his one-piece black suit. Angelo's gaze lingered for a second on the pistol with its barrel extended into a silencer, but it was the man's thin dark features that sent a chill down his spine. It was a face he had seen in a dream. No. A *nightmare.* A brief glimpse of an assassin who glanced his way deep in the hold of a dying ship. Incredibly it hadn't aged in more than forty years.

"I saw you on the *Andrea Doria,*" Donatelli said with wonder.

The man's thin lips curled into a cold smile. "You have a good memory for faces," he said. "But that was my late father. He told me he sensed someone else was in the hold that night. You and I, too, have a more intimate relationship. I talked to you once on the telephone."

Now Donatelli remembered the call coming late at night, waking him out of a sound sleep with the threats against him and his family.

"The *Brotherhood,*" he whispered.

"You have a good memory for names as well. It's a pity you didn't remember my warnings about what would happen if you couldn't keep your mouth shut. Normally I don't micromanage the everyday operations of my organization, but you've caused me a great deal of trouble, old man. Do you recall what I said?"

Donatelli nodded, his mouth too dry to reply.

"Good. Let me imprint it in your mind. I warned that if you
talked about that night on the *Andrea Doria*, you would go to
your grave knowing that you caused the death of every member
of your family we can find. Sons. Daughters. Grandchildren.
Every one. The Donatelli family will cease to exist except for a
collection of headstones in a family plot."

"You can't do such a thing!" Donatelli replied, regaining his
voice.

"You have only yourself to blame. There are great forces at
work here. No one forced you to talk to NUMA."

"*No.*" Antonio spoke for the first time. "The family was not
part of the deal," he said.

Angelo turned to his cousin. "What is he talking about?"

Antonio's battered face was contorted with guilt.

The man said, "Your cousin didn't tell you that he was working for me. He refused at first, but you have no idea of the pull
his homeland had on him. We told him that in return for keeping us informed through you about NUMA's activities, I would
solve his problems with the authorities back in Sicily."

"*Si,*" Antonio said, jutting his jaw out like Mussolini. "But
not the family. You get me back to Sicily. That was the deal."

"I keep my word. I just didn't say that you would be returning home in a pine box. But you first, Mr. Donatelli. *Arrivederci.*"

Antonio rose from his chair with a feral cry of rage and threw
himself in front of his cousin. The pistol made a *thut* quieter
than a door shutting. A red blossom flowered on the front of
Antonio's shirt, and he crumpled to the floor.

The gun coughed again.

With no one to block it this time, the next bullet caught
Donatelli in the chest and he crashed over backward in his chair
as Antonio reached back and filled his hand with the six-inch
Beretta from his ankle holster. He propped himself up on his
elbows and aimed the gun at Halcon. Magically, a neat round
hole appeared in the center of Antonio's forehead, and he
slumped forward onto the floor, his shot going wild.

The second figure stepped from the shadows, the gun in his

hand smoking. He glanced impassively at the man he had jus
killed. "Never trust a Sicilian," he said quietly.

"Good work, Guzman. I should have expected treachery. Sit
ting in an office has made me rusty when it comes to field opera
tions."

"You're welcome to come along when we take care of the res
of the family," Guzman said, his eyes glittering.

"Yes, I'd like that. Unfortunately it will have to wait. W₄
have more pressing business." Turning his attention to Angelo
he said, "Too bad you can't hear this, Donatelli. I've decided t₄
spare your family for a little while until we clean up the mes₄
you helped create. Don't despair. You'll soon see your loved one₄
in hell."

Voices were coming from outside the restaurant where Anto
nio's shot had caught the attention of passers-by. Halcon too₄
one last look at the still bodies, then he and his scar-faced com
panion melted into the darkness.

46

"HOW OLD DID YOU SAY THIS PLANE
was?" Austin shouted over the cockpit noise from the single
engine.

"About fifty years, give or take a few," Zavala yelled back.
"The owner says it's got all its original parts, too. Except for the
fuzzy dice hanging from the rearview mirror, maybe." Seeing the
alarm in Austin's face, Zavala grinned. "Just kidding, Kurt. I
checked. The engine's been overhauled so many times it's practically new. Hope we'll be in as good a shape when we get this old."

"If we *get* to be this old," Austin said skeptically, glancing out
the window at the inhospitable terrain below.

"Not to worry, old chap. The De Havilland Beaver was one
of the finest bush planes ever built. This crate is as tough as a
tank. Just what the doctor ordered."

Austin eyed the plastic statue of St. Christopher attached to
the control panel by a suction cup, sat back in his seat, and
folded his arms. When he suggested to Zavala that they find
something unobtrusive to fly, he hadn't envisioned the antique
Beaver with its quaint boxy lines, two-blade propeller, and blunt
unaerodynamic nose. He simply wanted an alternative to an
army helicopter that couldn't violate the airspace of Mexico's
neighboring countries without permission. Even a NUMA aircraft, with its turquoise paint job and big official lettering,
would have raised eyebrows.

They found the Beaver hidden by a painter's canvas drop cloth in the dark corner of a dilapidated out-of-the-way hangar at the Belize City airport. Zavala's eyes lit up like Christmas *luminarias*. He rubbed his hands together, itching to get them on the controls. Only one other plane would have elicited a stronger reaction, Austin thought. Luckily the Wright Brothers' invention was in the Smithsonian, which is where this plane belonged.

Like Shakespeare's Cassius, the Belizan who owned the plane had a lean and hungry look. He talked barely above a whisper and often glanced over his shoulder as if he were expecting unwanted visitors. He had been recommended to Austin by a former CIA colleague who served in clandestine operations helping the Contras fight the Sandinistas. Judging from his prudent suggestions about cargo handling and discreet landing areas it was evident he thought his two American customers were drug smugglers. Given the CIA's shady operations in Central America, that came as no surprise. He asked no questions and insisted he be paid what he called a security deposit, big enough to buy himself a Boeing 747, in dollars. As he carefully counted every bill to make sure he wasn't being cheated, he warned them to keep in mind Guatemala's territorial claims over Belize and do whatever they could to blend into the background. Austin observed that might be impossible with the bright mustard-yellow paint covering the old plane. The man shrugged and disappeared into the shadows with his wad of bills.

Austin had to admit the plane was better suited for the job than a newer and flashier aircraft would have been. It wasn't exactly the Concorde. Yet with a cruising speed of one hundred twenty-five miles per hour it ate up distance and was slow enough to serve as an ideal flying observation platform. Moreover, it was designed for short takeoff and landing on water or land.

Zavala was keeping the plane below three thousand feet. They were flying over the Peten, the thickly forested northern part of Guatemala that juts squarely into Mexico. The territory below had started as flat terrain and worked itself up to low rolling hills broken by rivers and their tributaries. It was once thickly settled by the Maya who used the rivers for intercity commerce, and several times they had glimpsed gray ruins through the trees. The distant peaks of the Maya Mountains rose from the haze off to the south. Austin marked their progress on a clipboard that held a map with the grid overlay on acetate. He referred constantly to the compass and the GPS finder.

"We're coming up on the junction point, where the jaws meet," he said, pointing to the map. He glanced at his watch. "Another thirty seconds should put us there." Austin peered out the window again. They were following a squiggle of river that meandered back and forth like blue Christmas ribbon candy and widened into the small lake dead ahead. Seconds later Austin pointed at the shimmering water. "That's it. The jaws of Kukulcan."

"We should have brought the mini-sub," Zavala said.

"Let's make a few runs around the lake. If we don't run into ack-ack fire we'll set her down."

Zavala breathed on his aviator-style sunglasses, wiped the lenses on a sleeve, and adjusted them on his nose. He gave the thumbs-up sign and banked the plane so the horizon tilted sharply. Zavala brought the same flying technique—a combination of F-16 jockey and fly-by-the-seat-of-the-pants barnstormer—to whatever vehicle he controlled, whether it was a submersible or an airplane that was built when Harry Truman was starting his first term as president.

The lake looked like a huge staring eye from the air. It was oval in shape and had a small island about where the pupil would be. It was small, about half a mile in length and half as wide. The river shot off at a sharp angle and curved around the lake until it intersected with water flowing from an outlet at the other end. Austin decided the lake must be replenished by springs or streams hidden by the trees.

The Beaver wheeled twice around the lake, but they saw nothing out of the ordinary. With the way apparently clear, Zavala pointed the plane down as if he wanted to drill a hole in the water. At the last moment he pulled the nose up like a dive-bomber and leveled off nicely until the white floats kissed the surface. The plane skimmed along like a flat stone, throwing off twin rooster tails before finally coming to a rolling halt about midway between shore and island. Austin kicked open the door as the propeller spun to a choking halt. With the engine stopped a palpable silence enveloped the cockpit. Zavala radioed the ship with a position report, and Austin scanned the lake, the low cliffs, and the island with his binoculars, taking his time until he was sure, as far as possible, that they were alone.

"Everything looks fine," he said, lowering the binoculars. He squinted toward the middle of the lake. "Something about that island bothers me."

Zavala leaned over Austin's shoulder and pulled his baseball cap lower over his forehead to shield his eyes against the sun sparkle. "It looks perfectly okay to me."

"That's the *problem*. The placement is *too* perfect. If you drew lines shore-to-shore from north to south and east to west, that island would be at the intersection, like a target in the cross-hairs of a rifle scope. Exact center."

Zavala restarted the engine and gave the propeller enough power to pull them along at a couple of knots. Then he cut throttle and let the plane drift closer to the island. They threw an anchor over the side and estimated from the length of the tethering line that the lake was more than one hundred feet deep. They inflated a rubber raft, climbed into it from the plane's pontoons, and paddled the short distance to the island, pulling the raft up onto the grass-covered mud. Austin estimated the island at about thirty feet across. It looked like the mis-shapen shell of a giant turtle, rising quickly from the water to a roundish summit about fifteen feet high. Undeterred by the thick growth of ferns and succulents, Zavala climbed up the slope. Near the top he let out a yell and stepped back as if recoil-ing from an invisible punch.

Austin's body tensed and his hand went to the pistol at his hip. "What's wrong?" he shouted. His first thought was that Joe had stumbled onto a nest of adders.

Zavala's peals of laughter startled a flock of white birds into the air like confetti blown in the wind.

"The island is *occupied*, Kurt. Come up and I'll introduce you to the landlord."

Austin quickly climbed the small hill and peered at the toothy skeleton jaw grinning behind the bushes, He pushed the leaves aside to reveal a grotesque stone head about twice life size, carved into the lintel over a squared-off opening. The opening was set into the side of a block-shaped structure that was buried in loose soil almost to the top of its flat, crenelated roof and decorated with a border of skulls similar to but smaller than the one they first saw. Using a sheath knife, Austin dug away at the dirt and enlarged the opening so Zavala could get his head and shoulders in.

Zavala flashed a light around inside. "I think I can squeeze in." He wriggled through the opening feet-first.

Austin heard a loud sneeze, then Zavala saying, "Bring a Dust Buster with you." Austin worked to enlarge the opening, then he followed Zavala inside.

He looked around. "Not exactly the Hilton." His words echoed.

The boxlike space was the size of a two-car garage. The walls were thick enough to repel a direct hit from a cannon. Austin's head almost touched the low roof. The plastered walls were plain except for dark blotches that covered most of their surface and four floor-to-ceiling portals like the one they had just come through. The doorways were clogged by root-bound earth that was as hard as cement.

"Dunno, Kurt. It's got a lot to offer. Water view. Simple decor."

"This is what the real estate guys call a handyman's special."

"Comes with a cellar, too." Zavala flashed his light into a corner. Austin knelt to inspect a massive flagstone in the floor. It was perforated by several holes along the edge. Using their knives, they pried it open and slid the flagstone aside to reveal a stairway spiraling down. Since Zavala had been first into the building, Austin volunteered to investigate. He descended the short curving flight of stairs to a passageway that went a few yards before it was blocked by a huge slab. Austin played the beam of his flashlight over the slab.

"You'd better get down here," he said quietly.

Sensing the seriousness in Austin's tone, Zavala quickly joined him. Lying on the floor in front of the slab was a pile of bones. Unlike the death's-head sculpture they had seen earlier, the six skulls they counted were once covered with flesh. Zavala picked up a skull and held it at arm's length like Hamlet contemplating the remains of Yorick.

"Sacrificial victims. From the looks of that hole in the skull, they were put out of their misery so they didn't have to starve to death."

"The executioners were all heart," Austin said, examining the slab for a seam. "The only way to get around this thing is with a jackhammer or dynamite."

Austin had seen enough. They climbed back to the upper chamber where Austin noticed several bleached white fragments on the floor. He picked one up only to have it crumble to powder in his hand.

"Freshwater shellfish," he said. "This place was underwater at one time."

Zavala brushed the dirty walls with his fingers. "You could be right. This looks like dried pond scum."

They climbed back into the fresh air and explored the perimeter of the structure. It was built onto a stone platform that had become the catchall for material floating in the lake. Seeds, probably brought in by birds, had sprouted, and their roots kept the dirt from blowing away. Looking straight down into the water at the edge of the island, it was possible to see a stone terrace. Austin kicked off his boots and slipped into the water, swam out a few strokes, and dove.

"This thing is like the tip of an iceberg," he said when he resurfaced. "It was probably a temple on top of a very big pyramid. Can't tell how far it goes."

"Told you we should have brought a submarine," Zavala replied as he gave Austin a hand back onto dry land. "So if what we think is true, and that building is a temple, we're at ground zero. The jaws."

"All we have to do is figure out how to get into the gullet."

"Lovely thought. We could try blowing that slab blocking the way."

"Yeah, we could do that, and it might even work. But it's not exactly a surgical approach. Our archaeologist friends would never speak to us again. Let's think about it while we look around."

They got back in the plane and taxied to the end of the lake, where they went ashore and made their way inland. The forest was in semidarkness except for the mottled sunlight filtering through the tree canopy. The trees discouraged undergrowth, making for an easy hike on a carpet of leaves. Austin followed a babble of water to its source and stopped where the river they had seen from the air was flanked by stone foundations. The riverbed between the foundations was filled with earth and vegetation, but several streams flowed from the substantial reservoir that had built up behind the crude dam and around the old barricade toward the lake. The main course of the river turned abruptly just before it hit the foundations and angled off into the forest. Austin followed the rushing waters away from the reservoir and stopped again at a similar pair of foundations.

"Just as I thought," he said.

Zavala was impressed. "How'd you know these things would be here?"

"Would you believe it if I said I was a *dam* genius?"

Zavala winced. "Of course I would. Now tell me how you *really* knew."

Austin picked up a branch, threw it into the river, and watched it disappear from sight in the fast-moving bubble and foam. "You remember how this river looks from the air? I think you said it had more wiggles than a belly dancer. Just before it comes into the lake, it angles off in a perfectly straight line. My first impression was that the section was too straight to be natural. Like that temple in the center of the lake. Nothing in nature is absolutely perfect. Maybe it was a canal, I thought. You know the Chesapeake and Ohio historical park north above Washington?"

"One of my favorite places for a cheap first date," Zavala said with a smile built of fond memories. *"Muy romántico.* What's that got to do with anything?"

"Think about that temple. Sometimes it's underwater. Sometimes it isn't."

Austin could almost hear the gears whirring as Zavala's brilliant mechanical mind processed the information. He slapped his forehead. "Of *course.* The locks."

Austin cleared a bare spot on the ground and picked up a short stick. He handed it to Zavala. "Be my guest, Professor Z."

Zavala drew a line in the dirt. "This is the Potomac River. You can't move boats up and down the river because of the rapids and falls, so you cut a canal around the white water. Here." He tapped the ground. "You build a system of gates and sluices to control the water level in the canal one section at a time. Let's see if I'm right." He drew an oval representing the lake. "In its normal state the river comes in here at the top, fills the flood plain to create the lake, then flows out the bottom, keeps going until it comes to the sea."

"Good so far, Professor."

"At some point unknown engineers put a dam here." Zavala drew a line across the top of the lake. "This blocks the water into the lake, but it's got to go somewhere or else it ends up sweeping around the gate." He drew a straight line away from the lake. "You cut this canal, and the water is diverted away from the lake to another riverbed." He looked up, triumph in his dark eyes. *"Now* you can drain the lake."

"And build the temple. Here." Austin drew an *X* in the dirt with the tip of his boot.

Zavala picked up the narrative. "After you lay the last stone of the pyramid, you close the canal sluice, open the lake gate. The lake refills in no time and hides the temple. Ergo . . ."

"Ergo, ipso facto, and voilà! Only problem is, the sluice gate is made of moving parts. In time the gate deteriorates with no public works department to maintain it. What's left of the Mayan civilization is being crushed into dust by the Spaniards. That curve is a natural catchall for anything floating down the river. Junk builds up in front of the lake gate like a dike, the canal sluice rots open, and the river is diverted away from the lake again. The lake is fed by a few streams, but eventually the water level drops, exposing the top of the temple. Which becomes overgrown with vegetation."

"So if we wait long enough," Zavala said, "the lake will eventually drop to where the temple is completely exposed again. Unless the water pressure from that reservoir busts through the old dam and raises the lake level."

Austin pondered Zavala's statement and nodded. "I'll tell you the rest of my theory on the way back."

As they walked through the forest Zavala got his revenge. "You've got to admit that's a *damn* nice piece of engineering."

It was Austin's turn to ignore the pun. "I agree. It allowed them to drain the lake again if they wanted to. That leaves open the possibility that they might want to reenter the temple. The entryway on top could be a blind. Like one of the false entrances they built into the Egyptian pyramids to fool grave robbers. I wouldn't be surprised if that's why they put the skeletons there, just for stage props."

"Some stage. Some props," Zavala said.

"Let's call in an air drop when we get back to the plane."

Minutes later, from the plane, Zavala radioed their wish list to the *Nereus.* He raised a quizzical eyebrow over one of the items Austin requested but asked no questions.

While they waited they had something to eat, then lounged in the shade until the radio crackled with a message. "Coming in, boys. ETA ten minutes."

Exactly on time a turquoise helicopter with NUMA lettering

on the side came in low over the lake, hovered near the plane, and dropped a large box wrapped in heavy plastic and buoyed by air-filled floats. The helicopter crew watched the men below snag the delivery, then waved good-bye and clattered off the way they'd come.

Inside the box were two sets of scuba gear and several cartons. Austin loaded the boxes in the raft and paddled back to the upper end of the lake while Zavala moved the plane to an indentation in the shoreline. Zavala knew better than to ask Austin what he had planned. Kurt would tell him when he needed to know.

Zavala covered the plane with a fishing net and was weaving branches into it when Austin showed up in the raft to help him finish the job. The cartons were gone. Satisfied their plane was well hidden, they piled their scuba gear into the raft and set off for the island, where they swept away traces of their previous visit. The raft was deflated and sunk in shallow water with rocks piled on top to hold it under. The water was warm, so they wore only lightweight black Lycra skins rather than the thicker neoprene wetsuits.

Without comment Austin tucked the small pouch he was wearing around his neck into a waterproof pocket. After a quick check of their equipment, they breast-stroked away from the island and, wasting no time, they let the air out of their buoyancy compensators and began to sink into the dark waters of the lake.

47

WITH SMOOTH, STEADY MOVEMENTS of their fins, they swam down and away from the temple at an angle until they were at the lake bottom, dwarfed by the imposing mass of tapering stone. The broad terraced levels spilled down the side of the pyramid like giant steps.

"That's some hunk of rock," Austin said, his awe undiminished by the metallic tone of his underwater communicator.

"Good thing we're not superstitious. I counted thirteen terraces."

"Knock wood on that score," Austin said. He glanced at his depth gauge. "One hundred fourteen feet. Ready to dive the plan?"

Long-lived divers remember the mantra: *plan the dive, and dive the plan.* Their strategy was simple. Explore each of the four sides top to bottom. They moved counterclockwise around the pyramid. It stood entirely alone, which made Austin wonder if the pyramid had been built with a single purpose in mind. The next side was like the first, and they spent only a few minutes exploring it. They hit pay dirt on the third try.

Where the other sides were relatively unadorned, this face was marked by a broad set of stairs running from the temple at the top down to what would have been ground level in drier days. At the foot of the stairs, standing in solitary grandeur like a doorman in front of a swank Las Vegas hotel, was a stone slab. The stela stood vertically in a foundation on the lake bottom.

Zavala played the sharp white beam of his hand-held halogen light across the dark surface. After a second he said, "Look familiar?"

Austin eyed the carving of a feathered serpent devouring a boat. "Small world. It's a twin of the stone from the *Doria*." He lifted his eyes to the stairway running up the side of the pyramid. "Reminds me of that slab that kept showing up in the movie *2001*. Maybe this little old billboard is telling us something."

With Zavala on his right and slightly behind, he drifted up the stairway like a lazy plume of smoke. The stairs were bordered with carvings, and in addition there were sculpted heads spaced every few risers. About halfway up, the huge stylized face of a serpent burst from its crown of feathers. The mouth, large enough to swallow a man, was wide open, in strike position. Thick blunt fangs about the size and shape of traffic pylons extended down from the roof of the mouth to meet a matching pair pointing up.

"Friendly-looking fellow," said Zavala. "You don't suppose he bites?"

"Meet the feathered serpent. Known in these parts as Kukulcan."

"He looks like a cross between a Rottweiler and an alligator. Ask him if he knows how to get into the pyramid."

"Maybe that's not such a dumb idea." With a few fin kicks Austin propelled himself closer to the yawning maw and probed the shadows with his light. "Say 'ah,' " he said, and headed straight in. His air tank bonked and scraped against the thick fangs, but once inside there was room to turn around. He stuck his head out of the mouth, invited Zavala in with a wave, then headed deeper into the pyramid, his light picking out footholds in the slanting floor. They swam down at an angle for about two minutes, slowly and cautiously, until the passageway ended in a chamber big enough for both of them to stand up. A set of stairs ascended into another passageway.

"I feel like a load of dirty clothes that's just gone down a laundry chute. That was too easy," Zavala said suspiciously.

"I was thinking the same thing. But remember, the people who built this thing knew it was going to be underwater. They probably figured that anyone trying to get in would waste time breaking through the slab just below the temple. And that even if they saw this entrance they wouldn't go into the serpent's mouth. Just the same," he added, "keep a sharp eye for booby traps."

They rose up the stairs like ghosts in a haunted house. Austin could hear Zavala grumbling. "Wish they'd make up their mind, man. Down. Up."

Austin sympathized with his partner's gripes. Even an experienced wreck diver can't always put aside those formless claustrophobic fears that the thousands of tons of rock overhead could come crashing down. Even worse, that they could be trapped, unable to move, doomed to die a painful suffocating death. He was glad when his head broke the water. Zavala popped up a second later. They flashed their lights around the circular pool. Zavala reached up to take his regulator from his mouth.

Austin's hand shot out and clamped Zavala's wrist. "Wait!" he warned. "We don't know if the air is good."

The atmosphere could be more than two thousand years old. Austin didn't know if any microorganisms, spores, or toxins could have been built up in all that time, but he wasn't willing to take the chance. He pulled himself out of the pool and removed his fins and belt, then helped Zavala do the same. They climbed the stairwell to where the floor leveled. The noise of their breath through the regulators sounded unnaturally loud out of the water.

The long, narrow chamber had a high vaulted roof supported by arches, built in the corbeled fashion that the Maya favored with levels of horizontally laid blocks. Austin's flashlight beam dropped from the roof and picked out an elongated head with pointed ears and flared nostrils.

Zavala said, "Is that what I think it is?"

"A horse is a horse."

"Of course, of course. But what the hell is Mr. Ed doing here?"

Austin lowered his flashlight so that the beam illuminated the horse's long wooden neck. "Well, I'll be . . . it's a figurehead."

The wooden sculpture of the horse surmounted the high sweeping bow of a boat with shiny dark red sides. The prow was extended into a pointed battering ram. The builders of this boat were true artists, Austin thought as they walked alongside the hull. The craft was a double-ender, long, narrow, and flat-bottomed, sweeping up at each end in graceful curves and tight as a tick from the looks of the well-fitted overlapping planks. The mast lay lengthwise on the deck.

Deck planks had fallen in to reveal dozens of amphorae in the hold. Scattered about were circular metal objects that may have been shields. Two long oars, their blades curled by age, leaned against the ship's backside as if waiting for the hands of long-dead steersmen. The boat sailed not on an azure sea but on a stone cradle. While most of the timbers were intact, some had rotted through so that the ship leaned at a slight angle.

"She's a lot prettier in person," Zavala murmured.

Austin ran his hand along the wood as if he didn't quite believe his eyes. "It's not just me, then. This is one of the ships pictured on the stelae and other carvings."

"What's a Phoenician boat doing in an underwater Mayan temple?"

"Waiting to overturn every archaeological assumption ever made," Austin said. "Wait until Nina sets her eyes on this lovely lady. We'll have to give her some specs to chew over until we can get a camera in here. What do you figure for length?"

"More than one hundred feet, easy."

Zavala almost bumped into one of four round pillars spaced alongside the boat. Another quartet of columns ran along the other side.

"Here's another spec for you to chew on," he said. "*Eight* pillars."

"Eight significant days in the Venus cycle," Austin replied. "Fits in."

They were at the boat's upsweeping sterncastle. Austin had expected the chamber to end in a blank wall. Instead there was another corbeled archway and beyond it a stairway leading upward. They climbed the stairs to a much smaller chamber whose floor was taken up largely by a rectangular sunken pit. In the pit was a sarcophagus whose lid was inscribed with repetitive carvings in the feathered serpent theme. They got into the pit and tried unsuccessfully to budge the lid with their knives.

"Maybe there's something on the ship we can use to pry it off," Austin suggested.

They descended to the large chamber. Zavala reached up to the boat rail and with a boost from Austin pulled himself over the side and into the boat. He held on to the gunwale and took a tentative step forward, testing his weight.

"The deck's holding, but I'll stay on the cross beam just in case." The wood creaked as he made his way across the deck. "Lots of amphorae. I—Jeezus." A pause. Then an excited exclamation. "Kurt, you've got to see this!"

Zavala came back to the side of the boat and helped Austin climb in. Through the centuries the deck had settled, and now the planking slanted down to the middle where most of the amphorae were concentrated. Austin followed Zavala on a cross beam to the middle of the deck. Although the hull rocked slightly from their weight, it remained solidly ensconced in its stone cradle.

Zavala bent over a big jar that had broken apart and came up with green fire sparkling in his hand. The elaborate necklace encrusted with emeralds and diamonds had come from a pile of gold and jewels lying in the artificial valley formed by the slanting planks. Austin took the necklace and decided he had never seen a piece of jewelry more beautiful. The intricate settings were painstakingly handcrafted. While Austin wondered, Zavala reached into an intact jar and pulled out a handful of loose gems. Diamonds. Rubies. Emeralds. Zavala's mouth dropped open in astonishment. "This must be the greatest concentration of treasure in the history of the world!"

Austin was squatting by an amphora that had split open. "It makes the British crown jewels look like play beads, doesn't it?" Stones the size of marbles ran through his fingers. "The international lawyers are going to have a blast figuring out who owns this stuff."

Zavala glanced toward the burial chamber. "Maybe the last owner of record is in that stone coffin."

Austin picked up a couple of spearheads. "Let's see if it's anyone we know."

They climbed out of the boat and went back to the burial chamber. The spearheads were strong, and the points fit under the lid. No combination of leverage, even in the hands of two well-muscled and resourceful men, proved equal to the skills of those who had designed and carved the stone coffin.

"Guess we'd better go back to grave robber's school," Austin said.

Zavala checked his pressure gauge. "No time like the present. We're going to have to switch to our spare tank if we stay much longer."

"We've seen all we need to see. Maybe the scientists can make sense of all this."

He started to lead the way back to the boat chamber when the unearthly quiet of the tomb was shattered by a thunderous explosion from above their heads. Austin had a fleeting vision of what it must be like under an erupting volcano. Synapses in their brains went crazy as age-old survival instincts clashed with conflicting commands.

Run. Hit the ground. Freeze.

They fought to keep their balance as the floor shook under their feet. The explosion forced air up into the enclosed chamber, creating a wind tunnel effect. The shock wave knocked Austin and Zavala back into the crypt. Arms flailing, they slammed against the sarcophagus in a wild clatter of tanks and air hoses, then slid into the space between the stone coffin and the wall that contained it. The fall cost them cuts and bruises but probably saved their lives. A piece of ceiling as big as a diesel engine block crashed down on the spot where they'd been standing. Sharp-edged rocks flew through the air as if they had been shot from a strafing fighter plane. A choking cloud of dust billowed into the burial chamber and covered everything with a fine whitish coating. Then a pattering of loose stones and dirt rained down.

Austin spat out a mouthful of dust and asked Zavala if he was all right.

Zavala made his presence and condition known, first with a coughing fit, then a string of curses in Spanish.

"Yeah, I'm okay," he sputtered. "How about you?"

"I think I'm in one piece. Wish I could stop the telephone ringing in my head."

More coughs. "What happened?"

"It sounded like a combination of Vesuvius and Krakatoa. My guess leans toward a few kilos of C-4 plastique explosive." Austin grunted. "I like you a lot, Joe, but I don't think we're ready to be engaged. Can you move?"

There was more cursing as they untangled arms and legs and breathing hoses, until they were able to stand. Zavala reached for a halogen lamp which had fallen within arm's reach. He flashed it on Austin then back at his own face. Their masks were askew but the lenses were unbroken and had protected their eyes from the blinding dust.

"You look like a disreputable mime," Zavala said with a laugh.

"I hate mimes, even reputable ones. You're looking a little pale yourself. I've got another revelation. We're breathing without our regulators."

Zavala held the half-mask that contained the microphone and regulator to his face and clamped his teeth on the mouthpiece. "Still works," he said.

"Mine, too. Looks like we won't need them. I feel fresh air coming in."

"That means somebody blew the top off the pyramid. Time to get moving. Can you walk?"

Zavala nodded and crawled from the pit, then leaned in and helped Austin out. They were covered from head to toe with whitish brown dust that gave them a zombielike look. Austin flashed his light back into the pit and saw that the heavy stone lid had been cracked open by the concussion. Austin knew they should be moving, but his curiosity got the best of him. He aimed the light at the figure inside.

The face was covered by a jade mask with round eyes and an aquiline nose. The corpse was dressed in a shroud of dark material that could have been velvet. Strands of whitish-red hair poked out from under an amorphously shaped hat made out of the same material. Austin moved the light down. The clawlike mummified hands clutched rolls of old parchment. Austin removed one of the rolls, examined it with wondering eyes, then tucked it back into the bony hands. He noticed a glint of yellow under the chin of the mask. The shape was familiar, but it seemed out of context. Austin wanted to take a closer look, but there wasn't time. The sound of voices was coming from the boat chamber.

THE ALMOST IMPENETRABLE CLOUD
in the boat chamber was dissipating rapidly, the motes swirling
against the sunlight that streamed down from a huge opening
that yawned where the ceiling had been. Great chunks of rock
had flattened the stern end of the dark red hull like a potato
masher. Columns had been knocked over and lay in fragments.
The chamber floor was littered with smaller pieces of rock and
coated with limestone dust. Austin had no time to mourn the
boat's destruction. A rope ladder dropped down from the ragged
hole. Two figures dressed in black were climbing down the ladder
into the dusty haze.

The first one to set foot on the floor reached up and steadied
the ladder. "Sorry about the mess, Don Halcon," came a voice
that was flat, unemotional, and unapologetic.

"It couldn't be helped, Guzman," said the slender-built dark-
haired man, surveying the wreckage. "The important thing is
that we reached our goal, not *how* we did it." He flicked on a
powerful flashlight and pointed it at the ruined boat. "My God,
what a fantastic sight!"

The intruders made their way through the rubble and climbed
over the splintered stern timbers to the less damaged section of
the boat. Moments later Halcon shouted with excitement. "Look
at this, Guzman!" he said with hysterical joy. "There are enough
jewels in my hand to outfit a whole new army."

Austin stood at the entryway to the boat chamber with Zavala and considered their situation. They were unarmed except for their sheath knives. Halcon and his henchman would have sidearms at the very least. If he and Zavala made a break for the ladder or the water entrance at the far end of the chamber, they'd be picked off like ducks in a shooting gallery.

He whispered his concerns to Zavala. "Maybe we can bluff our way through."

Joe had come to the same conclusion as his partner. "What have we got to lose?"

Just our lives and those of many others, Austin thought. "We've got to work our way back to where we came in. Get rid of our main air tanks. Keep the emergency tank and regulator with you." He tapped the pouch around his neck. "I've got a surprise that might distract them, but the timing has to be just right. It won't take long for them to find us. If we surprise them they may start shooting."

"Okay, let them know we're here. I'll take my cue from you," Zavala said.

Austin clapped his colleague on the shoulder, took a deep breath, and stepped out into the boat chamber.

"Hello, gentlemen," he said in a loud and clear voice.

The white-haired man with the scar quickly slipped a pistol from its belt holster and cocked it in Austin's direction.

"We're unarmed. There are just two of us," Austin said quickly, staring at the muzzle. He had gambled that the man was too much of a professional to let off a panic shot.

"Come forward where I can see you." Austin followed the order, he and Zavala closing the distance by several paces. The white-haired man climbed out of the boat wreckage, cautiously approached, and relieved them of their sheath knives. The livid scar on his face became more pronounced when he grinned.

"We really have to stop meeting like this," he said, tossing the knives out of range.

"Introduce me to your friends, Guzman." Halcon stepped from the wrecked boat, a gun in his hand.

"Please excuse my rudeness, Don Halcon. Allow me to introduce Mr. Austin and his NUMA associate Mr. Zavala, whom I met in Arizona. Zavala is the gentleman who was photographed by our surveillance camera."

"Of course, now I recognize him."

"You'll have to send me a copy of the picture, Halcon," Zavala said.

Halcon chuckled. "I'd be surprised if you resourceful gentlemen didn't know my name. Guzman told me about you. In fact I ordered him to kill you. You've been lucky; he rarely fails to carry out a task. Before he now redeems himself, I must admit you have me baffled at how you got into the temple."

"We were swallowed by the jaws of Kukulcan," Austin said.

Halcon studied Austin like an entomologist examining an insect in a killing jar. "You're either telling the truth or simply trying to be ironic," Halcon said. "Either way it doesn't matter. You won't be leaving through the jaws anytime soon."

"I'll tell you how we got in if you answer the questions of a couple of condemned men. I'm just curious if our theory is correct."

Halcon must have known Austin was stalling for time. Austin looked at it from a different perspective, the opportunity to set up an escape. He had no intention of dying in this tomb.

"A bargainer to the last," Halcon said, evidently intrigued with the game. "Go ahead."

"First of all, how did you find the temple?"

"The same way we knew about your *Andrea Doria* expedition. Mr. Donatelli's man, the Sicilian."

"Antonio?"

"His name is not important. When you told Mr. Donatelli you were headed for Central America we ordered our spies to follow you to Guatemala. That ridiculous little yellow plane was easy to keep track of."

So much for the Beaver's unobtrusiveness, Austin thought.

"I've generously allowed you a bonus question," Halcon went on. "I'm still interested in your theory."

"How's this for starters?" Austin said. "The Phoenicians

traded with the Americas for thousands of years. When the Romans besieged Carthage, a Phoenician fleet moved its treasure to the other side of the ocean. Centuries pass, Columbus arrives in the New World and hears tales of a fabulous treasure. He finds the talking stone, concludes it will point the way, and sets off on a last voyage to bring home the bacon. He misinterprets the information on the stone but comes pretty close."

"Almost as close as you have, Mr. Austin. Now will you reveal how you got in?"

"We came down that stairway," Austin said, glancing toward the burial chamber.

Halcon smiled and turned to his companion. "Guzman—"

"I'm not done," Austin interrupted. "Columbus has ties to a mysterious organization called the Brotherhood, so it is quite likely they knew of the treasure."

"*More* than likely." Halcon stayed his henchman's hand. "I'm truly impressed, Mr. Austin. The Brotherhood has been one of the best-kept secrets in the world. Not even when we sank one of the world's most famous ocean liners did anyone suspect our existence."

"You're telling me that the Brotherhood sank the *Andrea Doria*?" Austin said.

"Guzman, really. While my father and the others were dealing with the armored truck guards in the hold, Guzman was taking care of matters on the ship's bridge."

"It was an accident," Austin countered.

"So they say. It wasn't as hard as you might think. We knew the boats would pass close to each other that night. Guzman was prepared to kill everyone on the *Stockholm*'s bridge and ram the Swedish vessel into the other ship. As it was, he only took advantage of the mistakes made by others."

"If what you say is true, and the Brotherhood knew the talking stone pointed the way to treasure, why did they send it to the bottom of the sea?"

"Unfortunately the stone's value didn't become known until fairly recently. My father ordered the stone sunk. He was carrying out the original mandate of the Brotherhood, to destroy anything that discredited the discoveries of Columbus."

Zavala chuckled and said something in Spanish.

"You're quite right, Mr. Zavala, my father did, as you put it, screw up. But he couldn't have known that I would change the mandate of *Los Hermanos*."

"When did it change from sinking ships to starting revolutions?" Austin said.

A cloud crossed Halcon's pale thin face, then he laughed and clapped his hands. *"Bravo,* Mr. Austin. You have bought yourself more time on your death sentence. Tell me what NUMA knows of my plan."

"I will, after you fill in a few more holes."

"Your tongue would loosen if I started shooting holes in your colleague's arms and legs," Halcon said with a smile.

"You could do that, but let me offer another proposal. Tell me what your plan is, and I'll reveal a secret known to no other man on the planet but me. I give you my word."

"And I accept it." Austin had judged Halcon correctly as a megalomaniac who would want others to know of his mad schemes. "I can sum up my plan in one word. *Angelica.* The new country that will be carved out of the Southwest states and southern California. Those of Hispanic descent will take back what was stolen from them by force."

Joe chortled. "Good luck, pal. I know of a certain superpower that might object."

"Please give me credit. I'm well aware of the armed might of the U.S. and have no intention of going up directly against it."

"Then all those arms you're buying are for sport shooting?"

"Oh, no, they will be used for military reasons. You're of Spanish ancestry, Mr. Zavala, so you know what I learned in the bullring. With a few flutters and flourishes of a cape and deft footwork you can vanquish a much larger and more powerful foe."

"The U.S. isn't exactly a fighting bull," Austin said.

"The same principle applies. I have prepared the groundwork

well. I have moved millions of illegal immigrants into the old Spanish territories now occupied illegally by the United States, until they are on the verge of outnumbering the non-Hispanics. I have used my fortunes to acquire key businesses such as gas, oil, and mining. With my profits I have sponsored candidates pliant to my will for public office and bought and bribed others. Now I can put my plan into action. As soon as I leave here I will give the word. The army I have been training will move on the border towns. Others will conduct raids in the interior. There will be a backlash against Hispanics, much like that against the Japanese Americans in World War II. Although this time we will give them the means to resist against their Anglo tormentors, and a reason: to redeem the national pride that America has so often demeaned."

"You're talking bloodshed and chaos."

"My goals exactly! What can the U.S. do, free Albuquerque and Phoenix by nuking them? Conduct street-to-street fighting in the boulevards of San Diego? They will know a political settlement follows every armed conflict, and I will provide the way out. The governors I have elected will sue for peace and suggest that the U.S. turn to one of its citizens of Spanish heritage to act as mediator. I will negotiate *de facto* secession from the Union."

"There's no guarantee your scheme will succeed, in which case hundreds of thousands of people would have been killed for nothing."

"They will have served their purpose as a means to an end."

"Many of those people will be Latinos," Zavala said.

"What of it?" Halcon snarled. "My *conquistador* ancestors used warring Indian factions as their allies to defeat the Aztec empire, then made them slaves. I will offer those who survive the opportunity to relive the greatness of the past as I restore the glories of two great civilizations, the Indian and the Spanish."

"Glories like the ball court and the Inquisition?" Austin said.

"And more you haven't even dreamed of, Mr. Austin. *Much* more." His tone was ominous. "I tire of this game," he said impatiently. "What of this great secret? I wouldn't blame you for lying to me, but it won't save you."

"I'm not lying. It's in the other chamber."

Halcon exchanged glances with Guzman. "No tricks. Guzman has a hair trigger. Lead the way."

Austin went up the stairs first, with Zavala following, then Guzman and Halcon, until they came to the edge of the burial pit.

"You came in this way?" Halcon said, looking in vain for an entryway.

"I *was* lying about that, but not this."

The figure in the sarcophagus had engaged Halcon's attention.

"Who is it?" Halcon said.

"If I may?"

Guzman's cold eyes followed every move as Austin reached into the stone coffin and removed the shiny object from the bony hands of the mummy. He handed it to Halcon, who examined it, frowning with puzzlement.

"I don't understand," he said with suspicion.

"Consider this," Austin said. "You're the Maya, sitting on a pile of treasure for hundreds of years waiting for the men who brought it to you to return and reclaim it. One day a white man from the east shows up on your doorstep and says he wants his gold. He dies before you can accommodate him. You wonder if he embodies the Venus god, the feathered serpent Kukulcan, but you're not sure. So you hedge your bets, bury him with his treasure, and draw a map in stone in a way that only the Venus god will be able to understand. Those rolls of parchment he's holding are drawings of the inscription on the stone. But if that isn't enough to convince you, then tell me what a Christian cross is doing in a Mayan temple."

"It can't be!" Halcon said with disbelief.

"Don Halcon, meet the Admiral of the Ocean Sea, Christopher Columbus."

Halcon stared at the mummy a moment, then laughed without mirth and tossed the cross back into the sarcophagus. "Keep it, you poor fool."

While all eyes were on the coffin Austin squeezed the pouch around his neck. Seconds later came a distant boom, then several others.

"What's that?" Halcon said, looking about him.

Guzman moved to the stairway and listened. "It sounds like thunder."

While the henchman's attention was diverted, Austin reached down to the floor and in a single quick motion picked up one of the sharp spear points he and Zavala had unsuccessfully used to pry the lid off the coffin. He wrapped his brawny arm around Halcon's slender neck and jabbed the sharp spike deep into the skin.

Guzman's gun swung around.

"Back off or this goes into his jugular!" Austin warned. He pushed the spear in further. Blood trickled down Halcon's neck.

Barely able to speak with his throat crushed, Halcon hissed, "Do as he says."

"Put that gun back in your holster," Austin commanded. He knew Guzman would never give up his gun entirely, that he'd try for a head shot or plug Zavala first.

Guzman smiled, a hint of admiration in the curve of his thin lips, and slid the gun back into its case. Then Austin ordered Halcon to drop his weapon.

With Zavala staying close, Austin backed out of the chamber and dragged his human shield down the stairs into the main chamber. Guzman followed at a deliberate pace as they stepped over and around the rubble and stopped under the light streaming in from the ceiling hole.

Halcon had recovered from his surprise. "Looks like a Mexican standoff," he said, his voice choked but defiant.

A brief shower of water splashed down on them from above. Everyone looked up except Austin.

"That's not rain, in case you're wondering. Those booms you heard a few minutes ago were explosives. I used a remote detonator to blow up the dam that blocks water into the lake. Millions of gallons are pouring in."

"I don't believe you," Halcon snarled.

"Perhaps you should, Don Halcon," said Guzman. "It seems Mr. Austin was not lying about the detonator."

"You could never have foreseen events," Halcon said.

"That's right. My original plan was to blow the dam after we left to make it tougher for you to find the temple. This way at least we'll all die together."

They were suddenly drenched by another deluge from above, only stronger this time.

"My guess is that's only the first ripple from the explosion. The reservoir would have burst by now. More will follow. It won't take much to breach that hole you blew in the temple. I have no idea how long before this chamber fills, but I wouldn't stay around too long if I were you."

Guzman looked toward the ladder and seemed to lose some of his steely composure. "We must leave."

"Not without that treasure."

"Doesn't make any difference to me," Austin said. "Like you said, we're dead men."

Water poured down again, but instead of a brief burst, it continued to flow in a torrent.

"Don Halcon . . ." There was alarm in Guzman's voice.

"He's bluffing, you fool," Halcon replied with disgust.

"The treasure is of use to no one if he's right," Guzman said.

Halcon's eyes filled with hate. "You've always been nothing but a homicidal cretin from the day my father hired you," he said with contempt. "You can't see the glory!"

A hard smile crossed Guzman's lips.

Water was pouring in like a river now, directly on top of them so that it was hard to see each other, sloshing onto their feet, yet nobody moved.

"Quite a dilemma, isn't it, Guzman," Austin taunted, raising his voice to be heard. "Loyalty to your crazed boss and the Brotherhood, or death by drowning. I sincerely hope you resolve your family spat, but you'll have to settle it without me. That's the cue, Joe!"

Zavala ran toward the well at the far end of the chamber and dove in. Austin dropped the spear point, grabbed Halcon's butt, and with a powerful bum's rush threw him at Guzman, who'd been momentarily distracted by Zavala's sprint. They went down in a tangle, but even as he fell Guzman was pulling out the pistol. Austin dashed for the well. Guzman was up and got off a shot, but Austin was a poor target in the dim light, and the bullet missed. Austin dove into the well.

Guzman cursed and went after Austin. Buffeted by the flood swirling around his ankles and knees, he had taken only a few steps when he realized it would be suicide to stay in the chamber. This conclusion was reinforced when he turned and saw that Halcon had deserted him and was heading for the ladder. Halcon's dreams of glory had finally given way to his instincts for self-preservation. He slogged his way against the rising tide until he was under the ceiling hole where the water roared down in a miniature Niagara. Blinded by the force of the cascade, he groped for the ladder, but his hand slipped. He clenched his teeth with determination and tried again. This time he got a grip on a rung.

As he began to climb a hand grabbed him by the ankle and pulled him down. Guzman wrapped his arms around Halcon's knees and used the full weight of his body to pull him back into the chamber. Halcon held on with one hand and with the other pulled his pistol, which he had retrieved, from its holster and swung it with all the strength he could muster in his awkward position. The gun barrel struck flesh and bone, but Guzman desperately held on. Halcon raised the pistol again and brought it down twice more on Guzman's head with the desired effect.

Guzman's grip loosened. He lost his footing and was swept back into the chamber where his body came to rest against a pile of boat wreckage. Even then he wasn't through. He was on his knees, struggling to get to his feet, when a ship's beam as long as a man slammed into his face. Borne by the current, the timber had the effect of a battering ram. A fiery pain screamed in his brain. Dazed and blinded in one eye, arms flailing uselessly, he gasped for air, only to suck in lungfuls of foul water. His frantic movements eventually slowed and became more feeble, and the current drove him deep into the dark chamber.

Halcon was having his own problems. He had climbed only a few yards up the ladder when a wave surged over the lip of the gap in the ceiling and pummeled him like a giant wet fist until he was no longer able to hold on. More water poured in and knocked him off the ladder. Recognizing that escape by this route was impossible, he fought his way to the stairs leading to the burial chamber. With the water lapping at his heels, he crawled on hands and knees up the stairway.

Zavala had been treading water when Austin dove into the pool. As Guzman's bullet whistled overhead, they surface-dove and swam down into the shaft, buddy-breathing off one tank. Minutes later they emerged from the jaws of Kukulcan. They checked their compass and swam for open water, using every muscle in their legs to get beyond the current produced by the flooding temple. They surfaced near the cove that hid the plane. Within minutes they had cleared the branches away and started the engine and were skimming across the water for a takeoff. As soon as the plane gained altitude, Zavala banked it around the lake in a big circle.

The island that had built up around the temple was gone. In its place was a black hole. Lake water swirled down the hole like a bathtub drain and tugged at the mooring line of a seaplane that must have been Halcon's.

They had seen enough. They swooped in low over the lake for one last look at the vortex. Zavala couldn't resist temptation. He leaned out the window and shouted, "Good-bye, Columbus."

Then they headed back to the *Nereus*.

49

THE STUBBY-MASTED SAILBOAT WITH
the single oversized gaff-rigged sail cruised over the deep blue waters of Chesapeake Bay, pushed along from directly behind by a steady fifteen-knot breeze from the southwest. Austin lounged in the large open cockpit with one arm on the raised rail, the other on an oversized tiller. His eyes scanned the boat traffic, looking for prey.

His hunt was interrupted, not unpleasantly, by Nina, who emerged from the cuddy with two clinking glasses in her hands. "Pusser's rum and juice," she said.

She was dressed in a NUMA T-shirt and high-cut white shorts that emphasized her long legs and buttery complexion. Austin was not oblivious to her charms, but he was intent on his task. He murmured his thanks and kept his eyes glued on the sea.

"Aha, my pretty," he said like the wicked witch in *The Wizard of Oz*. He picked up a pair of binoculars and focused on a graceful sloop with a white fiberglass hull, about twenty-five feet long. Like Austin, it was loafing along, mainsail and jib set wing-to-wing with the wind behind.

Austin sipped his drink, set it in a glass holder, then moved the tiller so that the catboat came up parallel to the sloop. He waved at the two young men in the other boat's cockpit, jerked his thumb like a hitchhiker, then veered off into a broad reach with the wind on his side.

The sloop's crew took up the good-natured challenge for a race.

Austin pointed the bow closer to the wind, and the sloop followed suit. They were parallel now, maybe separated by a hundred feet, maneuvering for a start.

Austin tightened sail, putting the rail into the water.

The men in the sloop did the same with their main and jib, and soon the two boats were cutting frothy wakes across the bay. The sloop was sleek and fast, and the crew were good sailors, but before long Austin began to pass the other boat. He lay back against the rail, the picture of relaxation, sipping his juice until he left the sloop far behind.

"What did you just do?" Nina said with a smile.

"I taught a couple more sailors that just because this thing looks like a bathtub doesn't mean it sails like one."

"I think it's a *great* boat. Big deck. It's amazing the space you have below for a boat only eighteen feet long."

"I've overnighted quite often, and as you can see by the cooking and sleeping facilities, I like comfort and room to stretch. The catboat was originally built as a workboat. One person can handle the single sail, and it's big enough to catch a light wind at the end of the day. She's weatherly, too, in conditions that would sink another boat. Best of all, she's fast and doesn't look it. So I can sneak up on unsuspecting chaps like that sloop crew, and show them my dust. Here we are."

They had sailed off the point of a small island. Austin threw out the anchor and they dug into the picnic basket, enjoying lunch while the boat rocked slightly in the gentle swell. After lunch Nina sat close to Austin and leaned against his shoulder.

"Thank you for inviting me for a sail."

"I thought we both could use a pleasant diversion after the last few weeks."

She stared thoughtfully into the distance. "I can't stop thinking about those terrible men, though. What a way to meet the end."

"Don't feel sorry for them. Guzman had murdered hundreds

of people in his lifetime, not to mention sinking the *Andrea Doria*. In a way, drowning was a fitting death for him. If Halcon's scheme had succeeded, thousands more might have died. Guzman was lucky. Halcon would have had time to contemplate the error of his ways. The air in the burial chamber kept the water out for a while, but it was only a matter of hours before it gave out. Best of all, the Brotherhood died with him. I only wish he'd lived long enough to see what happened to his precious treasure."

"My hat is off to Admiral Sandecker," Nina said, eager to change the subject. "Suggesting that the treasure be put into an international fund to help rid the world of poverty and disease was an act of genius."

"The alternative would have been years of legal wrangling with no winners. Who were the owners? The descendants of the Phoenicians? The Romans? The Mexicans? The Guatemalans?"

"Or Christopher Columbus." Nina shook her head. "Ironic, isn't it? Like Halcon, his obsession with gold killed him."

"He wasn't in very good health even before he set sail, according to the autopsy. He might have died soon even if he never took his fifth voyage. At least this way he's become more famous than ever, whether he deserved it or not. Besides, I owe Chris one. If not for his obsessions we might not have met."

Taking Austin's hand in hers, Nina said, "If he only knew what would come from that voyage. Retrieving his body and the treasure will be the greatest archaeological project in history, with nations and governments all over the world cooperating. I can't wait to start work. He's done more in death to bring people together than he ever did in life. Too bad his legacy as the discoverer of America will be flawed."

"It doesn't seem to matter. I've seen the plans for the lavish tomb they want to build him in Madrid. They're bidding for his body in Washington and San Salvador, too."

"No one's suggested putting up a monument for those nameless Phoenicians and Africans who were the first to set foot in the New World," Nina said.

"Maybe they *weren't* the first."

She arched an eyebrow. "I beg your pardon. Do you have evidence to support that possibility, Professor Austin?"

"Maybe. I took another look at the boat carvings. Do you remember the picture of the man hanging from a diamond-shaped object?"

"Yes. I thought it might be a god of some kind."

"I came at it from a different way. I wondered how the Maya managed to get a bird's-eye view when they were laying out the pointers to the jaws of Kukulcan. I think they used huge kites."

"Flying Maya! That's a novel theory. Where would they have learned to do that?"

They were interrupted by the buzzing of Austin's cell phone. He dug it out of his waterproof pack and put it to his ear. His frown changed to a smile when he heard the voice on the line. He talked for a few minutes before hanging up.

"That was Angelo Donatelli calling from the hospital," he said. "He'll be out in a few days."

"It's a miracle he wasn't killed."

"More than a miracle. His cousin Antonio threw Halcon's aim off when he went for him."

"I'm glad. Mr. Donatelli sounds like a nice man from what you've told me."

"You'll get a chance to see for yourself. He's throwing a big family clambake at his Nantucket house. You're invited. Paul and Gamay will be there too."

"I'd love to come along."

"Good then, it's a date. Now would you like to hear the rest of my kite theory?"

Nina nodded.

"I think the Maya learned from the best kite fliers in the world. The Japanese."

She laughed. "I don't think I'll go there."

"Where would you like to go, then?"

Nina picked up the cell phone. "Someplace where you won't need this." She dropped the phone over the side.

Then, removing her sunglasses, she smiled and her lush lips parted invitingly. Austin accepted the invitation, which was as warm and sweet as promised.

"How would you like to go below and, what did you call it? Stretch?" Nina whispered.

Without a word, Austin took her hand, led her to the spacious cabin, and shut the louvered doors on the world. At least for a little while.